Precious Absence

A Novel

Ace Remas

PAGE PUBLISHING, INC.
New York, NY

First originally published by Page Publishing, Inc. 2016

This is a work of fiction, which is an official declaration that these events, persons, and places were imagined. Any similarity to actual people and conditions is purely coincidental.

ISBN 978-1-68348-709-8 (Paperback)
ISBN 978-1-68348-710-4 (Digital)

Cover Illustration
By Nevada artist Linda Burchard

Printed in the United States of America

"The absence of the dead is their way of appearing."

—Simone Weil

Chapter One

Before you meet Kostas Jack Wilson, you should know he is dead.

Ambushed.

On Valentine's Day.

By a gang of *sicarios,* as far as the police could determine, while he worked alone at his silver mining claim just northeast of the Honduran capital of Tegucigalpa.

He didn't go down without a fight. All six bullets in his .357 Magnum revolver had been fired.

Why the assassins didn't take the gun, the police could not understand. It was worth more than the missing laptop computer and cell phone.

The keys to his Toyota pickup were still in his pants pockets too. Maybe the bandits were surprised by someone.

Was it robbery? Or an assassination? When asked by the American ambassador, the police officer merely shrugged his shoulders. Who could tell in a country like Honduras? Maybe both, another policeman offered.

Kostas's Honduran partner and crew had already gone home for the holiday weekend. It would be their final time with family and spouses before starting the next long stage to excavate the mine after four years of surveying and planning.

Just the month before, Kostas had ceremoniously selected this spot for his first official penetration of the mountain. With one foot against the steep slope and the other on the dry bed of the creek, he was handed a brand-new pickax purchased just for this occasion, and he heaved it into the dried clay-like earth. It sank up to its shaft. They would need no dynamite to begin the mine. The little Kubota backhoe Kostas had purchased from a bankrupt contractor in Tegucigalpa would scrape down the sandy overburden to a wall of volcano-created rock; perhaps forty feet of easygoing before they would begin drilling to place the charges to crack open the mountain.

"Here," Kostas announced proudly, and pointed his right arm at a slight upward angle toward the center of the mountain, by his reckoning, about a quarter mile away through the rock and clay. His entire crew of twelve scrappy Lenca Indians, recruited especially by Kostas, had been assembled just for this momentous occasion.

The Indian mine workers from the local Lenca villages, not quite understanding the reason for such auspiciousness merely to dig a hole in the ground, still were caught up in the moment and cheered the blow Kostas had delivered to the mountain's flank.

"*Aqui!*" Kostas repeated in Spanish to acknowledge his crew.

They cheered again, grateful for the recognition of their contribution. In Honduras, for indigenous people, it was rare to find employment—and even rarer an employer who would treat them with dignity. They were as grateful for the respect they received as they were for the wages.

Now they mourned the loss of a good man. When Kostas's partner, Miguel Tavares, let them know the ambush had ended their jobs, without exception, they drove with their entire families to the mine. The body had already been taken to the morgue. The police were gone without even leaving evidence of their presence. Only Miguel sat alone in the shack that served as an office. He had no answers for their questions. Though he told them they would receive wages for one more week, this was small consolation for such a great loss.

Miguel treated the indigenous Lencas as other Hondurans did, indifferently. The Lencas would not miss Tavares, but they lamented what seemed like a golden opportunity to do a man's work for a man who respected their labor. Because losing a future to violence is all too common in Honduras, the Lenca crew was not angry, only dispirited. Theirs was a culture of accepting the bleak lot that afflicts most of mankind around the world, and especially in Central America.

Kostas's death was no random act of violence, in their view. It was a result of some conspiracy to control what must be a valuable asset—that hole in the ground they would never have the opportunity to excavate. Among themselves, they wondered what treasure lay buried at the mountain's heart to inspire murder.

Although the American ambassador to Honduras questioned the police about the unlikely coincidence of the bandits arriving only after Kostas was alone, the police did not seem interested. They patiently explained, as they had done many times before, that in their crime-ridden country, foreigners of all types, including tourists and drug lords, were murdered for their watches and pocket change. When pressed by the ambassador, they admitted they had not questioned Kostas's Honduran partner, Miguel Tavares, because, at least as far as they could tell, he had nothing to gain and, in fact, had much to lose by the crime. They had found him at home with his paramour in his luxurious apartment in the upscale Colonia Palmira district of Tegucigalpa when they came to offer official notification of their findings.

In Honduras, the distinction between crime and law enforcement often faded as the casual and distracted police perfunctorily performed their duties. This was not the first time the American ambassador had to report the death of an American, but this time, his suspicions would not go away. He had known Kostas since he had shown up in the capital four years earlier to register his intentions to develop a silver mine. Kostas was meticulous in complying with the complex array of Honduran regulations. Despite the advice of many locals whom he had to deal with, he never succumbed to the temptation of cutting corners, a common practice in Honduras when such actions were accompanied by an envelope stuffed with American dollars. Unlike the other mining operators in the country, Kostas made special inquiries into the environmental impacts of his project. He also relied on the local Indians in the area of the mine. Hardy men from the ancient tribe of Lencas, who once were neighbors of the Mayans just north in Guatemala, would be employed and receive the benefits of an increased standard of living Kostas had hoped to inspire for their community.

Kostas worked in Honduras for two months at a time, returning after each sojourn to his home turf in Nevada to manage his other mining properties there. While in the United States, Kostas raised the money and equipment for the small Honduran mining operation he had hoped eventually would employ perhaps two dozen Lencas. Though he was not required to include a local partner, he had recruited Miguel Tavares because of his connections in the capital. Kostas ignored the complaints about Tavares from some of the old-timers he had to deal with. Those seasoned veterans of other mining adventures implied Tavares was often involved with the profits of many enterprises but rarely with the work. At best, he seemed a slippery fellow.

That same morning, Valentine's Day, at home in Nevada, Kostas's wife, Grace, had no inkling of her long future of a life without him. No premonitory cold chill brushed her cheek. No sudden terror gripped her heart. The ambassador had yet to make the official call to inform her that her husband had been ambushed and murdered.

This morning, as was her custom, she walked from the small home in Schurz she shared with Kostas to the tribal health clinic on the Walker River Paiute Reservation, where she worked as the health nurse. This daily walk of a half mile or so was more than just exercise. She believed strolling along the irrigation ditch, waving to her Indian neighbors and spotting here and there a rabbit or hawk, brought her closer to the people she had chosen to serve. Her days were often long as a result, and one of her Indian patients, knowing of her customary morning walk, usually offered to drive her home in his or her pickup. Allowing herself to be given a ride, too, became part of her daily ritual because it gave her an opportunity to understand these simple folk. And for them to understand her.

Life is hard for Paiutes, as it is for most Indian tribes in the United States. Living in the gambling mecca of Nevada, and far away from any appreciable population of reckless tourists, it makes no sense, and it would be impossible in any case, they would try to establish a cash-cow casino to benefit the tribe as is common for other Indian tribes around the country.

The Paiutes in Nevada disdain such stratagems. They prefer the dignity of a poverty well earned by their patient acceptance of the disadvantages history has bequeathed to them. Lost in the modern world of the Internet and cell phones, cable television, globalization, and relentless bureaucracy, they find contentment in the vast and empty reaches of the Great Basin, home to their ancestors and the spirits who whisper secrets only they can decipher. Yet they need help and are glad recipients of it, especially when provided by a person who loved them as they are and not expecting them to become something other.

Grace was well named, they often remarked among themselves as they waited for her ministrations and advice in the anteroom of the busy clinic. Besides, they always noted to one another, she had married one of their own, at least by their accounting. Grace's husband, Kostas Jack Wilson, was the great-great-grandson of the most famous Paiute—Wovoka, the renowned Indian Messiah who inspired the Ghost Dance.

More than a hundred years ago, Wovoka was adopted by a Yerington rancher. Wearing a white man's garments, he was known as Jack Wilson. At tribal meetings, and when he was able to escape to the mountains and deserts, he became Wovoka. One fateful week in midlife, he had visions of a pure land inhabited only by Indians. All the white people had disappeared, and only animals and Indians shared the natural harmony of the landscape and sky. In his vision, when these simple and patient people needed meat for nutrition, deer and rabbits gladly surrendered themselves; fish obligingly swam into their tulle nets, and there was never a bad season for their annual harvest of pine nuts. In return, the Paiutes would protect the environment they and their families, animal and human, shared.

Dazed and weak from his long vigil with the spirits, Wovoka promised peace and happiness for all beings simply by fasting and dancing with devotion. Indians around the Americas were inspired by his message. They trekked hundreds of miles to join the Paiutes and other Indians for week-long festivals of spiritual celebration. Even the plains tribe of Sioux sent emissaries from the distant Dakotas on the iron horse of the railroad to learn what became known as the Ghost Dance. They danced and danced to purify the plague of ordinary view, the white man's view, that a material and visible life constituted reality. The real life of any being was invisible; it was the potential to become a perfect being, living in harmony with all other beings, seen and unseen, untroubled and unlimited by the coarse and, to their eyes, gross desires of a civilized existence.

The sad result of this collision of the invisible world of Wovoka and the materially evident world of the white man was disaster and death, culminating in the infamous massacre of hundreds of Sioux at Wounded Knee fifteen hundred miles away from Nevada in South Dakota in 1890. Defeated and dismayed, Wovoka dissolved into the shadows of history, occasionally supplementing his meager income with appearances as an Indian mystic in silent movies often filmed in the area.

Kostas was the son of Jack Wilson, Wovoka's great-grandson. A marine during World War II, Kostas's father had met his wife while on duty in San Diego. Of strong-willed Greek descent, she had insisted that her son possess a Greek name even though her husband, Jack, was of Paiute and Irish-American lineage. They compromised. Her son would have a Greek first name and an Irish middle name, and he could choose when he was of age which name he would prefer to be called.

He chose the diminutive version of his given name, Konstantinos. Kostas. He flaunted his Greek identity, but delighted in explaining his Paiute-Greek-Irish lineage as if something was revealed to him by all these cultures no one else could know. He had the natural view of a harmonious universe of the Paiutes, the philosophical wisdom of the Greeks, and the hard-living and aggressive impulses of an Irishman. He counted on such attributes to make him wise and lucky in the world.

At the University of Nevada in Reno, he had enrolled in the Mackey School of Mines to become a geologist. He explained to Grace, whom he met about then, geology was a perfect expression of his heritage. It combined the science of the Greeks, the natural visions of Paiutes, and the luck of the Irish. Any one of those traits, he surmised with enthusiasm, would direct him to some mother lode of precious ore somewhere in the world. His Greek logic would deduce the most probable landscapes to search for hidden treasures, his mystic visions would guide him to the specific mountain or plain within the vast landscapes of geology, and his luck would drive a pick in the spot where some natural treasure would fall into the palm of his hand.

Such aspirations often took Kostas away from Grace. Ten years before his enterprise in Honduras, while both were still in graduate school at the university in Reno, he had tried to induce her to join him in an old Airstream house trailer at the entrance of his most recent adventure in geology, a silver mine twenty miles northwest of Tonopah, Nevada, at the end of a rutted dirt road. He had licensed the claim with their collective savings of five thousand dollars, certain the previous mine owners had failed to read the clear signals that the tunneled rock had revealed to him. Grace refused to give up graduate school and remained in their Reno apartment. Kostas would then disappear for a week or so at a time to drill, dynamite, and muck ore by himself, sometimes with the help of his friends in graduate school. Ever devious and clever, Kostas had also engineered his investment in the mine as a research project for his graduate studies in geology. With such a qualification, his friends also earned credits while they mucked and hauled ore Kostas believed would make him rich.

The tunnel grew deeper, but the vein of silver ore Kostas was following never widened and enlarged as he had expected. Eventually, even the prospects of graduate school credits and cold beer could not convince his buddies to work for nothing. Grace, who had only once visited the lonely outpost of the Airstream in the dry, hot desert valley next to a mere knob of a hill, had firmly informed Kostas she would wait for him in Reno. Gradually, as they eked through their meager savings account, and his graduate school advisor got more impatient and suspicious of his reports, even Kostas began to lose hope.

Discouragement is a natural affliction of all prospectors. They must learn to deal with it despite all the sensible and visible signs it is time to quit a fool's errand and turn one's energies to an activity that was more practical and certain. At such moments, Kostas renounced his Greek logic, made prayers to his Indian spirits, and counted on his Irish luck. His friends from the university, his advisor, and eventually Grace, who supported all of his efforts, began to encourage him to recoup what he could from his investment by relicensing his claim to some other forty-niner sucker. The more they predicted gloom and failure based on the clear evidence of his hard work and investment over all this time, the more determined Kostas became. Although he could never explain it to himself, much less to anyone else, even Grace, who listened patiently to his extravagant justifications for his decisions, Kostas relied on a single moment of insight that revealed itself when he first inspected the mine in the company of its owner. In his heart, he saw a lode of treasure, sparkling, glistening, and pure. He touched the walls of the tunnel to see if its earthly vibrations would confirm this inner vision. There were no vibrations in the cool rock, which was as still as empty space. At that moment, Kostas laughed. *Of course!* he realized. How could the invisible be confirmed by the visible? The absence of any material sign was the very affirmation he was seeking.

Without further inspection, Kostas agreed to license the mine from the owner, who would be advanced the five thousand dollars and receive 10 percent of the revenue from the mine. The owner figured he had pulled a fast one on the impulsive young graduate student.

So for two years, Kostas spent weekends and breaks in his university schedule at the Tonopah mine. If he and Grace had accumulated a little more money, he spent it on dynamite, drill tips, and gas. They lived on a budget, normal for graduate students of any stripe, but even more stringent because he wanted to continue his quest. Grace never complained but made it clear that if he were right about the mine, its wealth would be organized by her and not by his ambitious geological strategies. Kostas agreed, as he always did with Grace. No one could disagree with her because she was so patient and wise, her logic and intentions so pure, that disagreeing with her could only arise from a very selfish and ignorant viewpoint. In addition, Kostas thanked his Irish stars for the good luck of finding such a jewel as his wife.

Then one magical day, Kostas's visions were proven true. As he loaded the ore cart with the large rocks from the end of the tunnel, he noticed a thin streak of slightly blue mineral that had been exposed by the most recent blast of dynamite. With his pick, he hacked away the surrounding hard rock to increase access to the soft blue ore. He slipped off the work glove from his right hand, and with excitement bursting in his heart, he reached out with his index finger and pressed it firmly into the blue mineral. The material gave under the pressure of his fingertip, and when he withdrew his hand, he had left a small indention in the clay-like substance. Forgetting even to replace the work glove on his right hand, he retrieved his pickax and furiously removed more of the hard rock between him and the blue clay. When enough was exposed, he heaved the pickax into the mineral, and it sank up to its handle.

Kostas had discovered the mother lode he had always expected to find. His Greek science had been proven right. Millions of years ago in the deep reaches of the Earth, water superheated by volcanic cauldrons and immense pressure had streamed toward the surface through fissures and cracks. As the water ascended, it leached minerals from the surrounding rock, including gold and silver. When the water cooled, these minerals would collect as veins of rich ore in the fissures of granite. Occasionally, these fissures would end in a round cavity, sometimes perfectly spherical, suggesting they once were bubbles of gas in molten rock. Suddenly stopped and cooled, the superheated water would cram the cavity full of valuable minerals, leaving behind a treasure chest of wealth.

It was this his Greek science had suggested when he licensed the mine from its owner. But it was his Irish luck that had him follow a single vein among the many that he might have chosen to this spot, a tiny corner in the entire solid core of the planet. Had he chosen another vein, he might have passed by this place with a tunnel just a foot away from the edge of the lode.

As he furiously scooped out the blue clay to load into an ore cart, he remembered his original vision, pure silver at his heart. This round ball of riches hidden deep in the body of the Earth was exactly what was predicted by his Paiute heritage of wonder.

He worked without resting until he collapsed with exhaustion. By then, it was nighttime outside the tunnel. He limped back to his Airstream and fell asleep in his bunk without removing his dirty work clothes. He was even too tired to take off his boots.

In the morning when he arose, he attacked the blue substance again and loaded it in the ore cart. Performing the function miners of old used to have mules accomplish, he pushed the ore cart to the entrance of the mine, a distance of some two hundred yards, to dump the mineral in its own collection pile at the front of the mine. He worked like this for an entire week, sleeping with his clothes on, eating quickly and voraciously on the run. He didn't leave to let Grace know of his find. When he had cleaned out the round cavity of its treasure, he surveyed and measured the pile of ore he had collected and thus was able to estimate his seven or eight days of incessant work had piled up about a hundred tons of rich ore.

He loaded up two burlap sacks of ore and drove into Tonopah with them to check with the assayer in town. While he measured and sampled the ore, the assayer sent him to the hotel to rent a room and clean up because he looked and smelled so badly. Kostas did not want to check into a hotel; in fact, he didn't want anyone to see him because savvy miners and prospectors would surmise by his appearance and excited behavior what had happened. They have seen it before—and they themselves would then soon be in their pickups and four-wheel drives to see if other claims were available in the vicinity. Kostas slept in his pickup while the assayer performed his duties.

The news was good, as Kostas knew it would be. The ore consistently assayed as silver throughout the collected samples at three thousand dollars a ton. If Kostas was right about his estimate, he had earned three hundred thousand dollars in one week.

Ten years after this bonanza, Kostas had travelled to Honduras to find another silver mine. For the past four years, he had been commuting to Honduras to develop his property with Tavares. Usually, he was gone about two months then returned to Schurz to work on his gold claim in Pine Grove Valley behind Mount Grant with his two partners in that venture, Jasper Heck and Tommy Hawkins. While he was away to Honduras, Jasper and Tommy made gradual improvements and advancements on their gold claim. When Kostas returned from his Honduras trips, they measured the gold dust and nuggets they had dredged from the sandy alluvial and split the few ounces evenly among the three of them.

Old man Jasper was the boss of this operation. A retired electrical engineer, a Libertarian, a Vietnam veteran, and a recluse, his goal was for each to make between one thousand and four thousand dollars a month through slow and steady work on the claim. When they divided the raw gold between them, each was free to sell it to a private collector, who paid premium prices and did not issue IRS Form 1099s to report the revenue. In this way, each of the partners earned tax-free income to supplement their other activities.

Tommy worked weekend evenings as a waiter in a high-end steak house in Reno while he continued his graduate studies in geology at the university. When he didn't have to attend classes at the university, he would drive to Yerington, pick up Jasper, and they would spend a day or two drilling and digging for gold. After building up a pile of ore, they would stop digging and process the earth and stone through a wooden sluice box they had built themselves to reduce the raw earth to the essential black sand, which was collected in the mats and riffles lying along the bottom of the sluice box. Working like this, in about a month's time, they would amass enough black sand to begin the next step of the process, panning.

During Kostas's long absences in Honduras, they would accumulate black sand for the duration of his trip. When he returned, the three of them would spend evenings at Jasper's ranchette panning the gold from the black sand. It was painstaking and backbreaking work. Jasper was accustomed to easing the physical pain and mental excitement of the hunt by sipping from his lemonade and vodka concoction he camouflaged in a hiker's water bottle. Tommy was too innocent not to be excited while in the company of the respected but cranky prospector, Jasper, who had found and staked the claim they worked together, and the proven success story of Kostas, who became locally famous at the university when everyone learned he had indeed struck it rich just like in days gone by. Kostas was all business. He panned expertly and quickly and made no special notice of the few flakes of gold he could transfer into the glass vial occasionally. Tommy would whoop and holler every time he found a little gold in his pan. Jasper just took more sips from his water bottle.

Because the price of gold fluctuated above a thousand dollars an ounce, it didn't take many flakes of gold over two months of digging and panning for them to collect enough to make each of them feel their work had not been in vain. Tommy was pleased his gold mining adventure paid as well as his waiter job. Kostas needed the money to continue to fund his big million-dollar strike in Honduras. And Jasper was happy there was no possible way the government could trace this income.

It was Jasper who originated this enterprise. Although he had planned to run the operation alone, it soon proved too difficult for him, both because of his age and his limited finances. An acquaintance of Kostas and recognizing his luck of the past, he invited Kostas to invest in the mine. Despite the modern insights of technology and science, all prospectors counted on luck.

Because Grace would not let Kostas invest their own money, he told Jasper he would bring in a partner who could contribute the resources they needed.

Tommy's father owned an equipment rental company in Sacramento, and thus Tommy had access without cost for all the equipment they might need, including the backhoe they used to scoop the sand and gravel, and the water pumps that flooded the sluice box. Kostas also required Tommy to give their operation fifteen thousand dollars in capital to fund the other expenses of claim fees, fuel, and payments to the drilling company, which had helped them select the spot for their excavations.

Tommy did not have fifteen thousand dollars to invest. How he got the money was a testament to Kostas's influence, Grace's wisdom, and Tommy's obedience to their collective wishes. And to the unlikely string of luck of their mutual friend and graduate school colleague, Dave Mogis.

Dave was an interesting fellow. Quiet, submissive, always in the background like the nagging presence of last night's dream, Dave worked hard at his studies. Methodical and, to Tommy's way of thinking, too cautious, Dave announced one day inspiration struck, and he had an insight about blackjack. He wanted to risk one hundred dollars on his theory. At Dave's request, Kostas and Tommy accompanied him on this excursion to Harrah's Casino in downtown Reno, just a few blocks south of the university.

Dave's first bet was an astounding twenty-five dollars; astounding because Tommy had assumed his

ever-cautious friend would test his theory with the minimum bet of five dollars. Graduate students worldwide
are famous for their poverty, and Tommy and his friend
Dave were no exception. They received nominal assis-
tantships at the university, which barely covered their
school expenses, and both had to hold down part-time
jobs as waiters, janitors, or night watchmen to make
ends meet. This sometimes angered Tommy because his
father owned a prosperous equipment rental business in
Sacramento and certainly had the wealth and income to
support his son in a more comfortable way. But his father
had earned his way up to wealth through hard work and
many sacrifices, which, he announced frequently to his
son, made a man of him; and he wanted Tommy to be
such a man. Much of Tommy's motivation for the gold
claim that he had later invested in was to find independence from his hard-hearted but loving father.

Much to the delight of Kostas and Tommy, however, Dave's first bet paid off. He doubled his twenty-five
dollars with a pair of kings, beating the dealer's pat nine-
teen. To Tommy's astonishment, Dave let the fifty dollars
ride on the next hand. Again, it paid off, and he doubled
his money again. Tommy pulled at Dave's sleeve, letting
him know he had indeed proven his point. He had made
a seventy-five-dollar profit in the space of five minutes.
Dave pulled his arm away from Tommy's tender touch
and signaled the dealer he was leaving the hundred dollars on the table.

When the cards were dealt, the dealer showed a queen. Dave showed his hand to Kostas and Tommy, a ten and a three. Kostas, always in command, told him to take a hit. The dealer showed a face card, and to win, Dave would most likely need at least a twenty. He should take a hit on the chance of drawing a seven or eight. Tommy agreed with Kostas by enthusiastically nodding his head. Dave refused. He slid his cards under the stack of four twenty-five dollar chips. The dealer turned over his cards, and the bottom card was also a three. He had to take a hit, drew a ten—the ten Dave would have received had he followed Kostas's advice and went bust. Now Dave had doubled his bet a third time, increasing his initial wager of twenty-five dollars to two hundred dollars.

Tommy pulled more urgently on Dave's sleeve. Now he had really proven his blackjack theories and did not need to take any further risk. He had increased his stake by $175. Tommy was fearful that the quiet mouse Dave had forgotten his humble beginnings, believing he was invincible, even in the face of the certain odds that to win four times in a row was, as Tommy reckoned to himself, just not in the cards. Kostas remained aloof and amused, curious to see how Dave's experiment would turn out.

There would be no story if Dave had decided, as so many might have, to withdraw with his winnings. The $175 was equivalent to a weekend's work in the kitchen of the Nugget Casino where he assisted the sous chef on the night shift. But there was a story because again Dave signaled the dealer he was letting the two hundred dollars ride. There was no suspense this time. He drew two face cards, and the dealer showed an eight. The dealer's eighteen lost, and Dave had increased his stake to four hundred dollars.

Now Tommy nearly jerked Dave off his tall chair. The dealer gave Tommy a hard look, and Kostas intervened by pulling Tommy away while whispering in Dave's ear that he had made the equivalent of two weekends of work. They should leave, and Dave could buy them all a beer while they regaled in his good fortune.

Whomever Kostas talked with, and especially when he whispered in the ear, was influenced by his forceful presence. Ignoring Tommy's frenzied stare, Dave turned around in his seat to look up at Kostas. After a moment of silence, Dave reduced his bet to the original twenty-five dollars, leaving only one chip of the sixteen on the table. But tantalizingly illogical, on this bet, he drew twenty-one, blackjack, and was paid one and a half times his bet. Had he left the four hundred dollars on the table he would have increased his stake to a thousand dollars.

Dave pushed back from the blackjack table and politely told his friends he would walk home that evening. They did not have to wait for him. Kostas and Tommy watched a couple of more hands, cautious bets of one hundred dollars each. Dave won one and lost one, remaining even. Convinced he would never again see Dave's original stake of one hundred dollars, much less his winnings of the last few minutes, Tommy turned to follow Kostas out the casino door.

Late that same evening, Tommy's cell phone rang. He woke up to see that it was three in the morning. The call was from Dave's girlfriend, Jackie. She was frantic. Dave was still at Harrah's, but now he had thousands of dollars in chips before him. He was betting two or three hands at a time, two hundred to five hundred dollars a hand. He was by himself at the blackjack table. A crowd of tourists and locals had gathered around him, cheering his every win and groaning with each loss. A casino manager stood next to the dealer, who was changed frequently, and monitored every move. The scantily clad hostess plied him with free beer. He had accepted a few since she had joined him, tipping the hostess with a twenty-five-dollar chip each time. Jackie was afraid Dave was about to lose all that he had advanced over the last few hours. She pleaded with Tommy to hurry back to Harrah's and rescue Dave from his dazed momentum.

Tommy hurriedly dressed and went outside across the stairway his cottage shared with the cottage of Kostas and Grace, who lived directly next door. He pounded excitedly on the door, and Kostas appeared in the doorway, groggy and clad only in his Jockey underpants. Tommy told Kostas of their mission. Kostas ordered him to wait outside. In a few minutes, both he and Grace emerged to join Tommy in Kostas's pickup.

It was easy to spot Dave on the casino floor. This late in the evening, or early in the morning, depending on how you see it, most of the casino was deserted except for a few desultory dealers standing unoccupied behind their blackjack and crap tables. But where Dave and Jackie sat, a crowd of curious onlookers blocked a view of them. As Grace, Kostas, and Tommy entered, they could hear groans and hurrahs as the cards were being dealt.

Unhesitatingly, as usual, Kostas sliced through the crowd surrounding Dave and Jackie to sit down in the empty chair beside Dave. Grace and Tommy followed in his wake and stood behind Dave. All three showed looks of astonishment when they surveyed the table before Dave. Neat and fallen piles of chips, in denominations of twenty-five and a hundred dollars, were scattered about.

Dave ignored Kostas and didn't turn around to acknowledge Grace or Tommy. Jackie, sitting on the other side of Dave, stood up and pushed Dave's shoulder toward Kostas.

"Listen to him," she commanded. "He's your friend."

Dave slowly turned in his seat to look at Kostas.

Kostas merely nodded his head toward the door. "Time to go, bud."

The casino floor manager, who stood directly behind the left shoulder of the dealer, stepped forward. He stared hard at Kostas, then at Grace and Tommy. "Need anything?" he asked Dave.

Grace moved in. "Here," she offered. "Scoop it all in here."

She opened her purse and helped Dave, who apparently decided to oblige his friends, slide the chips—dozens of them—into the wide gap of her open purse. When all the chips were cleaned from the table, Grace pushed shut the clasp on the purse and handed it to Jackie. "Take him home," she said quietly.

Jackie wrestled Dave by the elbow. The crowd, just as fascinated by this evidence of friendship as they were of the risks on the table, parted to open a pathway toward the door. Jackie maneuvered Dave off his chair and, with the trio of friends trailing behind, made their getaway out of the casino. She hugged Grace's puffy purse against her breasts.

Tommy offered to ride home with Jackie and Dave, as a protective bodyguard. Grace, who needed her purse back, said she and Kostas would follow them in the pickup. They caravanned to Dave's apartment near the university. Jackie let them all in with her key. Once inside, she and Grace took charge. They quickly straightened Dave's bed, still unmade from the day before, to empty Grace's purse onto the bedcovers. Jackie eagerly began sorting the chips into piles. Grace helped by transferring orderly stacks of chips to the dinette table. In the meantime, Kostas and Tommy maneuvered Dave into the bathroom to undress and clean up.

In a few moments, Dave emerged from the bathroom in his T-shirt and sweatpants. His friends, by now, stood in awe around the table. Grace announced there was $39, 975.

"All this from a hundred-dollar stake?" Tommy asked, incredulous that Dave's blackjack insights had been realized.

Dave bent over to inspect the stacks of chips lined up on the dinette table. He scratched his head, the hair still damp from the shower of a moment ago. "That much? I had no idea," he murmured dully.

Jackie retrieved a plastic grocery sack from the kitchen closet and slid all the chips into it. She took the bulging sack and buried it under Dave's pillow on the bed and then patted the pillow to let Dave know it was time for him to sleep. He gratefully lay down while Jackie tucked in the blankets around his body.

"I'll stay here until he wakes up," she announced in a businesslike manner. "Then we'll head straight to the casino to cash in the chips and to the bank to deposit the money. Don't worry, I won't let him make another bet."

Back in the pickup to drive home, Grace and Tommy began giggling.

"Well," Kostas said seriously, "looks like we found our investor for the Pine Grove claim."

Tommy's glee dissipated quickly because he knew Kostas's remark was intended specifically for him.

When he, Jasper, and Kostas planned the gold mining operation, Tommy was assigned the responsibility of lining up the equipment from his father's rental yard in Sacramento and raising the fifteen thousand dollars they needed for exploration drilling and other expenses. Tommy did not have fifteen thousand dollars, but he assumed Kostas expected him to ask his father for it. When Tommy confessed reluctance to do so, Kostas exhibited a diffident impatience. Tommy, who desperately wanted to be part of the team to work the diggings behind Mount Grant with Kostas and Jasper—looking forward as much to the adventure of it as well as the potential profit—agreed his contribution was fair and equitable. According to Jasper, they each could earn the amount of his investment in a year's time with the simple, part-time effort they had planned.

"And tax-free!" Jasper reminded him.

Tommy frequently thought Jasper got as much enjoyment in shortchanging the government as he did actually receiving the cash when he sold his share of gold.

Back at their cottage, Grace prepared coffee and breakfast for the two men. After breakfast, Kostas went back to bed, leaving Grace and Tommy alone at the dining table. Tommy worried out loud that Kostas's remark about an investment from Dave meant he was going to be replaced on the gold mining team.

Grace patted his hand. "No, no, that's not what he meant."

Tommy worried still. *What else could it mean?* he thought. He nervously twirled his coffee cup in its saucer. Grace patted his hand again as a signal to settle down.

"You have to remember, Kostas has been wheeling and dealing over mining properties all his adult life. He's very clever, and he sees ways to do things other people don't see. But he's a good friend, and loyal. So what he is asking you to do is to be creative."

Tommy wondered why Kostas just would not tell him what to do.

"Think, Tommy," Grace said thoughtfully. "Dave's got the money. You have the opportunity. Just borrow what you need from Dave. He won more than twice as much as you will ask for, and you'll be able to pay it back over time. You're his friend. He trusts you."

"That's what Kostas meant?"

"Kostas expected you to figure it out on your own."

Later that same day, Jackie called Tommy to report the money had been safely deposited in Dave's bank account. She told him Dave had kept out the hundred dollars he started with, but he promised Jackie he would stay away from the blackjack table. He was mostly happy, according to Jackie, because his blackjack theories had been proven correct—at least this one time; but he doubted they would work again. Part of his gambling strategy was observing the state of his mind as well as the mathematics of card counting. If his mind was positive, he could bet freely and with confidence, increasing the chance of winning, or at the very least decreasing the misery when he lost. But now his mind was not in the right place, so he would stay away from the casinos.

Tommy decided to waste no time. After confirming with Jackie that Dave was still at home in his apartment, he drove directly there to explore the issue of a loan as Grace suggested.

Simple friends are the best friends, and Dave was simple. He welcomed Tommy at the doorway of his apartment and thanked him for dragging him out of the casino while he was ahead. Still, he quietly expressed the wish that Tommy and his friends had arrived perhaps an hour or two later. He was certain he could have increased his winnings because he was feeling so good, despite the several beers he had consumed and the lack of sleep. This gave Tommy the opening to broach the reason for his mission.

"Everything in life is a bet," he said. "Blackjack is just more literal and immediate." Tommy realized he was avoiding the issue of asking for the money directly, but he couldn't bring himself to be more specific.

Dave saw no bait in his friend's remark so did not take it. Still exhausted from his long night's vigil at the blackjack table, he lay down on the couch and motioned to Tommy to sit in the armchair. He laid his forearm over his forehead and closed his eyes.

After a long silence, Tommy finally blurted out, "I need fifteen thousand dollars, and I'll pay you back."

Dave didn't move or open his eyes.

"It's for our project down by Yerington," Tommy continued. "I get a third stake in the mine if I can pony up fifteen grand. I could ask my dad for it, but he'll make it a big deal. Since your ship came in, maybe you can advance me the fifteen thousand for my project with Kostas."

Dave sat up straight on the couch. "You gonna work that claim for gold?" Like Tommy, Dave was also enrolled in the school of mines at the university.

"Yeah, and you know the gold is there. We've already pulled out a couple of thousand. I just need the money to secure my edge in the partnership."

"You don't want me as a partner?"

"Can't. Just three of us. But I'll pay you back."

Dave lay back on the couch. "Don't tell Jackie. And you have to pay it back when I ask for it. Okay?"

Tommy nodded to indicate he understood, though Dave had already closed his eyes and didn't see Tommy's agreement.

"I want to get some cash for my mom anyway, so drive me to the bank, and we'll take care of this right away," Dave added.

Tommy waited in the car as Dave entered the bank. A few minutes later, he was shocked when Dave slid into the passenger's seat and lobbed three bundles of hundred-dollar bills, each with five thousand dollars, into Dave's lap.

"Here it is," he announced simply. He showed another similar bundle to Tommy before stuffing it into the breast pocket of his jacket. "This is for my mom. I've decided to go to San Diego and deliver it to her personally. She'll get a kick out it. She's never had that much money before."

Still dumbfounded by Dave's lackadaisical handling of so much cash, Tommy drove Dave back to his apartment and then headed straight for his bank, where he deposited all of the cash in his personal account.

Eager to deliver a personal check to Grace, he raced up the stairway his cottage shared with Grace and Kostas and knocked loudly on the couple's door. When Grace appeared in the doorway, Tommy handed her the check. She inspected it briefly then stepped aside to show him into the apartment.

"That was fast," she observed as she gestured for him to join her at the small table in the dinette.

Grace took care of the administrative and accounting details of the gold mining operation. Each time Kostas sold a little gold from the operation to a local buyer, he dutifully delivered the cash to Grace, who deposited it in their joint account. Unlike Jasper, she kept accurate records of their income to be reported on their tax return each year.

"You were right," Tommy said. "He just threw the money into my lap when I asked for it. Just like that."

"Dave is a man without preamble. Simple and innocent. Don't disappoint him."

"I'll pay him back!" Tommy responded, slightly shocked to receive such an admonition from Grace.

"I'm sure you will."

As Grace patted the top of his hand, she promised Tommy he would receive an agreement to put in writing the terms of the partnership with her husband and Jasper Heck, but at this moment, he could consider himself a full partner.

Because Tommy wanted to show Grace he was an honorable man, he told her a formal agreement wasn't necessary. He trusted her and Kostas, just like Dave had trusted him. A handshake was good enough. He stretched out his arm toward Grace, hoping she would reach out and touch his hand, but she deferred with a motherly smile.

"Agreements make good business like fences make good neighbors," she said. "There's no telling what can happen in the future. Didn't you sign an agreement with Dave?"

Tommy shook his head in the negative as he drew back his hand, disappointed he had not the opportunity to feel the soft touch of her skin against his.

"Oh, you should!" Grace remonstrated. "Otherwise, he might make a claim on the partnership. To protect us, you need to sign a formal promissory note to him. Otherwise, if something goes wrong, he could say the partnership owes him the money. This way only you'll be liable."

Grace's words upset Tommy, but it took him a whole day to realize why. Her businesslike caution had erased the bloom of excitement and adventure. It was now clear to him that she, and probably Kostas as well, considered the gold mining partnership only as an ordinary business venture and not the lark he had made of it in his excited acquiescence to their wishes. Her apparent indifference to his eager aspirations cast a pall of discouragement, and he wondered if he had made a mistake to ask Dave for the money and then to give it all at once to Grace. He was sure his father, if he ever learned of these transactions, would be critical of his careless disregard of human intention—which, in his father's eyes, was always perverted by self-interest or the reluctance to act. It was one of the lessons his father continually repeated to Tommy. Business was simple when it was limited to self first, others second. Trust and kindness were for fools, and functioned only to add unnecessary complications.

If their mining hopes failed, Tommy would have to find a way to repay Dave himself. He quietly resolved never to rely on his father to absolve the debt. Until now, it had never occurred to him that there might not be any gold in the gravel of the Pine Grove claim. His faith in Jasper, the wizened prospector, and Kostas, the trained geologist, was complete. Because they never mentioned failure, Tommy never considered failure as a possibility. Suddenly, he felt quite naïve and regretted he had to agree with his father. Maybe he was too innocent for these kinds of adventures.

The next day, Tommy realized it was probably too late to ask Grace to return the check he had just handed over, even if he wanted to. She had probably deposited it and would then have to write him another check to reimburse the money, if she agreed to do that. He was saddened by the doubt her last words had inspired. *Only he was liable.*

His concern was not the money and how it could be repaid if the mining venture failed; the money was replaceable somehow. But he did worry about his father's reaction if the hasty loan from Dave turned out to be a problem. Even if he wanted the money back, he did not think he could bring himself to ask Grace for it or to confront Kostas if he became involved.

After much anguished speculation, the best course of action, he decided, was to do as Grace instructed, to prepare a promissory note to Dave and deliver it to him. At home, he found templates of promissory notes on the Internet and downloaded one he could revise for his purposes. After looking over it very carefully, he signed it. He printed out an additional copy for Dave and, after a moment's reconsideration, still another copy he could give to Grace to show her he had implemented her advice.

Dave did not answer his cell phone when he called to set a meeting time to show Dave the note and have him countersign it. That was strange. Dave was meticulous about his phone and accepting all calls. He often was so desperate for part-time work he answered every phone call, even in the midst of classes at the university, in hopes of lining up additional hours of work. Perhaps, Tommy thought, he felt wealthy enough now not to persist in such a habit, though that was unlikely.

Tommy wanted to get this matter out of the way quickly to show Grace he had followed her advice, so he tried Jackie's phone number. She answered and told him Dave had decided to fly to San Diego to deliver in person five thousand dollars of his winnings to his mother. He was to surprise his mother and so did not call ahead. He was so excited about being able to do this he had Jackie drop him off at the airport and bought a ticket at the airline counter with cash. He said he would be back the next morning in time for classes and his graveyard shift at the kitchen of the Nugget in Sparks. Jackie gave Tommy the number of the return flight the next morning and asked Tommy to pick Dave up at the airport.

The next morning, Tommy waited just outside the security stations at the airport for Dave to walk through. But he wasn't there. After trying Dave's cell phone, which again went straight to voice mail, he called Jackie at her job. She had not heard from him either. She could not tell him Dave's mother's phone number, and as they discussed this, she realized she did not even know her name. He knew she had remarried and had a different family name than Dave. She had moved to San Diego only recently. They concluded they would have to wait for Dave to connect with him.

By evening time, Dave still had not called. It was clear he would be late for work, which was so unlike him. Tommy decided to drive to the Nugget in case, through some miscommunication, Dave had returned and went directly to work. Since Tommy had shown up there once or twice to deliver Dave to work or pick him up afterward, the kitchen staff recognized him. They had not seen nor heard from Dave either. The kitchen chef came up to Tommy, a little exasperated that Dave had not called, but also showing concern because, according to the chef, this was so unlike Dave. He always had been dependable and considerate of everyone.

All the while, the promissory note had been folded in Tommy's shirt pocket. It had his signature on it, but remained unsigned and unknown by Dave. He was quite mixed about his efforts to track down Dave. On the one hand, he was sincerely concerned because Dave's unexplained absence was so uncharacteristic of his methodical behavior. On the other hand, he did not mind delaying the delivery of the promissory note, vaguely hoping some other resolution of the issue would develop, though he could not imagine what else could occur.

He called Jackie as he was leaving the Nugget to learn she had not heard from him either. Now they both were concerned. Jackie told him Dave had withdrawn the money he was to give to his mother from the bank account despite her advice not to travel with so much cash. She began to speculate something might have happened to him as a result. Dave was so innocent and guileless he may have even revealed his plan to someone he met at the airport or in San Diego before he reached his mother's house.

They could not check on this theory because they had no knowledge of who his mother could be. Briefly, they speculated about notifying the police in San Diego but decided to wait another day. Putting the best light on the situation, they concluded he probably forgot to charge his cell phone. The most likely explanation was that he was still with his mother, though this did not explain why he had not called in to his part-time job, which he treasured so much.

The next day at the university, Tommy could not find Dave even when he went to the classrooms and lab where he knew Dave had classes. He checked his apartment again, and nothing had changed there. Dave's motorcycle was still chained to the gas meter next to his apartment door as it had been when Tommy had dropped by before.

That evening, Jackie and Tommy met to discuss their concerns. In the time he had last talked to her, Jackie had become impatient and angry. She could not believe something terrible could have happened to Dave because such an outcome was so unlikely. She ranted about Dave's innocent forgetfulness, expressing concern that he had forgotten her as well. She began to wonder if Dave had detoured to Las Vegas with the money or had withdrawn more than he had told her about to gamble in Las Vegas. The longer he was gone, she thought, the more likely the result was good. He must be winning to be so uncaring. She could check this theory if she were able to find how much money was still in the savings account, but she had no access to it.

When she asked Tommy why he was so eager to find him, Tommy did not mention the promissory note but pretended his initial concern was caused by his absence at the airport. He did not mention to her that if she had been able to check Dave's bank account, it would show at least twenty thousand dollars missing, not just the five thousand he had told Jackie he was withdrawing for his mother. They talked about calling the police in San Diego, calling the airlines, and other stratagems. But they did not know where to start or if they should. After all, they were just friends, not family, and had no real authority to initiate any action.

During this entire time, Tommy had not communicated with Grace about the note or Dave. Kostas was away somewhere inspecting other gold properties near their claim in Pine Grove Valley.

That evening, he and Grace accidently met as they parked their cars on the street below their apartments, and Tommy described the mystery of Dave's disappearance. He leaned toward her, showing his wish to hear her advice.

As usual, Grace showed no inclination to make more of Dave's absence other than as an innocent act of forgetfulness or distraction. She would not accept that Dave had been so foolish to let some hustler relieve him of his five thousand dollars; nor did she think he was so reckless to have returned to the blackjack tables in Las Vegas or elsewhere with the money. She told Tommy to keep trying his cell phone and to leave a note at his apartment showing his concern.

On the third morning, Dave called Tommy. "I knew you tried calling me. Jackie too. Sorry about that," he started.

Tommy expressed his relief to learn Dave was safe. He explained all the imagined trouble they thought Dave might have encountered.

"Well, you were not so far off the mark," Dave replied. "I was afraid to call you and Jackie. I still haven't touched base with her. I don't know what to say."

Tommy's silence displayed his confusion, but Dave did not wait for his response. "When I went to the bank to get you your fifteen thousand, I got five for me too. Plus the five for my mom. Boy, was she happy to see that money! I am so glad I gave it to her. At least I used that much for a good cause. And I am so glad I loaned you the fifteen thousand. Otherwise, I might not have it anymore."

The implications shocked Tommy.

"Yeah," Dave continued, "my five thousand is gone. I lost it. That's why I was afraid to return your calls. I feel so stupid."

"In Las Vegas?" Tommy asked, incredulous that Jackie could have been so prescient to have explained accurately Dave's absence.

Dave recounted how good he felt after giving his mother the money and so he figured he was in a good frame of mind to gamble again. He bought a ticket to Las Vegas from San Diego and went directly to a blackjack table at the Bellagio, a luxurious hotel and casino on the Strip.

"When I exchanged my five thousand in cash for chips, they offered me a room for free!" Dave boasted. "I went up to the room just to check it out, but a lot of good it did me. I never even used it except to go to the bathroom once."

Dave informed Tommy he was arriving at the Reno airport and asked if he could pick him up and drive him to his apartment. He asked Tommy not to connect with Jackie and let her know what happened. He would find another way to deal with her.

When Tommy met Dave that afternoon, he still had the draft promissory note in his shirt pocket, but he did not mention it during the few minutes from the airport to the apartment. As they drove, Dave explained he was so happy Tommy had borrowed the money and removed it from his bank account; otherwise, he might have been tempted to withdraw more from his account.

"Funny," Dave mused, "when it's gone, it's safe. At least I can count on you."

As Dave expressed his remorse, Tommy was afraid to bring up the note, fearing Dave might change his view and ask for the money to be repaid. As a friend, he felt he should ask if Dave needed the money, but did not know how to phrase the question without risking an affirmative answer. He decided the best thing to do was to remain silent.

"I still have a little over thirteen thousand in my account, more than I had before. And you owe me fifteen, which is way more than I had. But I don't want you to give it back to me just yet, not until I can make sure I won't go again to the casino. I was so stupid."

Tommy smiled weakly, and not sincerely. As he patted Dave on the shoulder, he felt a great sense of guilty relief.

Later, he revised the promissory note to show only his signature. He signed one copy to give to Grace. He never mentioned it to Dave. If Dave ever asked the partnership for the money, Grace had the proof that would protect their interests. With Tommy, Dave would have to depend on undocumented friendship. Tommy felt lucky to have pleased Grace and Dave with one action, though from his side, the result was a complete accident, and he had exhibited no honest impulse. He could even refuse to repay Dave back, should he ever ask, to protect Dave from himself.

Chapter Two

The American ambassador in Tegucigalpa called Grace late in the afternoon. He had dialed her cell phone from a list of emergency numbers that Kostas had registered with the embassy. Grace was examining a young pregnant woman at the health clinic when the muffled sound of the phone emanated from her purse in the locker. As the ringing continued, she considered ignoring it; but thinking it might be Kostas, excused herself and rushed to retrieve the phone. Kostas had not checked in since the weekend, and she was eager to hear about his progress to open the mine. She knew this was the week that he had scheduled to begin actual excavations—after four long years of preparation. Though she doubted it, she thought he might also have remembered today was Valentine's Day.

Because Kostas had inspired such confidence and credibility in his Honduran activities, the ambassador himself, and not one of his assistants, made the call to

Grace. After following protocol to affirm her identity by comparing her responses to the emergency documentation Kostas had provided, the ambassador professionally but kindly relayed the difficult news, patiently pausing at her long silences. Still, he was busy and had other problems to solve, so he pressed her for an e-mail address one of his assistants could use to send her contact information. He asked if she wanted him to identify the body for the purposes of the investigation. Forgetting she was on the phone, Grace shook her head in the negative. She would come to Honduras. There was only silence on the phone line until the ambassador repeated his offer. This time, Grace spoke up and said she would come as soon as she could schedule a flight.

Grace absently replaced the cell phone in her purse, took her jacket out of the locker, and turned to walk home. The young Paiute woman, half dressed and still seated on the examination table, as she saw Grace preparing to leave, cleared her throat. Grace smiled weakly at the young woman and apologized for her forgetfulness. She removed her jacket and replaced it and her purse in the locker to finish her examination, which she accomplished with slow deliberation. As the woman dressed after the session, Grace conscientiously collected information on nutrition and prenatal care from the display rack mounted on the wall. She explained to her patient the function of each brochure and leaflet and dutifully asked if there were any other questions.

The Indian woman understood something terrible had happened and spontaneously reached out to hold Grace's hand. Grace burst out crying as the young Indian mother gently squeezed her hand.

The father-to-be was in the anteroom. When he heard his wife call out his name, he shyly poked his head through the clinic door and saw two women crying. Fearing for his unborn baby, he rushed in expecting the worst. Though he was aware of how unseemly and coarse it was to be relieved the bad news was not his bad news, he secretly rejoiced that his wife and baby were safe. Men died, babies arrived. Such was life in his rough world.

His wife took charge. She stood up and walked around the table to ease her shoulder under Grace's arm to support her. Following her lead, her husband stepped to the opposite side, and together, they escorted Grace out of the clinic and into the parking lot where his pickup was parked. Grace remembered her purse and jacket, and the young woman dashed back into the infirmary to retrieve them while Grace stood silently next to her husband in the parking lot. Putting Grace between them on the bench seat of the truck, they drove her down the country lane to her house. Hugging her jacket and purse to her chest, Grace had stopped crying and sat stoic and silent, staring out the windshield.

She refused their help when they arrived at the house. The young couple sat outside in the pickup while they watched Grace struggle to find her keys in the purse.

After she had let herself in and waved from the front window, the husband reluctantly started up the truck and backed out of the driveway. Feeling remorse for his selfish thoughts earlier, he asked his wife if she wanted to stay with Grace. His wife cradled the small mound of her stomach and said they just should go home and be thankful for what they share.

At home, Grace stood in the narrow hallway leading to Kostas's office to study the arrangement of photos she had collected over the years of their marriage and partnership. It was hard to imagine this Earth without Kostas poking its innards.

Despite the somber purpose of their mission, Tommy was excited to travel to Honduras with Grace. She had called him that evening and had asked him if he would accompany her to Tegucigalpa. The next day, they met at the Reno airport to fly to Los Angeles to connect with an American Airlines flight to the Honduran capital.

Grace had arranged and purchased all the tickets. When asked what he should bring, she simply told him not to forget his passport. Tommy arrived at the airport with only a small backpack containing a change of underwear and a clean shirt. Before they boarded the flight to Los Angeles, he stopped at an ATM to withdraw two hundred dollars, as a precaution should he need it to rescue Grace from some predicament. As Grace waited next to him, she gave him her ATM card and asked him to draw a like amount from her account. Tommy was shocked because she had to reveal her PIN number to him, which she did casually and without even lowering her voice, as if she did not care. Maybe she did not care, Tommy thought, as he typed in the number and extracted the cash, which he handed to Grace along with the ATM card and receipt for the transaction. Or, he suddenly speculated, his heart pounding with wonder, with Kostas gone, she had shifted her trust to him, and to be trusted by such a saint as Grace was a rare honor, or so he believed.

During the flight from Los Angeles to Tegucigalpa, Grace pulled a folder from her purse and handed it to Tommy. It contained the information she had printed out from the embassy's e-mail message. She asked Tommy to review it and help her find her way once they arrived in Tegucigalpa. A few tears began to well up. She did not have to explain to Tommy that she might feel overwhelmed as they approached the reality of seeing Kostas for the last time and therefore had no confidence in her judgment. Tommy did not know whether or not he should pull her close over the armrest and whisper encouragement in her ear. He realized in a moment of shame he wanted to be close to her, and secretly rejoiced these new circumstances would make something only dreamed about seem possible. He held back, unsure whether hugging her was for his benefit or hers. Grace patted his hand and smiled, as if she understood his dilemma. Tommy always believed she understood him better than he understood himself. Maybe that was the attraction.

Grace rarely met men who were not instantly smitten by her. She was not a great beauty in an ordinary way, but there was some superior aura about her that emanated an easy but exciting comfort. You could tell she was used to this reaction and could use this special quality to influence relationships, but also, she would only implement this power when a good purpose required it. Tommy was completely under her spell, and that was probably the reason she asked him and not Kostas's brother in Los Angeles to accompany her. When with Tommy, Grace was in control. Her husband's Greek-Irish-Paiute brother would not be so submissive.

Tommy pressed his head against the fuselage and peered through the window at the rough Honduran landscape below as the plane maneuvered to land. The night before, he had Googled Honduras to learn about the Tegucigalpa airport, which was considered one of the most dangerous in the world. A short runway surrounded by mountains and a sprawling metropolis, difficult crosswinds, and lax safety standards made each landing an adventure. He marveled a company like American Airlines found enough profit in their daily flights to take the risk. As he looked out the window, all he had learned about the hazards of this airport seemed evident. It did not help his confidence when the plane bounced up and down and weaved back and forth due to violent crosswinds. Grace grabbed his arm for security, and he willingly lent it to her. If they went down like this, he thought vainly, it would be a proper way to leave this world.

Of course they landed without incident. Still, Tommy's imagined excitement increased when Grace felt compelled to seek his support by hanging onto his arm as they entered the crowded terminal. Tommy straightened his back and peered straight ahead, as if on an important mission, despite all the distractions of the foreign airport. They had checked no bags so strode straight to the exit after clearing passport control, only to encounter a cacophony of noisy traffic and humanity. Taxi drivers pulled at their sleeves. Flower vendors pressed them to buy their posies. Beggars and thieves seemed to lurk in every shadow. Grace moved closer to Tommy, and side by side, they left the terminal to enter into the broad street outside. Tommy realized they were already near the center of the city.

Grace spotted an American in a short-sleeved white shirt and tie holding a sign with her name on it. The American saw them and came forward as he pointed at the sign in his hand. Grace nodded the affirmative, and the American showed them to a waiting SUV. He opened the door for Grace and Tommy to sit in the rear seat and himself took the front seat next to the driver. He turned to ask if she wanted to go to the hotel to freshen up and rest before moving on to the embassy. The ambassador himself, he said importantly, would be accompanying her to the morgue to identify her husband and to claim the remains.

Words like *morgue* and *remains* bothered Tommy. He instantly realized his understanding of Kostas's death had been merely theoretical. Subconsciously, he expected to find this adventure was some elaborate scheme of Kostas to induce Grace to visit him or to outwit some international law controlling the import of precious metals and money. Suddenly, he was afraid to accompany Grace to the morgue. He had never seen a dead person before, and to see Kostas as not the vital and handsome man he was might be just too much to bear.

Grace's response made it evident, though not to Tommy, that avoiding the truth of the situation was worse than actually confronting it. They drove directly to the embassy to meet the ambassador and to receive his guidance on the decisions she would have to make.

The SUV entered through an elaborate wrought iron gate into the courtyard of the American embassy. A marine with an M16 on his arm waved the driver through. In the shade of the tall building, Honduran families holding cardboard boxes and baskets huddled with their children. American tourists and businessmen were exiting the main building as the SUV pulled up directly in front of the steps leading to the embassy lobby. As Grace got out of the car, she noticed a tall Honduran woman holding the hand of a small girl. The Honduran smiled at her, as if in recognition, but the ambassador's assistant rushed Grace and Tommy past the woman before she could speak. Grace was reminded of the Paiute women she served in the reservation health clinic. As she was being pushed ahead by the embassy clerk, she turned to look again at the Honduran woman and her child. The woman had picked up the child and was following them into the embassy building.

Grace and Tommy were ushered into the ambassador's spacious office. The ambassador, a tall, handsome man with graying hair, rose from behind his desk and cordially held out his hand to Grace. She shook it briefly. Tommy stepped up and reached across the desk to introduce himself as a friend of Kostas and Grace, here to help.

The ambassador explained their schedule. They would drive together to the coroner's office to view the body. After certifying his identity for the local police, the ambassador himself would escort the two to the hotel, where they had already reserved two rooms on their behalf. He indicated that if she wished, he would stay and take dinner with her. Grace refused the offer of dinner, indicating that when she needed to eat, she would call room service.

There was another matter they had to discuss, the ambassador announced. Hesitating, he came around the desk to stand beside Grace in her chair. Grace straightened in her chair to look at him directly. The ambassador waited for her response.

"Go ahead," she announced finally.

The ambassador walked to the door of the office. He gave his secretary an instruction that was inaudible in the office where Tommy and Grace waited.

The ambassador returned to his desk but remained standing behind it. In a few moments, his secretary escorted the Honduran woman, still carrying her child, into the office. The secretary paused, looking to her boss for direction but also appearing hopeful she could stay to witness events. His nod indicated her to leave and close the door behind her.

"Mrs. Wilson," the ambassador said solemnly, "meet Pilar and her daughter Antu."

Grace stood up to honor the woman and took her hand to shake it. She leaned forward to look the small girl in the face and, despite her grief, gave the child a big smile. She had seen so many young Indian girls like this at the reservation in Schurz. The child smiled back but hugged her mother more tightly.

"Antu," the ambassador started, "is your husband's child. He registered her birth with us four years ago. Pilar, well, is her mother."

Grace backed slowly to her chair and sat down. As shocked as Tommy was about these revelations, his admiration for Kostas soared. If anyone could have had a beautiful Latin mistress, it would be Kostas.

"I've made arrangements for Ms. Chevez and her daughter to stay at the same hotel this evening with you so that you might decide how to handle this situation. That's, of course, if you agree as you'll have to pay their hotel bill. Antu is an American citizen, but Pilar is not, so it's a dicey situation to say the least. In his instructions in case of an emergency like this, your husband asked that we handle it in this way. He knew you would come to Honduras should something happen to him."

"Did he think something would happen?" Grace asked the ambassador.

Turning slightly to face Pilar, he then retook his chair behind the desk. "I'm sure, if you wish, Pilar will let you know what circumstances are like here in Honduras. She speaks excellent English and is a graduate of the local university. Among her people, she is an important person advocating for indigenous rights. She and your husband were quite involved in helping her native tribe, the Lencas, create an environmental safe zone around the many mining operations in the area. As I perceived it, your husband became quite passionate about conditions for her people, perhaps because his daughter was now one of them. But not everyone in government or the mining industry agreed with him, as you might guess. So, yes, he did think something could happen, and we discussed it. But he was determined—maybe a little foolishly—but determined to make a success of their plans for a good life as well as success of his mining venture."

Pausing, the ambassador turned to Pilar, implying she might want to say something to her lover's wife.

Pilar set her daughter on the floor. "He wanted her to be happy and safe," she said simply.

Tommy was amazed that though Kostas was literally absent from this earth, his presence exerted such a great influence on all the lives in this room. Unlike Kostas, Tommy was present but had as little bearing on these events as a fly on the wall.

Tommy's vision of a morgue was what he had seen on television, sterile hospital-like facilities with refrigerated bunks for the dead lined up on one wall, examining rooms with men and women in surgeon's gowns and masks over their faces. But that was television. Honduras offered a different drama. The Tegucigalpa morgue was a decrepit cinder-block building with bars over the few small windows. Some of the windowpanes were broken, and Tommy noticed flies freely buzzing in and out. A policeman leaned back in a chair next to the entrance as he read a local newspaper and smoked a smelly cigarette. More flies hovered about in the small lobby with a single wooden desk. A man, who could have been a pathologist or a mortician, came out of another small room when he heard the embassy's SUV pull up in front.

Inside the morgue, there was no refrigeration, just a large, plain room, its cinder-block walls painted military beige. A dozen tables were arranged in two rows of six. On five of the tables lay forms over which sheets, some stained with dirt and blood, were draped. Though the room smelled of formaldehyde and other antiseptic substances, they could not disguise the sweet perfume of decay.

As Tommy entered the room behind Grace, he knew under one of those sheets was Kostas, or what used to be Kostas. The medical-looking Honduran official led them to a table nearest the far window. After introducing himself in Spanish as the coroner, he explained this body had been here the longest; the others had just arrived earlier that day. Not too busy a week, he added casually. The ambassador translated for Grace and Tommy. Grace reached out for Tommy's arm, and he moved in closer to her, needing her support for this awful experience as much as she might need his.

The coroner stood at the head while Grace and Tommy moved to one side, the ambassador on the other. Then he lifted the sheet slightly to show the face. He said something in Spanish to the ambassador, explaining he could not show more without revealing the wounds. Grace reached out a hand but was afraid to touch the still, cold face. The eyes were closed, thankfully. The mouth was clamped shut with grim determination. Tommy only glanced at the face, finding it unbearable to look at, so turned immediately to watch Grace as if to help her, but mostly to take himself away from the terrible vision of Kostas frozen with fight, presumably for all eternity.

Grace nodded with recognition, and the doctor replaced the sheet.

In the office, they were given a large paper sack with the clothes, shoes, wallet, keys, and the pistol that had been found with Kostas. Tommy offered to carry the sack, but Grace hugged it to her chest as they left the morgue and climbed into the embassy car.

In the car, Grace leaned forward to talk with the ambassador in the front seat. "Has Pilar seen Kostas like this?"

The ambassador turned to prop his back against the door to talk with Grace. "She found him and called the police."

"Oh, how terrible!" Grace muttered.

"She knew we would call you," the ambassador continued. "She knew you would come."

"And her daughter . . . Kostas's daughter?"

The ambassador shrugged his shoulders to show he did not know the answer to her question and turned back to look out the windshield as the SUV slowly made its way through the crowded streets.

"We'll take you to the hotel now. The two of them will meet us there. Tomorrow, we can make whatever arrangements you wish with the funeral home."

When they pulled up before a modest hotel facing a pleasant plaza, Pilar and her daughter waited by the front door, a small suitcase on the ground by their feet. Grace walked directly to them, Tommy following behind. For a moment, the two women, both beautiful, dark, and appearing tall when compared to the Central Americans who thronged by on the sidewalk and in the plaza, stood face-to-face. Each gazed silently at the other then, in unison, they turned to look at little Antu standing by the suitcase. Grace knelt down and held her by the shoulders at arm's length to inspect the child's face. The girl smiled, and Grace pulled her close and hugged her tightly. Pilar knelt down to throw her arms around the both of them.

Tommy and the ambassador respectfully kept their distance, looking at each other with uncertain smiles on their faces. There is no explaining grief. Sometimes it can be joy, they seemed to say to each other. Tommy was suddenly overwhelmed with a sense of loss as he realized Kostas was gone. What he saw on the morgue table was not Kostas, but some cruel object that mocked life.

The clerk behind the hotel counter explained in Spanish there had been only two rooms reserved in Grace's name. Pilar translated for Grace. For a few moments, Grace, reflective and silent, studied Pilar and her daughter next to her.

"Tell him to make sure one of them has twin beds in it," Grace instructed Pilar.

Pilar smiled gently at Grace and took her by the hand as she turned to rattle off the instructions in Spanish to the hotel clerk.

The clerk handed Tommy a large iron key with a plastic tag dangling from it, and another to Pilar. Their rooms were next to each other. Pilar and Grace, with Antu in tow, disappeared into one. Tommy, suddenly by himself, opened the hotel door and let himself in his room, spacious and shadowy, overlooking an enclosed patio from the balcony. The french doors were open, and a slight breeze ruffled the curtains. He walked onto the balcony and saw Pilar and Grace standing on their balcony next door. Grace acknowledged Tommy with a nod of her head and went back inside with Pilar, out of sight.

Little Antu pranced onto the porch and waved gaily at Tommy. He waved back, wondering how much of Kostas she actually was. Would she have his spirit, his strength, his fortitude? He remembered the ambassador saying that her mother was an indigenous Honduran, of the Lenca Indian race. He marveled that the great-great-grandson of an American Indian, Wovoka the Indian messiah, had formed a union with an Indian two thousand miles away in Central America. Little Antu was a product of that union, now part Paiute and part Lenca, with Kostas's Greek and Irish lineage thrown in for good measure. A child of the world, he thought. Perhaps there was something good and important in her future as a result, he speculated. Curiously, despite the dire circumstances that had brought them to Honduras, he found himself envying Antu's legacy. When he remembered her mother, Pilar, a tall, beautiful Lenca, regal like an Indian princess even in her jeans, tank top, and flip-flops, he felt Kostas had inspired some great project. He was excited and happy to be part of it. He had found the adventure he had hoped their gold mine claim in Pine Grove Valley in Nevada might become.

But Kostas was dead. Such is the price of adventure!

Despite the ghastly environment of the morgue he had experienced earlier, Tommy was suddenly famished and could think only of food. He searched through his backpack for some snack he might have left in it, but there was nothing. He went to the balcony, but could spot no restaurant or shop near the hotel patio. He was afraid to leave the hotel to find some food without notifying Grace, but there was no phone in his room. As a last resort, he could call her from his room on his cell phone, but that even presented problems if making calls from and to another country other than the United States required some extra technical step that would sap his energy and challenge his patience. He marveled at how this one small matter caused such confusion, and mentally noted it might be a symptom of the grief and horror he had faced earlier. But he could not ignore the gnawing emptiness of his stomach, and its ache only increased the darkness he had encountered in Honduras. He sat on the edge of the bed for a few moments, trying to collect himself to think through this perplexing and agonizing problem. Now he was sorry that he had agreed to accompany Grace, that he had sought adventure with his friend Kostas, that he had not chosen the safe and comfortable alternative of keeping his nose to the grindstone at school, getting his degree and a job, and meeting an ordinary girlfriend whom he could marry and buy a house with. He realized in a moment of excruciating clarity everything he experienced was a result of the choices he had made in his life, and what he chose now was sure to have consequences he could not have imagined.

In such a state, he remembered his friend Dave Mogis and the fifteen thousand dollars he had borrowed from him. That money was now gone without Kostas to help Jasper and him manage the gold claim. Gulping with frightened frustration, he would have to face his father, confess his hasty investment in the claim, and ask him to repay Dave when Dave needed the money. He shivered with shame to remember he avoided giving Dave the signed promissory note, realizing that he had done so to give him some escape route or delay from repaying Dave. He slammed his knee with his fists as he understood the dishonest and disloyal nature of his mind. He wanted to avoid everything difficult, his father, his debt to Dave, the reality of life, death.

Then there arose memories of his fainthearted dreams of romance, adventure, success, and liberation from the droll life his father had lived and required. Who was he to challenge the rough business of getting through life? Afraid, confused, ashamed, and hungry beyond belief, he wanted to be home in his own Sacramento bedroom, showing up for work at his father's business without a care in the world. He had chosen uncertainty, which he had called adventure, over the certainty of the ordinary life his father had chosen for him, and now this was the result. He could not even figure out how to let Grace know he was hungry!

Grace solved his dilemma. She knocked on his hotel room door, softly calling out his name. Smirking with shame, Tommy rose from the bed and opened the door. What had kept him from just knocking on her door? Sad and straight, Grace stood before him. Pilar waited in the doorway of their room with little Antu clutching her leg.

"Pilar and I are going out and get some food for all of us. We thought you might be hungry, and Antu needs something before she goes to bed. Can you sit in our room with Antu while we're gone? It will only be a little while, maybe a half hour."

Tommy nodded meekly. Perhaps when the hunger was gone, the terror of the situation would subside a little. He patted his jeans pocket to make sure he had his room key with him and followed Grace into the next room.

Pilar explained something to Antu in rapid Spanish. The little girl looked at Tommy as she spoke and nodded her head with understanding. As she gathered up her purse, Grace knelt down to whisper something sweetly to the little girl, then both women left, Pilar carrying nothing with her. She walked with her arms swinging freely, ready for any eventuality.

When the hotel door closed leaving Tommy and Antu together, the little girl settled herself on the floor in front of the television, which was playing some Mexican soap opera. Tommy pulled a reclining chair off the balcony to watch with her. When the girl turned to check on his presence, he smiled weakly and, as always, she bestowed him with a wide grin. Adventure? He was babysitting!

By the time Pilar and Grace had let themselves back into the hotel room, Antu had crept close to Tommy, reacting with childish intensity to the suspense in the soap opera, and clung to his leg for safety and support. Surprised by this sign of familiarity, Tommy froze in place, afraid to adjust his leg for comfort, or to withdraw it. Occasionally, Antu would look up at him to make sure he understood the drama displayed on the screen, so Tommy would pretend he was watching, but he had no clue. All he knew was the women of the television drama were beautiful and strong willed, and the men intent and desperate. Not too dissimilar to the drama he was living, he thought woefully.

When she saw her mother, Antu leaped up to drag her toward the television, explaining something about what was happening in her rapid and sweetly childish Spanish. Pilar pretended interest for her daughter's sake. Grace followed with a cardboard box full of foil-covered paper plates of food, which she began laying out on the table by the window.

"*Baleadas*," Grace said. "A Honduran fast-food staple. Thick flour tortillas with meat, fish, beans, cheese, even scrambled eggs. We bought two of each, not knowing what you would like. But Antu gets at least one with eggs. It's her favorite."

Pilar set a plastic grocery sack with Coca-Colas and a small bottle of milk on the table. She peeked under each of the foil-wrapped plates to find one with scrambled eggs and cheese. She unwrapped one of those and placed it on the floor before Antu. The little girl tore off pieces of the tortilla, wrapping bits of egg and cheese in it and then popping the morsel into her mouth. Her mother opened the small bottle of milk for her, which she also placed on the floor.

Inexplicably, the pain of Tommy's hunger vanished. He felt light-headed and dizzy. Now all he wanted was sleep.

"Meat or fish?" Grace asked him.

He chose meat, and she handed him a plate together with a plastic knife and fork. She pushed the other plates of food out of the way so that he could sit at the table and eat his meal. He opened a Coca-Cola and gulped down half of the bottle. Pilar sat on the floor with her daughter and her plate of food. Grace took a chair next to Tommy at the table.

"Pilar tells me Kostas loved these *baleadas*," she told Tommy thoughtfully as she picked at her food.

Tommy's mouth was full, so he just nodded acknowledgement.

"Despite its problems, he loved Honduras too," she continued.

Tommy gulped down what was in his mouth and stopped eating to gaze at Grace. Grief had made her more alluring. She appeared wise and calm, almost spiritual. They both turned to look at Pilar and Antu eating together on the floor in front of the television. The girl laughed and her mother smiled as she smoothed down her long dark hair with her palm.

"He loved you too," Tommy found himself saying gently.

Grace set down her plastic fork and leaned back in her chair. She pushed away the half-eaten plate of food. Then she smiled sadly.

"I think Kostas loved everything! I'm just one object in a world full of treasures. I guess I always knew that but never understood until I saw Pilar and Antu. They should have been no surprise to me."

"You didn't seem surprised when you saw them," Tommy said earnestly. "You drew them close right away."

Grace raised her eyebrows. "What else was I to do? There's a lot of Kostas in little Antu, and I have to say that Pilar is not just a pretty little thing. You should hear her! When we went out for food, there was no talk of Kostas. Nothing about her own sorrow. She is out for justice and ready to get it. And I believe she will. I guess already I love her and Antu, not just because Kostas loved them, but because they loved Kostas."

The next morning, Miguel Tavares intercepted Grace in the hotel lobby as she and her entourage made their way to the street outside. He showed slight surprise to find Grace accompanied by a man but quickly recovered his demeanor as he removed his straw hat to introduce himself. Pilar abruptly stepped between Miguel and Grace and performed a perfunctory introduction before Miguel could speak.

Taking her cue from Pilar, Grace held out her hand and then withdrew it after the slightest of handshakes. Tommy wondered if the two women had spent last night planning the inevitable confrontation with Kostas's Honduran partner. So much was at stake for Grace and the Nevada investors in the Honduran silver venture. Since the energetic and impatient optimism of Kostas left no space for contingency plans, there was no person to assume control unless it was Tavares. Pilar's sterile politeness already suggested they had to seek other options.

Holding his hat at his chest with both hands, Miguel expressed in perfect English his elaborate condolences. Pilar did not wait but, taking Antu by the hand, went through the open doorway of the hotel and into the street to hail a taxi. Miguel seemed distracted by her action and interrupted himself to let Pilar know he had a car. She did not or pretended not to hear him but held out her arm for a taxi.

"But I have a car!" he shouted. His shout echoed in the plastered and tiled lobby, drawing the desk clerk's attention to them. Exasperated, he turned back to Grace.

"Please, let me assist you. I am at your service. It is the least I can do. I worked with Kostas for four years. He is my friend."

Grace nodded to Tommy to retrieve Pilar and Antu from the street. Tommy understood the silent command and left Grace and Miguel in the lobby to escort the mother and daughter back into the hotel.

When they returned to the lobby, Grace was seated on a couch with Miguel next to her. Miguel spoke earnestly, leaning close to Grace. In the midst of one of his long explanations, Grace stood up, interrupting him. Displaying repressed anger, he slowly rose from the couch, his hat still in his two hands. Clearly, he seemed like a man who expected attention and compliance to his wishes, especially by women. Though he was surprised and confused by Tommy's presence, his behavior clearly showed he had written him off as too young to be anything other than a helper to carry bags and run errands.

"Do you have a problem if Miguel helps us today?" Grace asked Pilar.

It was clear Pilar did have a problem but decided to deal with it directly as long as the problem had made its appearance. She understood sooner or later they would have to make appropriate business arrangements with Miguel. He was still partner in the Honduran enterprise, though with a minority share, but essential to making concluding dispositions of the property. Something of value was at stake, and since Miguel was tied to it by Kostas, undoing the knot would require Miguel's participation. Manifesting a clear signal of the nature of her thoughts, Pilar shot a fierce glance at Miguel, who was no taller than she was.

"Not today," Pilar replied.

Miguel's Land Rover—a new one, Tommy noted—was parked in the plaza in front of the hotel. Miguel opened the front door for Grace to sit with him, leaving Tommy and Pilar to decide on their own initiative to climb into the backseat with little Antu between them. Miguel pointedly made sure Grace had secured her seat belt before he put the car in gear, though he did not check to see if the passengers in the rear had done the same. Even so, Pilar spoke up in English to let him know they had all buckled up, as if to give him permission to drive off.

Their first stop was to visit a funeral home recommended by the consulate. Pilar and Grace had already decided during the long night to have Kostas cremated so that the ashes could be shared between his two homes, Honduras and Nevada, and his two families. Cremation also simplified the gloomy business of returning him to Nevada. Pilar suggested his ashes be transported in indigenous Honduran pottery, which could be packed safely in a suitcase purchased just for this purpose. As she had made these recommendations to her lover's wife, she let Grace know how much interest Kostas had in supporting local people and culture. This concern might have killed him as well, she had hinted, because his was a very unpopular example among the international mining companies, which were devouring the landscape in many places throughout Central America.

After making arrangements at the funeral home, which Grace had to pay for with her American Express credit card, Pilar directed Miguel to drive to a market area where they could select pottery to hold Kostas's ashes. They selected two of equal size, one for Pilar and one for Grace, and delivered them back to the funeral parlor. Although Grace was prepared to pay for both, Pilar insisted she purchase hers. She paid with the Honduran currency, the lempira, while Grace asked the clerk to accept credit card payment for the vase she had selected.

As the day progressed, it became apparent to both men the two women had extensively planned the day during their night together at the hotel. Tommy learned Antu already had an American passport, arranged by Kostas shortly after her birth. They were now on their way to the American consulate to obtain a travel visa for Pilar then to a travel agency to obtain tickets for the mother and daughter. Despite his polite but pointed suggestions, Miguel had been relegated to just a taxi driver, often left alone in the car with Tommy. They spoke little. Tommy did not know what to ask, and Miguel seemed uninterested in what he might have to offer.

Miguel stopped the Land Rover outside the gates of the American consulate to let Grace and Pilar walk through the plaza and up the stairs into the building, little Antu skipping along behind them. Finally, Miguel loosened his seat belt to face Tommy over the back of his seat.

"Have you plans for your return?" he asked.

Startled into action by the question, Tommy pulled his backpack across his lap to unzip it and find his passport and plane ticket. He pulled out the ticket to inspect it.

"You don't know when you're returning?" Miguel asked, incredulous that Tommy had to read the information from the ticket.

Tommy ignored the question. "It says here tomorrow afternoon, but I don't know if we'll make that."

"What else do you have to take care of?"

Tommy shrugged his shoulders. "I think Grace and Pilar have some business to take care of."

"Like what?"

Like murder! Tommy thought without speaking up.

Miguel turned back toward the front and gripped both hands on the steering wheel, one thumb beating impatiently on the soft leather.

By the end of the busy day, the two women informed Tommy of their plan. They were to fly home to Nevada while Tommy stayed behind to meet with Miguel over the technical issues of the silver mine. As a geology graduate student, he had the skills and knowledge to inspect the mine and the preparatory work of Kostas and to offer an evaluation of its prospects. Tommy agreed to do this though it meant that he had to stay behind alone in the murder capital of the world and to visit the place where his friend had been assassinated. He gulped a little to realize the thrill of adventure that he had hoped for when he formed his partnership with Kostas and Jasper came with the high cost of actual danger. Losing money was one kind of fear, but this was something entirely different. His risky loan and investment seemed like a minor concern now.

Always perceptive, Grace sensed his anxiety and reassured him he did not have to stay if it interfered with his own plans. There were other ways to accomplish the same tasks; it just seemed sensible to use his skills while he was here in Honduras. Tommy did not want to appear afraid to this strong woman, so he sat up straight and patted her hand. All of his senses were heightened, and everything around him, including the widow before him, seemed more radiant and beautiful. Sudden death, he realized, is always possible, even on the safe streets of his hometowns of Sacramento and Reno. If he just could remember this, everywhere he happened to be, life itself in all its small and normally unnoticed moments would become an adventure. In an odd and, to him, inexplicable way, he came to understand what Kostas had found in Honduras besides a silver lode.

Pilar and Grace, with little Antu in tow, left late the next morning for the airport. As they arranged themselves in the taxi, Tommy stood by the car door holding the small duffel bag containing the urn with Kostas's ashes. After Grace had settled in the seat, he gently handed her the bag, which she pulled close against her chest. Pilar carried her clay urn of ashes wrapped in a colorful Indian blanket. She motioned to Tommy to come around to her side of the taxi and thrust the bundle through the open window at him.

"He belongs here," she said. "Miguel will take you to where this must stay until I get back."

Cradling the urn in one arm, Tommy stepped into the street to make sure Grace could see him as the taxi moved through the traffic. Miguel, standing by his Land Rover, waved good-bye also as if he were a family friend. Only Antu returned the gesture, waving both small hands through the back window of the taxi. Grace and Pilar did not turn around but faced squarely ahead, each with an arm extended to support Antu as she leaned against the back of the seat to look out the rear window. Too soon for Tommy, the taxi was lost in the busy traffic. He was alone on a crowded Central American boulevard holding a clay pot containing the gray remnants of his friend and business partner.

Solemn and thoughtful, he stepped off the street onto the sidewalk. Cars whizzed by perilously close. Honduras was dangerous in many ways. Miguel, already exhibiting impatience, looked sinister and evil. His efforts to help seemed exaggerated to Tommy as if he had something to prove or disprove. Now he was alone with him in this crime-ridden country. It was only his desire to show Grace how brave and strong he was that allowed him to acquiesce to their plan and leave him behind. He was sorry now he had accepted the task. Everything happened so fast he had not even let his father know he had left the country. He fingered his cell phone in his jeans pocket and decided to call him immediately.

Motioning to fidgety Miguel to wait a moment, he dialed the country code and his father's number at work. Even though it was early in Sacramento, he knew his father would be in the office getting ready for what he hoped would be a busy day. For his father, each day was an opportunity to make new money and to avoid spending old money.

As he waited for the phone to be answered, he wondered how he would tell his father he was in Honduras and what his reaction would be. The first response, he surmised sadly, would be how much did it cost for him to get there and to ask if he was missing any of his classes. His father had the nasty habit of firing off questions and suppositions before his son could venture his business. Thankfully, the phone went to the office answering machine. Perhaps his father was in the equipment yard somewhere. He punched the phone to stop the call and decided not to try his father's cell phone. He would do it later when he was more prepared to respond to the barrage of questions and implied criticism he was most likely to receive.

At the advice of Miguel, Tommy had checked out of the hotel with Grace and Pilar. His backpack had already been thrown onto the backseat of the Land Rover. Miguel handed him a key to the apartment Kostas had rented for himself and Pilar. The apartment also functioned as Kostas's workspace and business office. His computers and files were still in place. Tommy could stay there while accomplishing his research. Pilar had left instructions to put the clay pot with Kostas's ashes on the bookshelf near a framed photograph of Antu.

The apartment was a pleasant twenty-minute drive along a wide freeway from the capital to Santa Lucia, a picturesque colonial town on the side of the mountain overlooking Tegucigalpa two thousand feet below. At night, Miguel explained to Tommy as they drove, the lights of the Honduran capital glimmered and twinkled like a night sky below them. Santa Lucia, he continued, was far from the madding crowd of Tegucigalpa, and many of the affluent business and government professionals commuted from there to their offices in the city.

But he preferred to be closer to the action so maintained an apartment in a good neighborhood near downtown. Kostas had chosen the apartment in Santa Lucia because it was closer to the mine.

Miguel continued to explain that silver had been mined on this mountain since the time of the conquistadores in the sixteenth century. Over the intervening centuries, 140 different mines had been opened and worked. All now were closed or inoperative. Either the mine owners, a landed class who had inherited them as family properties, did not have the capital to continue mining operations, or the mines had been worked to such depth that they had no answer to the engineering challenges of solving the problems of flooding and heat. No one doubted the presence of silver ore in the mountain, but none of the 140 previous attempts to extract it showed enough promise to risk the capital to allow exploration of the depths of the mountain. Increasing risk was the fluctuating and uncertain market price of silver. Tied to the price of gold, silver slumped as low as five dollars an ounce to as much as sixty dollars. Currently, silver stood somewhere in the vicinity of twenty dollars an ounce, a price Kostas had believed was high enough and secure enough to merit the million-dollar investment his project had become.

Sometimes, Miguel explained with mounting excitement, threads of pure silver were discovered. There seemed a promise of a huge cache of silver in this mountain, as he waved his hand at the crest above them, but until Kostas came along, no one knew how to continue explorations or how to finance them. The plan Kostas had devised was unique. Instead of mining, as did the sixteenth century Spaniards and their descendants, where the veins of silver were exposed at the surface, Kostas had determined to go beneath the mountain and tunnel to its core from below.

This was a brilliant deduction. All of the old mines were dug from above to follow a vein of ore whose ledges protruded from the side of the mountain. Consequently, the mine shafts gradually filled with water seeping from the rock. Moving ore up steep shafts was difficult and technically challenging. The deeper they penetrated the earth, the more extreme the heat became, making it difficult for the men hired as miners to work for extended periods of time. Seeping water gradually filled the shafts, requiring pumps and the sources of energy to run them. Finally, the early silver miners had to surrender the quest for riches and be satisfied with scouring bits of rich ore from the tailings and veins at the surface or near the top of mine shafts.

Years before he had begun this project, Kostas had been hired by an international mining company headquartered in Vancouver to investigate the feasibility of large-scale silver mining operations on the mountain. He very astutely visited many of the mines that had been opened over the centuries. It was then that he recruited Miguel as a translator and local administrator.

For five hundred years, the mountain had been punctured dozens of times by conquistadores and their Indian or Negro slaves, then by the Spanish colonists and their descendants, landed families claiming ownership of the land and the minerals that lay beneath them. Kostas explained to Tavares over evening meals and morning coffee, because these old mines existed, he could substitute their shafts for the expensive drilling that usually preceded any explorations. It was this observation that Kostas had used to convince the Canadian company with other mining properties in Honduras to fund his consulting contract. With Tavares as his assistant and translator, Kostas sought permission to visit all of the mines on the mountain, securing the right to inspect about a hundred of them.

In those early years, day after day, Kostas and Tavares pried open the old wooden or steel doors that closed up the mines, stepped inside, and inspected the veins of ore and their orientation within the mountain. They made precise measurements with hi-tech lasers and entered all the data into a computer, which Kostas had brought to Honduras for this single purpose. By determining the direction of the veins, their apparent size and nature, and calibrating their position in the mountain by GPS coordinates and altitude, Kostas was able to develop a computer-generated diagram of the core of the mountain.

This model showed veins of ore ascending to the top of the mountain, getting smaller and smaller as they gained altitude but showing an increase in size as they descended into the depths. The conclusion was simple. All the rich ore at the top, like the branches of a tree, arose from a thick, broad trunk at the center of the mountain. The early miners had merely harvested the easiest fruit. The source of those riches lay untouched at the heart of the mountain.

The president of the Canadian mining company praised the work, even agreed with its conclusions, but decided not to invest more. What Kostas's model also showed was the great bulk of the ore, estimated to be billions of dollars at current prices, lay directly beneath the town of Santa Lucia and the pricey neighborhoods that had grown up around this affluent enclave. Even with the efficacious application of bribes and a compliant corrupt government, the mining company could not hope to devour an entire town in pursuit of riches beneath it. Despite the hundreds of millions in future profit, the costs of replacing an entire town would add tremendously to the risk. The model Kostas had produced was still a guess, a highly educated guess to be sure. The only way to know for certain was to spend millions drilling to the core of the mountain to explore the extent of the silver lode.

Despite technology and its wondrous ability to see beneath the earth, there was still the risk that the ore did not exist in sufficient volume to justify the enormous investment required to find and mine it. Even if they were satisfied the ore body was large and rich enough, other risks had to be considered. In all decisions to mine the planet, the unknown always loomed large. Problems with heat, water, unstable rock, even occasional earthquakes could devastate the most reliable of predictions. There were also dangers not of earth and rock. The price of silver could fall during the years required to develop the property. Despite the elaborate prognostications of economists and bankers, there was no reliable way to predict future prices of precious metals. War, financial recession, political unrest, or new technology could impact value or the cost of exploiting that value. There was simply no small way a large international company could profitably mine. Their decisions were nearly all-or-nothing propositions: risk hundreds of millions of dollars or turn away.

Ending their commitment to Kostas for further exploration did not include abandoning the project entirely. As prospectors, mine owners, and mining companies frequently do, the president of the Canadian mining company found a way to continue control without further obligations. From his viewpoint, the silver was locked in the bank vault of a mountain, but he still wanted to possess the key.

When the president, Marc Cousineau, decided to end the contract with Kostas, he adroitly persuaded him to pursue his plan for the silver mountain independently. As had happened to Kostas in Tonopah when he invested in his first silver mine, something else had convinced him there was silver awaiting discovery in this mountain. Though his Greek science led him to his conclusions, and his Paiute intuition validated them, he counted on his Irish luck. When he shared his enthusiasm with his Canadian client, he was offered a loan of five hundred thousand dollars to give him the means to complete all of the permits and licenses required to stake a claim on the mountain. Kostas accepted the loan because Cousineau required only the mine itself as collateral. None of Kostas's other assets would be threatened because he could repay the loan simply by signing over the title to the mine, even if the project failed. If his project succeeded, repayment would be no problem because the mine itself would generate the income to cover the liability. The only other condition the crafty Cousineau attached to the loan agreement was that he retained first option on the property. As long as the Canadian was able to match the best offer Kostas might receive, Kostas had to sell to him. Ingeniously, Cousineau had engineered a way for Kostas to do the work he would have to do to continue development but still remain in ultimate control of the property.

Because Kostas had recommended to them, as their consultant, they tunnel from the base of the mountain to the rich and thick inner core of ore he thought lay hidden there, Cousineau encouraged Kostas to implement this plan. All he needed, according to the Canadian's estimate, was perhaps a half million more to cut a tunnel a quarter mile through solid rock on the basis of his computer-generated model. From such small-scale operations, big strikes had been discovered, he reminded Kostas. With a half million in his account to start, Cousineau had no doubt the energetic and persuasive Kostas could raise at least five hundred thousand dollars more. After all, he reminded Kostas, his silver strike in Tonopah a few years ago had made him locally famous and credible.

Cousineau had nothing to lose when granting Kostas all the rights to the silver mountain. If he failed, he would be proven right in turning down the proposal, and the loan would be paid back with interest. If Kostas succeeded, he could buy back the rights for a fraction of the costs of further exploration. If Kostas simply gave up the project for the lack of any meaningful result and released title to Cousineau, the Canadian was certain he could find another prospect to pay that much for the mining rights. The five-hundred-year history of mining on the mountain was a strong allure. Many other mining enterprises would jump at the opportunity to buy a shortcut to the permits and licenses, saving time and money.

Tommy understood instantly why Grace had delegated him and not herself for this mission as he entered the apartment Kostas had shared with his lover and daughter. Despite the businesslike office space in the front, the apartment showed a cozy and familial comfort. Antu's toys were still on the couch in the living room. The small bed in another room, definitely reserved for the child, was unmade; the rest of the room exhibited the pleasant chaos of childhood. The only other separate room in the apartment, the master bedroom, was spacious and comfortable, a large double bed in the center and a flat screen television on an opposite dresser. Patio doors opened to a shady garden with an elevated brick deck on the side facing down the mountain toward the capital city far below in the haze. Birds twittered outside. Pictures of Antu and Pilar graced the bookshelf and the work desk. Nowhere was there evidence of his second home and wife, though this did not suggest they were forgotten. Kostas lived in two worlds with two populations. Each world was real when he was in them, but like death and rebirth, one world disappeared when the other world appeared.

Tommy had carried the blanket-covered urn with him when he first entered the apartment. He immediately spotted the framed pictures of Kostas's Honduran family. He separated the pictures of Pilar and Antu to place the urn between them. Father and family together.

Miguel busied himself with turning on the computers and digging through a filing cabinet for the documents and information Tommy would have to inspect and organize. When the laptop screen came to life, curiously with a screensaver showing Grace standing in front of their home in Nevada, Miguel pushed Tommy into a chair and, leaning over his shoulders, clicked on the keyboard until the mining company's bank register appeared. The account showed a balance of slightly less than a hundred thousand dollars.

"We paid our miners a hundred dollars a week, twelve of them. We could have others who would have worked for less, but Pilar convinced Kostas this was the best. This is all that was left to begin the mine. It would have lasted about six months because we would have to buy dynamite, blasting caps, drill bits, and fuel. Kostas didn't think we could make a strike in that time, clearing fifty to a hundred feet per week. But he was about to return to the US to raise more money. We're already nearly a million dollars into this project, and this is all that is left."

Tommy noted the word *we*. "How much of that have you invested?" he asked Miguel.

Miguel shrugged his shoulders and raised his eyebrows as if surprised by the question. "I was a contractor. Kostas promised a bonus if we made a strike. Everyone was to get a bonus. Mine would have been one percent."

"How much were you paid?"

Miguel paused then leaned over his shoulder to click down the columns of numbers on the check register. "See, it's right here. Five hundred dollars a week."

"So now you're out of a job, a pretty good paying job?"

Miguel shrugged again. "That depends on what you and Grace decide. There are a few options in front of us. We can continue to develop the mine. Even without Kostas, I can run the operation. I did when he went back to Nevada. But you would have to raise more money."

"What else?"

"Your best option is to try to find someone who will buy your claim to recover some of the money, though I doubt you would get very much out of it. Maybe a hundred thousand at best, plus a royalty on earnings that may never come. Or you could take what you have and walk away from it. Remember, Kostas borrowed five hundred thousand from the Canadians. They'll want that back, and if you can't pay it, they'll probably take the claim, leaving you with nothing."

"Did what happened to Kostas have anything to do with any of these options?"

Miguel looked surprised. "What do you mean?"

"Was anyone else convinced, like Kostas was, there was value here for the taking?"

"Of course. Everyone knows there is silver in this mountain. Sooner or later, someone is going to figure out how to get to it. Kostas spent nearly a million trying to prove his point. Six months from now, we would have known the answer."

"Are you saying Kostas was killed too soon?"

"No! Of course not!"

Tommy paused for a moment to collect himself, pretending to inspect the check register. He was surprised by the strong and urgent sense of anger that had welled up in his heart. He could not understand, nor accept, Miguel's ordinary, nearly dismissive attitude that showed no grief or shock at the murder of his employer and partner. The kindest explanation Tommy could offer himself would be Miguel's concern for his own self-interest. Miguel's constant impatience suggested an alternative reason for his callous attitude.

Tommy turned away from the computer screen to look up at Miguel, who still stood behind him. "Why?" he asked simply. "Why then at the site of the mine?"

Miguel shrugged as if irritated by a question with an obvious answer. "It happens all the time in Honduras. Maybe the bandits thought Kostas had some cash for payroll in the office. They ransacked the place, you know. Ran off with a laptop and cell phone as far as we can tell."

Miguel said he would drive back to Tegucigalpa while Tommy spent the afternoon and evening reviewing the business and technical files of the mine. He walked Tommy outside and pointed along a narrow cobblestone street toward the town center to show him a restaurant where he could find dinner. When Tommy confessed he had neglected to exchange any of his American dollars for Honduran lempira, Miguel extracted his wallet and gave him a thousand-lempira note.

"Dinner will cost about a hundred lempira. Leave a tip, about 20 percent. You can give me the change back tomorrow when I pick you up."

After Miguel drove off, Tommy checked the small refrigerator in the apartment kitchenette and found only some old yogurt and a couple of bottles of beer. This caused him to inspect the kitchenette cupboards. He found some stale bread, a jar of peanut butter, and two cans of beans. Reluctant to take the walk down the street to the restaurant and to deal with the hassle of ordering a dinner in Spanish, he opened a can of beans and spilled it into a small pan on the tiny gas range. Though the bread was stale, he could find no mold, so he slathered two slices thick with peanut butter while his beans heated up. He was so hungry he munched on the crusty bread and sipped a beer while stirring the beans.

He sat at Kostas's work desk as the beans simmered. He used Kostas's computer to go online and e-mailed his father a vague summary of his circumstance. He promised to call when he returned home in a few days.

He found a small bottle of Honduran hot sauce in the cupboard and sniffed at the contents. It smelled spicy and familiar, so he sprinkled a healthy dose into the beans. When the beans were ready to eat, he took the saucepan, beer, and bread to the porch and sat on the small rock wall to watch the sunset in the west. Below, far below, the lights of Tegucigalpa twinkled. A warm and moist breeze fluttered the trees and bushes. The dark flank of the mountain was behind him. He turned to look over the roof of the house above the apartment at the dark shadows. There, deep in the earth, according to Kostas, was a treasure trove of silver.

Tommy realized as he sat there on the porch, if he had been able to accompany Kostas on one of his trips to Honduras, the focused earnestness of his friend would have been proof enough of the silver riches to be uncovered by his ambitious plan. Now without his presence, except in the otherworldly aspect of the clay pot of ashes, Tommy doubted how effective a plan—even one engineered by Kostas and his prescient way of accomplishing projects—it would be to continue the mine.

The next morning, Tommy was still asleep on the couch when Miguel let himself in the apartment.

Miguel kicked the couch. "Time to hit the road," he announced. "I suppose you want to see the mine."

"Is it safe?" Tommy asked, scratching his head.

"Safe as any place in this damned country. I have weapons in the car just in case."

"Your fancy Land Rover looks like an invitation."

"Actually, it isn't. It is too obvious. Sticks out like a sore thumb. If we were driving a broken-down Toyota pickup or Volkswagen, then that would be inviting. Besides, we're picking up a couple of the crew to accompany us. They'll have guns too so no one will mess with us."

After Tommy washed up and put on a clean shirt, he and Miguel walked uphill on the cobblestone street to the restaurant Miguel had directed Tommy to last night. Tommy returned the thousand-lempira note to Miguel, who accepted it without hesitation.

Over a breakfast of *baleadas* and excellent Honduran coffee, Miguel asked Tommy about his initial impressions. "What do you think? Continuing, or getting out?"

"Too early to know, don't you think? I haven't even seen the mine yet," Tommy answered.

"What's there to see? It's a hole in the ground. All you need to know is the model Kostas produced and the realities of the bank account."

"You have a suggestion?" Tommy asked as he sipped at his coffee.

"You're not going to hang around? Who's there to take the place of Kostas? Me? Maybe. But you'll have to raise more money, and that was Kostas's job too. Who's going to do that? His wife? I doubt it. Sell out? To whom? Not likely to get enough to pay off the Canadians. If you go to them, they have to take it off your hands as repayment of the loan, if you're lucky, leaving you nothing but what's left in the bank account. Kostas's investors in Nevada would be lucky to get ten cents on the dollar."

"So you're saying go to the Canadians and see if they'll exercise their option to buy it?"

"You have to do that first."

"What if they won't offer anything, knowing they have already given Kostas five hundred thousand dollars for it? Is it worth more than that?"

"You can try selling it here, to someone else."

"Who?"

Miguel leaned to one side to extract a folded sheet of paper from his hip pocket. He handed the sheet to Tommy.

"The Chinese. This is their offer. A million even. Half you use to pay back the Canadians. The other half to your investors. You come out clean, no profit, maybe a little bit of a loss, but off the hook."

"And all of Kostas's work for the last four years for nothing?"

"That's life. And, I might add, that's prospecting. Kostas was no fool. He knew if it didn't work out, he could convince the Canadians. And if not them, some other company to buy the results of his work to protect his investors. All he worried about was leaving them on the hook. It was his backup plan. He knew just having his claim, which took nearly four years of wrangling with the government to get, was worth at least as much as was invested in the venture. The Chinese will buy it just to avoid the bureaucracy and the bribes they'd have to endure if they tried staking a claim on this mountain. Everyone knows there's silver here. They just don't know yet how they are to get it."

"And Kostas found a way?" Tommy asked.

"He did indeed, and that's worth something to somebody."

"And you? What do you get out of it?"

"However it goes, I'm expecting my 1 percent."

"Ten thousand if it settles for a million? Nothing if the Canadians foreclose on the loan."

Miguel nodded his head. "That was my deal with Kostas."

"So you'll make more if we go to the Chinese and dump the Canadians?"

"So will you," Miguel replied.

As Tommy opened the door to the Land Rover for the trip to the mine, Miguel handed him a belt and canvas holster holding a chrome-plated .45 caliber pistol.

"Strap it on so it's handy in case we need it," he instructed Tommy.

Tommy stood outside by the open door of the SUV and self-consciously cinched up the belt over the belt he already wore for his jeans. He looked around to see if anyone was watching. It seemed strange to him that in the middle of the relaxed and pleasant environment of Santa Lucia, he would be standing on a public street arming himself. Miguel also strapped a holstered pistol to his hip before climbing in behind the steering wheel.

"Do you know how to use it?" he asked Tommy as they drove slowly down the narrow street between adobe homes and rock walls.

Tommy pulled the .45 out of its holster and held it up for Miguel to see. "Pull back on this to load it?" he asked.

Miguel nodded as he glanced over at Tommy.

"Do it now?" Tommy asked, incredulous that arming himself was a necessary precaution.

"If you need it, you won't have the time to do it."

Tommy pulled back the breech and slammed a cartridge into the chamber.

"It's got a kick when you fire it, so be ready," Miguel said matter-of-factly.

"This is normal? Did Kostas wear a gun too?"

"Always when he was at the mine. We spent a couple of thousand dollars on carbines and hunting rifles for the crew too. Basic materials for Honduran mining operations. All our crew kept a weapon close at hand."

They soon passed by the outskirts of Santa Lucia and drove down a narrow road to the main highway a few miles away. When he reached the main highway, Miguel turned right then very quickly turned down a narrow dirt road barely visible between the thick growth of trees. The road was bumpy, and Miguel slowed down to creep along between trees and bushes, nearly scraping the sides of the car.

"We planned on renting a Caterpillar D7 or D8 to widen and smooth this road before we could haul ore to the mill," Miguel said as he stared ahead at the road through the windshield. "But that's for later when there was ore to haul. A few months away under the best of circumstances."

Tommy spotted two men with rifles slung over their shoulders walking down the road ahead of them. As he fingered the unfamiliar cold metal of the pistol at his side, he looked at Miguel, who showed no concern. When the two men stepped to each side of the road to allow the car to pass, Miguel slowed and then came to a stop. The men reached for the door handles and let themselves into the backseat.

"These are our guys," Miguel said without introducing the two passengers. "You'll meet all the men who worked for us at the mine, and their families, I suppose. They've moved there temporarily to watch over the mine."

"You could have let me in on the secret," Tommy murmured. He turned around to see the two men.

Both smiled. One held out his hand. "Bienvenido a Honduras!" he said happily.

Tommy reached over the seat and shook his hand. The second man stared sullenly out the window by his shoulder.

"They're Lencas," Miguel announced. "Indigenous to Honduras. Here centuries before the conquistadores arrived. People believe they migrated up from Columbia ten thousand years ago. Neighbors with Mayans in Guatemala. I believe one of them is Pilar's cousin." He turned around to say something to the two passengers in rapid Spanish. The man who smiled replied.

"It's him. He's her cousin."

Tommy smiled and nodded his head at the genial Indian, but he kept his hand on the cold metal of the .45.

The dirt road ended at a dry creek bed. Miguel turned the Land Rover into the pathway created by the creek and drove slowly what would be upstream had there been water flowing.

"We're almost there. We were going to use the tailings from the mine to rebuild a dam across this creek. It was washed out in 1998 by Hurricane Mitch. A dam will stop flash floods and provide water for farms. It would also be a road over this creek." Miguel waved his arm out the open window of the Land Rover at the fields and forest along the creek bed. "Kostas had a grand plan," he continued. "He wanted to resurrect the small farming community washed out by the hurricane. He imagined the men we hired, all Lenca Indians, would live here. Their families would be close by so they wouldn't have to spend weeks away from home. It was his clever plan to get the license from the government permitting mining here. Instead of damaging the environment, which most international mining companies have done over the decades in Honduras, he was going to improve it. Even the mine itself would contribute to the improvements. The mine was designed to allow water seeping into the tunnels to flow into the stream behind the dam we would build with the mine debris. All the ore would be hauled out over the improved road to an established mill. The road would provide access and easy transportation for the Lenca families who lived in the rebuilt village. He even mentioned once a small hotel could be built to house international travelers who would have to pass through from time to time."

"Will that be part of the deal with the Canadians or the Chinese if they buy us out?"

"Are you kidding? It's an obstacle. They may say they'll support this plan just to keep the patents on the claim, but they are a long way from being missionaries. If the mine is what Kostas thought it might be, whoever takes over probably would want to build a mill on this site. Kostas was an outlier in the Central American mining industry. He seriously thought mining the natural resources of this country ought to benefit its people. Most mining companies will do only what they have to in order to hold their patents. Even less if they could bribe their way out of complications. I think Pilar had a lot to do with it. He was under her spell."

Miguel turned the car into a narrow canyon with a rough road that looked to be recently carved into the mountain. Alongside the road ran a ditch.

"See that?" Miguel said, pointing out the window to the ditch on the left side of the road. "That's for the water seeping out of the mine. We built that. As the tunnel gets deeper, more and more water will drain out of the rock.

The mine tunnel itself will rise upwards at a two-percent grade to direct the water to the ditch. Kostas designed the mine to supply water for the dam. By his calculations, we would be excavating about 250 thousand cubic feet of rock before we found ore. All that material was enough to build the dam down below. I even think he picked this spot with this in mind. You got to hand it to Kostas. He thought of everything. Including how to get rich with a good intention. No shortcuts for him."

"What happens to those plans if we sell to the Canadians or the Chinese?" Tommy asked.

Miguel shrugged his shoulders. "What do you think?"

Tommy turned his head to look over the back of the seat at the two Lenca Indians. They had leaned forward to peer ahead through the windshield as if eager to arrive.

A small gathering of people, including children and women, were waiting near the shed that served as an office, as they drove into the wide space carved out of the mountain to make room for the mine and its operations. Opposite the side of the mountain, where a mine tunnel had been started, was a collection of tents and temporary shelters built with tarpaulins and two-by-fours under the trees. Campfires with pots hanging from simple racks sent faint smoke into the air.

As the group waved gaily at the approaching Land Rover, two men with rifles hanging from their shoulders stood by the office shed. They seemed wary and moved their heads back and forth as if scanning the landscape. The two Indians in Miguel's car leaned out of their windows and shouted to the crowd. Two small boys ran forward to greet Pilar's cousin. Even before the car stopped, he opened the door and leaped out to hug both of the children at once. After stopping and getting out of the car, Miguel explained to Tommy all of their workers and their families had stayed here at the mine since the ambush.

"They knew someone from Kostas's family would be coming and wanted to be here to meet them. Kostas was very important to them."

Despite the somber reason he found himself here in the midst of the Honduran jungle, Tommy smiled broadly. Everyone lined up to greet him, men in front, women and children behind them. Tommy counted twelve men and twelve families. Including the children, there were nearly fifty people to be greeted. He waved to them, and all the children waved back. The women smiled shyly. The men stepped forward, each in turn holding out his hand to shake Tommy's hand. One spoke in English.

"This"—he turned to wave at the crowd behind him—"Señor Wilson family. Welcome!"

Tommy realized he had more to think about than just geological and financial conditions. He wished Grace were here to meet these people. He had no doubt she would have moved forward into the crowd embracing the women, leaning down and smiling at the children, shaking the hands of the men to seal her commitment to their well-being. He should do the same, he thought, but he was not Grace. Instantly, he was deeply touched with affection for these people. He wanted to help them as well as to help Grace.

Miguel came around the car and inserted himself between the group and Tommy. He held up his hand to show him into the office. Since Tommy appeared to be a bit confused or dazzled by the unexpected attention he was receiving, Miguel took him by the elbow and pulled him toward the shed.

"Let's get something done," he said.

To Tommy's way of thinking, a lot had already been accomplished. He had met the extended family of Kostas, and his heart already ached for them. He pulled away his arm.

"What happens to them?" he asked.

"They cost too much," Miguel said cryptically.

"You mean if we sell out?"

"They're not your problem," he said abruptly.

Miguel was right about the mine—it was just a hole in the side of the mountain, and not a very deep one. Only twenty feet of the overburden soil had been removed. According to the computer model Kostas had prepared, there was another twenty feet of overburden before they could begin the tunnel through the hard rock core of the mountain. Tommy had learned nothing new about the mine itself the model had not already described in detail.

But Miguel was wrong about the purpose of the visit at the mine site. Tommy had met the families who depended on Kostas for their livelihood. Had that information been omitted from Tommy's report to Grace, he would have committed a great error. She would be as interested in this aspect of the operation as the actual prospect of finding a silver lode or recouping their investment.

Miguel shrugged off Tommy's weak complaints that he hadn't revealed the whole picture. He responded to Tommy as if he was naïve and inexperienced, which of course he was.

"A mine is a hole in the ground with a promise of riches at the end. Everything else is a distraction," Miguel said as they returned to Santa Lucia.

As he listened to Miguel, Tommy patted his shirt pocket to feel the cell phone there. He was happy he had managed to take a few photos of the gathered community at the site of the mine. He looked forward to seeing Grace's reaction when he included the photos as part of his report.

Back at the apartment that afternoon, Miguel helped Tommy download a copy of Kostas's model of the silver lode buried in the mountain on a flash drive and collect other information on the operation of the mine. He also called the airlines and arranged Tommy's return the following morning. When they were finished, it was dinnertime. Miguel returned the thousand-lempira bank note to Tommy so he could order dinner at the restaurant down the street. As he prepared to leave for the evening, he hesitated in the doorway. Tommy looked up.

"Something else?" he asked.

"Am I still on the payroll?" Miguel asked.

"I suppose so until we decide what to do."

"How do I get paid? I can't sign checks."

"All the money is in a US bank account. I guess Grace can wire it to your account. Okay with you?"

Miguel came back into the apartment and wrote down his banking information on a slip of paper, which he handed to Tommy.

"I'd appreciate it every Friday if Grace can manage it," he said meekly. "Life goes on, you know."

Tommy took the paper and put it in his wallet. "I'm sure Grace will have no problem. What about money for the workers?"

"I gave them money for this week. We don't owe them more."

"But if Grace wanted to keep them on, how do we pay them?"

"You'll have to wire me the money, and I'll give them cash."

"Twelve hundred dollars a week? Is that right?"

Miguel nodded.

"Will they be staying at the mine?" Tommy asked.

"If you want them to."

"For now we do. I'm sure Grace will want to take care of them for at least a month. So count on your pay and their pay every Friday for a month."

"You coming back?"

"I suppose I will be. There's a lot to do whatever we decide. Pilar will have to return at some point. And I am sure Grace will want a hand in all the details."

"You work for Grace and Kostas now?"

"And Pilar."

Chapter Three

Grace, Pilar, and Antu met Tommy at the Reno airport the following evening. He sat in the front of the car with Grace as they drove him to his apartment. Grace explained they would meet in the morning at the apartment she and Kostas still maintained across the walkway from his.

"I'm not tired," Tommy said. "We can meet now if you want."

Grace patted him on the arm. "Tomorrow will be soon enough."

"What about Jasper? Does he know?" Tommy asked.

"I called him on our way back to Schurz. He'll join us for our meeting. He wants to help."

As they stood by the stairs waiting to walk up to their two apartments, Pilar quietly asked Tommy about her home in Santa Lucia. He confirmed for her that he had left the urn on the shelf next to their pictures.

"I should have called you while you were there," Pilar said. "Antu would have liked you to bring one of her dolls."

Tommy snapped his fingers. "I should have thought of that myself."

Pilar, like Grace, patted his arm, showing either gratitude or patience, Tommy couldn't tell which. He distinctly was aware he was treated with some condescension by both women, but he wasn't bothered by it. Though he knew Grace was a just a year older than he was, and Pilar was probably about his same age, both seemed considerably more experienced and wise in the ways of the world than he was. Or, he thought belatedly, he just felt younger and more innocent, like a boy, in their presence. He didn't know what to think. Nonetheless he was grateful to be in the company of such women and to have the opportunity to help them. Meeting the Lenca families at the mine in Honduras gave his understanding of Kostas's death a great significance beyond his own sense of loss. Truly, this was the beginning of an adventure and the very reason he had invested in the Pine Grove Valley claim.

From his apartment, he called his father in Sacramento to let him know he had returned to Reno. Uncharacteristically, his father patiently heard him out after he had learned that Kostas had been ambushed. When Tommy had finished his explanations, his father could hold back no longer.

"You aren't going back, are you?"

Tommy shrugged his shoulders even though he knew his father could not see his reaction. But his silence told his father all he had to know.

"You got your studies to finish. Don't sacrifice that for some wild goose chase in Central America."

Tommy wanted to say it was no wild goose chase, but he resisted and promised his father his studies would not suffer, though he was obliged to help Grace settle affairs in Honduras.

"Honduras is a dangerous place," his father continued. "I was ready to come and get you in case you got in trouble."

"Really?"

"Well, I am glad I didn't have to," his father said in response. "Just don't go again, okay, son?"

Tommy tried to remember the last time his father had called him son. He couldn't. Adventure had its rewards.

After speaking with his father, Tommy called Dave Mogis to explain his sudden absence over the last four days.

Dave couldn't believe it. "All the way to Honduras and back? Wow! What happens to the claim in Pine Grove Valley? Any way I can help?"

Despite himself, Tommy began worrying about his investment in the gold claim with Jasper and Kostas. He did not know if they could continue with their plan if

Kostas was not involved. Sooner or later, Dave would need the loan repaid, or least some of it, and Tommy did not have the money. It was too soon for Grace to have used it for expenditures for their operation, so he could ask for it back, thus excusing himself from the partnership; but he could not bring himself to even think about such a request. It would be like a rat deserting a sinking ship, and he wanted Grace to see him as anything other than a cowardly rat. He promised Dave he would call him after his meeting with Grace and Pilar the next morning.

"If you need someone to help, volunteer me!" Dave announced eagerly, almost with joy in his voice.

Pilar knocked on Tommy's apartment door early the next morning and asked him if he was ready for coffee.

"Honduran coffee. We bought some at the airport before we left," she added.

Tommy placed his laptop on the table in the kitchen of Grace's apartment and inserted the flash drive he had made of Kostas's model in Honduras. Pilar poured him a cup of coffee and set it on the dining table next to the computer. Antu sat in the living room watching cartoons on the television. Occasionally, she laughed out loud and clapped her hands.

Soon Jasper showed up at the front door, which had stayed open as Tommy carried materials from his apartment into Grace's for the meeting. Holding his old-issue army fatigue cap in hand, he sidestepped into the apartment and waited for someone to notice him. Grace was still in her room, out of sight. Pilar came up to Jasper and extended her hand to introduce herself. Without comprehending her place in this scheme, Jasper politely shook her hand and peered at the child laughing and giggling in the next room.

"Grace will explain," Pilar said.

Tommy nodded solemnly to Jasper, who nodded back. The old man raised his eyebrows as Pilar went into Grace's room, closing the door behind her. Tommy shrugged. It wasn't his place to explain this arrangement, at least not yet.

When Grace came into the room, she offered no explanation of Pilar and her daughter. She sat at the table and invited Jasper and Tommy to do the same. Pilar sat on the floor next to her daughter but positioned herself to listen to the meeting at the dinette table.

Tommy began by drawing out his cell phone and showing Grace and Jasper the pictures he had taken of the families guarding the mine. Pilar rose quickly from the floor by her daughter to see the photos. She pointed to one of the photos.

"That's my brother. And he's my cousin," she said.

She called Antu, who reluctantly left her place in front of the television; but when the young girl saw the photos, she immediately forgot her first distraction and urged Tommy to scroll through the pictures once again for her benefit by moving her finger back and forth over the phone. She squealed when she saw a friend in the picture and said something in Spanish to her mother. Both Grace and Pilar reached down to stroke her hair.

"In case you are wondering, Jasper, this is Kostas's daughter . . . our daughter now," Grace said. She reached up to touch Pilar on the arm. "Her mother, Pilar."

Jasper tipped his hat to the mother and patted the young girl on the head.

During the meeting in her apartment, Grace concluded everyone should drive to Schurz to meet with the investors Kostas had convinced to join this venture, including Tommy though he was not a member of the corporation. Most were Indian residents on the reservation. Of the five hundred thousand dollars Kostas raised over the four years to supplement the loan from Marc Cousineau's company, 150 thousand was contributed by Kostas and Grace. The balance came from forty-one investors on the reservation, who gave between one thousand and fifteen thousand dollars each. None could afford what little they had donated to the cause, but because they believed in the visions Kostas had shared with them, just as their forebears believed his great-great-grandfather Wovoka, they eagerly sought the pure land promised by exploiting the mineral wealth of the planet like the white man had done in their own native lands.

Grace seemed irritated when asked about the investment she and Kostas had contributed, and showed concern only for what was provided by her Paiute neighbors. During the meeting in her apartment, Tommy stood at the head of the table in the kitchenette and described the options available to them. They could cut expenses immediately, recouping the nearly hundred thousand dollars still in the account, which could be used to cut the losses of all the investors. If they convinced the Canadians to exercise their option, Grace would not have repay the loan advanced by the Canadians. If they were successful with the Chinese mining company, everyone could be repaid, including the Canadians. There would be no profit with the third option, but no one would lose money. As Tommy described these alternatives, he believed Grace would accept the last as it offered protection to her Paiute friends and neighbors, though it would end their dream of besting the white man at his own game.

As Tommy talked, Jasper sat in front of the computer and studied Kostas's model of the ore body locked in the mountain vault.

During most of Tommy's presentation, Pilar remained silent. When Tommy finished explaining these prospects, Pilar stood up to join Tommy at the head of the table. Jasper leaned away from the computer screen to watch her.

"Or we could keep the mine and prove Kostas right, for everyone," Pilar announced.

"But we'll have to raise more money to do that," Tommy reminded the group.

"How much more?" Grace asked.

Tommy shrugged his shoulders. "I don't know. We'd have to go back and make a plan."

"We have a plan," Pilar said, still standing. "Kostas's plan."

Jasper raised his chin at Pilar to show that she should continue talking.

"No one doubts there is silver in that mountain," Pilar began. "Everyone knows it is there. What they don't know is if they invest in the effort to get it, will it be worth it."

"You know something we don't know?" Jasper asked.

"I know it is too soon to give up," Pilar answered.

"What about Miguel Tavares? Do we need to keep him on?" Grace asked.

"He's part of the plan, the plan Kostas made," Pilar said.

"And that is?" Jasper asked.

"How do you think Miguel conveniently had an offer from the Chinese in his hip pocket?" Pilar said in response, but did not wait for an answer. "He works for them."

"Did Kostas know that?" Grace asked.

"Yes, that's why Kostas picked him and not any one of a hundred other 'consultants' who would have leaped at the chance to make five hundred dollars a week and a bonus when successful. That's the way Honduras works. Everybody is in everyone else's pocket."

Jasper laughed quietly.

Grace turned to look at him. "What's so funny?"

"I've heard this story before," Jasper told her. "A hundred times. You think prospecting and mining is a matter of luck and science? In reality, it's wheeling and dealing."

"Why did he need to use Miguel?" Grace asked, clearly mystified, though grateful, as was everyone else, that for a time their minds were drawn away from the dark clouds of grief hovering over them.

"I'll answer that," Pilar said. She pushed Tommy on the shoulder to sit down at the table while she stayed standing. "Kostas isn't a miner. He's a geologist and a speculator like most geologists hope to be. He just wanted to prove the mine was valuable and then sell that value to a qualified mining company, like the Chinese or the Canadians, but in such a way as to control their worst impulses. If they were convinced there were billions within their grasp, they would give us millions to get it. But the millions they give us would have to include conditions for taking care of the environment and employing our community, something the government or corporate headquarters would not do unless forced to."

"How much did Kostas talk about?" Jasper asked Pilar.

"Millions," Pilar answered.

Tommy sat silent and in awe. All of this was new to him.

"Millions?" Jasper pressed.

"Yes," Pilar said. "He told me his goal was twenty-five million dollars, maybe more."

Jasper whistled. Tommy rubbed his eyes. Grace smiled, though not at the promise of riches but at the clever stratagems of her husband.

"Not all for the investors in the project," Pilar added. "He planned setting aside some for the Lenca community we started there . . . for schools, homes, roads, health care. Also, he talked about doing the same for the people here in Schurz. Your investor group still multiply their investment by twenty to thirty times."

"And this Miguel character? What's he got to do with all of this?" Jasper asked.

"He's the conduit to the Chinese who have the money and the need. Miguel thinks he is their mole in our operation. But in reality, he is our mole, only he doesn't know it."

"You're not . . . Kostas wasn't . . . talking about fraud?" Grace asked.

"No. Everyone thinks the silver is there no matter what we say or do. If we say there's none, they won't believe us, the Canadians and the Chinese. We don't have to make any claims. We just say what we know. If we find silver, we let them know silver is there. If we find none, we let them know that too, only they'll think then we are hiding the real value. The Chinese and Canadians are responsible for their own beliefs. We're not. Whatever we reveal will be influenced by their own self-interest.

We can use the Canadians as our foil because Kostas agreed with them they have the right of first refusal. So we need an offer from the Chinese to set the value for the Canadians, if they decide to make an offer. Even if they do make an offer, as Kostas believed they would do, they really can't afford it because they're too busy with all their other operations around the world. For Kostas, they would put an offer on paper, but only if they could turn around and sell it to someone else, like the Chinese. If we ask them to make an offer, the Chinese will find out from Miguel's report to them, not from us directly. Miguel will believe, and consequently, the Chinese will believe we will be ready to accept whatever the offer is from the Canadians because we lost Kostas. The Canadians will go along with this because it is a way of increasing the perceived value of the property, which ultimately they control. They think they'll be using us to increase the value which the Chinese, in the end, will have to pay them for. They appreciate the chance, by the way, to stick it to their Chinese competitors this way."

Jasper laughed again. "Let me get this straight. Kostas is using Miguel to entice the Chinese. Miguel is using Kostas to make a buck both ways. The Canadians are thinking they're using Kostas to hoodwink the Chinese. Kostas is using the Canadians to get what he wants. And nobody knows what anybody else is doing except us. Is that about it? What did I tell you? Wheeling and dealing!" He slapped his knee.

"So?" Grace started. "I guess we will have to press on with the mine, is that what you're saying?" She looked at Tommy. "Can we?"

Tommy shrugged his shoulders. "I guess we could if we had enough money to pay expenses along the way."

"How much money?" Grace pressed.

Pilar answered. "Kostas was about to return to Nevada. To get another 250 thousand dollars."

"That's all?" Jasper asked, sounding skeptical.

"All? That's a lot. We don't have it. How do we do that?" Grace asked.

Pilar shrugged her shoulders. "I don't know," she said as she tapped the top of the computer screen where Kostas's three-dimensional model of the treasure hidden in the Honduran mountain slowly spun on its axis.

"Whatever we decide," Jasper said, now rising to his feet and indicating to Pilar she should sit down, "we keep this to ourselves. Not even to your investors, Grace. What they don't know won't hurt them. Because your intentions are good, they'll just have to think they've invested in an actual silver mine and not a scheme to trick two international mining companies. We can't go around saying we're digging into the pockets of the Chinese and the Canadians and not into a mountain in Honduras."

After Jasper and Tommy left, Pilar took Antu for a walk by the Truckee River three blocks from the apartment. For the first time since meeting Tommy at the Reno airport for their flight to Tegucigalpa, Grace found herself alone. She stood in the middle of the living room and stared at the walls and windows. Everything suggested Kostas's presence. She walked into the bedroom and opened the closet where Kostas kept his Reno clothes. She pulled a shirt sleeve up to her nose and sniffed it with her eyes closed. For a moment, she could almost believe he had walked into the room, but when she opened her eyes, nothing was there. She dropped the shirt sleeve and closed the closet door to walk to the bed they had shared, and sat on the edge next to the end table where she kept their wedding photo. He was so handsome! She picked up the framed picture and pressed it against her heart. She felt as if she would faint with grief and longed to lie down, close her eyes, perhaps sleep for a little while, then rise up to see all of this as a dream—as if she hadn't stood in a morgue to look upon his inert and cold body, as if she hadn't in her businesslike way taken care of details with a Honduran funeral director.

On the airplane as they returned from Honduras, Pilar had given her a photograph of little Antu. Grace had put that next to the wedding photo. She lifted it up with the other hand and held it close to her eyes. The little girl's black hair, her distinctive Indian profile, the tone of her skin were clearly those of Kostas. She pressed that photo against her heart next to the wedding photo. Despite grief, a moment of joy soared in her heart to know the child she never had with Kostas had finally arrived.

Not once was she angry or jealous of Pilar. As they spoke in the hotel room the night of her arrival in Tegucigalpa, Grace developed a great admiration for her husband's Indian mistress. She understood immediately why Kostas loved her. Grace loved her too. She, Pilar, and Kostas were cast from the same mold. She felt grateful Kostas had bequeathed her a family to replace him.

Giving in finally to the stress and strong bouts of turmoil surging in her heart, Grace lay down on the bed with the two pictures held under her hands on her chest. Like this, she fell asleep.

Pilar quietly let herself and her daughter into the apartment when they returned from their walk. She held a finger up to her lips to warn Antu to stay silent. They both tiptoed through the living room and peeked into the bedroom to see Grace sleeping with the two photos pressed against her heart. Pilar quietly squeezed the bedroom door shut and took Antu by the hand to lead her to the couch in the living room. There they lay down together. Pilar stroked her daughter's hair and whispered a Honduran melody into her ear, hoping she would fall asleep.

As her daughter nodded off, so did Pilar; and soon, all three occupants of the apartment were asleep and dreaming of better times, happy to be relieved for a while of the burden of a life without Kostas.

When Grace awoke, she found Pilar and Antu still asleep on the couch. She went back into the bedroom to fetch a blanket and came back to cover them. As she did so, the little girl opened her eyes and smiled to see Grace above her. She pulled the blanket up to her chin and snuggled back into her mother's bosom. Grace could not help herself. She leaned down and softly stroked the girl's hair, wondering as she did so if Kostas had also stroked his daughter's hair like this.

Suddenly, unexpectedly, without preamble or warning, without even a thought, a jolt of anger jerked her upright. *How could he have hidden this girl from me for four years?* she asked herself. She could understand his reluctance to confess his attachment for his mistress, but his daughter was her daughter too! Anger made Kostas seem present, as if he were standing behind her. She turned around abruptly to scold him, only to see empty space.

Dave Mogis invited himself and his girlfriend, Jackie, to the funeral for Kostas in Schurz and the investors meeting scheduled afterward in the tribal community room. They rode with Tommy for the two-hour drive from Reno. Jackie sat in the backseat of the car alone. In the front seat, Dave pestered Tommy about his trip to Honduras as he drove. Dave made Tommy promise that if he had to return to Honduras to help Grace, he would allow Dave to accompany him.

"I can afford it. I'll pay for my own ticket. We're both graduate students at the Mackey School of Mines. I can be a big help. And I'll carry a pistol if someone gives me one," Dave effused.

Jackie snorted disapproval at each of her boyfriend's remarks.

Though Tommy described conditions at the mine and the loyal Lencas awaiting some action by the corporation, he omitted any mention of the plan to develop the property as a ploy to entice the Canadians or the Chinese to purchase the mining rights. As Jasper instructed, he was determined to keep the plan Kostas had devised a secret. But he could not help expressing to Dave his negative impressions of Miguel Tavares. Now, in retrospect, he was gratified his initial insights seemed to be an accurate assessment. As he described this experience to his friend, Dave asked what appeared to him to be an apparent and logical conclusion. Did Miguel have anything to do with the ambush?

Tommy shuddered to think he might have been in the company of a conspirator to a murder. He could not believe that could be true. He preferred explaining the ambush as a random act in a country plagued by violence. He could see no logical reason Miguel or the Chinese would want Kostas dead, nor even believe their business ambitions included such an action. Strictly speaking, it was too soon. Kostas had not yet proven the worth of his claim in the Honduran forest. But if they had waited longer, Tommy thought fearfully, the offer for the property would have probably gone up as more value was proven or as more investment in the project was committed. Maybe, Tommy gulped to think this way, murder was a way to cut costs. He was confused. If he returned to Honduras as Grace requested, he would have to pretend ignorance of such thoughts when in the company of Tavares. He wasn't even sure he should, if he could, share these suspicions with Grace and Pilar. Perhaps with Pilar because she seemed inured to Honduran violence. But not Grace. She was too pure to be touched by such evil intentions. Or at least he thought so. On the other hand, Grace and Pilar might already have come to these conclusions and were saving Tommy from them.

A hundred people had already assembled at the cemetery when Tommy parked the car by the edge of the narrow gravel road. Other cars were parked along the street, and the parking lot within the fence line of the cemetery was full. In a corner of the cemetery a crowd quietly awaited. Everyone stood. A few women held umbrellas to protect themselves from the bright desert sun even though it was still winter in the Great Basin.

Grace, Pilar, and Antu sat in folding chairs next to a small grave site, which already had received the urn containing the ashes. None of the three wore hats to shade their faces. Behind Grace stood a few of her Paiute patients, young women, who positioned themselves so that the shadows of their bodies would offer some protection for Grace and her two companions.

Kostas was not a religious person and never pretended to have any interest in spiritual matters, though he often opined about the grandeur of the natural environment and the lessons to be learned by just observing the forces of nature, as if paying homage to his Paiute heritage. He also confessed admiration for the natural affection and compassion sensible Irish displayed toward others. But if one were to ask Kostas, it was Greek science he actually relied upon. For Kostas, a reasonable and scientific conclusion was to realize all creatures, human or otherwise, possessed a mind, the seat of experience. If the mind of Kostas wished not to experience harm or extinction by the actions of other creatures, then all other beings too, he concluded, must hold the same intrinsic wish. As a consequence of these observations, he showed patience and kindness for all creatures, human and animal, when witness to their needs. He never killed snakes as did most other geologists and miners; he let spiders weave their webs and, when possible, avoided destroying them; he rescued crippled birds; he would pass out dollar bills or lempira notes to beggars on city streets, in the United States or in Honduras; he opened doors for elderly people; he treated his Paiute elders with great respect and listened to their advice with the intention to put it into practice; and he treated women, old and young, with a gallant courtesy. Yet he was not sentimental. He killed rabbits and deer for their meat. He supplemented his diet on field trips in the wilderness with fish where possible. He was a fearsome opponent to those who threatened him. While in Honduras, it was evident he would use the .357 Magnum strapped on his hip if the situation demanded it, as the spent cartridges next to his body showed. No one could doubt the resolve of Kostas in any circumstance he encountered.

The ceremony for Kostas was no ceremony at all, as Grace had decreed. Everyone, except perhaps Tommy and his companions, understood. The entire crowd around the grave remained still and silent, their heads bowed, hats and caps held at the heart. Little Antu, sitting in a chair between her mother and Grace, was the only person besides Tommy who looked around curiously at what was transpiring. Grace reached out to put right her arm around Antu's shoulder, and when she did, Pilar extended her left arm and laid it on top of Grace's. Antu, to her credit, realized she had two mothers now and settled down. Tommy, still mystified, continued to peer around at the silent and immobile group. Even the children present imitated the posture of their parents.

Five minutes passed and the silence continued. Another five minutes passed. Tommy looked at his watch. Dave moved his head slightly to see Tommy's nervousness then resumed his quiet and respectful posture. He seemed to be enjoying it. Jackie put her arm around his waist and squeezed him a little closer.

After fifteen minutes like this, Grace stood up and turned to face everyone. She smiled as she wiped a tear from her eye. She nodded once, and the crowd parted to let her pass through, Pilar and Antu following. The few husbands and boyfriends of the Paiute women who had provided shade for Grace followed. They moved ahead, clearing a pathway. When they reached the car, one of them opened the rear door for the three passengers. Another moved to the driver's seat and started the car.

Soon a procession of cars followed Grace to the tribal community center about a mile away and closer to the center of the reservation in Schurz. The time for business had arrived. Nothing more could be done for Kostas. It was time to get on with the business of taking care of oneself and one's community.

As people gathered inside the community center, the hubbub and clamor of salutations and conversation increased loudly, welcome relief from the disciplined silence at the cemetery. Grace and her entourage of Pilar, Antu, Tommy, and Jasper waited in another room for the crowd to settle down. Dave and Jackie situated themselves against a wall, separate from the community gathered in chairs in the center of the room.

Grace had asked Tommy to export the photos he had taken of the Lenca families to his computer so they could be displayed on a large screen. As they waited, Tommy checked his work and reread the outline for his report. Jasper sat with Antu in his lap and listened to her explain something in Spanish, which he did not speak. Even so, he laughed at the appropriate places, and little

Antu seemed pleased to have such an interested audience. Grace was stoic and silent, staring at her feet as she sat in the uncomfortable folding chair. Pilar, on the other hand, was bright and alert, her head held high. As Tommy peered up from his concentration on the computer, he realized the people before him had now become his family, as important to him as his own mother and father. Noticing Tommy watching her, Pilar smiled at him. Tommy breathed in deeply and returned in earnest to the computer to review his work.

Though muffled by the closed door, they could hear the excited murmurs of the group waiting in the main room. Tommy looked at Grace to see if she would signal the beginning of the meeting, but she remained immobile and silent, her head bowed down so low her chin rested on her chest. Tommy thought she might be hiding her tears. Occasionally, she wiped her face with a tissue. He wondered if she was waiting for him to initiate the meeting. She didn't raise her head, and Tommy was left to decide for himself what he should do.

He knew had Kostas been here, there would be no question about who was to start the meeting, and no concern about its success. Kostas was a powerful figure among his Paiute friends. His family's heritage qualified him to be an elder in the tribe, a mantle that he had refused, though humbly so. His fiery Irish spirit invited all to enjoy life as he lived it. His Greek logic convinced nearly every one of the wisdom of his initiatives. But it was the serene competence of Grace that reassured them that if Kostas ever strayed from his good intentions or was on the verge of making a mistake, she would step in and gently correct his course.

Gradually, the buzz in the meeting room subsided. Soon it was dead quiet, as if everyone remembered why they were gathered together. Their friend was killed. Unlike the constant murmur of a few minutes ago, the absence of sound was haunting and unnerving. Tommy stood up and looked expectantly at Grace. She finally raised her head and smiled faintly at Tommy as she barely nodded to show her intent to rise and act. Pilar jumped up, and holding Antu's hand, she strode forward toward the door. Tommy fell in behind, Jasper behind him, and after a long pause, which created a gap between her and Jasper, Grace moved slowly toward the door. Without any bidding, everyone in the room stood up as she entered. Those who still wore hats quickly doffed them.

Tommy went to the table in front and connected his laptop to the television monitor. When he was ready to begin, Grace moved to the table and sat behind it, facing the crowd. Pilar put Antu in a chair next to Grace and sat down. Jasper moved away from the front and stood by Dave and Jackie at the wall. After Grace took her seat, the entire assembly settled into theirs.

Grace smiled uncertainly at everyone then turned to pay some attention to Antu. She brushed back the little girl's hair and straightened her blouse. Pilar scanned the entire group, making eye contact with whoever was watching her. Tommy busied himself with the computer to avoid the intense scrutiny. He had never addressed a group this large. He checked his notes again before standing up. Grace raised her left hand and motioned for Tommy to sit back down. She stood up.

"Thank you for coming," she began. "This is Tommy Hawkins, a friend of mine and Kostas. He's been of tremendous help and stayed behind in Honduras to assess our business situation there. I'll leave the business of mining to him." She raised her right hand toward Pilar and Antu. "This little girl is Antu, Kostas's child. Pilar is her mother. They are Lenca Indians, an ancient tribe in Central America with a long history of conflict with the white man, originally the Spanish conquistadores as far back as the sixteenth century, nearly three hundred years before the white man occupied your people's lands. I bring this up because these people were important to Kostas, just as you are important to me and Kostas. It is the reason for our venture in Honduras and why we are meeting here today. As you all know, Kostas is the great-great-grandson of your patron saint, Wovoka, who is buried not far from where my husband's ashes were laid to rest today. In the same way, Pilar and her family are descendants of Lenca royalty, Princess Antu Silan Ulap, who led the first indigenous rebellion against the conquistadores, a successful one by the way. So you can see"—she leaned down to take Antu's hand and stand her up from the chair behind the table—"little Antu here is now the inheritor of two lines of royalty, Paiute Wovoka and Lenca Princess Antu. It is for her we meet here today, not just for ourselves and not for Kostas. We're here to fight back like Wovoka and Princess Antu. To rebel but in a thoroughly twenty-first century way, with money. Our weapons will be ingenuity and cash. Victory will not be to see our opponents defeated but to establish security for ourselves." Grace motioned for Pilar to stand up. "Pilar will lead the charge like her ancestor did over five hundred years ago. It will be the plan Kostas created."

Not a soul in the room moved. Their eyes were transfixed on the two tall women standing behind the meeting table. Tommy's mouth was agape. He caught a glimpse of his friend, Dave, against the wall. His girlfriend, Jackie, had stepped forward, away from him, with excitement. Jasper leaned against the wall and smiled broadly.

Grace sat down, leaving Pilar standing by herself before the crowd. Everyone leaned forward with expectation. Pilar smiled then turned her attention to Antu, coaxing her to retake her seat. Antu shook her head. She didn't want to sit down, and everyone in the room laughed, as much from relief as from the delight of watching a child who knows she is the center of everyone's attention.

Pilar gave up trying to get Antu in the chair and let her roam behind the table as she pleased and asked Tommy to show everyone the photos he had taken at the mine. Tommy scrolled through the pictures of the Lencas whom he had met at the mine.

"My people," Pilar said simply.

Someone in the crowd said out loud, "They look like our people!"

"Exactly," Pilar responded.

By now, Antu had worked herself to the end of the table and spotted a few Paiute children about her age sitting together on the floor by the wall opposite Dave and Jackie. Shyly, she walked forward, completely ignoring the stares of the hundred or so people in the room, and stood by the group of children as if asking to join them. One of the Paiute boys slid his bottom across the wooden floor to make space for her, and Antu quickly sat down, her back to the crowd behind her. One of the Paiute mothers, recognizing the children had no interest in the business of the grown-ups, stood up and ushered the small group out of the room on to the playground outside. She turned around as if to ask Pilar if her daughter was permitted to join the group, and Pilar nodded her head and waved her hand at Antu to show her she could leave with the other children. Soon the noise of children playing outside echoed faintly in the meeting room.

Tommy had also prepared a few of the depictions in Kostas's computer model of the silver deposits in the Honduran mountain for preview on the large screen. He explained briefly the history of silver mining over the centuries and how Kostas had used the remnants of those previous attempts to plot a geological map of the mountain. He compared the silver mine in Honduras to the silver strike in nearby Virginia City, not even a hundred miles from Schurz. Anyone who grew up in Nevada, like most of the Paiutes in the audience, understood the significance of this comparison. The silver mines of Virginia City, Nevada, produced in present-day dollars billions in riches over the few years of its existence. That wealth spawned the fortunes that became the modern-day institutions of the Bank of America, Wells Fargo Bank, the Western Pacific Railroad, and Stanford University and made the city of San Francisco the financial capital of the American West.

An old man in the front row stood up and signaled for attention. Tommy paused and waited for him to speak.

"Kostas said this, not you?" he asked.

Tommy could not say he had repeated what Kostas had asserted. He could only say that was what he surmised from the computer model he had showed and explained to the group.

"What did Kostas say?" the man asked.

Tommy looked to Pilar for help. "He didn't say that," she announced loudly so everyone could hear. "But I know what he did say."

Everyone waited.

She paused to look around the room. "He said, his words, 'Twenty-five million.'"

"Dollars?" the old man asked.

"Of course dollars. He also said 'Maybe more.'"

A great stir animated the room. Another man, much younger, stood up and signaled for attention. Pilar nodded in his direction.

"Is that what we invested in?"

"Yes."

"So what happens now?"

"We press on," Pilar said simply.

Grace stood up and motioned for Pilar to sit down. She briefly explained the three options that had been discussed at her apartment. The best case of those three was recovering the original investments.

Another person stood up. "You mean the best we can do is just get our money back? That's no victory."

"It is," Grace answered, "if you need that money or are afraid to lose it."

"What would Kostas say about that?"

"If Kostas were here, we wouldn't even be talking about such an alternative. The only reason we have brought it up is because he is not here. You have a choice. Quit now or risk a little more and move forward."

"If we move forward, does that mean twenty-five million dollars?" the man asked.

"Maybe, maybe more, maybe nothing if we fail." Grace shrugged her shoulders.

Pilar jumped up from her chair. "It's more than just what we want." She asked Tommy to bring up one of the photos of her people gathered at the mine. "It's what they want . . . need, too."

"Just like us," the old man who asked the first question said. He turned toward the crowd behind him so they could hear him.

The younger man spoke up again. "Did they invest too?"

"They have nothing but their strong backs and a stronger will," Pilar answered. "They're investing sweat and blood."

After the meeting, Grace invited Jasper and Tommy to her home in Schurz. Because Dave and Jackie were dependent on Tommy for transportation, they accompanied Tommy to Grace's home and so were included in the discussion about the results of the meeting with investors at the tribal community center.

Of the forty-one original investors Kostas had recruited over the four years of the project, thirty-nine were able to attend the meeting. Of those, thirty-two indicated to Grace they could add to their investments. When Grace totaled these promises, it amounted to 165 thousand dollars, short of their goal by 85 thousand dollars. When Grace asked Pilar if that would be enough, she merely shrugged her shoulders. She could only report what Kostas had told her.

Jasper tapped Grace on the shoulder to get her attention. Grace stopped her speculations and turned toward Jasper.

"We have the fifteen thousand Tommy just added to our Pine Grove Valley claim partnership. Let's throw that in, if it is okay with Tommy," Jasper suggested.

"Is it okay with you?" Grace asked Jasper.

"Our claim is peanuts," Jasper replied. "The best we'll get out of it will be just one or two times of our investments. And just for ourselves. Honduras promises twenty or thirty times the investment. And benefit to so many more than ourselves. It makes sense, business sense, and good sense."

Dave, realizing it was the fifteen thousand dollars he had loaned Tommy they were speaking about, squirmed in his seat. Because she knew him so well, Jackie grabbed him by the arm to hold him back, but she failed.

"I'll throw in ten thousand dollars," Dave said loudly, drawing everyone's attention to himself and away from Tommy.

For a moment, Tommy was grateful for the interlude. It allowed him to reflect on why he hadn't thought to make the suggestion Jasper had. He would have liked Grace to know he held the same good intention, and was sorry he had not spoken up sooner.

"Good," Grace said quietly. "That adds twenty-five thousand, making our total a hundred and ninety." She paused for a moment. "Kostas and I still have some of the money from his original strike ten years ago. We can contribute twenty-five more too."

Tommy, seeing his chance to be part of this discussion, said, "That's two fifteen total. Should be enough."

His comment, though, had all the power of a footnote. He felt deflated and frustrated his acquiescence to Jasper's suggestion was accepted by others without awaiting his direct approval.

After everyone had left to return to Reno or Yerington, Grace found Antu standing before the collection of photographs hanging on the long wall of the hallway.

"Papa?" Antu asked as she pointed at one of the pictures.

Grace knelt down to hold Antu close to her. Antu laid her head on Grace's shoulder and whispered again, "Papa?"

Pilar emerged from Kostas's office where she and Antu slept. She too knelt down on the opposite side of the little girl and put her arm around her daughter and over Grace's shoulder. She whispered something in Spanish Grace did not understand. Antu smiled uncertainly, trying to look as if she understood, but it was clear she had not, or did not want to understand.

Grace stood up suddenly, as if angry, and strode directly to the door of the bedroom she had shared with Kostas at the end of the hallway. She shut the door behind her and sat on the bed. Four years he had kept this secret from her! A daughter!

She had never wanted children, and to her understanding, neither did Kostas, though they rarely spoke about the option. As a nurse practitioner specializing in reproductive and women's health, Grace was always prepared and cautious. She had assumed Kostas had accepted this fact because his frequent forays into the field or other countries would have made family life difficult. Grace wondered if Antu was an accident or a clever strategy of her husband's beautiful mistress to capture a future with him. Grace was wounded in the heart because Pilar shared secrets she did not know with her husband.

If Kostas were present, she would scream at him. She wanted to slap his cheek, to wake him up. How dare he keep such a beautiful secret from her! She lunged off the bed and went to the door to confront her husband's mistress. As unfamiliar as anger was to her, Grace now found purpose and initiative in it. But Pilar had returned to her room with Antu. She had closed the door, and Grace knew if she opened it, Antu would be frightened by the angry distortion of her appearance.

Instead, she went outside and tried to stare at the sun. It hurt her eyes as she expected, and after a few seconds trying to endure the pain, she lowered her head and cried. She wanted to shout, to shake her fists at the universe and let Kostas know he had disappointed her. But she was ashamed of herself for allowing such negative and, to her mind, self-centered thoughts to contaminate the ever-present waves of grief coursing through her. She shook uncontrollably and finally collapsed onto the sand. As she lay there, she pounded her fists against the earth as if she could shake loose the spirit of Kostas it now contained.

Pilar had come out of the office and stood by the window inside the house to watch Grace. Normally brave and resourceful in every circumstance, she didn't know what was right. She had usurped the marriage of a good man and a good woman, and if it hadn't been for Antu, she would feel some guilt. But Antu was a gift to Grace, a bit of her husband reincarnated in the flesh. Someone to love and to cherish, to care for, to protect. It mattered little in the end that Antu had emerged from her loins and not those of Grace. Her husband had planted the seed. Grace would reap the crop.

As Grace struggled to stand up, Pilar went outside to help. Grace refused the extended hand, brushing it aside. Antu came to the doorway. Her presence stopped Grace. She knelt down to hug her close to her body. Pilar stood behind watching. She ventured a hand to touch Grace's shoulder, and this time, Grace did not turn it away.

Monday morning, Grace drove Antu and Pilar in her Subaru station wagon to the health clinic. They deposited Antu in the preschool in the building next door and together opened up the clinic. The waiting room was full, mostly young women seeking advice for their pregnancies or other women's issues. Grace put a white smock on Pilar and instructed her how to offer assistance. When Grace was busy in a private meeting with a patient, Pilar sat in the waiting room with the Paiute women and chatted with them. By now, they all had heard about the investor's meeting and the great riches promised by their scheme. The whole tribe was abuzz with the prospect of finally beating the white man at his own game. They made no secret of it despite the plea by Grace to keep gossip to a minimum.

Pilar showed them the pictures on her cell phone of her Lenca family and friends in Honduras. As she scrolled through the pictures to the delight of her new Paiute friends, it was inevitable pictures of Kostas and his daughter would come up. Repeatedly, she was asked to pause at these pictures while the Paiute women whispered their condolences for her as well as for Grace. That Kostas essentially had two wives did not seem to them strange or even unexpected. In fact, they acted as if a man who lived in two countries would certainly have two lives. Pilar wondered if she could ever explain this to Grace, or whether she should try. Perhaps the presence of Antu was explanation enough.

They managed a whole week of this routine. Antu became increasingly eager to attend preschool with her new friends. Each day, she came back with a new word in English and soon was constructing simple sentences in English.

Chapter Four

Since Tommy's departure from Honduras, Miguel Tavares hadn't returned to the mine to meet with the Lencas staying there. Without direction, it was doubtful the Lenca crew made any progress. Yet everyone was being paid weekly wages for at least a month as Tommy had promised them. Jasper was confused why no one just continued performing the functions they were being paid for.

"Do you think Kostas would have used this as an excuse to take a vacation?" he asked Grace as they met with Pilar and Tommy at her Reno apartment the weekend after the funeral.

"It's not exactly a vacation," Grace responded. "For none of us, even if we're not doing much."

"I'm sorry to be so blunt. But you've got money in the bank and the go-ahead to implement Kostas's plan. So why wait? Lowering our heads and just forging ahead with life won't solve any problems."

Tommy was shocked at Jasper's brusque words and tried to intervene by coming to Grace's aid.

Jasper ignored him. "We're lollygagging. Let's send me down there to kick some butt."

Where Tommy had failed, Pilar stood in to face Jasper. "I'll call Miguel right now and tell him to get started," she offered.

Tommy held up his hand. "Let me call him. I know what has to be done, and besides—"

Pilar put her hands on her hips and stood in front of Tommy. "Besides what?"

Tommy knew she understood what he didn't say directly, but he was sorry he had brought it up. "You know," Tommy deferred.

"Because he's chauvinist Latino?" Pilar pressed.

"If we send Jasper to Honduras, do we need to keep Miguel on?" Grace asked.

"Of course," Pilar replied. "He's the key. As soon as he sees our progress and commitment, the Chinese will learn about it. Then they'll understand their plan didn't work."

"What plan?" Grace gasped, though she understood Pilar's implication.

"In Honduras, all you need to do is let someone know what you wish would happen and what's that worth to them. Then someone will take the initiative and, viola! Your wish is fulfilled."

"And Miguel knew this?" Grace continued.

"Miguel is a babe in the woods. Completely in the dark. He thinks he's smart and clever because he's working both sides of the street, but he doesn't know what either side is doing. He's just an echo chamber and will tell any side what they want to hear. He's not brave enough to know the truth."

Pilar was fierce. She sounded like the princess from whom her tribe had descended.

"When do we contact the Canadians?" Jasper asked.

Pilar pressed Tommy's arm, perhaps to show him he was forgiven. "Let Tommy do that. You're too savvy for them. They'll like Tommy. They have dozens like him on their staff. Eager graduate students ready to strut their technology for the old geezers."

Tommy didn't know whether this was a compliment or not coming from Pilar. She herself seemed so knowledgeable about the world of prospectors and their elaborate schemes to raise money or market their discoveries.

"This old geezer will need Tommy to come along. Technology has sort of left me behind," Jasper inserted into Pilar's impassioned commentary. He looked at Tommy. "You willing?"

Tommy was eager to let Jasper, and Grace and Pilar, know he was willing, but he hesitated because he recalled his conversation with this father on the phone when he returned from Honduras. Only too late did he realize his failure to accept the challenge from Jasper as soon as it was offered made him look timid. He tried to think of a way to overcome the error, which, much to his frustration, caused him to hesitate even more. Finally, he nodded his head glumly.

Grace reached out and put her hand on his arm. "Are you sure?" she asked.

Tommy nodded his head again, this time slightly more vigorously, which he hoped would show some enthusiasm. But he stayed confused about how he would let his father know he was headed back to the murder capital of the world.

"Dave Mogis wants to go too," he said.

"You mean instead of you?" Grace asked.

"No, I mean with me. He made me promise I would ask you if he could go if I returned to Honduras."

Jasper spoke up. "Maybe a show of force would be good. It will let the Chinese know we're serious about developing the property. As if Kostas had planned this the whole time. What do you think, ladies?"

"We shouldn't use the money for another plane ticket," Grace said.

"He would pay his own way!" Tommy said.

They concluded Tommy would call Miguel to instruct him to reopen the mine and begin working it according to the plan interrupted by Kostas's death. Pilar would get in touch with the Lenca workers and assure them their employment would continue for as long as the refinanced corporation was able. Contrary to her wishes, Pilar was convinced to stay in Nevada with her daughter and Grace for the next few weeks. Tommy was glad Pilar wouldn't be accompanying them. To him, she seemed too headstrong and bold for what had to be accomplished in the near term. All they needed to do was to continue the excavations at the mine following the plan Kostas created. Since their goal was to convince, or fool, the Chinese, he forgot they actually had to find the vein of silver ore the computer model predicted was there. Otherwise, the whole operation was a bust, and the only people to benefit would be the twelve Lenca families who would be earning good wages during this campaign.

And Miguel. Tommy saw the absurdity of it. No matter what the outcome, Miguel would profit. He would earn his weekly consulting fee for as long as the plan was implemented. If they found no silver, he still earned a good wage in Honduras. If they did strike a rich vein and were able to liquidate their interests to the Chinese for millions, in addition, Miguel would receive 1 percent of that windfall, possibly 250 thousand dollars if they had achieved Kostas's goal of twenty-five million. It was also likely the Chinese were paying him for his espionage. Tommy made a secret promise to himself not to let Miguel profit by the death of his friend. But how he was to accomplish this he could not imagine. He wondered if he could share these thoughts with Grace, deciding ultimately he could not even if it was revealed Miguel was an accomplice to murder. But Jasper would listen. He could tell the Vietnam vet about these thoughts, and the gruff old man would know what to do about it.

Grace purchased airline tickets for Tommy, Jasper, and Dave. When Tommy told Dave he would have to reimburse the corporation for his ticket, Dave was more than happy to do so. Both of them visited their geology professors to explain their absence. Dave had the idea he could make his journey to Honduras a field trip for credit with his instructors as long as he brought back a report. When Tommy demonstrated the model Kostas had devised, his teachers were more than interested. One of them even offered to consider investing in the enterprise. They all were aware of Kostas's good fortune with the silver mine in Tonopah, and some, it could be said, envied him. He had practiced what they preached. Tommy politely turned away these requests because he didn't want to feel any further obligation to his teachers than was required by his studies.

When the three arrived in Tegucigalpa, Miguel Tavares was there to meet them in his Land Rover. Jasper raised his eyebrows at the expensive car. Tommy and Dave deferred to their elder and let him sit in front with Miguel, forcing Miguel to speak to Tommy over his shoulder while he drove them to Kostas's apartment in Santa Lucia. Jasper said little and only nodded when Miguel addressed him. Tommy could see Jasper was showing Miguel what he actually thought of him, but he did not know if Miguel noticed. If he did, then Miguel was a wiser conspirator than Pilar had indicated.

When Miguel let them into the apartment, the first thing the three travelers noticed were three pistols in holsters lying on the kitchen table. Dave eagerly strapped on one and pulled the gun out of its holster. Jasper pushed down on his arm and made him put it safely back in the holster.

As it was early evening, Miguel left the three alone to plan their sleeping arrangements in the apartment. Jasper took the bed in the master bedroom, Dave took Antu's small bunk in the corner, and Tommy settled for the couch, which he didn't mind. Together they walked up the street for dinner. Jasper let Dave know there was no need to wear the gun as long as they were in town. Dave reluctantly set it back down on the table.

Tommy called Grace when they returned from dinner to let her know Miguel was coming tomorrow to take them to the mine. Since none of the three spoke Spanish, Miguel would have to stay with them as long as they were managing the workers. In the background, he could hear Pilar saying something to Grace.

"Ask for Jorge," Grace said. "He speaks enough English to be quite helpful."

Pilar said something else to Grace, which she repeated to Tommy.

"Jorge has Kostas's pickup. Tell him to give it to you, and you won't have to depend on Miguel for transportation."

"What is Miguel supposed to do to earn his keep?" Tommy asked.

Jasper nodded his head to show agreement.

"He has to do anything you ask him," Grace replied.

Tommy heard noises on the phone as if it had been dropped and then retrieved again. Pilar came on the line.

"Tell him to call Grace tomorrow. She'll set the record straight. He works for us. You're the boss. Grace will tell him that."

Tommy understood Pilar would be telling Grace what to say to Miguel.

Jasper knew how to kick butt, and the Lenca mine workers appreciated it. They were grateful for the opportunity to work hard when it appeared their efforts would be productive and paid well. While the men removed the overburden at the mouth of the mine and installed the support timbers, their families transformed their temporary shelters into more permanent dwellings. They began clearing land and turning the soil to prepare fields for vegetables and corn. Some planted melons, a lucrative cash crop to bring them additional income. With Miguel's help, a contractor was hired to widen and grade the road from the highway to the mine and to flatten the bed of the dry creek in preparation for the dam to be built there. A mining supply company delivered a stack of rails and two ore carts. The rails were quickly installed from the mine to the site of the dam. Lenca miners, equipped with hard hats and goggles, drilled into the hard rock of the mountain for the first dynamite charges. Everyone, including the families of the miners, cheered as the blast blew dust out of the mine. The diesel generator Kostas had installed earlier was wired to provide power to the homes of the miners across the dry creek bed from the mine. The office shed was expanded to include a small kitchen and space for sleeping when the three Americans did not want to return to the apartment in Santa Lucia. One of the wives of the Lenca workers was hired to be a cook and housekeeper for the men. Though her Lenca husband was shocked to learn she would be paid the same wages as he was, Tommy couldn't believe, even in Honduras, people could work as hard as the Lencas and still be happy they earned only a hundred dollars a week. The wages their project paid seemed a pittance to him, even though the average income for a Honduran was less than two hundred dollars a month. Miguel was politely critical of Tommy and told him he should use him to make these kinds of arrangements. Jorge became the foreman of the Lenca crew.

Because Jasper, Dave, and Tommy were so eager to be involved in all aspects of developing the mine and helping the Lencas build their village, Miguel's duties were relegated to running errands and dealing with the mining supply companies. He was clearly dissatisfied with his diminished role and showed it whenever the opportunity arose.

Tommy called Grace each day to give her reports. Pilar sometimes took the call and was more eager than Grace to listen to the details of their activities, especially the reports about Miguel's activities and comments.

Just a week after their arrival, the mine had penetrated the mountain through one hundred feet of the solid rock of the mountain. Dave Mogis was invaluable. His measurements with the laser plotted their course through the mountain and at the right angle of ascent toward its center. He showed an unexpected knack for the placement of the dynamite charges, which he explained was the result of a summer field trip and internship at a lead mine in Colorado. He also exhibited great interest in the dam. Kostas had engaged a civil engineering firm to prepare engineering drawings of the dam and irrigation ditches to guide its water to fields where farms would eventually appear. Unlike almost all other mining operations in Honduras, this mine was contributing to the environment and to the well-being of the local inhabitants by providing a source of clean water, free electrical power for part of the day, and comfortable living conditions, at least by Honduran standards.

Unlike Tommy, Dave, and Jasper, Miguel never stayed at the mining camp but returned each evening to his apartment in Tegucigalpa. The three Americans stayed at the apartment in Santa Lucia two or three times a week, mainly to shower and get their laundry done. As they penetrated more deeply into the mountain, Jasper let everyone know because it was always the dark of night inside a mine, there was no reason not to work twenty-four hours a day. They hired four more Lencas to make a total crew of sixteen, all earning a hundred dollars a week. As a result, many Hondurans began showing up at the mine, lining up to be interviewed for a job. It tugged at Tommy's heart to see so many needy and desperate people. He often chatted with Jasper about this, but Jasper reminded him theirs was not a welfare program.

Once, an entourage of Chinese mining executives arrived in their Toyota Land Cruiser accompanied by a Honduran official from the office of Secretariat of Environment and Natural Resources and two Honduran military officers armed with automatic weapons. Through an interpreter, the Chinese made polite inquiries. Jasper invited them to tour the mine and explained patiently and clearly their plan to access the silver core of the mountain. He frequently mentioned the similarity of the silver opportunity of this mountain to the Comstock Lode in Virginia City, Nevada. Any geologist or miner engaged in silver exploration understood the significance of this comparison. In the period between 1860 and 1890, the Comstock Lode produced seven hundred million dollars in silver, when one dollar would buy a steak dinner. Tommy marveled at how adept Jasper was at implying great value while at the same time acting as if they themselves were naïve treasure hunters. Miguel was especially solicitous of the Chinese. He explained later it was his job to develop interest in the mine from any and all parties.

Despite the apparent progress of the mine, there was no evidence of silver ore; but at this point, none was expected. According to the model Kostas had developed, they still had at least another fifteen hundred feet to tunnel. In fact, if silver ore had been detected in these early stages so close to the surface, there would be cause to worry, according to Tommy, because silver ore in a place where it was not mapped by the computer would indicate the computer model was inaccurate or flawed in some way. Thus assured that finding nothing was what they needed to find at this point in their project, they pressed on with confidence. Only Miguel doubted the wisdom of this view.

Grace began to worry that the three hundred thousand dollars in the bank account, when Tommy returned to Honduras with Dave and Jasper, would soon be depleted. In just three weeks, they had burned through over a fifty thousand. At this rate, they would be out of money in twenty to twenty-five weeks, little enough time to dig a tunnel a quarter mile in length. During that period, they would have to strike the vein of silver ore, if the model Kostas had produced was accurate. But also, there was the chance that after weeks of more drilling, blasting, and mucking rock, there would be no cache of silver and no money left to explore further. Grace did not want to go back to the Paiute investors in Schurz to raise more money.

Tommy had difficulty explaining to Grace and Pilar why not finding silver was, at this point, a sign of encouragement. It proved Kostas's model was correct. As she listened to these explanations, Pilar wondered out loud if they could use the absence of silver ore as proof of the value of their claim. Because such an idea was so contrary to ordinary thinking, one evening as they rested in their bunks at the mine office, Tommy asked Jasper if Pilar's intuition had some merit. The thought made Jasper laugh out loud.

"Yes, we have no bananas!" he retorted.

Tommy remained intrigued with the idea, however. He got out of his bunk and turned on his laptop to check the model again.

"Of course, this is just an estimate," he said to Jasper as he tapped the computer screen with his forefinger.

"A guess," Jasper corrected.

"A prediction," Tommy answered. "Like the weather. No one second-guesses weather predictions anymore. Farmers plant their crops according to weather predictions. People invest in commodities based on weather predictions. Ships and planes plot their routes based on them. People even plan their vacations by checking the weather. Predictions based on computer modeling are a new reality. Why wouldn't that be true inside this mountain? Kostas took hundreds of measurements. He plotted the pattern of silver ore in the mountain. He knew the geology of silver, how it is leached from the earth by superheated steam and volcanic action. We techies know these things. It is just not seat of your pants, maybe like it was in your day. So we can say, based on what we have found so far, Kostas is right. His model is right on. If the weatherman says there'll be no rain today, and I poke my head out the window and see there is no rain, then I have to say the weatherman was right. The same is true with Kostas. He said there would be no silver here, and there isn't."

"So what do we say to the Canadians or the Chinese? We stuck our head into the mountain and there was no silver, so Kostas was right. Trust us."

"Trust his model. The Canadians know him. They know his work. They paid him to do this kind of work and made decisions based on it. I bet if we went to them right now, they'll nod their heads and agree."

"Sure, for a little, but not for a lot. If we could show them a chunk of argentite, the price would go up."

Tommy stood up with excitement. "What if we told Miguel we're making an offer to the Canadians based on this evidence and they accepted it? Would he buy it and go to the Chinese with it?"

"We're going to use nothing to prove we got something, is that it?"

"But our nothing means something."

Jasper scratched his head.

Tommy continued. "If we make our nothing seem like something to the Canadians, Miguel, who's interested in feathering his own nest, will make it seem like really something to the Chinese. And then we'll have a bidding war."

"Over nothing?"

"Nothing yet. But something soon. Isn't all of life like that? Don't we speculate about what we are going to get because we don't yet have it?"

"That's gobbledygook. No one is going to buy that. Not in a million years."

"Jasper, listen to me for a moment. Everyone knows if we found silver, the costs of dealing with us goes up. So they'll automatically think, when we don't have it, the costs will be lower. They'll assume buying before we find silver is cheaper than buying after we find it. So they'll be more eager and able to make an offer now than waiting for us to find what we're looking for. I think Pilar is on to something. I really do."

When Tommy tried to explain this new concept to Grace, she confessed she found it difficult to understand. But Pilar saw its merits immediately and urged Tommy to fly back to Nevada for an appointment with the Canadians. She would call to schedule a meeting in Vancouver. After consulting with Dave and Jasper, Tommy agreed to return to Reno. He asked Dave if he was to come home with him, and after a thoughtful pause, Dave reluctantly decided he should return and show his face at the university.

Dave and Tommy worried about leaving Jasper alone at the mining camp. After all, that was the location—and the cause, apparently—of the ambush. Jasper assured the two young men the prospect of death for an old man was sometimes alluring, not frightful.

"Especially in a blaze of glory," Jasper said as he patted the pistol he had taken to wearing on his hip.

Jasper's response mystified Dave. He realized in a moment of illumination that he actually feared failure more than death. Death was out of mind even though his friend, Kostas, had recently been murdered at this very place. The thought of failure was always present in his mind. He instantly saw the folly of his view and how upside down it was. His failures and his successes faded in importance when he understood the specter of death hovered nearby. And it was more exciting.

As he fingered the .45 caliber strapped on his hip, Dave changed his mind and told Tommy he would stay with Jasper at the mine. There was no one else to equal his skill at placing the dynamite charges. The efficient distribution of dynamite charges in the rock wall at the end of the tunnel created rapid and predictable progress. A misplaced charge could actually delay progress. He told Tommy he could e-mail his report and correspondence to his instructors at the university and did not need to be present. Besides, since he was paying for his own plane tickets, he didn't think returning was a good use of his money.

"In actuality," Dave told Tommy as they were driving in the Toyota pickup to the apartment one evening, "I think I'm a better student when I'm absent from the university. The professors are more interested in what I am doing here than what I could be doing by attending classes."

"Absence makes the heart grow fonder?" Tommy speculated.

Dave waved his arm out the window on his side of the pickup to encompass the rough landscape of Honduras.

"We would be bored in school, don't you think, after all of this?" he said quietly. "And because we were bored, our teachers would be bored with us. When they see the empty chairs in the classroom that used to be ours and remember us, they're excited because we're excited to be here. We're actually practicing what they are preaching. I bet they feel like they accomplished something with us. Imagine their reaction with me sitting there taking notes and staring at the blackboard. It's laughable when you think about it. We're better students when we are absent. Who would've thunk it?"

Tommy had to laugh at the absurdity of Dave's observation because it was so true.

PRECIOUS ABSENCE

Tommy did not often talk to his father during his few years at the university in Reno, so when he left for his second trip to Honduras, again he deferred connecting with him despite his father's admonitions during their last conversation. When he called his father from his apartment in Reno after returning from his latest sojourn, he hesitated to confess he had spent the last few weeks in Honduras and, in the end, failed to mention it. Instead, he let his father know he was traveling to Vancouver, British Columbia, to visit an international mining company about the property in Honduras his friend, Kostas, had been developing. He was distinctly aware that his omission was tantamount to a lie and resolved when it was necessary to return to his duties in Honduras, he would definitely inform his father. But he could not be sure he would fulfill this resolve when he remembered his father's likely reaction to the news.

During his two day's rest in Reno before flying to Vancouver with Pilar and Grace, he visited his university professors and delivered a report on his findings at the silver mine. He especially wanted to consult with them about the model Kostas had developed to see if they saw any fault in it. When they praised the model, Tommy asked them specifically if finding no silver ore where the computer model said it would not be found was a sign of progress. One professor shrugged his shoulders with surprise. He never thought to make such an observation himself but could find no fault with the logic of it. Thus encouraged, Tommy was prepared to explore the interest of the Canadians on this basis.

On the plane, the three of them planned their respective roles.

Grace would lead the delegation by first acknowledging the debt owed to the Canadian company and their gratitude for it, hoping to avert an immediate demand for repayment. Pretending, if by chance she actually didn't feel that way, she was overwhelmed by the prospect of carrying on the work of her deceased husband, she would remind the Canadians of their past confidence in Kostas and their promise to make an offer when it was appropriate to do so. She would also share a financial statement to show what they had invested in the project and what they had recently raised from their shareholders.

Pilar objected to this last bit of strategy. Knowing that they had more than two hundred thousand dollars in the bank, the Canadians might make a demand for a substantial payment against the loan. Grace disagreed. She believed it showed their own willingness and ability to continue the project and reminded Pilar that their and the Canadian's interests were mutual, according to the plan by Kostas. The Chinese were the target, not just the liquidation of the mining interests they controlled. Just how the Canadians would secure an edge in that plan was unclear to Grace, but she insisted one of the goals of the meetings was to prove the Canadians did have this interest and were willing to pursue it. If they did indeed want to continue the original plan, that goal would open the door for more assistance from them. At the minimum, it would protect them from facing a demand for repayment of the loan.

Pilar's role in the meeting would be to make a case for the environmental and social commitments required by the plan developed by Kostas. She would explain Kostas always planned that the development of the mine would be a contribution to the indigenous community, and any offer the Canadians made would have to include provisions to carry on those intentions.

Tommy would demonstrate the model and cover all of the technical considerations of the project.

As it turned out, they did not need their plan. Marc Cousineau, though he had lieutenants in the meeting, took control and made a direct and forthright offer. His company would buy the rights to the mine for twice the amount that had been invested in it, $1,430,000, less whatever of their original investment remained in the account, and forgiveness of the loan, in total an offer of nearly two million dollars.

"We know Kostas's main concern was protecting your investors. This way, they double their money," Cousineau explained. "To obtain the licenses and permissions Kostas had spent four years acquiring would cost us more than this."

He also said, almost offhandedly, everyone knows there is silver in the mountain; and eventually, someone is going to mine it. The obstacle wasn't finding it; it was obtaining the patents from the government permitting the search for it. Since Kostas possessed that, they were willing to take over immediately.

Pilar tried to make her case for the environmental and social conditions, but the Canadians treated her with such indifference she did not believe if they made promises they would keep them. She whispered to Grace that in her eyes, the Canadians were as bad as they believed the Chinese must be.

Grace quietly turned down the offer. Doubling their investment, as clever and as tempting as it was, wasn't enough. If obtaining the license to mine the mountain was so difficult, expensive, and time-consuming, then other parties should be interested.

"You mean the Chinese," Cousineau blurted. "Ultimately, they will be getting this property, but we can work together and both make money out of it if you want. Isn't that your plan?"

Grace was startled by Cousineau's directness. "You mean you would be selling it to the Chinese?"

"We mine deep pockets as well as mountains," Cousineau replied. "And we can work together if you want to do this."

Grace looked to Tommy and Pilar for help, but both were silent. She bowed her head solemnly for a few moments before replying. "Thank you. This is a lot to absorb. We're not used to 'wheeling and dealing' like this.

Can you give us a few days to think on it? I am sure Kostas would want us to work with you, but we also have to consider our investors."

Cousineau reached across the coffee table between them and patted Grace's hand. "Of course. We didn't expect anything else. Also, remember this is a very painless way to get rid of the bothersome detail of repaying the half million you owe our company."

"So you want your money back?" Grace asked quietly.

"It's part of the legacy, isn't it?" Cousineau replied.

Grace raised her eyebrows as if surprised to hear the word. "Legacy?" she repeated.

"What Kostas left behind," Cousineau clarified.

"You mean what he started," Grace corrected.

Cousineau nodded his head. "That's a good way of putting it." He stood up suddenly as if to close the meeting. "Be careful in Honduras. It's a rough place. A lot is at stake. And we can help there." He paused to nod to one of his associates standing behind him near the door to the office. "This is Benvolio. You can call him Ben. I'm assigning him to you. When you return to Honduras, let us know, and we'll send him along with you or your crew."

"Why?" Pilar asked.

"He knows how to handle difficult situations," Cousineau said quietly.

The next day in Reno after returning from Vancouver, Pilar announced to Grace and Tommy she was going to accompany Tommy to Honduras.

"What about Antu?" Grace asked quickly.

"She'll be with you."

Grace seemed satisfied and turned around to glance at the little girl sleeping on the couch in the Reno apartment. "She'll be okay with that?" Grace whispered.

Pilar nodded her head. "She knows she has two mothers now and two countries, and she likes her new friends at school. She's learning English, and she is safer here than in Honduras. Kostas would want nothing else."

"Did he plan on ever letting me know about Antu?" Grace continued.

Pilar nodded. "Of course."

"When?"

Pilar turned to look at her daughter napping on the couch. Facing Grace again, she shrugged her shoulders but said nothing.

Tommy didn't know whether to speak up or not.

"Will you let Cousineau know you're going to Honduras?" Grace asked to change the subject.

"So he can send along his bodyguard? Or spy?" Pilar replied.

Grace nodded then looked to Tommy, expecting him to add something to the conversation.

"How will Miguel react to Benvolio—Ben?" Tommy responded dutifully.

Pilar chuckled. "Afraid and happy at the same time. Afraid because Ben is there to protect us and our project, and happy because his presence signifies the value the Canadians have placed in it. Cousineau is a clever man. The Chinese, as a result, will get an earful from Miguel. But because of that, we do have to be careful. After all, it is Honduras."

For this trip, his third to Honduras in just a few weeks, Tommy realized there was no evading a call to his father. He left Grace's apartment to cross over to his own where he could talk on his cell phone in private. As he dreaded, his father vehemently demanded he not go.

"Your friend was murdered there. You won't be safe. How can you even think of going?" his father yelled in the phone. After a moment's silence, in a quieter tone he added, "What will happen to your studies? You don't want to screw up your chances for that master's degree. You've spent years in school working for that. No, I can't permit that."

Tommy listened patiently, not responding at the frequent silences punctuated by the heavy breathing he could hear over the phone.

"Well?" his father finally demanded.

Tommy whispered into the phone. "I got to go because my friend was murdered there. Don't you see?"

"Are you sure? Maybe you're involved just because you're an extra hand."

"Of course I am. They need me."

"What happens when they don't need you anymore? What do you get out of it?"

Tommy couldn't tell him he had invested in the venture through his partnership with Kostas and Jasper because he couldn't tell his father about the fifteen thousand dollars he had borrowed from Dave Mogis.

"I'm not doing it for me," he said sullenly into the phone.

"Even so, it's going to cost you something. Your master's degree maybe. Maybe your life. Did you stop to think of that?"

"Kostas was my friend. Grace is my friend. I can't just desert them."

"There are other ways to help. You don't have to be there to help them. To risk your neck."

"But I want to be there. Don't be so gloomy about it. Everything is risky. Just driving on the freeway is risky. So why let potential trouble rob us of something worthy? Safe is sorry, in my book. A sorry life."

As Tommy ended his minor speech, which surprised him, he suspected his father might have understood it as a criticism of the choices he himself had made. There was a long silence on the phone before his father responded. When he did speak, he sounded defeated, something Tommy had never before detected in his father's voice.

"If you need me, call. Make sure you call. You're my son, my only son."

"You're my only dad," Tommy discovered himself saying.

He wished he had thought to drive to Sacramento and meet with his father instead of enduring the unnerving abstraction of a long-distance phone call.

Ben joined Pilar and Tommy at the Los Angeles airport as they boarded the American Airlines flight to Tegucigalpa. Their new traveling companion was dark complexioned and appeared as if he were of Latin descent. He spoke English with a slight accent, though Tommy thought it might be more Quebecois than Latin. He soon revealed he was fluent in Spanish and chatted animatedly with Pilar as they boarded the aircraft. On board, Pilar took the seat between Ben and Tommy. Because Tommy rarely had much to say, when conversation arose, it was between Pilar and Ben, both of whom were clearly more comfortable speaking Spanish. As a result, Tommy was ignored for much of the flight. Though he was determined not to take note of this innocent slight, by the time they had landed in Tegucigalpa a few hours later, he was unhappy and grumpy. By now, Pilar and Ben were comfortable with each other; and to passersby, it was Tommy who looked to be the odd man out. Cousineau, Tommy reflected, was a clever conspirator because he had selected exactly the right kind of man to accompany the energetic Latina. What a sorry show Tommy imagined himself to be in contrast! Both Pilar and Grace, it seemed, treated him like an afterthought or as an errand boy. Maybe his father was right. He was invited into this adventure because he was useful. When his usefulness ended, so would the adventure. Once again, he allowed himself to long for the pleasant oblivion of an ordinary life, though he knew such a desire was what he was determined to resist. Unlike his father, he knew, though perhaps subconsciously, he would never be satisfied with mere contentment.

As was expected of Miguel by now, again he registered the unmistakable expression of surprise and shock to see yet another man accompanying Pilar and Tommy. As he shook hands when introduced by Tommy, he did not remove his straw hat, as Latin decorum might decree, so had to tip his head past the brim to look up to see the face of the much taller Ben. Though obviously aware of the slight, Ben smiled genially and squeezed the Honduran's hand with emphasis.

"From Vancouver," Pilar said emphatically.

Ben reached into a shirt pocket to extract a business card, which he handed to Miguel. Miguel received it cautiously and spent a moment to study it.

"Global Resources Ltd?" he said, peering up again at Ben.

Ben leaned down a little again as if to hear and smiled broadly. "You know who we are," he said quietly. "We've been with Kostas since the beginning, just as you have. When you worked with Kostas on the surveys we hired him to conduct, you were working for us too."

"And you're here for?" Miguel queried.

"Silver, of course. Why are we all here?"

Miguel turned to Tommy. "You didn't say anything about this."

Tommy shrugged his shoulders, and before he could speak, Pilar stepped between them.

"They called us because Kostas had asked them to if something ever happened, so we invited him to come to Honduras and look things over. There's no commitment yet."

Clearly agitated, Miguel led the trio to his Land Rover parked on the street outside the terminal where a young Honduran stood guard over the vehicle. He tipped the guard, and the party climbed into the SUV with Ben taking the front seat across from Miguel.

"Will you be staying at the apartment too?" Miguel asked.

Ben shook his head in the negative. "At the mine. Pilar too."

"How long will you be here?"

Ben shrugged. "That's up to Pilar."

Pilar leaned over the seat to give instructions to Miguel. "Drop Tommy off at the apartment. He'll rest up there, and Dave or Jasper can bring him out in the morning. Also, I have to pick up some things for me there before we head out to the mine."

"You won't be staying at the apartment?" Miguel asked as he negotiated through the traffic on the crowded street.

"With my brother's family at the mine. Ben too. Later, Ben will rent a car if he needs it."

As Pilar rummaged through closets and drawers for clothing, Ben asked Miguel to open the rear hatch of the Land Rover so he could extract something from the baggage he had checked on the airplane. Miguel got out of the car with Ben and opened the rear gate. He watched as Ben opened a suitcase and extracted a holstered pistol wrapped in a wide belt.

"I suppose we'll be needing these," Ben said casually as he strapped on the weapon.

"You've been here before, I take it?" Miguel asked as he squeezed shut the hatch.

Ben answered in Spanish, letting Miguel know he had met with Kostas a few times right here in Santa Lucia.

Also in Spanish, Miguel replied, "And I didn't know about it?"

Ben shook his head. "It was our secret," he said mysteriously.

Before Miguel could respond, Pilar showed up with a duffel bag. She threw it in the backseat and climbed in beside it.

Miguel drove in uncharacteristic silence, his two hands tightly squeezing the steering wheel. Pilar laid her head on the duffel bag next to her and closed her eyes.

Ben smiled slightly as he glanced at Miguel from the corner of his eyes.

Jasper arrived at the apartment late that evening just as Tommy lay down on the couch to rest from his trip. Dutifully, as he had promised his father, he had just called to let him know he had arrived safely. His father had asked him to call each day, and if he happened to be unable to answer the phone, to leave a message. It was the only way, his father had confessed, he could quell the constant worry of having his only son traveling in the jungles of a hostile and outlaw country. Not used to such soft requests from his father, Tommy acquiesced. When he called to make his first report, he felt gratified to understand his past view of his father might have obscured the truth of their bond. He was grateful Kostas had influenced his world in such a way that he had rediscovered his father. Had he stayed in school, fulfilled all the functions ordinary life demands, and received his master's degree, he doubted he and his father would have experienced anew the pure joy a father and son can share.

"That Ben fellow is already shaking things up," Jasper said as he smacked Tommy on the rear to rouse him from the couch. "Pilar too. A firecracker of a couple, those two."

"What happened?" Tommy asked as he sat up straight to make room for Jasper on the couch beside him.

Jasper ignored the implied invitation and remained standing in front of Tommy as if to emphasize the importance of what he was to say.

"And Miguel, you can almost see him pulling out his hair. I think he's afraid we've hired Ben to take his place."

"But we need to keep Miguel on the payroll, don't we?"

"We know that, but he doesn't. Ben wasted no time. He inspected the mine, talked with the Lencas we've hired, found a place to sleep in Pilar's cousin's cabin, and let everyone know how much confidence his company has in Kostas and his plan. He told everyone, except Miguel, not to worry about their job. When Grace and Pilar were ready, his company would take over operations. He had Miguel scratching his head and sulking around. He didn't even leave until I did. Pilar put him out of his misery finally. She told him they had no plan to gyp him out of his deal. One percent."

"Did Miguel seem happy about that?"

"Nope. Seemed worried. I'm sure Ben and Pilar cooked all of this up on the airplane. I bet Miguel is meeting with the Chinese right now."

"So what will happen now?"

"We'll see. Can hardly wait to get back tomorrow. Getting something for nothing is pretty interesting right now. Seems possible, as hard as it is to understand and accept. Still no silver ore though we've already gone three hundred feet into the mountain."

By now, Tommy was wide awake. He stroked his chin as he ruminated about Jasper's comments. "So you think finding nothing right now is still the best thing?"

Jasper shrugged his shoulders. "The way I see it, according to this plan of Kostas, we can't lose. If we find silver, we got something to bargain with. If we don't find silver, we still got a bargain to make. Pretty sweet. Wished I'd thought it up myself."

"What will Miguel report to the Chinese?"

"He'll let them know the multinational mining company, Global Resource Limited, is going to take the mine off our hands. After all, they've already invested in Kostas for thousands to survey the mountain. That's the reason Kostas staked his claims. Everyone can understand then why the company couldn't commit to further exploration. Too risky for a big company but maybe just the ticket for an independent prospector like Kostas. After all, he does have a history of successful silver mining, and he is from Nevada, the site of the world's largest silver strike. I think Miguel and the Chinese will even think the Canadians manipulated Kostas to do the additional survey and permitting work on his own nickel to reduce their own risk. Very clever from a wheeling and dealing point of view. Since they've retained the right for first offer, they could get what they would have had to risk their own millions to have if they had done it themselves.

The crafty Chinese will admire their cunning and thus convince themselves that the Canadian's plan worked. If the Chinese or Miguel had anything to do with Kostas's death, they will be slapping their foreheads now because it dragged in their fiercest competitor. I guess they thought the Canadians would just kiss off this opportunity without Kostas. But they didn't count on Pilar. She's a fighter, I tell you. She understands completely the situation, and voilà! Ben shows up. Tall, dark, and handsome as if Kostas resurrected, only now with the quite visible support—and interest—of the Canadians. Now the Chinese have to act. And we got Miguel to thank for that because his worries will be their worries. If they want the mine, they'll have to make a move. We'll see soon enough how effective Miguel is and how sound Kostas's plan was."

"Ben knows we've found nothing so far?"

"Of course he does. To hear him tell it, Kostas's model is the work of genius. He said this in the presence of Miguel. If we had found silver ore in these first three hundred feet, it would defy the model. Since we haven't found it, he has great faith in the model."

"And how did Miguel react to that?"

"He's a parrot. He repeated it to make sure he had heard Ben right then left immediately. I think he was anxious to get the news to his other employer."

"What does Miguel think the Canadians are going to offer?"

Jasper chuckled. "This Ben guy is great. He let slip, as if by accident, that he was here to certify what his company was going to receive for a million and half bucks and forgiveness of the loan, almost two million. You could see Miguel's eyes light up when he overheard that."

"That could be twenty thousand dollars to Miguel according to the contract he had with Kostas."

"And I bet he multiplies that by two when he tells the Chinese what offer would do the trick," Jasper added.

"Forty thousand dollars . . . four million?"

Jasper chuckled to himself at the thought of earning four million dollars. "Already we're talking millions, just like Pilar said at the meeting in Schurz, and not even a day has gone by since your return."

"You think the Chinese will fall for it?" Tommy asked.

"For them, Ben is proof enough. And our naïve cold shoulder. Pilar let Miguel know, in no uncertain terms, as soon as negotiations were finished, we were finished with him as if we would entertain no other offers, as if we're not interested in hearing from anyone else, maybe even pretending we don't know anything about the Chinese and their interest in the mine. Playing real dumb like a real hustler she is. According to her, the grieving widow and the grieving mistress just want to be out of Honduras, fat and safe in America land."

"So you think the Chinese don't credit Pilar or Grace with the ability or willingness to 'wheel and deal'? And that the Canadian's are taking advantage of them?"

"In the eyes of the Chinese, Pilar is an indigenous native, a second-class citizen, and a woman to boot. Grace is a spoiled American woman. The fact that Ben showed up proves to them the Canadians think like they do. There's an opportunity to pluck the fruit from these naïve and weak women. They won't be able to resist getting involved somehow."

"Won't they question the four million dollars?" Tommy asked. "Seems like a lot for what has been accomplished. After all, Grace and Kostas only have about seven hundred thousand of their own into the project, plus the loan from the Canadians. How can they justify nearly a three-time markup?"

"A million and half dollars in our small, local operation is like five and half million to a giant company like Global Resources and the Chinese company. Both would have spent that much to get where we are now, probably more. So two million from the Canadians seems like a bargain."

"And four million is a bargain for the Chinese?"

"Yes, from their perspective. They need the silver more than we or the Canadians do. If this mine turns out as everyone expects, it will have a major impact on the worldwide silver market. Silver is used in the manufacture of electronics. Cell phones, computers, everything electronic. Where are the most electronic products in the world manufactured today? In China. They need a resource to feed their own industrial complex. Mining silver in Central America is a low-cost way for them to ensure a constant supply of a vital resource. It will make their manufacturing prowess more competitive because other countries will have to pay the market price for the silver they need while the Chinese get it for the low cost of mining it. For the Chinese, silver mining is more than just making dough out of a mineral resource. It is a strategic economic move to make sure their industrial complex controls the resources they need to remain competitive in the global economy, and at the same time because they control so much of the supply, they can jack up the price of silver on the world market to make the manufacturing capabilities of other countries less able to compete, to say nothing of the profit billions in silver will produce for them. For such an advantage, four million bucks, even more, I hope, is a drop in the bucket."

"And Kostas realized all of this?" Tommy asked, awed at the grand scale of his vision.

"Of course. Geologists long ago migrated from lucky fortune hunters to global businessmen. It is the world market that determines value, not the mineral itself. Haven't you learned that yet at the school of mines? You don't make money just by digging holes in the ground. As I've said again and again, you make money wheeling and dealing. The only difference today from my day in the past is that you manipulate on an international scale. Panning for gold in Nevada and selling to a couple of local jewelers is chicken feed and old fashioned. What we're doing here is the real prospecting, only the vein of ore we're looking for is in the pockets of international bankers and economists. Yes, Kostas knew what he was doing. Why else did he come to Honduras and risk his neck? Because he learned from the Canadians and knew what the Chinese were after and figured out a way to make them compete for the results of his work and vision."

"But to make this elaborate plan work at some point or another, there has to be silver, doesn't there?" Tommy wondered out loud.

"Of course. That's why Kostas picked this mountain. Everyone knows there is silver here. They've been mining it for nigh on five hundred years. Have you ever talked with anyone who doubted that? No."

"Are you saying Kostas picked this mountain, this place, for this scheme?"

"Of course."

"It is almost as if the actual silver is an afterthought. Without all the other elements—the Chinese and their need to remain competitive as a manufacturing juggernaut, the world economy, and the Canadians—the undiscovered silver has no value."

"Why do you think it stayed in the ground for five hundred years when everyone knew it was there? Before now, there was no way to turn a shiny piece of dirt into money. Now there is, and that's what Kostas actually discovered. That's why we're here."

"And the Chinese don't know this?"

"What difference does it make whether they do or not? Kostas showed them how to get what they wanted, and of course they'll have to pay for that service."

"Why don't the Canadians just take over? Why do they need us?"

"The Canadians are using us, using Kostas." Jasper paused to stroke his chin thoughtfully. "This is the plan Kostas sold them on. To accomplish what Kostas could would've cost them millions, and they would have to justify that investment to their board of directors and shareholders as a mining venture, not as a scheme to entice the Chinese. By using Kostas, they did not have to venture any capital, so did not have to explain to their shareholders what they were doing, and at the same time using Kostas as a convenient foil to the Chinese. They can't lose."

"And the loan to Kostas? The five hundred thousand? That didn't need approval by the board?"

"For a company whose gross revenues is measured in the billions, five hundred grand is chump change. They dump that kind of money all the time into projects they option. It's their way of keeping their fingers in a lot of pies at once. And it gives them ultimate control over unrealized assets. If a venture is successful, they will make that much in one day of mining."

"Wouldn't the Canadians make more if they developed the mine themselves? After all, to hear you tell it, the million and a half they may give us is not such a big deal. Then they could control the silver market themselves, maybe even improve the product enough that the Chinese, if they still wanted it, would have to buy it for hundreds of millions, not a measly few million like we're talking about now?"

Jasper laughed. "You're so naïve. Do you believe Kostas's model is a true picture?"

Tommy looked shocked. He had never doubted Kostas and his geological abilities or good fortune. On the basis of this faith, he had borrowed and invested fifteen thousand dollars in the Pine Grove Valley enterprise. Even his college geological professor could find no fault with it.

"Don't look so surprised," Jasper said as he sat down on the couch next to Tommy. "No one knows for sure the prognostications Kostas created with his model are actually true. Only more tunneling or drilling will reveal the truth, and even if there is a lode of silver in the mountain, there are so many other factors to consider, not the least of which is the actual price of silver years from now after the mine is sufficiently developed. Don't you see? It doesn't matter to us or the Canadians if silver is there or not. It matters only to the Chinese.

Who knows what headaches they'll run into when they begin mining? Sure, there's silver, but no one can project what it will cost to get the silver out of the mountain and to the market. It's the same problem everyone who has dug in this mountain has had for five centuries. Silver is there, yes. But getting it out of the mountain is risky business. What Kostas understood—and you and Pilar figured this out for yourself—we don't need to grasp at it and to hold it in our hands to appreciate its true value. Look at history. For centuries, people made money on this mountain merely by the promise of riches at the end of a mine tunnel. And, yes, they made money by digging silver out of the mountain. But the real inheritors of that wealth were the people who speculated on the basis of this promise. They never needed to possess the silver. In fact, like the Comstock lode in Virginia City, real wealth arose for those who never lifted a shovel. They understood what we understand now. Silver—all minerals, gold included—intrinsically has no value. The value arises in the minds that desire it, not in the thing itself. The Chinese desire it. We don't. Let's not forget this. We'll make millions even if there is no silver. Kostas's model is a magical hologram, a brilliant one, that entices and invites, but it has no more reality than the movie screen temptress we fall in love with. It is a symbol of desire, not of reality. Let's stick with reality."

"But there's gotta to be silver there," Tommy responded. He leaned over to place his elbows on his knees and held his head in his two hands as if suffering a headache.

"Of course. There has to be the basis for what is absent. Otherwise, how would we know what is not there?"

Chapter Five

Grace was slightly amazed Pilar could leave behind her daughter with her lover's wife for a treasure-hunting trip to Honduras. Alone with the small girl, Grace cared for her as would a mother, watchful, tender, admiring. Antu was a delight. Together, they patched together a patois of Spanish and English expressions to satisfy every moment. If she had known Kostas as a child, Grace often imagined, he would be just like Antu despite the child's gender.

Antu's father was her husband, Grace thought to herself, so did that make his daughter hers? She opened Antu's American passport to make sure the last name beneath the picture of the young girl was Wilson, the same last name as hers. So why could she not claim to be Antu's mother? Who would question her when documentary evidence seemed to offer confirmation? Why would a baby have to slip from her loins to be her child?

The young Paiute women who had come to Grace for prenatal treatment and examinations always returned after their babies were born to thank Grace for the precious result of their pregnancies. They often handed their newborns to Grace, and Grace cherished these moments. At such times, she felt like a mother, a mother to the newborn and to its birth mother.

When she recalled from time to time the young women, many still in their teens, she had served at the health clinic, Grace realized she had treated them as if they were children who needed her motherly advice and love. She often chuckled to herself to think that the babies of her patients could be considered as her grandchildren. Indeed, many of the Paiute women regarded her as an elder in the tribe, seeking her blessings and guidance. Like children, her patients were reckless and ignorant of basic health and hygiene needs. She coaxed them to adopt new habits, trained them in nutrition and exercise, counseled them in how to face and overcome their fears. They needed protection, care, and love, which she was happy to provide. These relationships were the most important part of her job. Her biweekly paycheck and career status were of little consequence to her. She worked for these people just as a mother worked for her family.

This maternal attitude did not end with her patients. When she strolled to the clinic down the country lane from her home, her heart generated the same warmth toward the animals she spotted from time to time. The rabbits and birds, the field mice, the hawks cruising above, the grasshoppers and bees, even the occasional garter snake, needed and received the same affectionate protection she was ready to bestow. In her eyes, they were all lovely beings in a universe saturated with affection. These creatures too were her children, she often felt. She just could not help herself. True happiness, she had come to recognize, arose from cherishing others over oneself.

Though Kostas would often tease her about these displays of excessive empathy, at the same time, he understood this quality to be the best part of his wife. He too benefited by her grand heart. It was what he admired most about her. He was convinced she was one of a kind, and no matter what sin or mistake he committed, she would still cherish him. This made him very confident. For Kostas, Grace had manifested a universe that forgave every being and every deed. She was well named for her gift was grace.

Now Antu, this child, this twenty-first century version of a Lenca princess and a Paiute messiah, had been entrusted to her care. As Kostas secretly predicted, she forgave him this trespass because had Kostas lived, he would have sooner or later shared this rare treasure with her. He knew she would adopt this lovely incarnation of their destiny as her purpose in life. This was the very reason she had trained as a nurse practitioner and accepted employment in a relatively low-paying position as a public servant. Antu arrived as the symbol of her purpose, representing her husband's grandiose humanity and her patient acceptance of his reckless intentions.

Once every month, a doctor employed by the Indian Health Service would drive from Reno to the reservation and spend a weekend to meet patients with problems Grace could not treat. She brought Antu to the clinic with her this weekend to ask the doctor to examine the young girl.

"She's Paiute?" he asked as he sat down on the narrow stool in the examining room.

He asked because, technically, he was limited to offer services only to members of the reservation.

Grace shrugged her shoulders. "Yes, I believe so," she replied. "Her father was Paiute."

"And her mother?"

Grace paused for a long while, causing the doctor to halt his examination of the little girl.

"Me," Grace whispered at last.

The doctor smiled and turned his attention back Antu. "That's news to me! I've been visiting here for two years, and this is the first time you've mentioned it. What's going on?"

Grace pulled Antu's passport from her purse and opened it for the doctor to read. "See, Wilson. Her father is my husband. Doesn't that make her my daughter?"

"Her birth mother might have to something to say about that," the doctor replied as he handed back the passport.

Antu sat silently on the examination table, kicking her feet back and forth. Grace reached over to stroke her black hair.

"She's got two mothers. Isn't that better? Wouldn't everyone be better off with two mothers?"

"Eventually," the doctor said as he pulled his stool closer to Antu, "you'll need a birth certificate. What will that say?"

"My husband's her father."

"Well, I hope you get away with it. Everyone is better off when you take charge."

Dave adored Ben.

"Actually, his name is Benvolio, of Italian descent," Dave informed Tommy as he arrived with Jasper late the next morning at the mine. "He was born in Argentina but moved to Montreal with his parents when just a kid. He's fluent in four languages, Spanish, Italian, French, and of course English. He has a master's in geology from McGill University and has been all over the world for Global Resources. And he was friends with Kostas. He came to Honduras a couple of times to help him out. It's very auspicious to have him here. Something's going to happen."

"Why do you say that?" Tommy asked.

"Did you ever read *Romeo and Juliet*, Shakespeare's play?" Dave waited for Tommy's response, but getting none, continued. "I did, believe it or not, in my English lit. class I had to take to fulfill my humanities requirement. Benvolio—his name means 'goodwill' in Italian—tries to keep the peace between the Capulet and Montague families, but he fails. Do you think that's why Ben is here? To keep the peace?"

"Or fail?"

"What do you mean?"

"Is goodwill a good intention?"

Dave stepped back and, exaggerating his expression, wrinkled his brow to show Tommy how confused he was. "I don't get it."

"Don't forget why we're here. Kostas was killed. Now there's going to be a fight for what he created."

"And Ben is part of it?"

"Why else would he be here? He works for the Canadians."

"I thought he was here to protect Pilar, Kostas's partner."

"She doesn't need protection. She can take care of herself. Besides, every man and woman in this camp hangs on her every word. She can't go anywhere without an entourage. She's the boss lady, I can tell you that. She even tells Ben what to do, and he hops to it."

Dave fingered the holstered sidearm strapped to his hip. "Like this kind of fight?"

"You've seen too many movies. Did Ben have anything to say about your work on the mine?" Tommy interjected, impatient with Dave's confused excitement.

"Yeah, a lot. He said go wide, not high. Should have thought of that myself. He says if we cut the tunnel a little wider, we increase our chances to intersect a vein of ore, which will most likely be trending vertical, according to Kostas's model. Going high with the tunnel makes it easier to work because we don't have to bend over, but that ain't going to help much if we don't find anything. By going a little wider while reducing the height of the shaft, we will excavate the same amount of material but increase our chances of running into a vein of ore. With Ben's help, we will reset the dynamite charges to do that. A terrific suggestion! He's a real pro!"

Tommy had to remind himself Dave had no knowledge of their ultimate aim to set the stage for a buyout from the Chinese. He looked over his shoulder at the shed where Ben sat in the shade of the porch as he ate the breakfast the Lenca cook had prepared for him. He gave Tommy a cheerful wave of the hand as he sipped his coffee.

"He seems at home already," Tommy murmured to Dave.

"Pilar too," Dave said. "She's right at home. Despite what happened to Kostas, she looks happy."

"Happy to be doing something, I imagine."

"Happy to have Ben doing something," Dave corrected.

Miguel arrived in his Land Rover, unmindful of the cloud of dust he brought with him to shroud the porch where Ben sat.

"Where's Pilar?" Miguel asked Tommy as he rushed toward him.

"What's up?" Tommy replied.

Miguel patted his hip pocket. "I don't think Ben ought to listen in to what I've got to say. It seems like Pilar has taken over anyway."

Jasper came out of the shed holding a cup of coffee. Seeing Tommy, Dave, and Miguel standing at the mouth of the mine, he shuffled forward, looking stern and preoccupied. Tommy nodded in the direction of Miguel and told Jasper the Honduran wanted to see Pilar. Jasper looked into his coffee cup and swirled it a couple of times to cool, then sipped it as he peered at Miguel over the rim of the cup.

"Here she comes," he said as he nodded in the direction of the village the Lencas had constructed in the last few weeks.

Pilar's stride was long and purposeful, despite her flip flops, as she approached the group standing by the entrance of the mine. She stopped directly in front of Miguel without acknowledging the other men.

"Well?" she said to Miguel as she planted her hands on her hips.

"What about him?" Miguel asked as he pointed to Ben still sipping his coffee on the porch of the shed.

Noticing everyone looking his way, Ben waved cheerfully again and invited the assembly into the shade of the porch with a wave of his arm. Dave and Tommy started to move that way, but Miguel pulled Tommy back.

"Okay, just us, right here," he said seriously. He reached back at a folded sheet of paper in his back pocket. "I got a call last night you should know about before you make any decisions with your friend from Canada over there." He handed the paper to Pilar, who snapped it from his fingers.

"You misspelled *conditions*," she said as she scanned the letter. "You left out the *i* in the middle of the word." She handed the letter back to Miguel.

"What about the rest of it?" Miguel exclaimed with disbelief. "Did you read the whole letter? It's an offer to take this project off your hands!"

"We got an offer," Pilar replied, still holding the note up for Miguel to take.

"But this one's better!"

"How do you know?" she asked.

"Well, I guess I don't exactly. I'm just presuming on the basis of what Ben said yesterday."

Pilar pulled back the letter to reread it. "This a Chinese company?" She pointed to the masthead of the letter then held it up again for Miguel to take.

This time, Miguel snapped it out of the woman's hands and extended the letter to Tommy. "See! It says four million dollars!"

Tommy leaned over to read the letter while Miguel held it up, but Miguel forced him to accept it. His heart pounded with excitement. He found it hard to believe that the ruse he and Jasper had discussed last evening was actually working and so quickly. He didn't know what else to do but repeat Miguel, as if to confirm the offer was actually four million dollars.

Jasper snapped the paper from Tommy's hands and forced it upon Miguel, who accepted it reluctantly. "If this is an official offer, you might as well tell those folks we already have an offer." He turned to look at Pilar, and she nodded her head in the affirmative, so he continued. "We ain't going to grab at a pig in the poke for a measly couple of million extra. Ain't very insightful of these Chinese fellows if they think we can be persuaded to turn our backs on a reliable company like Global Resources. If it weren't for them, none of us would be standing here."

Ben left his perch on the porch and approached the group standing in the shade at the entrance to the mine. Miguel folded the paper and returned it to his hip pocket as if to conceal it.

"Miguel brought us another offer," Pilar told him as Ben came close. "We turned it down, of course."

Smiling broadly, Ben put his arm over the shoulder of the much shorter Miguel. "That's his job. He has to promote your best interests. We wouldn't expect anything less. Whose offer is it?"

Reluctantly, Miguel pulled the paper from his pocket again and handed it to Ben, who unfolded the paper quickly. He laughed as he gave it back to Miguel.

"You'll have to do better than that, I'm afraid. Doesn't seem too attractive or too worrisome. For a Chinese operation, I'm a little disappointed. It's not exactly like they don't have the wherewithal to ace us out of a deal."

Miguel appeared totally bewildered. "I guess I'll call Grace."

"Go ahead," Jasper said, "but she'll just call Pilar to find out what she thinks."

"Who do you work for?" Pilar asked Miguel.

Miguel was taken aback by the direct question, especially from a woman. He raised his eyebrows and stepped away as if to defend himself from the small group standing in the mouth of the mine.

"Everyone knows I represent you. That's why they come to me. Who are they going to call? You?"

"Every million dollars is ten thousand for you, is that it?"

"Of course! Why not? It's my job. It's our agreement. I can't control what they offer. I just receive offers on your behalf and bring it to you." Miguel glanced around at the one woman and four men standing around him, as if trapped.

Dave looked confused. "What's going on?" he asked.

"Wheeling and dealing," Jasper answered.

Jorge, the crew foreman, emerged from the darkness of the tunnel. He said something to Pilar in Spanish. Pilar translated for the group, informing them the charges had been set, and they would have to move away from the mine. Two more Lenca miners followed Jorge from the tunnel.

As the group retreated to the shady porch of the shed across the clearing, Jorge took a position against the mountainside away from the mouth of the tunnel. After checking the area, he signaled he was ready. He pressed the button on the electrical detonator, and a muffled blast followed by a small cloud of dust emanated from the mine. After a few moments, a group of Lenca miners in their yellow hard hats disappeared into the lingering cloud of dust in the mine.

Miguel seemed beside himself that business as usual had not paused for what he took to be an astounding event, an offer of millions for this hole in the ground that had yet to produce an iota of value. Without any comment, Pilar headed back to the collection of shelters across the creek; Jasper and Dave went into the shed to finish their breakfast. Ben and Tommy stood by awaiting some response from Miguel.

Holding up the paper containing the Chinese offer, Miguel waved it in front of the two men. "Cash!" he said emphatically. "Right now!"

Ben smiled patiently and gestured for him to return the paper to his pocket. "We offer more than just cash," he said to Miguel. He pointed to the impromptu village that had arisen across the stream near the dam, which already was showing some progress. "Your Chinese are going to take care of them?"

"So I say no to them? Shouldn't we be more thoughtful, more strategic about a response?" Miguel asked, barely audible.

Ben laughed. "You want me to give you advice on how to take over our deal? That's loco!"

He turned on his heel and strolled back to the shed to join the others there. Miguel looked at Tommy as if he were his only friend. Tommy didn't know what to do but smile weakly. A few weeks ago, he was talking with his university professors about geological field research projects and class schedules, and now he was asked to evaluate offers of millions of dollars. They didn't teach this at the school of mines, but should because it was apparent to him in this moment that so much of mining and geology was exactly as Jasper had predicted, wheeling and dealing. His father would be proud of him if he could share with him this wisdom of the real world his trips to Honduras were gradually accumulating.

Feeling a bit sorry for the frustrated and confused Miguel, Tommy reached out and tapped him on the shoulder. "Miguel," he started, "you can't lose, can you, no matter what deal is accepted. Don't be so miserable.

At least you're earning a weekly paycheck the longer this project goes on. Why are you so eager to end it?"

"You don't understand Honduras," Miguel replied quietly. "It's not as simple as that. There's more at stake than my paycheck."

"For you?"

"For all of us," Miguel said ominously.

The more Tommy thought about their plan to use the absence of silver ore to prove the mine's value, the more confused he became. That Kostas could conceive of such a plan and work on it for four years absolutely astounded him. Where did he find the mindfulness and confidence to grasp such a contrary view? As it did in the ambassador's office when he found out about Kostas's Latin mistress, his admiration for his dead friend soared again. Such a plan possessed an otherworldly quality, hardly believable to the ordinary intellect. For all his young life in geology, value was found in the things uncovered in the earth. Finding nothing, as so often happened to miners and prospectors, was failure. Here in Honduras, finding nothing was success, a completely contrary view. In addition to creating and holding such a view, Kostas had persuaded a huge intercontinental corporation to accept it, though in retrospect, perhaps those involved with large economic issues would be more inclined to understand since money itself was inherently a valueless commodity except where people agreed to assign it certain powers.

Despite this confusion and the doubts it caused, he could not be shaken from the sensible nature of the enterprise. Kostas had created a project that could not fail. If his original plan to market nothing failed because they did find something, that something was worth a great deal. On the other hand, if—as he had projected—nothing was to be found, that too was success because, as Jasper had intimated last night, the absence they discovered proved in a very abstruse and subtle way there was something that was gone, and the something that was gone was what people desired. Only Kostas saw beyond the object of desire to realize its true nature. Nothing was as it appeared. With this simple realization, he had started a business.

Tommy was conflicted. As much as he admired this esoteric plan of Kostas, he himself hoped they would find the rich vein of silver ore. That seemed more certain. Yet at the same time, to realize that value would take years of work in the uncertain worlds of nature and economics. Nature might reveal insufficient or scattered quantities of ore, making further investment unfeasible; earthquakes and other seismic shifts would bring danger and expense to the project, increasing costs and making profit far more arduous and uncertain. Wars or overproduction of silver in other parts of the world could devalue the thing they had risked so much to find. Technology could eventually invent a less costly replacement material for silver. It was far easier, Tommy concluded, to market nothing than it was to grasp at and market something. This was Kostas's wisdom.

Poor Miguel! He didn't have a clue. His Land Rover, his plush downtown apartment, his constant preoccupation with money would fail him. None of these objects would bring him the satisfaction he sought. In fact, they created dangers he otherwise would not have to confront. Tommy wished he could lecture Miguel on the wisdom of Kostas, but he knew even if Miguel would listen to him, he would react as if Tommy was crazy or was trying to bamboozle him. There was no winning with Miguel, and Miguel could never win in this battle. He had already trapped himself in a hopeless quagmire of greed for things.

Pilar's long relationship with Kostas must have educated her too. It was evident she wanted nothing for herself. She participated in this plan to bring well-being to her people and had hooked her wagon to Kostas's star to achieve that aim. Tommy wondered if Kostas was used by her for her own aims, and supposed it was so, though he could find nothing wrong in this action since her intention was to benefit others. Perhaps, he thought in a moment of brilliant insight, Kostas was using Pilar to guide his own intentions. Their mutual good purposes were manifested in the form of Antu, their daughter, the inheritor of his royal Native American lineage.

Since Antu was one with Pilar's tribe and with Kostas's tribe, helping the tribes was protecting their child. All this was so beautiful to Tommy. He could hardly contain himself, but who could he explain it to in order to share? Who would understand? Dave and Jasper, as well meaning and honest as they were, could rightly be said to accept this plan for the pure adrenalin rush of being involved in a plot. The Canadians, by their own admission, saw a way to make a few millions with no risk on their side. Grace, as wise and kind as she was in every circumstance, seemed overwhelmed by the abstract nature of her husband's plan. She was so generous she wilted at the thought of taking advantage of others on the often flimsy excuse their intentions were good. Tommy did not think he could explain to Grace in a way she would fully comprehend. In fact, he was afraid that if he tried, she would require some adjustment to the plan to make it more ordinary, such as telling everyone the plain truth. That truth? There's nothing here. But that is the truth of every moment. There is nothing here in every moment because every moment immediately transforms into the next moment and what once was is gone, always.

Tommy's head ached with such thoughts. His father? Would he understand? Uncharacteristically, remembering his father calling him son in their last conversation, he wished his father were here to explain the plan Kostas had created. Tommy felt his father, the experienced and crusty businessman, would understand because he understood money. Money was the perfect metaphor for the value of absence. By itself, money was nothing—numbers on a check register, slips of paper, or cheap metal coins good for nothing other than pleasing children who used them to fill their piggy banks. Yet money was something, such a something that men killed for it, sacrificed their health for it, separated themselves from family for it, argued, passed laws, cheated for it. All in the name of—what? Safety? Happiness? Comfort? Reputation? Certainty? It never worked. Through all the ages of man, things did not give them what they sought. Usually, those things killed him. Kostas was so smart. He wanted none of the things, and yet he was willing to use them to bring some measure of safety and comfort to the people he loved.

When Pilar joined Tommy and the others in the shed after Miguel had driven off in a cloud of dust, Tommy quietly insinuated that she might have been a little too abrupt with him. After all, Tommy speculated, doubling the value of the mine was a considerable accomplishment, at least in the eyes of a Honduran. Miguel, who probably spent his entire life like most citizens of his country, scrambled constantly for money. Not just for money, Tommy added, but for survival.

Jasper answered for Pilar. "She gave him what he deserved," he blurted.

"But he seemed nervous," Tommy replied. "Even scared."

Ben rose from the table the crew used for eating and working. "Of course he's scared. What happened to Kostas was no coincidence."

"You mean the Chinese?" Tommy gasped.

"They say in Asia, life is cheap," Ben mused. "In Honduras, it's cheaper."

"But Kostas raised the price," Pilar said. "And they'll have to pay it."

"Someone going to call Grace?" asked Jasper.

"I'll let Marc know our plan is working," Ben said as he went outside with his cell phone.

"Working? What's working?" Dave asked, looking plaintively at everyone in the small room of the rickety shed. "What's working?"

Jasper patted him on the shoulder, pushing him back down into the chair by the table. "Your investment. Now you're learning about real prospecting. We're increasing the return on your investment."

Tommy held up his cell phone to let everyone know he would call Grace. He went outside to make the call but walked away from the shed to put some space between him and Ben, who still talked animatedly on his cell phone.

When Grace answered the phone, he explained the offer that Miguel had presented and their response to it.

"Does that mean the Canadians will offer more to match the Chinese?" she asked.

"It means whatever the Canadians do, the Chinese will match or increase. So I guess the Canadians will do something to make the Chinese believe how confident we are that we have something."

"Do we have something? I mean, silver? Is there silver?"

Grace sounded plaintive, uncertain, but Tommy did not know how to offer reassurance or even if he should try.

"Not yet," he muttered into the phone.

"So how can we make them believe we have something when there is nothing we can show for all this work and investment?"

"That's the beauty of Kostas's plan. We don't need anything to prove we have something."

"So why is a Canadian mining company interested if we have found nothing? It just doesn't make any sense."

"They know how to make something out of nothing. That's their business."

"I thought their business was digging ore out of the ground."

"Digging is the easiest part. After they dig it, they have to sell it. To sell it, they have to refine it. To refine it, they have to build a mill and refinery. To build a mill and a refinery, they have to commit millions of dollars. To commit millions, they have to convince their stockholders and board that it is a worthy risk. To convince them, they have to foretell the future price of silver. In the end, it is all guesswork. It's far easier, and safer, to make someone else do the guesswork, the Chinese. That was the plan Kostas created."

"Are you sure? What about Pilar and the Lencas? How are they protected by this plan?"

It was clear to Tommy his answers did not satisfy Grace. "They get some of the millions," he said finally.

"Money? That's protection? Sounds like the beginning of their problems."

Tommy's father immediately came to mind. Could Tommy say his father was happy because he was financially successful?

"You're saying money is the problem?" Tommy asked after a moment's contemplation. "Are you saying it won't help the Lencas, your Paiute investors, you, Antu, Pilar?"

Grace replied to Tommy's question with a quiet determination in her voice, which surprised him.

"Kostas learned when he hit his first strike in Tonopah that the money we received wasn't a gift. It was a curse. He knew from then on he would never be satisfied as a result, no matter how many millions he dug out of the earth."

"So why are we doing this?" Now Tommy was even more confused.

"Antu doesn't need money. She needs a mom and a dad, a family. Pilar doesn't need money. She needs the power to protect her people. If money is the object, it's not worth the pursuit. We won't sell out to the Chinese if all we get is a big paycheck. To make it right, they'll have to invest in the community. The environment. We're protecting them as much as we are our own. Don't you see?"

"But why all this talk about investment, budgets, cash flow, market evaluation, and so forth? What's that all about if it isn't about money?"

"Money gives us the energy to accomplish our goals, but it's not the goal."

"You're wrong!" Tommy responded, more heated than he intended to. "It's the goal for the Canadians. It's Jasper's goal. Dave too. And it sounds like it's Pilar's goal too."

"Pilar doesn't want money. She wants revenge."

After his phone call with Benvolio in Honduras, Marc Cousineau called Grace to let her know he was ready to take the plan to the next step. The Chinese, he told her, had taken the bait, and now it was time to set the hook.

Grace was offended by the explicit language. To her, it sounded cruel and merciless, but she remained quiet. Her many years with Kostas had taught her the difference between a man's view of relationships, generally confrontational, and a woman's, usually sensitive to a broader range of issues than a one-on-one tug-of-war. She let Cousineau know she was not so overcome with grief, as he might have supposed, to listen to his proposal. What offended her more, however, was that already Kostas was consigned to the past, now merely a historical incident in the centuries-long history of silver mining in Honduras. Cognizant and savvy about this history, Cousineau was ready to take advantage of his knowledge, and of the ambush that killed his friend.

"We're going to send you a new proposal," Cousineau explained. "I'll let you forward it to Miguel Tavares as if you'll be consulting him on the merits of our proposal. He will think you don't know any better or that you're completely innocent of any intrigue, perhaps even a little bored with the details of business. Act like you don't care. That's understandable, given the circumstances. Though the contract will be marked confidential, he'll go right to the Chinese with it, I'm sure. We're upping the ante. We're adding a royalty to the original sum of a million and a half plus forgiveness of the loan, which the contract will promise upon consummation of an agreement, and another five million to be paid based on future production. To the eyes of others, this will provide you and your investors an income for the next few years. To the Chinese, it will say we're offering you about seven million dollars in total. It will convince them we know something they don't. They'll have to do better. When you talk with Tavares, let him know how much you don't like the royalty extended payment plan, as that keeps you and your investors involved with the risks inherent in any mining venture, and would prefer all of the cash up front. The Chinese will read this and promise at the least to match our total of seven million or close to it. They'll probably make it an all-cash proposition, hoping you will be enticed with all the cash in front and no risk. Then we'll have them on the hook. After that, we'll take it to the next stage. You good with that?"

Grace recognized Cousineau was on familiar ground. He probably had several discussions and deals like this going on simultaneously all over the world. Though she did not quite understand the implications of his proposal, she told him she would review it with her crew in Honduras.

"Ben's there with them," Cousineau reminded her. "He has my full confidence and can work out all the details that concern you."

"But you are not actually going to give us seven million dollars, are you?" Grace asked.

"No, this is just a ploy to get you—and us—millions out of the Chinese. We really cannot take on this project at this time, as much as I would like to. We know silver is there, and Kostas had a good plan. But we still have first rights to an offer, and we can make money, make money back, that we invested in Kostas years ago when we hired him to do the original surveys he used to create his computer model of the silver deposit. As long as we match any other offer you may receive, you cannot refuse us. That's our contract with Kostas. I can send you a copy if you wish, but take my word for it. We'll make money because we'll make the Chinese pay us for the right to pay you."

"Did Kostas devise this plan with you?" Grace asked, a little shocked that her husband, whom she thought she knew so well, could have carried this secret for all these years. She thought he was intent on mining the silver mountain in Honduras like the old Comstock Lode prospectors and miners of Virginia City did 150 years ago. He had other secrets too, she remembered, as she looked up from the phone to see Antu playing outside with a new friend who had been dropped off by her parents.

"He didn't 'devise' this plan with us. He did it to us," Cousineau corrected. "We were roped in by his shenanigans as if we were suckers. But in a good way. He made it a deal we couldn't turn down because it is so damn easy, and it won't cost us a cent even if at some point you get millions. That money will come ultimately, one way or the other, from the Chinese, but because of our contract with Kostas, it will have to go through us. We'll take our cut off the top."

"It all sounds so mysterious and secretive. Is all business like this?" Grace inquired, feeling naïve.

"Successful business is."

"Is that so? What about Pilar and the Lencas. Did he rope you into that too?"

"That's his business. What he was to do with the money is his business. Ours is just to turn a buck."

"You don't have any conscience about how your operations affect the lives of others, their environment?"

"Of course we do, but within limits. There's only so much we can do. If we get too charitable or too green, it will cost too much, and there won't be enough profit to take the risk. Everything has to be balanced."

"There's no other way to find balance?"

Cousineau, despite himself, chuckled at what he took to be a question from an innocent do-gooder. "Maybe Kostas did," he said at last.

"Maybe we will," Grace replied firmly.

The next day, Grace received an e-mail from Cousineau's office with a ten-page contract in the attachment. She noticed that Ben in Honduras was copied on the e-mail, but not Pilar or Tommy. By addressing her exclusively, in his own way, Cousineau, the president of a billion-dollar international mining company, had designated to others she was the cornerstone of this particular operation. She understood this was most likely a strategic means to make the Chinese believe the naïve and grieving widow would be easy to outsmart.

Without opening the attachment, she forwarded her e-mail to Miguel, copying Pilar and Tommy. She composed a short note to Tavares, asking him to offer his advice to her and to the team in Honduras. She also was prescient enough to remind him that it was best if he kept these negotiations confidential. She imagined, as she did so, Miguel would forward his copy of the contract to the Chinese company without compunction.

Even though she had followed Cousineau's instructions, she felt guilty participating in this elaborate subterfuge. She recognized her role was to play the bereaved widow, impatient and ignorant of the details of high finance and wishing desperately to separate herself from the horrors of Honduras. That was easy enough to do, and she did not have to pretend. But she was concerned that their actions ultimately would provide an adequate return to the Paiute investors who had believed in her husband.

As she contemplated this, she turned in her seat to see Antu playing with her friend under the cottonwood tree by the irrigation ditch, which ran behind their house in Schurz. Beyond the two girls drawing figures in the sand extended the rolling hills of the Great Basin desert toward the Wassuk Mountains in the south. Kostas loved this country, she remembered, and she started crying. What had driven him to the wet jungles of Central America, away from his desert homeland? It wasn't the ambition for personal wealth, of that she was sure. Though he rarely talked expansively of his grand plans, it had been clear to Grace he wanted his tribe, the descendants of his messiah great-great-grandfather Wovoka, to realize the pure land he had visualized in the desert 150 years ago. That vision ultimately cheated the Paiutes of a place in history, sentencing them either to death by the hand of the white man, who feared a tribe dedicated to a vision of purity, or to banishment in a remote corner of the desert.

She was struck with how similar the Lenca history was to her husband's tribe. Conquered, enslaved, impoverished, cast aside. His mistress was the female incarnation of rebellion that inspired Wovoka's commandments and the Lenca princess Antu Silan Ulap's resistance movement against the conquistadores. Kostas's union with her forged a bond with the tribe in the north and the one in the south. And the symbol of that union played in the sand with a little Paiute girl outside her home.

Grace got up and went outside to call Antu. In simple English, which by now the child understood quickly and easily, she asked if the two girls would like some cookies and milk. Milk was a favorite of Antu. Grace had earlier learned from Pilar that, often, fresh milk in Honduras was a difficult commodity to find, and cookies were nonexistent. Antu's favorites were double-stuffed Oreos. The environmentalist in Pilar complained about the sugar, so Grace promised her she would ration the cookies and other sweets.

"And no candy," Pilar had insisted. She grimaced to show her white teeth and tapped them with her forefinger. "It rots the teeth."

Before Pilar left for Honduras, Grace had purchased an electric toothbrush for Antu and showed her how to use it. "For the teeth!" she had emphatically announced to Pilar.

"Still no candy."

Pilar had left her laptop in the apartment she had shared with Kostas so had to rely on either Ben or Tommy to obtain a printed copy of the contract. Tommy was disappointed she asked Ben to print out a copy for her, and not him. Quietly and happily taking charge, Ben produced one for her and Jasper to review. If Tommy was to read a paper copy, he would have to print out his own, but decided just to read it on the computer screen.

"I suspect we'll be seeing Miguel soon," Ben announced as he handed out the copies of the contract.

"With a new 'offer,'" Jasper muttered.

No one spent any time laboring over the dense type on the ten pages. Ben outlined it for everyone without looking at the contract.

"Actually, this was written for Miguel," he announced as he waved the paper copy of the contract in the air. "Marc and I figured this out on the phone yesterday."

"Already you have a contract?" Tommy was incredulous.

"It's mostly boilerplate. Plus we already had a contract with Kostas for first rights. All we have to do to get this property is to match whatever offers you may receive. Whatever the Chinese offer, we'll match. They'll have to keep increasing the offer to chase us off. At some point, we'll take a cut off the top—our profit—so you can close the deal with the Chinese without us. This is business for us. We're not doing you any favors. We've maneuvered a way to be involved so that we have to be bought out. That's always been the plan. We want the Chinese and Miguel to think we have a stranglehold on this property. Because we can keep matching whatever they offer, they'll have to keep increasing the offer until they think it is out of our range. They're counting on Grace and Pilar, the principals, to be sort of innocent bystanders, discouraged women weeping over the loss of their man."

"You think Miguel thinks that after he has met Pilar? And Grace?" Tommy asked Ben.

"I admit, Pilar, you have to tone it down a bit. Don't want to scare him off," Ben said as he turned toward Pilar.

"He's not scared of me—yet," Pilar replied.

"Is he scared of the Chinese?" Tommy interjected after a long pause in the conversation.

"He should be," Ben replied.

By now, the mine tunnel had extended past five hundred feet into the mountain. The dam at the end of the ore cart tracks was taking shape. Already water dripped down the face of the rock in the tunnel, and a small trickle flowed down the indention in the floor of the mine to the ditch running along the tracks. Puddles of water were starting to accumulate behind the partially built dam.

"Still no silver ore," Dave lamented.

Dave sat with Tommy and Ben at the wooden table in the office shed. They sipped coffee the Honduran cook had prepared for them.

"Ain't supposed to be any silver," Tommy replied. "Not yet."

"When? Is there enough money to keep going? Seventeen hundred dollars a week for the crew, plus Miguel's pay. Thousands more for dynamite, drill tips, equipment, fuel, food."

"You worried about your investment?" Tommy asked Dave. "It's a better bet than blackjack."

"More work too. You worried about your investment?" Dave retorted, a little too negatively Tommy thought.

For the first time, Tommy perceived an indirect reference to the loan Dave had given him. If Dave had not provided the loan, Tommy would have no stake in this enterprise, and Dave's stake would have increased by a 150 percent. As it was now, if Tommy merely paid Dave back the loan after the mine produced some dividends for its investors, Dave's "investment" in Tommy was no better than a push on the blackjack table, even money, no loss, no gain. Dave's own investment of ten thousand dollars in the mine, on the other hand, a sum much smaller than he had lent Tommy, could possibly become a two thousand percent return. Tommy had no idea if Dave had figured this out for himself. He hoped his simple friend never indulged in such calculations. Sitting at the table with Ben on one side and Dave on the other, Tommy felt a strong sense of guilt. He should have given Dave the promissory note, and he should have let his father know about the loan. Without warning, he suddenly longed for the comfortable oblivion of graduate school, beer with buddies on Friday nights, and steady progress toward his master's degree.

Through the window of the shed, he could see the mouth of the mine. Two miners, still in their yellow hard hats, sat by the mine drinking water from a canteen. He envied the Honduran Lencas. Their lives were simple: work and family. Without exception, every man employed by the mine had at least two children. Most had more. The boys played soccer in the dirt field of the clearing in front of the mine and shed. Young girls scampered to and from the shed where he sat to fetch things for their mothers, sometimes stealing a tortilla from the kitchen.

Tommy was saddened to think his appreciation of this blissful environment was contaminated by his guilt over the way he had handled the promissory note and the implicit lie of omission by not consulting with his father. The reward of integrity, he realized, was peace of mind, and he did not have that. He resolved to find a way to reform his past deeds, though he could not see how to do that without just plainly confessing to both Dave and his father what he had done. But he could not imagine doing that. If he did, he quickly realized, he possibly could lose his stake in this enterprise. Like Jasper and Dave, he was alternately consumed by the potential for profit for all of them, and by the circumstances that endangered them. Kostas's absence and the cause of it cast a gray cloud over the excitement of their adventure. Tommy had a hard time convincing himself this morning he was a good person. He took advantage of his friend, he lied to his father, and he was afraid. How could he escape the boxed-in feeling this frame of mind had created?

One of the cook's daughters, a beautiful teenage Lenca, came in with a coffeepot and offered to refill their cups. Ben held out his cup so the girl would not have to lean over the table to pour. Dave shook his head and covered the cup with the palm of his hand. Tommy copied Ben and held up his cup. With the other hand, he signaled a small amount to be added to his cup and thanked the girl in Spanish. Despite the refreshing vision of this young virgin, he stayed gloomy and preoccupied with his own low opinion of himself.

Ben slapped Tommy on the shoulder. "Don't be so glum!" he said heartily. He waved his arm toward the miners still sipping their water by the mine, the boys playing soccer in the clearing in front of the shed, and the cook in the kitchen helped by two of her daughters. "We're family. Isn't it great?"

Tommy smiled and with his eyes followed Ben's extravagant gestures. "Actually, it is," he murmured. "I never thought geology could be so social. We're surrounded by people almost all the time. On all my field trips, we camped out in lonely places with no one except other grad students or scientists. And to think we all could be making good money doing this!"

Ben moved his chair closer to the table and leaned over it toward the two young men across from him. He held his coffee mug in two hands under his nose, his elbows planted on the table. He sniffed at the coffee and smiled. "And good coffee too!" he announced.

Dave tipped his cup toward Ben to agree.

"But?" Ben paused.

Tommy and Dave straightened their backs and pushed back into the chair, waiting for Ben to continue. Ben stayed silent.

"But what?" Dave asked.

"This is Honduras," Ben replied.

Miguel's Land Rover sped up the canyon road to the clearing where the boys played soccer. They had to stop their game to make way for the car, which drove past the young men too quickly. Some of the boys shook their heads with dismay to see such indifference on display. As usual, Miguel was unmindful of the dust he raised. The boys on the improvised soccer pitch waited for the dust to settle before resuming their game.

As the Land Rover came to a stop by the porch, the cloud of dust followed, flowing over the car and into the front door of the shed where Tommy, Dave, and Ben were sipping their coffee. Miguel leapt out of the car holding a sheaf of papers in his right hand.

"I've talked to Grace," he announced to the three at the table as he came through the door. He pushed the contract toward them. "About this. She said you have copies too. What do we do? Where's Pilar?"

As he stood up, Ben waved his hand in front of his face to disperse the dust still hanging in the air.

"I'd say you're sitting pretty. Nearly seventy thousand to you when we consummate this deal," Ben said to Miguel. He turned around to see the reaction of Dave and Tommy, who remained seated at the table.

"I know I shouldn't talk to you about it, but what about the Chinese?" Miguel said. "We can't just leave them hanging. Shouldn't we respond in some way?"

"Why?" Ben asked. "It's none of their business, is it?"

Miguel looked at Dave and Tommy still seated at the table. He pointed to Ben, who had moved outside to the porch to watch the boys playing soccer.

"Of course that's what he has to say," Miguel said. "It's his company making the bid, and he has to support it. But don't you think you ought to see if a better deal can be made?"

Tommy shrugged. "I can't imagine the Chinese could do better. Nearly seven million for a mine that has yet to produce any evidence of a strike seems pretty good to me. It nets the company ten times the original investment."

"But it could be better," Miguel insisted.

"How do you know? Did you already talk with the Chinese?"

Miguel pointed to the contract again. "No, I didn't. Not yet. Grace said this was confidential, so I didn't do anything except drive out here."

"So let's keep it confidential then," Tommy concluded. It was evident to Tommy his reply didn't satisfy Miguel. "Are they expecting your call?"

Miguel looked at his feet and nodded his head. "I have to call them."

"Why?"

"Why wouldn't I? They've made an offer in good conscience, and it is only natural there would be some bargaining going on back and forth. It would be foolish not to ask what more they might wish to do."

"You know something we don't?" Dave asked, also standing up because of the excitement gradually building.

Pilar showed up at the door. "Do you?" she pressed Miguel.

Feeling hemmed in by the three people in the small room, Miguel backed away and threw his copy of the contract on the table as he sat down. He carefully removed his straw hat and set it on the table next to the contract, then turned in his seat to look at Pilar. He peeked around her to see where Ben stood on the porch outside. He nodded in the affirmative and gestured to ask Pilar to sit across the table from him.

"It's my job to know," he started.

Dave and Tommy pulled up chairs and leaned in to listen.

"And what do you know?" Pilar replied.

"They have cash. You won't have to wait for your money."

"Seven million?" Pilar asked.

Miguel nodded.

"But we haven't shown any evidence of a strike just yet. How could they be so certain as to make such an offer?" Pilar asked pointedly.

Miguel hesitated, looking at each person across the table as if debating his own response to the question offered by Pilar. Finally, he spoke up, though quietly as if he did not want Ben standing outside to overhear. "They've seen the model Kostas created. That did the convincing."

Pilar gasped as if surprised by this information. "You showed it to them? Without our knowledge?"

"Kostas told me to show them a long time ago. I just never told you that."

"And what did they say about the model?"

"What everyone says. Everyone knows there is silver in this mountain. Kostas showed the best way to get at it."

"And they believed it?" Pilar asked.

Miguel glumly nodded his head.

"Don't they need more proof than a highly educated guess?" Tommy asked, astounded over the elaborate subtleties of the plan Kostas had created.

"History is proof enough," Miguel responded. "They're here in Honduras only because they know, everyone knows, there's silver in this mountain. They just got here a little too late. Kostas staked his claims and got his permits before they were able to. They saw no reason to spend years getting their own if they could just buy it from Kostas."

"Of course," Pilar said, leaning back in her chair, "they must have known they would have to compete with the Canadians."

"They figured they could outspend them, and it wouldn't be all that much. Seven million is a drop in the bucket to them. They would spend twice that to find their own claim and get the permits. Half of it would probably be bribes anyway. They figured Kostas would be easier to deal with than the Honduran bureaucracy. In their eyes, he is a small operator. It would be easy to buy him out."

Pilar spoke softly as if to prevent Ben just outside on the porch from overhearing her question. "But the Canadians?"

"I guess they figured without Kostas, the Canadians would back off."

"Did Kostas tell you why we're doing this?" Pilar started. "About the Lenca community, about the responsibility to the environment? The Chinese are among the worst polluters in the world. Why would they agree to such terms?"

"They haven't agreed to those terms. They think if they throw enough money at the problem, you'll just go away."

"Did you tell Kostas that?"

Miguel nodded. "He knew."

"What did Kostas say?"

"'There's more than one way to skin a cat,' but I don't know what that means," Miguel replied.

"Did Kostas tell you how much it would take for us to 'go away'?" Pilar still pressured, speaking nearly in a whisper as she bent over the table to be closer to Miguel's face.

Miguel cocked his head and raised his eyebrows.

"How much?" Pilar kept pressing.

"Twenty-five."

"Twenty-five million?"

"Yes."

"And they agreed to that?"

"They think seven million is enough to entice you."

"What are you expecting? One percent of seven million or one percent of twenty-five million?"

Miguel stood up and carefully placed the straw hat on his head. "Whatever I can get. Kostas knew that. Now

I'm thinking, in retrospect, the one percent was his way of getting me to encourage the Chinese to up the price. It worked."

"Are the Chinese paying you a finder's fee too?"

"I'm an independent contractor. I do what I can."

"If we stick with the Canadians, what happens then?"

Miguel looked out the door again to see where Ben was standing. He turned around to face Pilar and her two companions. He shrugged his shoulders. "It wouldn't be good. They need this for a lot of reasons. Their necks are on the chopping block too."

"So it's true," Pilar said, standing up to confront Miguel, her hands planted on her hips. "The ends justify the means. They figured we would walk away happy with a little cash in our pockets when Kostas was gone, did they?"

Jasper was upset the discussions about the contract from the Canadians and Miguel's response to it had occurred without his participation. Because his few weeks in Honduras had taken a toll on his aged body, the day before, he had let everyone know he was going to rest in the apartment in Santa Lucia for a few days, hoping to refresh himself so that he could continue in Honduras. If he didn't recover, he would have to return to Nevada.

Jasper didn't want to read the proposed contract from the Canadians and refused the copy Tommy tried to hand to him. He believed it was just a prop in their ploy to increase the offer from the Chinese and not a serious proposal from the Canadians. Still he wondered if the Canadians really had an interest in investing in their enterprise, or why they agreed to get involved at all.

"What's in it for them?" he asked Tommy and Dave.

Both young men shrugged their shoulders.

"Doesn't make sense, does it, that they would go through all this trouble and send Ben down here just to be nice guys or to needle a competitor," Jasper continued.

"Maybe"—Dave began stroking his chin—"maybe they're using us."

"How?" Tommy asked. "They have no stake in this. Unless you count the loan they gave Kostas. At least not yet."

Jasper pulled out a chair and sat down with the two young men. "They've got something up their sleeve. They're not the type of men who are interested in doing good if it doesn't make them money. Maybe it's revenge."

"Revenge? For Kostas?" Dave blurted.

"That doesn't make sense either," Tommy replied. "Big multinational companies like them don't engage in petty behavior."

"They don't?" Jasper queried. "This Cousineau character seems too savvy to me just to be involved for the fun of it or to do some good or for revenge. It has to be money. They see a way to make money off this deal. You have to remember, Kostas's first trips to Honduras were under contract with them to assess this silver mountain. When he finished, they made a decision not to pursue this opportunity. Perhaps that's what they wanted people to believe. Maybe they were using Kostas as some kind of front, knowing all along there would be a way to turn their preliminary investment in Kostas to some good advantage in the future. Maybe they knew then the Chinese were coming. Maybe they set this up and not Kostas. Maybe Kostas was duped by them."

Tommy shook his head. "That couldn't be! That is just too complicated, too devious, too clever. How, four or five years ago, could they read the future? It's just too unreal!"

"That's what mining companies do," Jasper answered. "They have to read the future. You can't invest hundreds of millions of dollars in a project without knowing in advance that the price of gold or silver or whatever is being mined will be enough to show a return on that investment. They have to read the tea leaves. In fact, now that I think of it, it would be pretty easy to figure out the Chinese, one day or another, would come here where the silver they need is. But you could never convince a board of directors or shareholders to underwrite a plan like this. In fact, you couldn't even mention it because that would spill the beans to the whole world. You would have to keep it a secret in your own company. This is Cousineau's baby! He dreamed it up. He is taking it step by step. He needed Kostas as a front."

"Do you think Kostas knew this?" Tommy asked.

"It doesn't matter if he did or did not. It is apparent by now that Kostas had other aims, the ones he and Pilar pegged on the project. Employment for her tribe, controlling the environmental effects of a large-scale mining operation, enriching his tribe in Nevada. For Kostas, however it turned out, it was a win for him. He couldn't lose. No silver, no sweat. He and the Canadians had a way to dump the property on the unsuspecting Chinese. And if silver was there, as the model shows, then billions will spill out of this mountain. In mining and prospecting, everything is one-upmanship."

"So how do we one-up the Canadians?" Tommy asked.

As Tommy and Jasper talked, Dave watched and listened with wide open eyes and a dropped jaw, incredulous at what he was hearing. "This is a little more complicated than panning for gold out of a little creek behind Mount Grant," he muttered.

"Panning for gold is a hobby, not life. This is life," Jasper whispered.

"And death," Tommy added. "It killed Kostas."

"The stakes are high," Jasper confirmed.

When Tommy informed Jasper that Kostas had instructed Miguel to show the model to the Chinese months before the ambush, Jasper slapped his knee and chuckled.

"He did set this up! Right from the start!" Jasper exclaimed, standing up as quickly as his sore legs would allow. He paced back and forth behind the table in the shed at the mine. "He set this up!" he repeated with admiration. "So beautiful! Maybe you fellows do learn something in graduate school!"

"I never learned this," Tommy replied. "Never even heard of it."

"Haven't you ever read about the Comstock Lode and all the tricks they played to make money off the backs of Irish immigrant miners?" Jasper asked. "The bankers and politicians never dirtied their hands with a shovel or a drill. They traded, speculated, spread rumors about the fortunes to be made to make their own fortunes. Their product was promises, not silver. The poor men who actually dug and mucked ore in the mines made four dollars a day. Even the saloonkeepers made more than them. No, you don't make money in prospecting by digging. You make it by wheeling and dealing, and it appears Kostas was a master at that. He was using the Canadians and the Chinese."

"But the Canadians believed they were using Kostas?" Tommy speculated.

"And through Miguel, they both drew in the unsuspecting Chinese," Jasper added.

"I guess Kostas read the books about the Comstock Lode," Tommy offered meekly, feeling a bit ashamed to be so ignorant of the actual business of mining and prospecting.

"I'll bet my shirt he did. Must have been the reason he came to Honduras in the first place." Jasper paused to point to the mountainside across the clearing. "He probably scoured the world looking for a place he could pull this off. A place where everyone knew there was a silver strike waiting to happen. It would be easy enough to have found this place." He stamped his foot on the floorboards for emphasis. "Five hundred years of silver mining, and still not one great fortune made of it. Yet everyone knows there's silver deep in this mountain. How else could it have leaked out of the cracks and crevices at the surface to entice us all? The Spaniards and their descendants only harvested the low-hanging fruit. Sooner or later, someone was going to come in and go for the source of all that wealth. That's why the Chinese are here. They need silver for their manufacturing empire. They searched the world over for a place to dig. Like Kostas or the Canadians, they saw the potential here by just studying the history of the place, and they moved here to do what Kostas did. But Kostas beat them to the punch. I bet he even knew someone besides himself would come to the same conclusion. That's why he started here four years ago. To sit on an undiscovered fortune."

Tommy replied as he just now understood the implications of Kostas's scheme, "So you're saying Kostas never intended to mine this mountain. His plan all along was a scheme to sit on an ore deposit until someone like the Chinese would show up."

"Maybe he didn't know about the Chinese at first, but he certainly knew the Canadians were interested. The Chinese showing up was just a stroke of good luck. I'm sure as soon as he saw them arrive on the scene, he upped the ante because now he would have two enterprises competing for the right to mine this mountain."

"It seems so obvious when you explain like this," Tommy mused.

"Obvious now, but how obvious was it four years ago?" Jasper replied.

"Four years ago, it wasn't here at all. So how did Kostas see it when others did not?"

"I guess he had a vision like his great-great-grandfather. Maybe it was in his DNA. A Paiute vision."

"But a Greek scientist to figure it out," Tommy added.

"And don't forget about his Irish luck. He was always lucky," Jasper added thoughtfully.

Seated at the table, Tommy looked solemnly between his legs at the floor under his feet. "Maybe not so lucky," he mumbled.

Ben leaped onto the deck of the porch and strode through the door of the shed. His broad smile quickly faded when he saw the somber faces of Jasper and Tommy.

"The Chinese are coming to inspect the mine," he announced. "Miguel just called Pilar. They'll be here in a couple of hours. They're going to inspect the mine."

"Why are they doing that?" Jasper asked. "Ain't nothing to see."

"What do you mean there's nothing to see? You've dug five hundred feet into the mountain. You have sixteen miners at work. There's four of us Norte Americanos on the scene. You spent nearly a million dollars on this place. It shows you are committed, that you're convinced there's silver in the mountain. That you believe in Kostas's model."

"But there's no silver to show them," Tommy said.

"Why would there be? You knew that going in. Pilar said to show them the model, and overlay on it the course of our mine, which will show you're just a few hundred feet from a strike."

"According to Miguel, they saw the model already," Jasper said.

"You're not supposed to know that. So let them pretend to be surprised by it," Ben replied.

Pilar arrived at the door and immediately took over the meeting. "I told Miguel to bring them here. They can check out the mine if they want to. Like Jasper said, there's not much to see except that we're committed. But we can show them the dam, the irrigation ditches, the village across the way, and the people we have here. I'm going to explain the conditions of a contract. I asked Grace to call Cousineau and have him modify the showpiece contract to include provisions for these added features. Employment for the Lencas, a responsible environmental plan, and continued support of the dam and village."

"What will Cousineau say to all of that?" Jasper asked.

Ben spoke up. "He called me already. He says it's a brilliant ploy. It increases the commitment the Chinese will have to match or surpass. It makes Pilar and Grace look like a couple of naïve do-gooders, and the Chinese will agree to anything because they know they can get away with ignoring these conditions in this corrupt country. It'll make them lick their chops with anticipation to beat out us Canadians."

"They're not going 'beat us out,'" Pilar insisted.

"Not you, anyway," Ben answered.

The Chinese arrived in two Toyota Land Cruisers following Miguel's Land Rover. Two distinguished Oriental gentlemen looking uncomfortable in khakis and hiking boots and ill-fitting baseball caps emerged from the rear doors of the SUV in the middle of the caravan. Their clothes appeared to be brand-new as if they had selected what they thought would be an appropriate costume for an on-site visit to a silver mine in the Honduran jungle. Both smiled genially and bowed slightly to greet Pilar and the others waiting in front of the office shed.

Another man of Hispanic descent climbed out of the front door. He introduced himself as the translator.

The second SUV parked behind the first, and two tall Chinese men emerged with automatic weapons hanging off their shoulders. The translator explained these were bodyguards. Their charges were never out of their sight, he added in perfect English.

One of the Chinese executives said something to him, and he translated for Pilar and the others. "They ask you don't take offense at the protection they brought with them. They heard what happened to your predecessor and thought it advisable they were prepared for any eventuality."

In Spanish, Miguel introduced Pilar as the principal spokesperson for their operation. He continued to explain that the chief of the operation, the wife of the late manager, operated from their headquarters in Nevada. Pilar looked askance at the use of the word *headquarters*, as if the exaggeration wasn't needed. She pushed Miguel aside and in Spanish directed her words to the Chinese executives to introduce Tommy and Dave as mining supervisors. She added they were graduates of the Mackey School of Mines at the University of Nevada in Reno, Nevada. This was Jasper's idea after his talk with Tommy. Any silver mining conglomerate such as the Chinese were evidently proposing would recognize the name and its association with the world's largest discovery of silver ore in Virginia City, just twenty miles south of the university. As the translator relayed the message in Chinese to the two executives, they raised their eyebrows to show approval and nodded their heads as they bowed slightly toward Tommy and Dave.

Unable to contain his excitement, Dave reached out to shake the hand of each of the Chinese men. One of the security guards stepped between Dave and the Chinese, and Dave pulled back his hand. He shrugged his shoulders to show innocence. But he stayed excited. The guard looked down at the pistol strapped on Dave's hip then said something to the translator. The translator chuckled and in English asked Dave if he could take his weapon into the office and leave it there.

"He says," the translator said as he nodded toward the bodyguard, "there's already enough firepower here to take care of any problem that might arise."

Dave sauntered through the office door as he undid his gun belt. He threw the loaded holster onto the table and came back out with his hands spread out to each side. The bodyguard nodded approvingly as he smiled slightly.

After this interlude, Pilar introduced Jasper as an experienced miner from Nevada whom they had retained to manage the Lenca miners. When they saw the cars approaching, Ben had left to wait out of sight in the shelter where he slept. While the bodyguards stayed outside stationed by the door, Pilar escorted the entire party into the shed and asked Tommy to demonstrate the model, which had become the inspiration of their plan.

Before they could move toward the door, one of the Chinese executives held up his hand to stop everyone and turned toward the SUV. He opened the tailgate and came around the back of the car holding a large bouquet of colorful flowers. With exaggerated courtesy, he bowed toward Pilar and presented her with the bouquet, saying something in Chinese as he did so. The translator leaned toward him to hear, but the Chinese man had spoken so softly he could not hear. The translator started to ask the Chinese to repeat himself, but Pilar told him it wasn't necessary.

"We know what he said," she said as she accepted the flowers. "Tell him we are grateful for his condolences and his interest."

Pilar gave the flowers to the cook in the kitchen as the group entered the shed. The two bodyguards stood outside on the porch by the door. The boys playing in the clearing stopped their soccer game to stare at the two strange men, not because the men were carrying automatic weapons, but because they never had seen Chinese as big as these two. The guns themselves were not an uncommon sight in Honduras.

Tommy's laptop was already loaded with the model. He began with a map of the mountain itself. The map displayed 140 dots showing the location of the mines created over the four-hundred-year history of silver mining in the district, including the pattern and direction of the shafts on every side of the mountain. He paused while the translator explained what was being demon-strated. One of the Chinese waved his hand impatiently for Tommy to move to the next image, this time a pro-file of the mountain showing the altitudes of the many mines on one side of the mountain, mostly at the higher altitudes. The Chinese executive waved his hand again for Tommy to move on, as if he was familiar with these images. Tommy moved to a three-dimensional picture rotating around the entire mountain festooned with arrows pointing to show the paths of each of the shafts, more than a hundred of them. All the arrows, it was soon clear, aimed directly at the center of the mountain. This time, Tommy was not hurried along. One of the Chinese moved closer to the screen and traced along one of the arrows, following it to beyond its end in the center of the mountain. He looked at Tommy as if to confirm his unspoken observation. Tommy nodded his head. He saw what was obvious to all. The core of the mountain was the source of all those ledges, veins, and outcroppings of silver. It would be easy to deduce from such a diagram its clear implication. All the silver previous miners had discovered in dozens of places had been exuded over mil-lions of years from a single source.

The next diagram overlaid on the three-dimen-sional model was the course of the mine shaft they had been digging for the last few weeks. It too pointed to the heart of the mountain, but from below and not from above. Using his knowledge of silver geology, Kostas had projected a cone of silver ore rising from the mountain's base. As the cone ascended, it narrowed, showing that its edges had been mined by all the centuries' previous endeavors, but the source of this wealth had not been touched. The mine shaft the Lenca miners had excavated these last few weeks headed directly toward this source.

The Chinese mining executive touched the screen at the blank space between the cone of silver ore and the end of the mine shaft. Tommy did not need a translator to answer his question.

"Seven hundred and fifty feet," he said slowly so that the translator could repeat in Chinese.

The two Chinese straightened up from their awkward postures posed over the computer screen and replied to the translator, who told the assembly they were now ready to see the mine shaft.

Jasper ushered everyone out the door and led them across the clearing toward the opening of the mine. Jorge and some of his daytime crew handed out hard hats to each member of the party. Pilar followed along and introduced the Lenca mining crew to the Chinese. She added that all the work had been accomplished by the Lencas, and it was their plan to continue to employ them, which they wished to make part of a contract with whomever was to take over the mine. Whether or not the translator included all this information, Pilar and the others could not tell, but his response to her lengthy explanation seemed too short to have contained all the information she had included in her remarks.

With Jasper at his side, Jorge proudly led the group into the cool darkness of the mine. As Jasper spoke, his voice echoed. They had to pause many times to accommodate the frequent requests of the Chinese, who inspected the timbers shoring up the mine. Pilar had stayed behind at the mine entrance though she had received a hard hat and put it on.

When the group reappeared after their visit to the end of the tunnel, Pilar took charge. She pointed to the ore cart tracks leading out of the mine and down the dry creek bed alongside the steep side of the mountain, explaining as she did so that the material from the mine was put to good use to rebuild a dam that had been destroyed during Hurricane Mitch over fifteen years ago. She paused while the translator spoke. He too pointed to the tracks and then downhill toward the creek where the dam was slowly taking shape. Pilar backtracked a little toward the mine to point to the slight indentation on the left side of the mine to channel water to the ditch outside by the tracks. The Chinese nodded to show their understanding, but she could tell they were impatient with this portion of the tour and were just behaving politely.

When the translator finished his response, Pilar walked along the tracks toward the dam. Earlier, she had asked one of the Lenca miners to station himself at the end of the tracks with an ore cart full of crushed rock from the mine. When the group stopped, she nodded to the miner to dump the ore cart. Rocks and dirt poured out on top of the pile that was to become a dam. Another miner on the backhoe began distributing the rocks along the top of the dam.

She paused here to offer an extended explanation of the irrigation system. She pointed to the village growing up across the creek and to the fields already tilled and showing stalks of corn, melon plants, and vegetables. Apparently, she had forgotten she would have to pause to allow the translator to speak to his two clients, and when he tried to speak, the Chinese signaled him to stop. It was clear the Chinese knew what Pilar was explaining.

All the while, Miguel lingered at the back of the group, not adding to or interfering with the presentations. When it was apparent the Chinese had seen enough, he hastened forward and indicated to Pilar he should take over. Pilar looked to Jasper for guidance, and he shrugged his shoulders to show it mattered little to him. Back at the shed, Tommy gave the Chinese a flash drive with a copy of the computer model. No longer was there a reason to keep their plans a secret.

As if he received a signal from Pilar, which he might have, Ben appeared at the door of the hovel where he had chosen to stay and walked purposefully toward the group standing on the porch of the shed. He manufactured the appearance of an angry or irritated man.

"What's going on?" he asked Pilar.

This surprised Jasper, Tommy, and Dave, though they suspected Pilar and Ben had cooked up this staged confrontation to drive home the point that there was serious competition for this venture.

Pilar grabbed Ben by the arm and led him away from the group, all the while talking rapidly and heatedly in Spanish. The translator could not hear, and when the Chinese glanced at him for an explanation, he held up his hands to show his confusion. The two Chinese looked at each other seriously but waited patiently to see what result would come from this unexpected disturbance. Tommy wished that Pilar had given him some hint of this pretense so that he could support it, but he did not know what to do. Maybe his shock at Ben's unexpected appearance was exactly what Pilar had planned.

Miguel, of course, was flustered. He had been promised earlier that Ben would be absent during the visit. When Pilar returned after Ben disappeared among the dwellings on the opposite bank of the creek, he rushed toward her to ask why Ben had been allowed on the premises during the visit from his competitor.

"Don't worry," Pilar replied. "It'll help, not hurt. I thought it would be good to show we have a serious contender and that we are quite familiar with him. Drive home the point with them that we're serious about the environmental and employment conditions of a contract with them."

"But that may kill the deal," Miguel protested.

"That's okay. We still have an agreement with the Canadians. Nearly seven million dollars. We're happy with that."

"You don't want more?" Miguel asked as if shocked to believe Pilar was satisfied.

"Not under the wrong conditions. It's not our purpose. Grace is ready to sign with the Canadians, if you want to know the truth. The Chinese are in your hands, not mine. You do what you can if you want. Basically, I'm not counting on them even to make an offer. They seemed pretty skeptical about the dam and other considerations."

"Of course they're skeptical. They're engineers, not philanthropists. It's money and nothing else that will make this deal."

"Tell them that and see how far that will get you," Pilar replied, sounding impatient with Miguel. "And the flowers? Whose idea was that?" she added.

"It was a surprise to me," Miguel answered.

"Maybe they'll surprise you some more."

That evening after the Chinese and their bodyguards left, Jasper, Tommy, and Dave drove back to the apartment in Santa Lucia, the three of them jammed together on the bench seat of the old Toyota pickup. Jasper had interrupted his rest to meet with the Chinese but still needed more time to restore his aching body. Dave was too excited to stay at the mining camp. The nights there were dark and lonely, and he needed company. Tommy sought relief from the tension of these intrigues.

After taking turns using the bathroom to clean up, Dave convinced Tommy to walk up the street to the restaurant for a couple of beers. Jasper stayed behind to rest. He flopped on the king-sized bed in the master bedroom and turned on the television with the remote control.

Dave was anxious to clarify his understanding of the Chinese visit. He still had no concept of the scheme Kostas had created and which appeared to be so ably managed by Kostas's Latin paramour and his wife in Nevada.

"It looks like we landed smack-dab in the middle of an international intrigue," Dave started as he sipped at a bottle of beer. "Canadian manipulators, greedy Hondurans, Chinese geologists, Lenca Indians, the Paiute nation, and us. What's going on? Are we in trouble?"

"I guess you and I are the babe in the woods," Tommy replied. "My father would get a kick out of this. I think he would understand better than I do."

"And appreciate it. But I'm just either confused or scared. I don't know what I should do. In a way, all this makes me sad. I like digging into the mountain, blowing things up, looking for a buried treasure. That's exciting. But this." Dave paused to wave his hand in the air to indicate all of the world. "This is scrapping for a piece of thin air. I'm kind of ashamed of myself right now. Just money ain't worth all this, don't you think"

"You were pretty excited when you piled up thirty-eight thousand dollars in casino chips on the blackjack table."

"That turned out to be the effect, not the purpose. I was testing my theory and got great delight in seeing how it worked out. Losing and winning are just matters of luck. I was more interested in how I would manifest action from an abstract idea. That was interesting. The result, money. Yeah, that was nice but not necessary. I guess I am not just practical enough like other people. I didn't choose geology as a way to make a fortune. I chose it because I like the mixture of science and guesswork. It never occurred to me I might strike it rich one day. That seems more like an accident."

"But you invested your money in this enterprise when Grace asked for it. Didn't you do that to make money?"

"Not really. I was just excited to be part of it, and still am. I just don't want it to turn into something that is only about money. If it becomes that, then we'll be arguing with one another. Some may even start shooting over it like already has happened here in Honduras. Do you believe Kostas was here only for the money?"

Tommy shook his head. "No. He was here for the adventure of it. He made it an adventure to use this situation to the highest advantage of others. That's what I think."

"So why can't we do that too?"

They put down their beer bottles and looked at each other across the dining table. Dave held up his hand and Tommy reached across to shake it.

"That's what we'll do," Tommy said.

The solemnity of the moment made Tommy think he could now reveal how he avoided giving Dave the promissory note for the loan. He stared at his friend, who joyously dug into the meal that had been placed before him by the Honduran waitress. But Tommy decided he didn't want to alter the joy of their mutual pact with such a pedestrian confession. Instead, he reached across the table again and patted Dave on the shoulder. Dave looked up and smiled genially.

"You really ought to start eating before the food gets cold," Dave said. "It's really good."

After the Chinese left the mining camp, Grace received phone calls from Pilar and later Miguel to report the results of the meeting. According to Pilar, it was evident the Chinese were going to return with an offer, one that probably bested the Canadian proposal.

"I don't understand," Grace said to Pilar. "They didn't see anything that proved there's silver there. Why would they act so quickly?"

"It was Kostas's model. It has been the whole time. He directed Miguel to show it to them a long time ago. All the rest of this activity—the mine, all of us here on site, the investments we've made, all that was to make them believe we believe silver is there. Why else would we be here?"

"Do we believe silver is there? Did Kostas believe that?"

"It's science, but still it's guesswork. Kostas just wanted a plan that made sure we couldn't lose, silver or no silver. If it's there, then we've done a service for whoever takes over the mine. If it is not, we've done a service for your investors and for us here in Honduras."

"I don't understand why the Canadians are being so helpful. What do they get out of it?"

"They're clever enough to get something, quite a bit I suppose," Pilar replied. "Ben is very involved, yet he hasn't whispered a word about his company's ambitions."

"I know we'll get money, for our Paiute investors and for your Lenca community, if we're successful with this scheme, but what will the Canadians get out of it?"

"There's a price tag on their service."

"They'll do all this just for a little more money?" Grace asked.

"Well, they liked Kostas. Trusted him. Maybe they're just getting back at the Chinese. Plus, it's probably a lot more than 'a little more money.'"

"You think the Chinese had something to do with the ambush?"

"I don't know. It could have been just like the police said, a gang of *sicarios*."

"Or Miguel?" Grace asked quietly.

"He's too meek to think of such an action. I doubt he had any knowledge of it though I still think he hasn't been forthright. It is clear he has some commitment to the Chinese. I suspect they are paying him and will give him a finder's fee if they make a deal with us."

"So Miguel will profit one way or another, from us and the contract he signed with Kostas? And from the Chinese?"

"That's the worst part of it. I don't want him to make a penny from this. I'm ready to dump him right now."

To Grace's ears, Pilar sounded cold and resolute. "But you yourself said we need him," she reminded Pilar.

"As long as he is useful in this scheme, yes, we need him. But I'm hoping when we cash in, we can find a way not to pay him, even one percent."

"One percent is seventy thousand dollars if we receive seven million."

"That's a fortune here. Enough to retire on. I'd rather give that money to the Lenca miners who have worked so hard. They deserve it."

"We can't just cheat him," Grace said. "That wouldn't be right, even if we don't like him."

"Then we'll have to outsmart him."

Not long after her telephone conversation with Pilar, Grace received Miguel's call. According to him, the Chinese were impressed with what they saw and were meeting to make an offer. He had let them know the basis of the Canadian proposal without revealing all the details. Grace asked him why it wasn't a problem that they could show no evidence of a silver strike. Like Pilar, he explained the model Kostas had created was convincing enough.

"That's just a picture on a computer," Grace answered. "It's no more real than a movie is real life. Don't they see it as just a guess? Or a clever ruse?"

Miguel explained that they had used their scientists and geologists to reconstruct the model based on the results of Kostas's four years of measurements in over a hundred previous mining attempts, and they had come to virtually the same conclusion. Geologically, it made sense; historically, it had always been true that silver was abundant in that mountain; and it was cheaper, and faster, to buy out the work and claims of a company like theirs than to resort to staking new claims elsewhere on the mountain and engaging in drilling surveys. All of that would require as many millions as they were willing to risk by making an offer to them but would be ultimately a more uncertain and much longer process. No matter the outcome of their negotiations with them, the Chinese were committed to a long stay in Honduras.

"And you have to remember the pressure on these Chinese executives," Miguel added. "They were sent here to get a result. They probably have a budget of tens of millions of dollars. This is the quickest way to get that result."

"What would happen if we didn't sell out to them or to the Canadians?" Grace asked.

Miguel asked her to repeat the question because he couldn't believe that such a thought was being entertained.

"You mean continuing on your own?"

"Wouldn't our project be worth more if we could actually show silver?" Grace added. "It makes sense if everyone was sure the value is actually there."

After a long silence on the phone, Miguel responded quietly. "And the reverse if you found nothing."

"Isn't that the risk all miners take?"

"But you don't have to take that risk. What you have now is perceived as valuable. If you continue working on the mine and continue to find nothing, then you may change perceptions, possibly lowering the price, maybe even showing it is worthless."

"So nothing now is worth something, and nothing later is worthless. I don't understand."

Miguel's response urged Grace to accept his view. "Right now, what you have is worth something. That's the perception."

"All of this is no more than a mirage. The mine, the silver, Kostas's model, the global Canadian mining company, the Chinese, us, you, the Lenca miners, my Paiute investors—just a mirage? Why are we doing this then? What makes us think something tangible is going to rise up from something so intangible?"

"Isn't everything like that? Once there was nothing, and now there is something. Even the universe."

"I don't understand how that can happen."

Miguel muttered into the phone. "Aren't you interested in making money? This is how it is done."

"Money, is that all there is that's important?"

"It's hard to survive without money. Survival is important."

"How you survive is also important," Grace said, ending the telephone call.

Chapter Six

When Grace included Antu in her morning walk to work, neighbors noticed. Because other children were on their way to school at the same time, their mothers pushed them out the door to join Grace and Antu instead of driving them as they usually did. Before Antu arrived, it did not seem appropriate to saddle Grace with babysitting responsibilities if they had allowed their children to walk with her. But Antu opened the door, not just for other children, but also for some of the mothers who joined the group. In the few weeks since Antu had been in Grace's care, children ranging from Antu's age to middle school students and several mothers had made a ritual of the morning stroll. Grace realized Antu had inspired within her community a healthy exercise program, something Grace herself had preached many times to her clients. Her instructions and encouragement in the sterile environment of the clinic had little effect, but tiny Antu, without a word—at least in English—skipping along the roadway and pointing out the marvels along the way, animals, birds, insects, flowers, and, of course, the many neighbors who came to their front doors to wave to the cheerful group, seemed to inspire merely by the purity and simplicity of her happy spirit.

Even inclement weather was no impediment. Late in the spring when an unexpected light flurry of snow swirled in the air, children and mothers alike raced back and forth with their mouths open to catch a few rare snowflakes. Everyone was delighted when Grace, usually reserved and determined, joined them in their futile quest. They all laughed to see stately Grace chase a snowflake with an open mouth. That morning when they arrived at the clinic where Grace separated from the group as the rest continued on to the schools nearby, several mothers leaned forward to give her a tender hug. Smiling to herself, Grace realized her decision with Kostas to delay or avoid having a child was one of the few mistakes they had made as a couple. But now that error had been corrected.

Every evening at seven o'clock, Pilar called Grace on her cell phone to speak with her daughter. Antu never exhibited much appreciation of these exchanges. Though from the cell phone emanated something that could be taken for her mother's voice, she sometimes held the phone away from her ear to look at it quizzically, as if wondering why her mother had been crammed into the small device.

When Grace took the phone from Antu to receive Pilar's daily report of activities in Honduras, Pilar frequently asked for reassurance that Antu was safe and healthy. Grace wondered out loud why she inquired so often as if she were implying Grace was not capable of caring for her, and Pilar replied that was not the issue, but something else had changed.

"Of course something's changed," Grace responded. "You're not here. Her father is not here. You're both absent. A disembodied voice on a tiny device she holds in her little hands must seem strange. Maybe she's wondering why her father isn't calling her."

Pilar stayed silent when Grace talked like this. Sometimes she would ask if Antu ever talked about her.

"She sees your picture, and his, every day in her room."

"But does she say something?"

"She's a happy girl. Everyone loves her, and she has lots of friends. She is a very busy little girl."

"But does she ever ask about me?"

Grace found it difficult to answer the question because she could not remember a moment when Antu did make an inquiry about her parents. The only words she could recall was when Antu murmured "Papa?" as she looked at the pictures of Grace and Kostas in the hallway of her Schurz home.

As soon as the phone conversation switched to the business of the mine and the complex stratagems to entice the Chinese and fend off Cousineau's aggressive impulses, Pilar's voice lost its uncertainty and became hard and focused.

This week, Pilar reported there had been no word from the Chinese since their inspection of the mine the previous week. Miguel had no explanation for this unexpected lack of response. Ben was pessimistic they could make an offer, blaming not a lack of interest but the complicated nature of Chinese bureaucracy.

After two weeks had passed since the Chinese delegation had visited the mine, there was still no response. Pilar grilled Miguel, reminding him of his own words that it was his job to encourage a counter proposal. As he shrugged his shoulders and frowned to show dismay, he confessed they hadn't even returned his phone calls or e-mail requests for a meeting. All he was told, he informed Pilar, was that they had not completed their analysis, and it was too soon for them to consider another offer.

Ben and Marc Cousineau had no explanation either.

"Maybe you're stuck with us," Grace said once to Cousineau during one of their infrequent phone interchanges.

Cousineau chuckled. "They're a crafty lot, and much more patient than us eager-beaver Westerners. I should know better than to expect quick action from the Chinese. Maybe this is their plan, to put you on edge."

"On edge? Why would we be worried? You put on paper you're going to give us seven million dollars. How can I complain or worry? We stand to get nearly ten times our investment."

"Without the Chinese," Cousineau enunciated slowly as if carefully considering each word, "there is no higher offer to match."

Pilar had no explanation either for the sudden stalled negotiations. When Grace repeated Cousineau's last words, Pilar could not respond. Grace pressed her for her thoughts.

"For the first time," Pilar said, "I feel like we're over our heads. How bold we've been!"

"And foolish?" Grace asked.

Grace could not see Pilar shrug her shoulders.

Jasper decided he had to return home for a long rest and to visit the VA hospital in Reno. His stomach often ached, and he felt unusually depleted of energy. Using the excuse of returning to their classes for a short while anyway to complete their reports and projects and to meet with their instructors, Dave and Tommy agreed to accompany Jasper back to the United States. Tommy's father was delighted to hear his son was safe and would soon be out of Honduras. He told Tommy he would drive to Reno and meet him at the airport. During Tommy's five years in Reno, his father had never once visited him even though Reno was only a short two-hour drive from Sacramento. Tommy happily passed along the arrival details and told his father he had a lot to talk about. He looked forward to the opportunity to describe the negotiations for the silver mine, and hoped that during these talks, he could finally reveal the loan from Dave and his investment in the project in Honduras because he had given all the money to Grace for the Pine Grove Valley claim with Jasper and Kostas.

Pilar was then left alone, with Ben, at the mine compound. Because the apartment in Santa Lucia was now available, Pilar offered it to Ben. He gladly accepted and told her he could stay at the mine in the accommodations added onto the office shed when she wanted to rest or relax in a more comfortable environment. Pilar shook her head in the negative. She wanted to stay with her people, close to the action and to their needs.

After three weeks had passed since the visit of the Chinese mining company executives, Miguel still had no explanation of the absence of any communication whatsoever from them. Pilar asked him one day if he was still being paid by the Chinese, to which Miguel feigned shock and insult, but he could offer no credible response so merely shrugged his shoulders as if to laugh off the intended slight. But he must not have been paid, it was clear to Pilar, because he seemed sincerely concerned.

"Did they dump you?" she pressed him. "Maybe we ought to talk about your responsibilities here," she continued. "With Tommy, Dave, Jasper, and Ben, seems like we're overloaded a bit at the top."

These observations forced Miguel to act. "I'll go to their office in Tegucigalpa. They'll have to see me, even if it is to say their plans have changed."

Three days later, Miguel returned to the mining camp and slouched into the office where Pilar sat at her laptop.

"Well?" she asked as she pushed the laptop away.

Miguel held out his hands. "They weren't in."

"In the office or in Honduras?"

"I don't know. I was told they weren't in. That's all. I couldn't get any other information from the office staff."

"Chinese office staff? Or Honduran?"

"Mostly Chinese. A few young men, who looked to be graduate students like Tommy and Dave. Very industrious but without a clue."

Ben reminded Pilar the contract from Cousineau contained a deadline for the offer they had made, one month from the date of the contract, and already more than three weeks had passed.

"Then what?" Pilar asked him.

"We start over. If there is no counteroffer, there is nothing to match."

"Are you saying the price drops?"

"Of course it does. We aren't competing against ourselves."

Pilar called Grace to report Ben's words.

"Cousineau hinted the same," Grace replied. "Their deal is to match an offer, and if there is no offer to match, then they're free to set the price."

"Are we back to zero?" Pilar asked.

"Maybe not zero, but not seven million. Maybe their original offer. Twice our investment and forgiveness of the loan."

"At least we're not losing money that way."

"Neither are we making it. We promised more to our investors, and there will be none for your Lenca community."

"So we don't have a choice. We have to keep digging."

"Until we find silver?"

"I guess finding nothing actually means we found nothing," Pilar concluded glumly. "Maybe it was too good to be true. We got distracted by what we wanted rather than paying attention to what is."

Despite the disappointing reality of Pilar's assessment, Grace had to laugh. "I feel kind of silly right now to think we could have pulled this off. You're right. We were—are—over our heads. What would Kostas do?"

Because phone calls from Honduras had become a daily occurrence, plus her urgent wish to stay in touch with the babysitter she had hired to sit with Antu after school, Grace carried her cell phone in the pocket of the white lab coat she wore at the clinic. Before this, when the only calls she could expect were from Kostas—and they were infrequent—she considered answering the phone while with her patients a sign of disrespect. Everyone at the reservation had by now learned of her duties to carry on the work of her late husband, and the potential profit that might come to many members of the tribe as a result, so they were as eager as she was for her to stop her examinations and meetings in order to take any call, whatever it interrupted.

"All the way from Central America!" they occasionally whispered loudly to one another as Grace hunched over the phone.

At such times, Grace would wave a hand or press an extended index finger against her lips to silence the admiring murmurs. On many occasions, the young Paiute women would lean in to listen. Grace would then turn away, sometimes walking to a deserted corner of the clinic with one hand pressed against an ear to shut out the noisy young women.

As she lifted the phone from her pocket and glanced at the screen to see where this call originated, she did not recognize the telephone number. The area code showed Northern California, where she had no business or friends. She pressed the button to answer the call with some dread, supposing the strange number signaled some unexpected complication or concern.

An official- and efficient-sounding woman asked for "Ms. Wilson."

"Yes?"

"Ms. Grace Wilson?"

"Of course. Who's calling please?" Grace looked up at the two young women who were in the office at the time and gestured for them to step out of the office into the waiting room of the clinic.

"Hold on for Mr. Emerson Smith."

Grace had never heard such a name.

Sounding distinguished and, as Grace imagined, older thus wiser, Emerson Smith announced he was calling on behalf of the Yin Plata Mining Company, which his consulting firm, Asia Americas Strategies in San Francisco, represented.

"Yin Plata? The Chinese?" Grace asked.

"Yes. You don't recognize the name? *Yin* is Mandarin for 'silver,' and *plata* is Spanish for 'silver.'"

"The Silver Silver Mining Company. Catchy!"

"Appropriate, I would say," Emerson replied. "We are representing their interests in the proposal to acquire the rights to the mine you and your group are managing in Honduras. They've come to us with instructions to deal with you directly rather than your representatives in Honduras. They saw little to be gained through second-hand negotiations."

"So they are interested still?"

"Of course. But there is a matter that concerns them deeply, and they asked me to confer with you directly on it before taking further steps. Can you meet with me?"

"What concern?" Grace imagined finally the absence of even a trace of silver had injected a measure of reality into the negotiations.

"It's complicated. Can we meet in person?"

"When?"

"As soon as possible."

"I can't leave my work here at the clinic without some arrangement."

"No need to leave your work. We will meet at your office."

The next afternoon, Emerson Smith and an assistant, a young man who drove the car, both wearing suit and tie, arrived at the clinic on the Paiute reservation in Schurz. The small anteroom of the clinic was crowded with several young Paiute women waiting to see Grace. Included among them was an older woman, a tribal elder, who steadied herself with a cane. When the two men came into the room, they approached the desk where Grace's part-time assistant sat to register arrivals and gather medical records while the patients waited. Grace had neglected to mention to her she had a business appointment. The young woman assistant stood up behind her desk; she was so surprised. The older man, Emerson Smith, reached into his shirt pocket and extracted a business card. He gave it to the assistant, who turned on her heel and rushed through the door to the examining room where she passed the card to Grace. Grace accepted it and smiled, dropping the stethoscope she was holding against a woman's chest to let it dangle around her neck.

"I didn't think they would be here so soon," she told the assistant. "They must have left very early in the morning. Tell them I'll be there in a moment when I'm finished here."

Grace lifted the head of the stethoscope and continued her examination of the young woman. The assistant returned to the waiting room to inform the two men that Grace would wind up her consultation with a patient as quickly as possible. She beckoned toward two empty chairs lined up against the wall. On each side of the empty chairs, Paiute women sat. All of them gawked at the two men.

The old woman, leaning forward in her seat to rest her chin on her hands supported by the cane, spoke up so that everyone in the room could hear. "Nobody here wears suits like that."

"And ties!" a young woman added.

As Emerson and his assistant looked down at their ties, Emerson held his up for everyone in the room to see. "Too dressy?" he asked the group.

Someone chuckled out loud. "A mite!"

All the women laughed easily. Emerson sat down on one of the chairs and patted the one next to him with his hand to indicate to his assistant that he should take his seat also. The assistant looked concerned and confused, though Emerson seemed to be enjoying the gathering.

The old woman asked Emerson if he was here on business.

Emerson nodded his head to show that he was. "And you?" he asked the old woman.

"My back," she replied. She removed one hand from the top of the cane and pressed the small of her back. "Killing me! Can hardly walk."

Emerson bent forward to put his hand on the small of his back. "Sometimes my back acts up. Hardly can get out of bed when it does."

"But you don't have to do the laundry."

Emerson laughed and punched the assistant next to him with his elbow. "Nope, fortunately. Probably couldn't do it if I had to. Never acquired the skill."

"But you got to do other things, I suppose, things I couldn't do," the old woman said as she straightened to push her back against the chair.

"You can talk, can't you?" Emerson asked her.

"Yup. Too much." The old woman looked around to all the young women in the room, who were focused on the interchange between the two oldest in the group. Everyone laughed or smiled quietly.

"Me too, sometimes," Emerson added when the laughter subsided a little. "But it's my job."

"Talking is a job?" the old woman asked him.

Emerson nodded his head. "I guess you can more accurately describe my job as knowing what I am talking about."

"Do you?"

The woman's question made Emerson's young assistant smile broadly, as if suppressing a more obvious outburst. Turning toward him, Emerson also grinned and patted his assistant on the knee, then he faced the woman. He held up the tie again to show it to the old woman.

"Some people think so," he said.

"Can I get a job like that?" the old woman returned.

Emerson reached again into his shirt pocket and extracted another business card. "I'm sure you could. You must know a lot that other people will find helpful and valuable. Give me a call someday if you wish."

The woman took the card and squinted her eyes to read it. "Asia Americas? Americas? Does that include Honduras?"

"Yes. You know about Honduras?"

The easy levity of a moment ago disappeared as Emerson and his assistant became serious.

"Yup," the woman said as she stuffed the business card into a pocket. "I've invested in it."

"With Ms. Wilson?"

"Twice. Once with her husband. And again with her."

One of the younger women in the group lined up against the wall in the waiting room chairs raised her hand for attention. Emerson turned and motioned for her to speak up. "Us too," the woman announced. "My dad said Kostas was going to make us rich."

Emerson spent a moment to look at each individual. "Anyone else here invested in Honduras?"

One other woman raised her hand. "We gave him a thousand dollars."

Feeling she had been duped into revealing secrets that they had been warned by Grace to avoid exposing, the older woman asked abruptly, "Are you lawyers?"

Emerson smiled to ease the rising tensions. "Accountant is a better word for what I do. Number cruncher. Henry here is the lawyer. Our job is to help people get rich."

"Are you going to help us too?" the first young woman asked.

"That's up to Ms. Wilson," Emerson replied.

As if called into action by the man's words, Grace walked through the door behind the Paiute woman she had been examining. Everyone in the waiting room, except the older woman, stood up. Emerson stepped forward and held out his hand.

"Emerson Smith. My assistant, Henry." He swung his arm around to include the entire assembly in the room. "All these ladies are waiting for you?"

Grace nodded without saying anything.

"Should we come back later when you're not so busy?" Emerson continued, showing genuine concern that his arrival interfered with local priorities.

Grace was touched by this show of gracious consideration. She looked out at the group of women, still standing except for the elder.

"We can wait," one of the women offered.

From her seated position, the tribal elder nodded thoughtfully. "Yes," she said, "we can wait. Take care of your guests."

Tommy's father, Billy Hawkins, stood in the baggage claim area of the Reno airport when Tommy walked in followed by Jasper and Dave. His father started to shake Tommy's hand as he usually did, but instead held up his arms to hug his son. After a moment's hesitation, Tommy leaned in and allowed his father to wrap his arms around him.

"I'm glad you're safe and home," his father whispered into Tommy's ear.

"Honduras isn't that bad," Tommy replied, slipping out of the embrace.

His father shook his head to disagree. "I guess you don't read the news."

As Tommy introduced his father to Jasper and Dave, Jasper patted Tommy on the shoulder. "He's a good kid. You ought to be proud of him."

"Should I?" Billy Hawkins replied and, realizing the gaffe, hastily added, "I am." After a moment of reflection, he repeated, "I am."

Dave's girlfriend, Jackie, came through the glass doors of the terminal and gave Dave a quick kiss on the cheeks.

"I was so worried," she said to Tommy's father. "Weren't you? Honduras! What a place to hang out!" She turned back to her boyfriend. "You aren't planning on going back, are you?"

"If I can get away from my classes," he told Jackie. As if making a resolution, he added, "I will go back."

Tommy rode to his apartment with his father while Jasper joined Dave and Jackie in their car. Jasper was to stay in Dave's apartment while he was visiting the VA hospital in Reno. Jackie let everyone know she was taking Dave home with her, embarrassing Dave.

"And you?" Billy Hawkins asked his son as they drove to Tommy's apartment.

"And me what?"

"Are you going back to Honduras?"

"Maybe. But we should talk about it. I have a lot to talk about."

"Me too."

The next morning, Tommy awakened to smell coffee brewing in the kitchenette. He came out of the bedroom to see his father, already dressed, fiddling with the toaster oven on the counter. Tommy went over, peeked through the window of the toaster oven to see a couple of frozen waffles, and showed his father how far to turn the dial. As the waffles slowly browned, Tommy returned to the bedroom to shed his sweatpants and dress in his usual Levi's and T-shirt. His father stood up from the kitchen table to fetch a cup. He filled the cup with black coffee and pushed it toward Tommy. As Tommy gazed contemplatively into the black liquid swirling in the cup, his father slowly cut his waffle into small pieces.

"I guess you don't have any maple syrup," his father observed.

For the next several moments, neither spoke or seemed inclined to speak. Billy finished his breakfast and stood up to place his empty plate into the kitchen sink. He turned and leaned against the counter as he wiped his face with a paper towel. Uncharacteristically, he waited for Tommy to start their discussion. Tommy fidgeted in his seat and took frequent small sips of the hot coffee.

After a few moments of the difficult silence, his father gave in. "How's the coffee?" He returned to his seat at the table across from his son.

Tommy nodded his head as if appraising the coffee and then held the coffee cup high in the space between them. "It's better in Honduras, but this is pretty good."

"It'll do the trick? Wake you up?"

Tommy shook his head again and raised his eyebrows to show he was alert. He didn't know whether to start by telling his father about the loan from Dave Mogis, or the exciting nature of the negotiations at the silver mine in Honduras. Appearing unusually patient, his father leaned back in his chair as if to give his son the space to consider his responses.

"How's Mom?" Tommy asked instead.

"Busy. As usual. She was worried about you. You should've called her a couple of times."

"She could've called me. I would've taken the call."

"I wouldn't let her."

"Why?"

"She would just worry out loud with you. Like she always does."

"I could handle that."

His father fingered the paper towel he still held in one hand. "I don't think she could have. She watches the news too."

"Honduras is in the news?"

"Not often, but enough. Drug smugglers, murders, desperate families fleeing to the US. Sometimes they send their children unescorted all the way through Central America and Mexico to see if they can sneak in the US and be taken care of here. That's been in the news a lot. They fear for the life of their children. For us, it was the opposite. Our child, our only child, went to Honduras, into the thick of it, where his good friend was murdered. What were you thinking of?" It was clear as he spoke Billy could not resist the momentum of his words. "Didn't it occur to you we might worry ourselves sick about you?" He slammed the tabletop with the palm of his hand and stood up suddenly.

Tommy looked down into the dark cup of coffee and did not watch his father pace back and forth in the tiny kitchen. He didn't have anything to say.

"Well?" his father asked, stopping his pacing and standing before him, his arms crossed over his chest.

Tommy pushed the half-full cup away from him. "I'm sorry. I was just trying to be a good friend."

"How about a good son?"

"Nothing happened! I'm here!"

"And you're staying here?"

Tommy shrugged his shoulders. "I don't know. It depends on what happens."

"What about your classes? Are you going to get your master's degree? You didn't screw that up, did you?"

"Dad! That's my business. I'm twenty-eight years old. Whatever my situation is, I put myself here." He paused, contemplating his next words before speaking them. "On my own," he said at last.

His father slumped, losing the momentum that had propelled him. He pulled the chair away from the table and sat back down. After a long silence, he looked up and gazed at his son.

"I did what I thought was best for you."

"Well," Tommy started, finding some new energy, "I did what I thought was best, and I don't think I did all that bad, if you want to know the truth."

"So you're going to get your degree after all?"

"Sure I am. Most of what I did in Honduras is the equivalent of a field trip. My professors will accept my reports and findings. A few tests, a couple of more papers, and I'm nearly finished."

"That's all you had to tell me."

His father said nothing more, making it obvious he was waiting for his son to speak. Clearly, this was an invitation to reveal all that he had held back about his investment in two mining projects, one in Nevada and one in Honduras. But to explain that, Tommy would also have to say where he had obtained the fifteen thousand dollars he had given Grace. He was sure his father would criticize the loan and the way he had handled it. His father, sullen and silent, appeared to be determined to wait for a response.

Instead, Tommy began by explaining how Grace had asked him to accompany her. He described the visit to the morgue, meeting the mistress and daughter of Kostas, and Grace's request that he stay behind to assess the situation since he was qualified to do so because of his training at the Mackey School of Mines.

"Is she paying you for that professional service?" Billy asked.

Again, an opportunity arose to slip in the information about his investment, together with Jasper, in the Honduran silver mine, but he could not bring himself to confess the truth of the situation. He deferred by telling his father he expected some profit from the venture.

"You have something on paper?" his father pressed.

"I suppose I will get a fair share, like all of those who invested in the project," Tommy replied.

"What share? And share of what?"

The only way to answer the question was to explain the entire scheme involving investors, the Canadian and Chinese offers, and his personal investment with money borrowed from his closest friend. Tommy couldn't understand what was holding him back. Did he fear his father or whatever his reaction might be? What could his father do? He had done nothing before to help him with such matters, always insisting that his son, like he did, pay his own way through life.

Tommy's heart was frozen. His stomach ached. Strangely, he felt more threatened here in his own apartment with his father than he had been in all his days in Honduras. He recognized at the core of his relationship with his father that his father wanted something from him, but what that could be, Tommy did not know. As the man's son, did he owe him something? Was he obliged to surrender to his father's priorities or to try even when he didn't understand what they were? When was he free of his father? Did he belong to him for as long as his father lived? Did Tommy's accomplishments, and his failures, belong to his father and not to him, and that is what his father demanded? Was a son's life the father's life? The jumble of confused thoughts cleared for a moment, and Tommy could see that no matter the success a father might enjoy in his own strivings, if his son failed, then that father had failed. Tommy realized with a jolt, despite his father's urgent demands, his father feared his own failures would be revealed by his son's.

Tommy stopped his contemplation and smiled weakly at his father across the table. "Dad," he said softly, "everything is okay. Really!"

Tommy understood his father wanted his son to make the choices he had failed to make in his own life. His heart opened up. For the first time in the presence of his father, Tommy was not confused.

With Tommy and the crew back in Nevada, Kostas's battered Toyota pickup was ceded to Ben since he had to commute between the mine and the Santa Lucia apartment. Occasionally, Pilar required the pickup for a trip into Tegucigalpa and visits to other Lenca communities. At such times, she would ride with Ben to the apartment, where she left him as she continued on her errands. Ben always asked if he could help by accompanying her, and each time, she refused the offer.

Though Pilar would sometimes enter the apartment when they arrived, her stays were brief and businesslike, either to use the bathroom or to pack a few extra clothes. When she did, she noticed that Ben had moved the photos of her and Antu, and the urn containing the ashes of Kostas, to a windowsill above the nook that contained Antu's bed, well out of sight.

When Pilar returned from her trips to Tegucigalpa the next morning, she always stopped at the apartment to pick up Ben. This morning, she was earlier than usual. Ben greeted her at the door shirtless and his hair tousled as if he had just emerged from the shower. He stepped aside to usher in Pilar.

"Mission accomplished?" he asked her.

She nodded and looked away, as if embarrassed to be in the same room with a handsome half-dressed man.

Ben retreated to the bedroom and came out again as he buttoned up a shirt.

Pilar smiled. "I think I'll take a shower before we head out to the mine. Did you leave behind any clean towels?"

Ben went to the small linen closet next to the bathroom door and extracted two soft towels. He handed them to Pilar. With two arms, she pressed them against her breasts and attempted to ease herself past Ben. He held up his hand to stop her and reached into the linen closet to bring out a folded robe.

"You might need this," he said as he handed it to her.

She accepted it as she closed the bathroom door behind her.

"Want me to make you some coffee?" Ben asked, raising his voice slightly to compensate for the closed door.

Pilar cracked open the door and peeked past its edge. "That would be nice. It was a long night."

Ben reached up to prevent Pilar from closing the door too soon. "Breakfast too?"

Pilar paused as if considering the request. "You'll fix that for me?"

"Of course. Why not?"

"This is Central America. Men don't fix breakfast, especially for women."

"I'm not from these parts. Norte Americano."

"Kostas never fixed breakfast for me."

"I never fixed breakfast for anyone before either."

Pilar smiled and squeezed shut the door without further response.

When Pilar emerged from the bathroom dressed in the robe and barefoot, a towel wrapped around her wet hair, Ben was at the stove in the kitchenette, his back to her. He was attempting to fry some eggs in a large flat pan. The table between them had been set for two. She tapped him on the shoulder and leaned over to peer into the frying pan. Ben threw down the spatula on the counter next to the stove.

"I can see why you've never cooked breakfast for anyone," Pilar said pleasantly. "You don't know how."

She pushed him aside with her hip and took up the spatula to scrape the overcooked and broken eggs onto a plate. She lowered the flame on the gas burner, cleaned out the frying pan with a paper towel, and with the end of the spatula, sliced a slab of butter from the cube and dropped it into the pan. With one hand, she cracked an egg and dropped its contents, yolk intact, into the simmering butter, then added three more eggs.

"How do you like your eggs?" she asked Ben as she carefully tipped the pan to keep the melted butter next to the egg whites.

"Scrambled," Ben answered.

"I can see why."

Ben laughed.

Grace led Emerson Smith and his assistant, Henry, into the examining room and closed the door behind her. There were only two stools and the examining table to sit on. She slid onto the table and gestured to the two men to take their places on the stools. Henry indicated he preferred standing and asked Grace if she would be more comfortable on one of the stools. She alighted from the table and took a seat to face Emerson. Henry leaned against the wall behind his boss. The three smiled at each other as they noted the babble of muffled voices in the waiting room beyond the closed door.

"They seem quite devoted to you," Emerson suggested.

"I am very fortunate to have them," Grace replied. "So what's your business?"

"The Yin Plata Mining Company sees great value in the work your husband has accomplished," Emerson said. He turned on the stool to look over his shoulder at his assistant.

Henry pulled a sheet of paper from his suit jacket pocket and handed it to Emerson.

"This letter confirms our status with Yin Plata. We're authorized to negotiate on their behalf. Anything we offer has been approved by them, and thus tantamount to acceptance. Of course, any modifications we make to the offer as a consequence of our meeting here in Schurz will have to be reviewed and approved by them. But I'm sure we'll have no problems in that regard."

He handed the single sheet of paper to Grace. She unfolded it and glanced at it briefly. "You said something on the phone about a problem?"

"Please excuse our boldness, but before we can move further on negotiations, we need to give you a piece of advice."

"Go ahead." Grace motioned with her hand as if to dispense with the formalities. "I can use all the advice I can get."

Emerson smiled as would a kind father who approved of an accomplished daughter. "Actually, it's a very serious matter."

"Seven million dollars sounds serious to me," Grace replied.

"This is not about money."

Grace cocked her head to look at Emerson with surprise.

"We came here to advise you to terminate Miguel Tavares. Immediately. Otherwise, we cannot continue our negotiations."

Grace sat up straight on the stool and wrinkled her forehead. "We don't have much love for him either, but felt he was a necessary foil as a conduit to the Chinese, who I guess are your clients now."

"Our clients have been paying him consulting fees too. But they stopped as soon as they learned he also was on the payroll of the Canadians."

"Cousineau?"

"Yes, Marc Cousineau. He's known throughout the mining industry in Central America for his crafty and aggressive methods."

"And his purpose?"

"We believe he was using your husband's endeavor to increase the perceived value of this property. He had a stranglehold on it. Since you were required to give him the opportunity to match every offer, he effectively was driving up the cost to our client until our client was priced out."

"So how would that benefit Cousineau?"

"If our client withdrew their offer, there would be no offer he had to match. It is our belief he planned on you, the grieving widow, to give up, and he would buy it from you for a song, perhaps a couple of million, then turn around and offer it to the Chinese at the highest price they themselves had set in the previous negotiations."

"Leaving us out?"

"Yes."

"How far was your client willing to go?

"Approximately twenty-five million dollars."

"Kostas knew this? It has been reported to us that was his goal."

"Your husband was very skilled in these kinds of matters. He understood Cousineau would drive my clients out of the bidding and put him in an indefensible position."

"And Cousineau knew Kostas had figured this out?"

"Of course, but we can't know that for sure."

"And Miguel? What was his role?"

"Everything your husband planned and may have shared with Mr. Tavares was reported to Cousineau."

"And?"

"We can't know for sure, but our client does not believe your husband's death was a random act."

"Cousineau?"

"As I said, he is well known for his aggressive and crafty schemes. For him, more than twenty million dollars was at stake. And your husband was an obstacle."

"Is Miguel still on Cousineau's payroll?"

"We think so. At any rate, it does you no good to keep him around, and I am sure now that we have shared our suspicions with you, you will wish to separate from him as quickly as possible."

"Did Miguel . . . did Miguel—" Grace could not complete the terrible thought.

"Perhaps not directly, but surely he suspected something, and he did not share that information with you or the police who investigated the crime. You might say it was profitable for him to remain ignorant."

Only a few times in her life did anger distort Grace's self-control, and when it arrived, she was always shocked to experience it, even when it seemed an appropriate response. She realized in this moment with Emerson Smith that regarding her husband's ambush as a random act of violence was protection against the terrible vision of intentional murder for the sordid purpose of increasing personal wealth. She stood up suddenly and paced back and forth in the examining room. The chatter of the women in the waiting room had diminished to a barely audible murmur. With those women, she dealt with protecting life and bringing life into this world. To take a life seemed so contrary to the vivid and wonderful urgency of existence that she always felt, even in her worst moments. She breathed deeply to collect herself and turned around to face Emerson.

"If I tell Pilar this," she said to him, "I'm afraid she'll kill him."

"Tell her that will solve nothing," Emerson said as he looked up from the stool where he sat. "But I'm afraid even without your husband's fiery mistress, Mr. Tavares will have plenty to worry about on his own. After all, it is Honduras." He paused for a moment to contemplate his next words. "In fact, I suggest you don't tell her, not just yet. As long as she remains in Honduras, her safety is at risk too."

"And Ben? Benvolio, Cousineau's man who accompanied her to Honduras. Is he privy to Cousineau's methods?"

"We doubt that. Cousineau couldn't let anyone know what he was doing. As I mentioned, he is well known in these parts and has many connections. He wouldn't have to do or to say much to make some bad people eager to please him."

"After we get rid of Miguel, then what?"

"We've thought this through. That's our job. But you'll have to trust us. I know how disturbing all this intrigue may be for you. You may want to take it just one step at a time."

Grace stood up quickly and gazed longingly at the closed door, behind which her patients awaited her ministrations and care. "Did Kostas suffer?" She turned to face Emerson.

Emerson rose from his stool and came toward Grace as if to allow her to rest her head on his shoulder. Grace refused the implied consolation Emerson's posture suggested.

As she stepped back, Grace told Emerson, "Once, I asked Cousineau if this is how business is done. By 'this,'

I meant all this wheeling and dealing. He said yes, if it is to be successful."

"For Mr. Cousineau, success means winning. He likes to win."

"At any cost?"

"At any cost. You can understand now how futile your partner's effort, Ms. Chevez, to protect the environment and her people would be with such a man."

"Are your clients any better?"

Emerson spread out his arms. "We're here. That should tell you something."

"I don't know who to trust anymore."

"I can understand. Our client selected us because of our record in Central America. You can check us out if you wish."

"What would I find?"

"Our name Asia Americas Strategies spells it out. We look to the long term and tell our clients to do the same. Protecting the environment is protecting their business. Being a good neighbor and benefactor increases productivity and profits. Partnership, not greed. Look me up on the Internet and read some of my papers and interviews. We've presented to the United Nations, to the World Bank, and many national congresses and parliaments. I'm quite proud of our role in the world. If you haven't already, you should do the same for Mr. Cousineau. He is the poster boy for the evils of corporate malfeasance." Emerson paused and took in the spare medical environment of the examining room they stood in. He spread out his arms. "Some people would call you a do-gooder. In fact, that's how Cousineau has referred to you, as if it is a fault or a weakness. In our view, it is a virtue and a strength."

Grace smirked slightly. "So you're a do-gooder too."

Emerson turned to face his assistant still standing in the back of the room. "What do you think, Henry? Am I a do-gooder?"

"I wouldn't be here if you weren't," Henry replied seriously.

"So how do we 'do good'?" Grace asked.

Both took their seats again on the stools and leaned in toward each other. Henry moved closer to stand directly behind his boss and listen in. Emerson began.

"We've put some thought into this plan. Before Miguel is ousted by you, our client will formally inform him they have terminated their interest in this project. There'll be no explanation why. The Chinese suffer no fools. When he shows up on your doorstep, you tell him you can't afford to pay him anymore, and you'll have to terminate his contract as well."

"We don't say anything about his working with the Canadians?" Grace asked.

"You play dumb."

"That'll be hard for Pilar. She'll want to let him know what she thinks."

"Maybe we give Ms. Chevez all the lurid details later, after we're on track with you. That's up to you, but there's no purpose to let Tavares know what we know about him or Cousineau. Patience. He, and the others, will get what is due to them. Let's just keep this between you and us."

"All our eggs in your basket?"

"They won't be broken, and they'll hatch into lovely birds."

Grace smiled at the analogy. "Why didn't you present all of this to Kostas? It might have saved him."

"It was his death that brought the Yin Plata executives to us. They smelled a rat and asked us to find it. I wished we could have been involved earlier. It just wasn't to be."

"Miguel is gone. Then what?"

"He'll go straight to Cousineau. He'll be desperate because Cousineau will be his only client and source of income. For all intents and purposes, he'll be out of a job, and to him, it will look like you're practically out of business. No interested buyer other than Cousineau, no silver yet as we understand it, and no more money. We expect Cousineau will pounce then. He'll foreclose on the loan and make life so difficult you'll accept a handout to be rid of it and Honduras. Tavares will clamor for his one percent of whatever the Canadians offer and threaten legal action to get it. Cousineau is counting on you and Ms. Chevez to throw up your hands and hunker down here in Nevada, far from terrible memories of Honduras. That's what we expect."

"How does your client get involved?" Grace asked.

"Everyone imagines you cannot run a silver mine and don't want to. It's a multimillion-dollar enterprise. So it is natural that you would sell your interest in it. But that sale, if it should occur, is subject in essence to Cousineau's oversight. He can hold it up by claiming to equal the offer. He won't, of course. It is just a tactic. Tavares too will be hanging around thinking he can force you to pay him one percent of whatever he expects you to receive from the Canadian company. I understand Cousineau has offered you approximately two million, which includes forgiveness of the loan. Technically, maybe legally, you would owe Tavares twenty thousand dollars. I know you don't want to pay him anything now that you know how he has been playing not just both sides of the street, but all three sides. So with our help, our client has a plan that will avoid all of these issues. But to implement them, we want to make sure Tavares is gone."

"What about Ben—Benvolio? Does he have to go too?"

"Right now, he works for Cousineau, so certainly he can't stay around. But if my suspicions are correct, once he learns of these details, he may not want to continue his relationship with his employer. But he isn't your concern, nor ours."

Grace leaned forward toward Emerson and asked quietly, "Do you want to share your plan with me now?"

"Not yet. It is better you don't know. The more oblivious you appear, the more convincing it will be to Cousineau and Tavares that you're over your head."

"That'll be easy. I am over my head. What about Pilar? What do I tell her?"

"Ms. Chevez has made strong demands on the environmental and social conditions of this project. Your husband was in full support of them and shared these requirements with my client. I think she'll want to make sure those conditions are met. So we've included in our plan a way to do that. But first things first. We're here to take the first step. When Tavares is out of the picture and Cousineau reacts, we'll be right here to take that next step with you. Our client has given us firm direction and license. That's why we're here."

The muffled clamor behind the closed door to the waiting room increased in volume as more patients arrived.

Emerson nodded toward the door. "They're still waiting for you."

Grace glanced at her watch. "Can you wait? You've driven a long way to give me this . . . advice." Grace went to the door and cracked it open to speak with her assistant.

The assistant looked harried. "The room is getting full. Shall I reschedule some appointments for you? It's getting late," she offered as she stood up quickly.

Grace turned to look back at the two men and shrugged her shoulders. "Duty does call. Can we meet later? Perhaps at my home."

"We've reserved rooms at the El Capitan in Hawthorne. Can you drive into town and meet us there this evening? Or should we come to your place?" Emerson asked.

"Hawthorne is a half-hour's drive from here. If you can sleep on a couch, you can stay at my place, and we can meet there when I'm finished here."

Emerson turned to Henry, his assistant. "What do you think? Bring a sleeping bag?"

Henry laughed. "Wish I had!"

Grace went to her locker and pulled her house keys from her jacket. She gave them to her assistant and asked her to show the two men the way to her home. In the meantime, she would call Antu's babysitter to alert her that visitors would be at the house.

The old woman with the bad back and cane watched these preparations unfold. She slowly made her way to Grace and took the house keys from Grace's assistant. "You need your helper," she told Grace. She turned around to look at the dozen women waiting in the anteroom. "I'll take Mr. Emerson and his boy. They can follow my car. He said he's going to help me get a job talking."

Emerson stepped forward and extended his arm to the old woman. "Lead the way. I'll ride with you so we can talk. Henry, you follow us in the car."

As she started out of the office holding on to Emerson, the old woman patted Grace on the arm. "I'll make them coffee and fix them a snack if they need it. Don't you worry. We'll figure this out."

Grace was still at the clinic when Pilar called at seven that evening.

"I have a confession to make," Pilar started even before asking about her daughter. "I didn't go to work today. I spent the whole day in Santa Lucia at the apartment just relaxing."

"What's wrong with that?" Grace consoled. "You deserve it."

"Ben was here too. He's staying at the apartment, and I stopped by to take a shower on my way back from Tegucigalpa."

"So you had company. What's wrong with that?"

"He took me to lunch. Actually, we had a lovely time."

"Are you still confessing?" Grace asked, now curious.

"I like him, I guess."

"That's natural. He seems like a nice fellow."

"But it's only been a few months . . ."

"You would have liked him if Kostas were still with us. There's nothing strange about that."

"I shouldn't feel this way."

"Antu is well," Grace interjected, now feeling uncomfortable with Pilar's confession. "And I had visitors today too. The Chinese sent their consultant from San Francisco to see me."

Pilar's tone changed on the phone, suddenly all business. Grace noticed she had not yet inquired about her daughter.

"So they are interested?" Pilar asked.

"Yes. But not as long as they have to communicate with us through Miguel. And he was working for them. They told me so." Grace had decided to take Emerson Smith's advice and avoid telling Pilar about Miguel's relationship with Marc Cousineau. "All we have to do is terminate him, something you've wanted for a long time."

"Done! I'll call him right now."

"It's important how it is done. Maybe you should tell him in person—with Ben. Just say we can't afford him. That we're out of money."

"Are we?"

"We will be soon if something doesn't come of all of this. But just make sure Miguel thinks it is because we're giving up the ghost. Sound defeated."

"You have a reason for saying that, do you?"

"Like Jasper said, this mining business is mostly a matter of wheeling and dealing. Just 'wheel and deal.'

You can even say we're over our heads, we're sorry we've taken it this far, you're ready to come back to Nevada to take care of your daughter, and you never want to see Honduras again. Just make it clear we want to put all of this behind us."

"Like we're giving up?"

"There's no reason for him to know what we really think."

"What do we really think?"

"Keep it a secret: we are not over our heads."

The next morning, Grace, surrounded as usual by a group of children on their way to school, was joined by Emerson Smith. His assistant, Henry, followed slowly in the car. When a few curious mothers asked about Emerson's business suit, he apologized he had not packed anything else for his overnight trip to Nevada, but he boasted genially that he did not put on his tie as he fingered the open collar of his white shirt.

Old Sarah, the tribal elder who had chauffeured Emerson to Grace's home the previous evening, returned in the morning for coffee. Emerson had invited her after asking Grace for permission to do so. Since she could not walk with Grace and Emerson, she rode with Henry in the car. Occasionally, Henry pulled the car alongside Emerson and Grace so that Sarah could talk to them through the open window.

"I think Sarah's excited," Emerson explained to Grace when the car dropped back behind them. "She wanted a job talking, so I dreamt up one for her. It's a job you can give her."

Grace stopped to look at him. "What can she do?"

"Become an advisor like I am. Put her on your board of directors. You don't have one yet, do you? Let her recruit a few others. They'll vote you chairman of the board."

"That's a good idea. Can we include outsiders, like you?"

Emerson politely deferred the invitation, citing a conflict of interest for obvious reasons, but he did affirm that it would be best if others outside the tribe were also included, especially someone with business and financial experience.

In addition to terminating Miguel, formation of a guiding board of directors was Emerson's last piece of advice. He explained it also would ease Grace to know the burden of future decisions would rest on the shoulders of others and not exclusively on her own. Emerson's recommendations included an offer to send her instructions and documents to transform their careless alliance with the many investors into a valid and functional corporate entity. His staff would guide her through the process to incorporate. This was a necessary step if she was to continue negotiations with his client. The Chinese, he added, were meticulous bureaucrats.

"Good fences?" Grace interjected.

"Make good neighbors," Emerson concluded. "There's too much at stake to do otherwise."

Emerson and his assistant left soon after arriving at the clinic. Already, the waiting room was crowded with women and two men. Grace's assistant informed her most did not have appointments. There was such a buzz in the community about the visitors from San Francisco they were anxious to learn what they could. Grace presumed most in the waiting room had invested in the Honduran project, or knew someone who had. She instructed the clerk to send in patients one by one as she slipped on her white lab coat and draped a stethoscope over her neck.

As she cycled through the patients, others arrived and added their names to the waiting list. The assistant began quizzing them more thoroughly since most of the complaints they had registered with her were for colds, sore muscles, or headaches. A Paiute herself, the assistant recognized these ills were common and usually were accepted patiently and without complaint until they disappeared on their own. Life was hard in the hot, dry Great Basin. Nature was the ultimate refuge of the Paiute nation, but also its chief challenge. They were used to the raw necessity to endure. Where she could, she handed out aspirins and asked them to come back if the symptoms persisted. But even those who accepted the aspirins stayed behind in the waiting room to talk with the others. As it was a pleasant day, some moved to the benches outside the clinic and visited with one another.

Henry had dropped off old woman Sarah at the clinic. She waited there for her son to arrive with her car to take her home. Everyone outside crowded around to hear what she might have to say, but Emerson persuaded her to resist revealing their plans until she had affirmed with Grace she was to be on the board of directors, and her first assignment would be to select nine others with an investment in the project. For once, she enjoyed remaining silent, recognizing it enhanced her position more than talking might have. She remembered Emerson explaining that talking wasn't really a job; it was knowing what you were talking about. Silence implied knowing, and she was grateful the white man Emerson had shared this wisdom with her, though she felt a little admonished. She squirmed in her seat when pressed by others to tell them what she knew.

Her son was late, and she went inside to warm up in the cozy confines of the waiting room, but also to escape the press of neighbors who pestered her about her conversation with the "two white dudes." She reprimanded the young man who called Emerson and Henry "white dudes."

"Dudes they may be, and they're certainly white, but they are on our side. Be respectful. White people have elders too."

The young man laughed. "Yes, ma'am!"

His friends patted him on the back as if to congratulate him. He was the only one of the group the old woman had responded to despite their entreaties.

When Grace saw Sarah in the waiting room, she invited her into the examining room.

"So you think it's a good idea? To have a board of directors? With you part of it?" Grace asked.

"It's the way we do things, isn't it? A council of elders. He told me to find nine others who have invested."

Grace nodded her head in agreement. "And he told me we should add someone outside the tribe, people with business and financial experience. Five more. That'll make a board of fifteen."

"We'll vote you chairman—chairwoman, of course. You have the most to lose," Sarah replied as if reassuring Grace.

"Not really. I've already lost. All I want is for all of you not to suffer. That's all."

"That's why you'll be the chair . . . person. You're the only one looking out for everybody. Take a peek out there." The old woman pointed to the door to the waiting room. "They all are waiting for you to take care of them. You'll be doing just what you do here—taking care of us all."

"Kostas is taking care of you all, not me. He created this."

"And he died for it, I reckon."

"I 'reckon' so," Grace imitated quietly.

"And for your daughter," the woman added.

Grace sat back, shocked to hear, for the first time, Antu referred to as her daughter. It pleased her. She wondered what Pilar was trying to tell her when she confessed that she had spent the day with Ben. Until now, she had always presumed Pilar would come to Nevada and live with her so that Antu would remain in their mutual care. It had never occurred to her before that Pilar may choose to stay in Honduras or to move somewhere else. Grace never thought Pilar would ever replace Kostas in her heart, just as she was sure there would be no man to replace Kostas in her own. Now she feared the alternatives Pilar might choose.

Sensing Grace's tense distraction, Sarah reached out and touched her arm to get her attention. "Little Antu is a lovely girl, fits right in. She is where she belongs," she said, as if divining Grace's thoughts.

Grace turned away to wipe away a tear in her eye.

When Grace called Tommy to report her meeting with Emerson Smith, Tommy and his father were still at his apartment. Billy Hawkins listened to his son's half of the conversation, and when Tommy ended the call, Billy immediately quizzed him about it.

"A board of directors? For what?"

Tommy's grin showed excitement. "I guess we're still in business. A Chinese company sent a representative to visit Grace and make arrangements for further negotiations. Isn't that great!"

"Chinese? What's going on?"

"She wants me to be on the board, as the chief technical advisor."

"Who else will be on the board?"

"Grace, of course, and I guess Pilar. Jasper and Dave. Members of the Paiute tribe who have invested in the mine. And we need one other, someone experienced in business and finance."

Billy sat up straight as if to call attention to his presence. Tommy noticed and smiled at his father.

"Someone like you, I suppose," Tommy told him.

"You recruiting me?" Billy asked his son, amused and impressed by how his son had turned the tables on him. "It would give me a chance to see you in action."

In the five years Tommy had studied in Reno, his father never once took the opportunity "to see him in action." Tommy realized he had counted on what he took to be his father's lack of interest in his son's affairs. If his father was guilty of some neglect, Tommy was too. He had never volunteered reports about his activities, successes, and difficulties. Their relationship had dulled into a cold and formal reserve that protected each from their own feelings and angst. It never occurred to Tommy his father had depended upon him. His view was the reverse: his father expected Tommy to depend on him. Now Tommy could see why he craved adventure.

Adventure was independence, freedom. Dependence on his father was safe and comfortable, but in the last analysis, it imprisoned. Tommy wanted anything other than a dull life. He realized in a moment of clarity as he smiled genially at his father, this was his father's failure. Now his son had brought the scent of adventure and his father was for a moment liberated by the brief taste of another life, the innocent and eager, even careless, energy of youth.

"You want me to suggest that to Grace?" he asked.

Billy feigned reserve and caution, but his heart, emboldened by his son's accomplishments in Honduras, surged with excitement. "If you think I can help."

Tommy knew now was the moment to tell him everything about the loan from Dave, his investment in the Pine Grove Valley gold claim, and the negotiations for the silver mine his dead friend Kostas had created. He reached across the table for his laptop computer to begin with the computer model of the ore deposit locked in the heart of the mountain. For the first time, Tommy led the conversation while his father listened attentively and with respect.

After several questions about the technology that had constructed such a marvelous glimpse into the bowels of the earth, Billy scratched his head. "But you still have no silver ore, is that right?"

"That's the beauty of it, and the mystery. That's how original Kostas was. He made it real without a lick of reality to it except what we imagine."

"And others agree with him? The Chinese, for example? And the Canadians you mentioned?"

"On this basis, we've raised nearly seven hundred and fifty thousand dollars and got a five-hundred-thousand-dollar loan from the Canadians. And not much of it is left by now, I presume."

"One and a quarter million for a hole in the ground? Are you crazy? Shouldn't there be some evidence of silver ore?"

Billy wondered how a business could be created on such an abstract basis. There was nothing to possess or to control except an idea, a hope, a promise. For Billy, business was attending to the details of things. He could hardly comprehend attending to something that was not there.

"Is this what you learned in graduate school?" he asked as if a new esoteric technology had been invented.

Tommy shook his head. "I never heard of such a plan either. This scheme was created by Kostas four years ago before anything was done. Out of thin air. He was counting on history. People have been mining silver here for more than five hundred years."

"And they didn't get it all?"

"What miners in the past found came from someplace. We're digging a mine to access that place."

At this point, Tommy had to explain his investment in the mine, a one-third share of fifteen thousand dollars contributed by the Pine Grove Valley operation.

"One third? You invested five thousand dollars? Where did you get that money?" his father asked. "You didn't tell me anything about it."

"Actually, Pop, the whole fifteen thousand dollars from the partnership came from me. I put up the money."

"Fifteen thousand! Where did that come from? Fifteen thousand dollars for an empty hole in the ground? What were you thinking?"

Tommy tapped the computer screen. "I was thinking of this."

"But there's nothing there!"

"That's why it is worth something. We're small potatoes. We could never run a silver mine. It would be a huge operation. We have to sell it."

"So why would people pay you for something you haven't found yet?"

"Because they know as soon as we tap into the ore body later, the price will be higher, much higher, and there would be many more bidders for the project. So it's cheaper now."

"Cheaper? If you're so certain you will find silver, why don't you wait until then and get a higher price?"

"Because right now our 'nothing' may be worth twenty-five million dollars, and that's enough for us. Besides, we don't know for sure the ore is really there. We could be wrong. Hanging onto the property is risky."

Billy shook his head as if to clarify his understanding. "So what you're really saying is that you don't know if the silver ore is there or not, and the only way to find out is to keep digging, which costs money, so the more you dig, the deeper the hole gets. But you can sell them what you don't know because they don't know for sure but are making a bet Kostas is right. Is that about it?" Billy scratched his head again for a moment. "I got to hand it to you, son. I guess you did learn something at college." Billy interrupted himself to chuckle loudly. "I never knew you could figure out things like this. This is amazing! What you've done is amazing!"

He paused to do some quick math on the calculator on his cell phone. "Your fifteen thousand is 2.1 percent of the total investment. That's worth nearly $525,000 if the Chinese or Canadians give you 25 million. Your one-third share of that is about 175,000. Are you telling me you've made $175,000 by investing $5,000?"

Tommy nodded. "Yup, if everything turns out that way. But maybe it won't. Who knows?"

"How did you come up with the fifteen thousand dollars? You didn't make that waiting on tables. Why didn't you come to me with this proposal? This is real business!"

Tommy was grateful for this question and did not hesitate to tell his father he had borrowed it from his best friend.

"You said he put in ten thousand too?" Billy asked.

Tommy affirmed the response with a nod of his head.

"So he could have invested twenty-five thousand dollars if he hadn't loaned you the money? Why was he willing to shortchange himself like that?"

"I borrowed the money before all of this happened. For the Pine Grove Valley project, to be partners with Jasper and Kostas."

"Didn't he ask for his money back when he knew what he loaned you went to a project he was willing to invest in?"

Tommy shrugged. "It never came up."

"You used your friend's money. I guess that's what banks do. You'll be profiting at his expense."

"It just happened. Don't make it sound like I planned it this way. It just happened."

"Well, make it unhappen," Tommy's father said emphatically.

"How?"

"Give him back his fifteen thousand dollars so he can put it in the project. If this project is as lucrative as you've said, he'll more than double the return he'll receive."

"I don't have it anymore," Tommy confessed, a little shocked at his father's words.

"You could have asked me for it."

A melancholy laugh slipped from Tommy. "Really? Would you have believed all of this before now?" He pointed to Kostas's model of the ore deposit slowly turning on its three-dimensional axis on the computer screen.

"You're right. I would have tried to bring you to your senses, but I see now I would have been wrong not to trust your judgment. So let's make it good now with your friend. Be an honorable friend and pay back the fifteen thousand. Tell him to invest that too in the project. I'll give you the money to do it." Billy paused as if to think through his next words. "If he does, that brings the total to 730,000 from investors. If Grace will let me, and if they need it, I'll invest another 20,000 to make the total a neat $750,000. That way, I'll be an investor, and she can put me on the board of directors . . . that is, son, if you want me to."

Tommy sat down and put his head in his two hands, his elbows propped on his knees.

"You're quick, I got to say that. Is that all there is to it? Just acting without thinking."

His father sat next to him on the couch and threw an arm over his son's shoulders. "We are thinking, but together. I'm just sad you didn't think I would listen to you, but I know that's as much my fault as it is yours. This project is more than an investment. It's my son's project . . . and I trust my son." Billy took a deep breath. "I love my son," he added quietly.

Father and son stood up abruptly and faced opposite directions. Billy turned around and stuck out his hand.

"I'll expect you to pay back the fifteen thousand dollars."

Relieved, Tommy shook his father's hand and told him he would sign a promissory note if it made him feel better.

"That's just good business. It's not about feelings," his father admonished.

When Tommy handed Dave a check for fifteen thousand dollars to repay the loan, Dave hesitated before accepting it.

"Why are you doing this now?" Dave asked.

"So you can invest it with Grace if you want. I felt bad I was able to put in more than you, and it was your money all along." Tommy held up the promissory note he had composed weeks ago. "I never gave you this, and I should have. I apologize for delaying this. But my father says you should mark it paid."

"I trusted you. I didn't need something written down on paper."

"My father, and Grace too, says it's better to be clear about things like this. Who knows what can happen in the future?"

"Should I turn around and add this to my investment with Grace?"

"If she'll take it, and I think she will. She wants everyone to profit by this enterprise. This will increase your standing a lot." Tommy paused to reflect on his next words. "It's a better bet than blackjack."

Dave let out a forlorn laugh as he extracted the check and promissory note from Tommy's extended hand. He folded the check and put it in his shirt pocket and leaned over to sign the note pressed against the top of his knee.

"My father is going to put in an additional twenty thousand, and he'll be on the board too," Tommy said as he accepted the signed note.

Grace was happy to receive the additional thirty-five thousand dollars contributed by Dave and Billy Hawkins. She agreed Tommy's father would be a welcome addition to the board of directors and asked him to begin working immediately with Emerson Smith and his staff to oversee all of the preparations to establish the corporation and firm conditions for all of the investors.

Tommy and Dave were distracted by their duties in graduate school. Their instructors were not as lenient and understanding as they had originally believed, or hoped. When Tommy told his father he was planning on returning to work as a waiter to replace the income he had not earned during his sojourns in Honduras, Billy told him because he had a new, possibly more lucrative job with Grace, he would advance Tommy the money he needed so he could concentrate on his studies.

For a short while, it was easy, even desirable, for Tommy and Dave to forget the intrigue and excitement of the enterprise in Honduras because of the work required by their graduate school advisors and professors. For the first time in his college career, Tommy recognized the value of the degree he was pursuing. He realized until now he had signed up for graduate school as a means to extend his college life. The degree was important to his father, but for Tommy, it was just fulfilling a filial responsibility. Now that he had some experience in the real world of geology and mining, he savored the authority his degree would give him. His professors made comments about this surge of energy and insight, perhaps feeling gratified that it was a result of their example.

Dave too discovered the same dedication to his studies, but his purpose was to end them as soon as possible. He was eager to return to Honduras where the real work, and the real world, was. Slowly, Jackie began to perceive where Dave's heart really lay and began to question him about his devotion to her. Dave remained oblivious to her concerns, frustrating her even more. Unable to conceive that Dave's infatuation might be with Honduras or the work of mining, she supposed he was smitten with Grace. When she indirectly offered this as her explanation of his frenzied attention to matters other than her, he laughed.

"Grace? She's way out of my league, and older than me, and who could ever follow Kostas?" he retorted.

Jackie wasn't satisfied with his response. To her, he protested too much. "Maybe Pilar?" she added quietly.

Dave struggled to hold back a big guffaw. "Pilar! That's even crazier! She is out of everybody's league. She acts like the princess she is. Gets her own man, and her own way, by just being there."

It never occurred to Dave that Jackie was pleading for some direct manifestation or declaration from him about their relationship. She liked it when Dave's life was humdrum and predictable. Since winning a small fortune at the blackjack tables, his life had become risky and unpredictable. It was clear he never left the gambling table after a taste of its excitement, and she was worried she had lost him.

Jasper hibernated at his ranchette in Yerington, strangely separate and seemingly disinterested in the increasing activities required to establish a legitimate corporation and negotiations with the Chinese through the San Francisco consulting firm headed up by Emerson Smith. Concerned something had gone amiss in Honduras, or that Jasper was suffering silently some illness or disability, Grace asked him to come and visit her in Schurz. He reluctantly accepted the invitation and coincidentally showed up at the reservation clinic the same day the physician from Reno was attending to his Indian patients. When Grace introduced Jasper to the doctor, as the doctor shook his hand, he pulled Jasper toward him to look into his eyes.

"You're in pain," the doctor said bluntly as if without a doubt.

Jasper smirked. "You've seen more than my doctors at the VA hospital. They prescribe Percocet and send me on my way."

"Your stomach hurts?" the doctor asked as he pressed his hand against Jasper's abdomen.

"Now it does, but not always."

"Are they treating you for ulcers?"

Jasper shook his head. "That's not my problem."

"It will be," the doctor said as he sat back down on the stool next to the examining table. "Talk to your doctors and get off the Percocet. It has a history of side effects, which include stomach ulcers. I'm guessing that's why you're so uncomfortable."

After the doctor finished his examinations and treatment of his Indian patients and departed to return to Reno, Jasper thanked Grace for making him drive from Yerington to meet her. He learned more from the few minutes with this doctor than he had in his several visits to the VA hospitals over the past few weeks.

"It was just coincidence he was here when you came," Grace replied. "I had nothing to do with it."

Jasper shook his head as if disagreeing with her. "I think you had everything to do with it. Somehow, you manage to make things better for everyone you meet. Maybe that's why we call you 'Grace.' I feel better already just being here."

Grace made it clear she wanted to get down to the business of the mine in Honduras and let Jasper know

Emerson Smith of Asia Americas Strategies had informed her the Chinese had terminated Miguel Tavares, and now it was time for them to do the same. Since Pilar was so eager to confront Miguel, she worried giving her the responsibility for terminating him might result in some violent confrontation even with the presence of Ben. Nobody from Nevada was there to support her.

"I wish I were there to do that," Jasper said as he stroked his chin. "But you're right. I don't think Miguel believes she has the authority to do it. He'll have to hear from you directly. You'll have to call him yourself. But let Pilar know first that's what you're doing." He paused to reflect for a moment. "I wonder how fast Cousineau will hear from him."

After alerting Pilar, Grace immediately called Miguel. As she had earlier instructed Pilar, she blamed their shrinking bank account and implied much uncertainty about their future plans. Miguel said little, and Grace presumed he was unprepared for this news following so quickly his termination by the Chinese. As she hung up the phone call, she felt sad to know that she had brought trouble to another person, even one who may have conspired against her and her companions. She still could not accept that the ambush of her husband was anything other than a random act of violence in an outlaw country.

She confessed these bad feelings to Jasper, but he gave her no sympathy.

"He deserved what he got." He looked at his watch to check the time. "I bet within the hour, you'll get a call from Mr. Cousineau."

But it was Pilar who called. "I told Ben."

"Told him what?"

"About Miguel. That he was working for Cousineau. Ben was shocked. And angry. He's going to call Cousineau right now."

"He didn't know?"

"The way he acted, I'd say so. And I trust him."

"So Cousineau knows we know."

"I didn't think of that. But I can't stop Ben now. He's mad."

Grace hung up the phone fearing its next ring. Everything had spun out of control, she told Jasper, who stood by as she talked on the phone.

"The jig is up," Jasper said solemnly. "Let the chips fall where they may." He let out a forlorn laugh. "Enough clichés! What's next?"

They didn't have to wait long. Grace's phone rang, and it showed Cousineau's Vancouver number. Grace hesitated before punching the dial to answer.

Cousineau was not apologetic. "Let's get down to business," he started. "My first offer stands. Double your money in the project and forgiveness of the loan. I'll handle this from here on out on my own without bothering you folks with it. It's a good deal. You should accept it, and put all of this behind you."

"Thank you," she said as sterilely as she could manage. "I agree it is a generous proposition, at least from your viewpoint. But we'll continue on our own. You forget we do believe, thanks to my husband's work, there is silver there and we intend to find it. We'll stake our future on Kostas, not you."

"Then I'll foreclose on the loan. With interest. Six hundred and thirty thousand, one hundred and thirty-eight dollars and ten cents."

"I see you prepared yourself," Grace replied. "I'm not surprised."

Cousineau was not deterred. "Through the end of this month. By then, or I bring legal action."

"And when we repay the loan, then what?"

"Can you? I doubt it given the state of your finances."

"We'll find a way."

"You are on your own, but we still have first rights on the property. When you fail, it'll be ours, and you have just doubled your loss."

Grace noticed the absence of any attempt from him to change her mind on his original offer. "Our gain is to be rid of you." Grace hung up.

A few minutes later, Pilar called again. "Ben quit. I knew he would. He thinks his boss is a crook. He'll work with us."

"Why?" Grace asked.

"I asked him to," Pilar confessed.

As Grace contemplated Pilar's response, she thought of Antu. And Kostas. "What about Kostas?" she asked Pilar.

"Kostas?"

"Does Ben believe Cousineau had anything to do with the ambush?"

"He doesn't want to think that. He can't believe a large international company like Cousineau's would stoop to such criminal behavior."

"What do you think?"

"I think they're capable of anything to get their own way. They don't have to murder people to kill them. They do it by poisoning the water, the air, the land. They bring misery to countless others to fill their own pockets with ill-gotten gain. That's what I think. If they did not kill Kostas, they're still killers."

The board of directors had not even met yet, and the company was now faced with a six-hundred-thou-sand-dollar obligation due by the end of the month. Billy Hawkins slapped his forehead when Grace reported by phone the results of her conversation with Cousineau.

"You turned down doubling our money and no obligation?" he asked, exasperated. At the minimum, he had expected to double his twenty-thousand-dollar investment based on the reports he had received from his son. Despite the excitement of this new enterprise, his central responsibilities in it, and his newfound faith in his son, he now felt he had made a mistake to act so hastily, and so out of character for him. He wondered what kind of magic or delusion had enticed him into this new world so quickly. When he confronted Tommy about his fears, his son merely shrugged his shoulders, seemingly unconcerned. He told him not to worry. Grace would find a solution—she always did, he reassured his father.

"Grace? She's a nurse! What does she know about dealing with these robber barons?"

Tommy patted his father on the shoulder and smiled genially. "We still have the mine, and there's a billion dollars of silver in there someplace. Six hundred thousand dollars is a small price to pay, don't you think?"

"It isn't small when you don't have it! And you're not going to get it from me or the investors. They're tapped out. And we only have a couple of weeks."

"Grace will get it. Kostas always came through. So will Grace."

But Emerson Smith solved the problem. The Chinese agreed to advance the funds to cover the obligation.

"It was Grace's idea," Emerson told Billy. "She expected Cousineau to act quickly, as he has. So did we. Have you completed the corporate papers and filings yet? Has the board of directors met yet?"

Billy ignored what he considered Emerson's routine questions as if to distract him from other suspicious issues. "What do the Chinese get out of it?"

"It's a loan like the one the Canadians gave you. The only string attached is you have to pay it back. That's all," replied Emerson.

Billy didn't believe Emerson because the Chinese were so famous for the abstruse methodologies they brought to business and national policies.

"They must have an ulterior motive," he pressed Emerson.

"Of course they do. If you default, they get the mine, not the Canadians. Grace said she didn't want Cousineau to get it no matter what he was willing to pay. And I agree with her. She's a smart but principled cookie. You should listen to her. She'll make a wonderful chairperson for your board of directors."

Admonished, Billy understood Grace and his son, Tommy, operated on a different level, more refined and considerate than the narrow plateau of self-interest he typically stood on to justify his own business decisions. When he put down the phone to end the call, he turned around to apologize to his son.

"You were right. Grace had a plan, a big plan, all along. You young'uns are showing me up."

A Federal Express truck rolled to a stop in front of the reservation clinic, and its driver rushed through the doors with an overnight envelope in his hand as if he held something unusual and portentous. The clerk behind the waiting room desk reached for the envelope, but he pulled it back and announced sternly that Grace herself had to certify she had received it.

It was not unusual for Federal Express to make deliveries to the clinic, but except for some prescriptions, none of the deliveries had to be signed for; and if so, normally the assistant could accomplish that without interrupting Grace. Reluctantly, Grace's assistant stood up to peek into the examining room.

"Sorry," the driver told Grace as she came out of her office. "It doesn't look like good news. All the way from Honduras."

"I was expecting something from Canada," Grace told him as she signed for it.

The FedEx driver looked surprised. "Canada? Honduras? What's next? China?"

"You're not so far off the mark," Grace said over her shoulder as she took the envelope into her office.

The driver raised his eyebrows at the receptionist. "What kind of international business are you guys running way out here in the middle of nowhere?"

"Nowhere is our home," the receptionist said coldly, indicating he should mind his own business.

The letter was from Miguel Tavares. It included a copy of the contract he had signed more than three years ago with Kostas. Grace studied her husband's signature at the bottom of the agreement. She touched it with her fingertips. His scrawl was so familiar. As a result of the longing inspired by this unexpected artifact of her husband,

Miguel's concerns seemed shallow and unimportant. He was formally laying claim to the 1 percent commission he was to receive when the mining property was sold to another party. The cover letter, obviously prepared by a lawyer but not a very competent one—nor someone fluent in English—clumsily demanded payment as if its authors presumed they had sold the property already. It was so pitiful Grace threw down the papers on her desk and went back to her patient waiting on the examination table in the alcove.

Terminating Miguel was not to be rid of him, she realized glumly. She just wanted to put him out of mind. She found it difficult to understand why people like Miguel and Cousineau were so obsessed with accumulating wealth. Such attitudes banished Native Americans like her Paiute friends and patients to the edges of society. When the white man invaded their pure lands, the Indians who owned nothing had lost everything. Once owning nothing was glorious freedom, daring freedom, unattached to the burden of possession. Before the conquistadores conquered and enslaved the Lencas in Honduras to mine silver and gold for their national treasuries, the indigenous of Central America faced only natural, external problems and not the painful inner demons of civilized greed.

Poor Miguel! From his vantage point, the most he could expect from Grace and her investors was perhaps twenty thousand dollars at its present valuation, a small amount. Dave Mogis had made nearly twice that much in a single session of blackjack. Miguel had lied, cheated, and possibly was associated with worse crimes for this pittance. Again, Grace felt the unfamiliar energy of anger rising in her heart. She stopped her examination of the young patient and went back to reread the cover letter then to look again at her husband's signature on the bottom of the contract. She could probably dispose of Miguel's claim with a simple payment of ten thousand dollars immediately, without the burden of continued legal action and its myriad and time-consuming complications because it was clear Miguel was so desperate. There was enough money in the account to do that, but despite this wisdom, the painful burn of anger at her heart denied him any profit at all. Pilar, of course, would object to any settlement with Miguel except to exact the most painful form of revenge. She took the papers and its FedEx envelope to the waiting room and handed them to her assistant. She told her to call Sarah into the offices and tell her to fax the letters to Emerson Smith and Billy Hawkins.

Since the business of the mine became a daily occurrence in the clinic, and feeling self-conscious about using the receptionist, who was on the clinic payroll, as her assistant in these matters, Grace had invited Sarah, the elder with a cane, to come by the clinic from time to time to manage these business affairs. Sarah was more than happy because she could read every bit of correspondence, talk with important people on the phone about the project, and later relay what she knew to her neighbors and family. It became a custom in the evening for the Paiute investors and their friends to find an excuse to stop by Sarah's dilapidated prefab on the road between the clinic and the cemetery to chat over coffee. Soon the whole reservation was apprised of the problems and successes of the mine.

"We keep calling it 'the mine.' Doesn't the corporation have a name?" her son once asked Sarah.

"Grace asked us to think up one," Sarah answered. She peered around at the group assembled in her home. "Any ideas? We need it to finalize the papers Billy Hawkins is working on."

"Members of our tribe are the principal owners?" someone asked.

"And the Lencas? Principal workers at the mine?" someone else added.

"Yes to both questions," Sarah answered, "as far as I know."

"Let's not be 'white' with a name," the first questioner offered.

"Let's be Indian?" another person queried.

Although nothing yet resulted from this chatter, everyone who participated in the contest to throw out prospective names felt part of the process, whether or not they had invested personally in the project. Though many were enamored of the eventual profit, counting the proverbial chickens before they hatched or daydreaming on how they would spend their winnings, as if their investment was the equivalent of a lottery ticket—vain fantasies to be sure—they legitimately were grateful that their late friend, Kostas, and his competent and good-hearted wife had given them a means to combat their sense of banishment that life on a lonely and dusty reservation miles from any white man's town inevitably instilled.

Someone learned, probably from Sarah, that the Chinese company competing for the mine was named Yin Plata Mining Company. Like Grace had earlier observed, they chuckled at the "Silver Silver" appellation.

"Let's copy the Chinese," Sarah's son suggested.

Everyone in the assembly in Sarah's front room turned to look at the young man seated cross-legged on the floor in the corner.

He smiled. "Silver is the color of the full moon. In our language, moon is *muha*. The Spanish word for moon is *luna*. What about Luna-Muha, or Muha-Luna?"

"Or Lunamuha, all one word?" someone else suggested.

"Or Muhaluna?" another announced.

"Either way," Sarah postulated, "it means Moon Moon, or Silver Silver. Just like the Chinese name."

"I like Muhaluna, all one word," her son announced. He scribbled something on the yellow writing pad in his lap and held it up for everyone to see the word written out. "It looks like it means something, even if you don't know the language."

Sarah tallied everyone's preferences and settled on Muhaluna Mining Company. They urged Sarah to suggest the name to Grace.

Sarah had her son drive her to the clinic for the single purpose of revealing to Grace their inspiration. By then, it was early evening, and Grace was about to walk home. She rode with Sarah and her son instead. In the car, Sarah turned around in the front seat to give Grace the name for their enterprise. Sarah showed her the name her son had written down.

As Grace repeated the word to herself, she smiled then leaned forward to pat Sarah on the shoulder. "Muhaluna it shall be. I think Kostas would have liked it. And I am sure Pilar will appreciate it. There is no Lenca language anymore, so Spanish will have to represent the interests of the Lencas. Muhaluna Mining Company it is."

In that moment, the elder Sarah realized her talk had created something, just like Emerson Smith had intimated a few weeks ago. She and her tribe had moved a bit closer to the rest of the world. The vast and empty reaches of the Great Basin valley spread out before them as they drove along the sagebrush-lined country road no longer symbolized her tribe's remote separation from the rest of the world. Instead, it was clear in her eyes this place, these people, her people, were part of a global community. Isolation was a state of mind, not a fact. The wisdom of Grace and her husband Kostas had reached out across a continent to embrace new friends. Inspired by this vision, she turned around again to face Grace in the backseat.

"The full moon, the silver full moon, will be our sign!" she announced joyously.

But wealth, even just the promise of it, corrupts. Sarah's enthusiasm for the project made many of her tribe quite miserable. They either lacked the will to invest when there was an opportunity to do so, or they did not have the money even if they wanted to. Only forty-one individuals of the more than seven hundred who lived on the reservation were going to profit if the project was successful. Many of the forty-one already acted as if they had earned thousands and had gone into debt on that presumption. Those who had nothing pestered friends and relatives who had invested for loans so they could share in the good fortune Sarah had predicted.

Not all members of the Walker Lake Paiute Reservation lived in Schurz. In fact, many, especially the younger, the children and grandchildren of the reservation residents, had moved away to Reno and California, or to college. As word spread of the impending wealth some of their tribe were expecting, these expatriates too began to clamor for participation. As a result, a delegation of dissatisfied Paiutes showed up one morning outside the clinic to await Grace's arrival. Grace had to delay seeing her appointments, which distressed her, as the group demanded a meeting then and there outside the clinic.

Some had come with their checkbooks or cash, which they wanted to give to Grace as their investment in the project. Others postulated that the structure of the Muhaluna corporation had to be modified to include every member of the tribe even if they did not invest or did not have the means to invest.

Grace was taken aback. She reminded everyone there was no profit to share, and it was just as likely those who had invested would lose their money as they would profit. Those who had invested decided to accept this risk while others, like members of the crowd addressing her, turned away from the risk or had no means to take it.

There still was no firm evidence the mining company had succeeded. The mine had yet to show a trace of silver ore. The Chinese had not yet revealed their plans. The Canadians were dogging their every move in the hopes of stealing the claim from them. They were nearly out of money from the original investors and had a six-hundred-thousand-dollar loan with the Chinese to be paid back somehow, at the worst case, by turning over the mining claim to them, leaving their corporation with nothing. In such an event, everyone would lose. How, she paused to ask, would those who had not invested, members of the tribe, share in the loss if they had not invested their own money and had nothing to lose?

"You stand to make the most," a young Paiute man, who had driven from Reno where he attended the university for this meeting, objected angrily.

Others in the crowd supported this view with grim faces and angry-sounding agreement.

This reaction saddened Grace. She didn't blame those who confronted her, though it would be easy to condemn their foolish and blind self-interest. She blamed herself. Although she never thought of money or wealth as a source of happiness, at least for herself, she realized now she had allowed herself to believe that the potential wealth promised by the silver mine would make her friends, so long disadvantaged in a society indifferent to them, if not happy at least temporarily relieved of their burdens. Pilar held out the same aspiration for her Lenca compatriots. Grace had forgotten that throughout the ages, the urge to increase wealth had created misery for those without the power to resist its disastrous effects.

Grace had no adequate response to the demands of the crowd. She checked the time on her watch and told everyone she had work to do. Sarah stepped forward to lead her into the clinic. Not satisfied, the crowd tried to follow them into the clinic. Sarah turned on the steps of the clinic and told them to leave Grace alone. This was not the time nor the manner to make their demands.

"Maybe this is my fault," Sarah whispered to Grace as they walked into the clinic. "Loose lips sink ships. Mr.

Emerson should have warned me. I got carried away with it all."

Grace moved in front of Sarah to stop their progress.

"We both are a little over our heads, don't you think?" she said.

As usual, Sarah was reminded of how grateful her tribe was to be blessed with such a saint.

"We'll figure something out," she told Grace.

Emerson expected such a development.

"It happens wherever a few of an indigenous group have good fortune. Capitalism is a dangerous wild animal when not caged."

He presented his solution as part of the agenda for the first board meeting of the Muhaluna Mining Company. In addition to the routine items was a proposal to signify Pilar as representative of the Lenca tribe and Sarah as the representative of the Paiute community in Schurz. Pilar owned no stock in the corporation since she had no money to invest, and Sarah's investment could be returned to her. Like Pilar, Sarah could represent the interests of her constituency without any compromising self-interest. Instead, each was to earn an annual stipend for their service, which would replace any profit they might have realized from an investment. Emerson's plan, created after discussions with Grace, proposed that the corporation would assign to each tribe 10 percent of the shares, entitling 10 percent of the profits to be distributed by the two nonprofit entities headed up by

Pilar and Sarah. None of this money was to be granted as income to any member of the respective tribes. Instead, the money would be used to benefit each tribe at large, through support of education, health care, and other community programs. Each tribe would select a council of elders who would decide how the money would be allocated. Through action by their own council, each tribe could decide to invest further in the Muhaluna Mining Company if they wished to share the risks inherent in any commercial enterprise.

For the first board meeting, Pilar was required to travel to Nevada. After consulting on the phone with Grace, she designated Ben as supervisor during her absence. He refused any pay for the service, telling her it was his way of correcting the misdeeds of his former employer.

The first board meeting of the Muhaluna Mining Company was held on a hot July day, nearly six months to the day since the ambush that took away the favorite son of the Paiutes, in the community center at the reservation in Schurz. Pilar had arrived from Honduras a few days earlier to make up for the lost time with her daughter. Dave, accompanied by Jackie, who rarely let him out of her sight since he had returned from Honduras, joined Tommy and his father in the car from Reno. Jasper had come from Yerington a day earlier for the chance to see the doctor who had helped him before. Though it was a weekday when she normally saw her patients, Grace closed the clinic and had her assistant reschedule all of the appointments.

Emerson Smith and Henry drove that same morning all the way from San Francisco. Earlier, they had turned down Grace's invitation to stay at her house and instead would make the half-hour drive to Hawthorne, the town nearest to the reservation, to check into a motel after the meeting.

Somehow, Cousineau had learned of these arrangements, and he too showed up in Schurz with two rough-looking cronies. He had not called ahead and so surprised Grace and Pilar. Feigning goodwill, he approached Grace outside the community center and asked to be introduced to Emerson Smith.

"So you got the Chinese on the hook?" he asked Emerson after a brief handshake.

"Off the hook," Emerson replied.

His remark made Cousineau chuckle. Cousineau nodded toward Grace and the group surrounding her as they waited to convene the board meeting.

"Well, no matter what you do, she's still on my hook," he announced, clearly satisfied with himself.

Pilar came out of the center dragging little Antu by the hand. When she saw Cousineau, she passed her daughter's hand over to Grace and strode directly to the Canadian mining executive. As usual, she was dressed in her Levis, tank top, and flip-flops. Her skin glowed with the warm tan of the southern latitudes. She stepped between Emerson and Cousineau and put her hands on her hips.

"I'll call the reservation police if you don't get on your way," she snarled.

Cousineau held up his arms as if surrendering. "Strictly business. I'm here to make a proposal to your board. They're fed up with your goody-two-shoes approach."

Emerson stepped forward and gently pushed Pilar to one side so that he could face Cousineau directly.

"You are not on the agenda. Sorry. Since you seem to be so well informed, then you must know there has been no offer and therefore nothing for your company to match. There is no reason for your presence here, and we are well aware of the legal obligations of the Muhaluna Mining Company. So, please, we have business to conduct, private business, and you can be on your way. If you wish, you can meet with me in Hawthorne when we're finished here."

Emerson gave Cousineau his business card. Cousineau turned it over in his hand and inspected both sides of the card.

"I've heard of you. You've been around the block. Well, so have I. But I was invited to attend your meeting."

"Invited? Who invited you?"

"One of your shareholders. It seems word got out we have made an offer, a good one that doubled everyone's investment, and they want to know why that was turned down. Why you left money on the table when the results of your efforts so far have been inconclusive."

"So you expect to make a presentation to the board? Just like that?" Emerson replied.

"Why not? It's out in the open. If you are concerned about your investors, and they had the opportunity to make their own valuation, shouldn't that be allowed? I thought you would be eager to hear me out."

"And you're expecting a vote on this? Today?"

"I didn't come all the way from Vancouver just to sightsee in this godforsaken place." Cousineau waved his arm at the grounds of the reservation as if dismissing the dusty environment around them.

Uncharacteristically, Emerson seemed at a loss, but Pilar stepped in.

"Who invited you?" she asked.

Cousineau turned to one of his assistants and held out his hand for the note the assistant passed on to him. He unfolded the paper and read aloud the name.

"Mr. Eddie Tom, it says here, of the Walker Lake Paiute Indian Reservation. He called us, I understand."

Pilar turned to ask Grace if she knew Eddie Tom. Grace nodded. He was well known in the community for his harsh views on how his tribe had been dealt a losing hand by the cheating white man.

"I shouldn't have accepted his investment," Grace confessed. "I knew it would be trouble. But I didn't know what else to do. I was afraid if I left him out, he would cause problems. And I was afraid if I included him, he would cause problems. It looks like I was right on both counts."

"How much did he invest? Do you remember?" Pilar asked.

"The minimum. One thousand dollars."

Emerson motioned to Cousineau that he should wait where he stood while he, Grace, and Pilar moved away to discuss their options. Both women remained silent as Emerson wrinkled his brow, appearing to think deeply. After a few moments, the skin on his forehead relaxed, and he let out a faint chuckle.

"You got to hand it to this guy. He's nothing if he's not persistent," he told Pilar and Grace. "But look at it this way. He's persistent because he perceives value here though we have nothing yet to prove the value of the mine. If we let him make a presentation, I think he'll be just shooting himself in the foot. He'll press the shareholders to accept a doubling of their money, which will prove to them the value of what we have. All he will have done without us saying a word is to prove we do have something of value."

"What if some want out now and will sell their interest to Cousineau?" Grace asked.

"We can't stop that, but that doesn't make much sense to him. He can't buy enough to get control. We'll just be obligated to treat him like any other shareholder. I don't think he'll shell out money for the few pittances he may be able to convince others to sell. It wouldn't buy him anything."

"So you're saying just let him say his piece?" Pilar questioned.

"Why not? He'll prove for us how valuable this enterprise is or can be. Act like this is normal."

Pilar looked unhappy with Emerson's suggestion. "But he is a crook . . . maybe worse!" she said after a long silence.

"I don't think any of your people will be fooled by him," Emerson answered soothingly.

Eddie Tom came to the board meeting drunk. He was often inebriated, but this time, he seemed especially under the weather. Throughout Cousineau's explanation of his offer to double everyone's investment, Eddie Tom grunted angry support. Those who had happened to sit close to him moved their chairs away. Cousineau was clearly upset and soon realized that his hasty plan to disrupt the corporation had been a wasted effort.

After Cousineau had finished, everyone except Eddie Tom remained passive and silent. Eddie Tom raised his hand to offer his share, asking for ten thousand dollars for his one-thousand-dollar investment—clearly an absurd proposition when Cousineau had offered only to double everyone's investment. Pilar leaned close to Grace next to her and whispered what a good idea it was to include at least one rotten apple in the barrel. She chuckled at Cousineau's obvious frustration.

When it was clear Cousineau had finished his efforts and was ready to leave, Eddie Tom got up to depart with him as if the meeting was concluded. Sarah's son, after she had elbowed his ribs, escorted Eddie Tom out of the room.

Grace stood up to apologize for the delay of the meeting and explained this was an unexpected complication and they wanted to resolve the issue as quickly and as transparently as possible. A middle-aged Paiute rancher stood up, his cowboy hat in his hands, and signaled for Grace to recognize him.

"We're in it for the long haul," he said as he turned to make sure everyone in the room could hear him. "Grace, we know you'll take care of us." He lifted his chin toward the door that Eddie Tom and Cousineau had just exited. "And we know what he will take care of."

As the rancher sat back down, a satisfied murmur echoed in the room.

Chapter Seven

After her several months in Schurz, Antu was as fluent in English as a child her age could be. After their long separation, her mother was shocked at the transformation. Adding further to her mother's amazement, Antu asked her, in English, to speak "American," not Spanish. When Pilar asked why, Antu held out her arms and twirled her body around.

"Because we are here," she happily announced to her mother.

Out of curiosity, Pilar responded in Spanish to make sure her daughter had not forgotten her native tongue. Displaying some impatience, Antu repeated in Spanish her request to speak "American."

Antu had changed in other ways too. She was taller, a little stouter, and had abandoned the clinging reserve, which characterizes so many young girls in Honduras. She had many new clothes that Grace had purchased for her, and was as eager as any young American girl to sport the styles and trends of her new culture. Without presuming her daughter's adjustments were improvements, Pilar asked Grace on more than one occasion if Antu had talked about her. Grace always gave noncommittal and vague responses to these inquiries because she could not remember even once when Antu expressed any longing about her absent birth mother. Once, she even asked Antu if she wanted to call her mother to answer a question she had put to Grace. Antu's response was simply a puzzled look.

"Always you help me," Antu had explained.

As the day Pilar was to return to Honduras neared, it became evident to both women that Pilar had become despondent over this issue. Grace's tension gradually increased because she feared Pilar would take her daughter to Honduras. It was evident Pilar was considering this option. Since Grace herself could not bear to be without Antu, she sympathized deeply with Pilar's predicament. She longed for a solution that would make everyone happy, and the only one she could muster would be to suggest that Pilar stay in Nevada and not return to her homeland. Even so, she understood such a decision would deprive Antu of her ancestral home. There seemed to be no satisfactory solution.

Pilar recognized her wish to keep Antu with her was principally selfish, for her benefit and not her daughter's. Antu was safer, healthier, and had the benefit of an organized and qualified education, all very difficult issues to maintain in Honduras.

Grace was a competent guardian. Honduras offered only uncertainty and difficulty. Grace offered the opposite. She was certain to provide for her child. As Pilar reflected on this and the promise of wealth from their enterprise in Central America, she came to the unavoidable conclusion that her daughter had a future here in America. She daydreamed of her daughter as an American teenager, complete with smart phone and a savvy appreciation of modern culture. She imagined her daughter in an American college. During the few times she and Kostas talked about the future they wanted for their daughter, Kostas gave her glowing reports of college life in the United States. He wanted his daughter out of Honduras, but did imagine she would someday return as a savior for her desperate homeland. Such a future Pilar wanted also, and living in Honduras would not provide that. With such thoughts, even without bringing up the subject to Grace, Pilar sadly concluded she could not take her daughter back to Honduras. If she wanted to be with her, she would have to stay in Nevada.

Though when the project in Honduras came to some resolution, she could return, it could be a year or longer, and she would have to satisfy herself with occasional visits. Pilar was afraid her daughter's growing dependence upon Grace would replace her attachment to her mother.

It was not wealth that motivated Pilar as she struggled with these decisions. She feared the consequences of the mine and the powerful influence of promised wealth on her Lenca tribe. Of her group, she was the only one who had been able to attend the university and obtain a degree. Her community relied on her for guidance. She also felt she must protect her guileless compatriots from the dangerous actions of the faceless international corporations, which had already raided so much of the Honduran mineral wealth at a terrible cost to its people.

Benvolio, as Pilar came to call Ben—because she preferred the Italian over the North American version of his name—reported daily to Pilar; though from Grace's vantage point, there was not much new in the daily reports. Pilar's telephone conversations in Spanish with Benvolio seemed much longer than the brief summary of activities she later transmitted to Grace. Gradually, Grace suspected there was much more to the relationship than merely business. She suspected part of Pilar's confusion about Antu resulted from worrying about Antu's effect on her relationship with Benvolio.

Perversely, Grace was pleased to think Pilar had encountered a replacement for Kostas. It helped cleanse the memory of her husband by making the affair a mere flirtation and not a commitment of the heart. Happily, a child had resulted from that dalliance, an unexpected gift from her husband. The only other acceptable alternative would be her not having any knowledge whatsoever of

Pilar and her husband's romance, which of course was impossible in any case. It was obvious Pilar was lost in Nevada. She was separated by thousands of miles from her purpose in life, from her new love, and to regain that, she would have to be separated from her child. As Grace contemplated Pilar's predicament, she generated a deep sympathy for her. Despite herself, she began to think of Pilar like she thought of the many Paiute women who were her patients, someone to care for.

Pilar sensed this and reacted haughtily to being regarded sometimes like a daughter herself by Grace. It soon became evident to both women it was time for Pilar to return to her mission in Honduras without her daughter. Like so many quandaries in life, this issue seemed to resolve itself with no direct action or communication by either Grace or Pilar. It was evident to Pilar her daughter's well-being was ensured by Grace and would be endangered by a return to the homeland. It was also evident to Pilar that she longed to be with her people and engage in the fight to bring them safety and happiness. As she had with Kostas, Pilar found strength and purpose in the companionship of Benvolio.

The day before Pilar was to fly from Reno to Los Angeles for the flight to Tegucigalpa, Grace and Antu drove her to the Reno apartment. Dave and Tommy came by that evening to give her instructions on the information they required to finish their field trip reports. Of course, they also wanted to keep abreast of the mine's progress and made arrangements to receive weekly reports until they were able to return.

The mine had by now penetrated past the quarter-mile mark, and still no sign of silver ore, as was predicted by Kostas's computer model. But a strike was anticipated within the next hundred yards, only a week or so of more excavation. Dave wondered out loud if they could slow down a bit, which made everyone laugh, until he was ready to return so he could be there when, as he said, "We strike it rich." He could finish up his summer term and examinations within two weeks. Tommy observed he could be there when they "went broke" too. Dave reminded him and the others that at least he could see the dam, which was nearing completion. He had ingeniously included the dam as one of the field trip projects he could use to qualify for additional credits at the university.

"I want to show my mom what I helped build," he explained enthusiastically.

Dave's innocence and energy lifted everyone's spirits. Even Pilar began to regard the project as an adventure in which she met her romantic hero. Grace enjoyed talking about the benefits of the project on the Lenca community. Only Tommy remained serious.

"What if we run out of money before we run out of tunnel?" he asked somberly. "My dad isn't so happy about our progress. He keeps saying we just keep digging our hole deeper."

Grace reassured him, and the others, that she and Emerson Smith had worked out a solution. The Chinese mining company would take over operations even without evidence of silver ore.

"But what if there is still no ore?"

"You mean," Pilar asserted, "what if Kostas was wrong?"

"Well, sure?" Tommy raised his arms as if that was obvious.

"Why do you doubt now? After all this time? And effort?" Pilar asked.

"And money?" Tommy added.

"Do you think we should've sold out to Cousineau?" Pilar pressed.

"No, but—"

"But what?" Pilar pressed Tommy.

"We've been dealing with nothing for so long I'm tired of it. Everything is still so uncertain. After six months since I started in Honduras, the only silver I've seen is this shiny dime." Tommy reached into his jeans pocket to pull out a handful of coins though no dime was included. He laughed forlornly. "Not even in my pocket."

Everyone else chuckled with relief.

Grace reached out and gently touched Tommy's outstretched hand.

"You have forgotten our purpose," she began. "We started with nothing. And we knew we were going to have nothing for a long time. But what we did have was some-thing of value. It's a very rare state of mind. Something Kostas was capable of and something he is teaching us now. Tommy, you and I started in Honduras with loss. We lost Kostas. Even so, we found Kostas. All of us." She paused to look at Pilar and Dave, then over to Antu who sat at the dinette table with a coloring book. "He wasn't wrong. He wasn't right. He just was. And is. We just are. And will be. Just imagine what he imagined. A mountain full of silver. Everyone knows it is full of silver. Scientists and geologists know it is full of silver. The Canadians know that. The Chinese know that. We don't need silver in our hands to be certain. When we get certain, we die a little to the real magic of life. Real life is uncertain—"

"But," Tommy interrupted, "you told everyone who put money into this project they would reap benefit. You sounded certain."

"I sounded certain that we have to make the effort to remain uncertain. That's all," Grace replied.

"And that's something somebody could invest in? I think not! Not if they understood what was really going on," Tommy said, sounding desperate and confused.

"Look what good uncertainty has created. Pilar's friends and neighbors are working and living happily. Our Paiute neighbors are excited to be part of something beyond the borders of this reservation. You two have made a career out of it. Tommy, you even got your father involved. What was happening between you two before

325

Kostas's model bloomed on your computer screen? Dave built a dam. Jasper found something greater than his own preoccupations. I have a new family." Grace leaned close to Pilar to lay an arm over her shoulders. "We don't need to be certain, do we?"

"Still, it would be nice to know everyone won't be disappointed," Tommy mumbled.

"Believe me, our problems begin when we find silver."

Dave was confused and shook his head. "At least we got a dam out of it," he said. "I'm going back to take pictures of it and watch it fill up with water, and see the water flowing down the irrigation ditches to the fields of corn, beans, and melons. That's something for certain!"

When Tommy and Dave left, and Pilar had put her daughter to sleep on the cot Grace had brought to the living room, Pilar sat on the couch and patted the cushion next to her. Grace sat down and turned to face Pilar. They were silent for a few moments.

"Antu will be in good hands. Loving hands," Pilar finally said. "You're her mother too."

Grace nodded acknowledgment.

"You've reminded me of my purpose," Pilar continued.

"You never really forgot it."

Pilar made a tight fist and pounded her thigh. "Sometimes I get angry. Angry at Miguel Tavares. Angry at Marc Cousineau. Angry at the world."

"Change the word," Grace suggested gently.

"What word?"

"*Angry*."

"To what?"

Grace put her hand over Pilar's closed fist. "*Wrathful.* You're not angry because you've been slighted. You're wrathful because your people have been treated so unfairly. Wrath is good energy. Anger is bad energy. Defend, not destroy."

By the time Billy Hawkins had completed all the administrative requirements to establish the Muhaluna Mining Company as a legitimate corporation, of the seven hundred and fifty thousand dollars that had been raised for the enterprise, less than one hundred thousand remained. Operating expenses in Honduras required about ten thousand dollars a week. Travel to and from Honduras and other administrative costs in the United States added to the overhead. At this rate, Billy presumed they would be out of money in less than two months.

The Chinese had loaned the corporation the exact amount required to meet the obligation with Marc Cousineau, but the sum remained on the books as an obligation. It could be repaid in only one of two ways— with silver or with a deed to the mine itself. In the latter case, everyone who had invested would have no opportunity to recoup, much less profit from their bold risk.

Despite continued progress at the mine, no trace of silver ore had yet been detected. Even though this result, or lack of one, was as Kostas's model predicted, Billy wasn't the only one who allowed himself to worry their efforts would amount to nothing more than a folly.

Losing money was one kind of pain, but losing face was another. There were moments of abject terror Grace allowed herself to suffer when she imagined disappointing her Paiute neighbors and Pilar's Lenca community. Such a result would tarnish the memory of her beloved Kostas. The native people in Nevada and Honduras revered him as a shaman who would conjure up wealth from a patch of dirt. Like his great-great-grandfather, Wovoka, he was expected to perform miracles. The computer model of the mountain of silver turning on its three-dimensional axis was nothing more than a twenty-first century version of medicine man Wovoka's legendary illusions.

At such moments, it helped Grace to muster up images of Kostas. If he were present, the situation would be identical to what it was now—no silver and hundreds of thousands of dollars that had disappeared into a deep hole in the side of a mountain—but no one would be worried or anxious because Kostas himself would be so positive and confident even in the face of unexpected problems and dangers. Grace aspired to rekindle that confidence within herself by calling upon her partner. She dredged up memories and visions of him directing his Lenca crew, panning for gold in Nevada, dealing with prospectors and mine owners, working at his desk in their Reno apartment or their Schurz home, and sharing a morning's cup of coffee with her has he chatted about the day ahead. She didn't realize it then, but she knew now she had never been afraid or worried even in his most extravagant moments. She never doubted him during the many months he depleted all their savings in the quest for silver in the mine at Tonopah years ago. Somehow, she understood because he believed whatever could happen would be, in a word, okay. *Okay*—a small word, a casual word, but a wonderfully complete and descriptive word. In the world of Kostas, everything, even unexpected complications and challenges, was okay. She supposed, as she thought with a grim smile creasing her face, even as he defended himself against the *sicarios,* he himself was okay. He brought joy even to the worst of moments.

With Kostas, life was okay. It always was, during good times and bad times, when times were rough, and when they were smooth. In actuality, she realized as she devoted herself to his image, it didn't matter what happened. What mattered was how she and he met what happened. That was life—real life. It was exciting, loving, and though it was utterly free of concern, its main quality was quiet exhilaration.

Kostas thrived on uncertainty. He never wanted to be certain, and that was the energy and thrill others found in his company. That was his magic. She recognized her occasional descent into fear and anxiety was a resurgent attachment to certainty. Life with Kostas cleansed her of that fault. Remembering him like this also cleansed.

Billy was not so easily dissuaded of his bleak misgivings. He often wondered out loud with Grace if they should have accepted Marc Cousineau's original offer, when they could have doubled their investment and be rid of this uncertainty. At such times, Grace would remind him that their aim was much greater than personal enrichment or lazy acceptance of an unencumbered life. It wasn't right, she found herself saying, to shift their burdens onto the shoulders of others. They had an obligation to see this through so others would find benefit and relief. That was the real result, she affirmed sternly.

Though generally of a good heart, Billy didn't accept Grace's altruistic motives as sufficient rationale for their decisions.

"It's money, our money, their money," he asserted. "We're its guardians. We should have remembered that instead of shooting for the stars."

Emerson Smith limited his counsel to Billy Hawkins to the routine administrative requirements of establishing a basis for the corporation. For all else, he met with Grace, and was eager to do so whenever the need or opportunity arose. In the few weeks it took for the mining enterprise to arise as a qualified business entity, he had been also grooming the Chinese executives for the offer they eventually would make. For the requirements of that offer, he consulted with Grace and accepted her views seriously. Even though most of their meetings were over the telephone, he had become enamored of her. During this time, she kept her schedule at the clinic in Schurz and was as busy as she normally would be. When he did have to meet with her personally, he convinced her to drive to Reno, where he could fly to. They met in Grace's Reno apartment, sometimes with Billy present, sometimes with Tommy or Dave, and sometimes just the two of them.

His trips over the last weeks had become so frequent that he rented a condo in Incline Village at Lake Tahoe, which was actually closer to Schurz than Reno, and invited Grace to meet there instead. As it was just the beginning of fall in the Sierras, some of the most pleasant times of the year, they often would spell themselves with long walks along the sandy Tahoe beaches.

Emerson was a widower, but his infatuation with his new client was from a father's perspective. He and his late wife had not the good fortune of children. Like Grace had found with Antu, he felt blessed to find the daughter he and his wife would have had if such good fortune had come to them.

For all of her astuteness and powers of observation, Grace remained unaware—one could say blissfully unaware—of Emerson's doting attachment. She freely shared with him her concerns, her aims for the company, her interest in the welfare of her Paiute patients and friends, Pilar and her Lenca community, and, sometimes, her grief. She gave Emerson a picture of Kostas so that he could remember their mission was inspired by his magical powers. Emerson learned of Kostas's mixed heritage of Native American, Greek, and Irish blood. As a result, he scoured the Internet for information about Wovoka and the deplorable and horrifying results of the massacre at Wounded Creek in 1890, indirectly caused by Wovoka's messianic teachings of the Ghost Dance. He also delved into the history of the Lencas in Central America and came to appreciate and understand the role Pilar had cast for herself, as the princess savior of a people oppressed by European, that is to say *white*, civilization.

Of much of this history, especially the plight of the indigenous of Central and South America, he was already knowledgeable. But Grace, and his few meetings with Pilar, had strengthened his resolve to help his Asian clients resist their bureaucratic impulses to cut costs by exploiting the land and its people. He credited this renewed pledge to Grace. Her example, her devotion to her late husband, the care and concern she exhibited for her patients, and the soft acceptance of her husband's mistress and her child galvanized his resolve.

But Billy Hawkins could not restrain his misgivings. He pressed Emerson for some concrete proposal from the Chinese, in Billy's eyes, the only way they could succeed other than actually finding silver at the end of the mine tunnel. Billy came to believe the Chinese were delaying their offer because they had disposed of the threat of Marc Cousineau with the loan but, like Cousineau, would count on foreclosing on the loan as a means to acquire the property. Emerson assured Billy he did not believe that was the case. But Billy could see no alternative. If they ran out of money before finding any silver ore and had no means to repay the loan, then the Chinese would get for a pittance, which they once considered to be a twenty-five-million-dollar value. Emerson reminded Billy they could not assume ownership without first allowing Cousineau to top that offer, which he most certainly would. Therefore, they were in the same position as before, but without the power or money to influence results. It would then be between the Chinese and the Canadians. As Cousineau had projected, Grace and her investors would be deprived of any profit for all their hard work and money. Billy could not visualize an alternative to this dilemma. Emerson promised him, without revealing any details, that he and Grace had a plan that would avoid all these problems.

"How is that possible?" Billy asked. "I can't see any other alternative except to sink more money into the project, money we don't have. And if we get it from you or the Chinese, we're just digging our hole deeper!"

Emerson reminded Billy there were issues other than the financial details and corporate arm wrestling over possession and control.

"Like what?" Billy asked.

"The environment, the Lenca, the Paiutes."

"You mean the investors?"

"I mean the communities," Emerson pronounced.

"You mean you're holding up the Chinese until these side-issues are resolved in some way? Issues that have nothing to do with the value of the property and may even burden it with expenses they don't want to bear?"

"Of course."

"Why?"

"That's what Grace and Pilar demand."

"Don't the other investors have something to say about this? The board of directors?" Billy asked.

"Most of them are Paiute, original inhabitants of this land, just like the Lenca, as you will remember, and I think they're fully in line with Grace. And Kostas. It is what he wanted as well."

"Kostas is gone."

"That makes no difference. His purpose remains."

"I never met the man."

"But you have." Emerson paused to consider these words then offered an amendment to them. "We have. Just now."

Kostas's great-great-grandfather became famous when he died. Just before New Year's Day of 1889, he fell into an inexplicable death-like coma. "Stiff as a board," someone said at the time. His family moved his body to a shelter and began their grieving ritual. The following day,

New Year's Day, the sun went into total eclipse. Wovoka's Paiute tribe believed the sun was dying and an apocalypse would end all life. As the moon moved across the face of the sun to usher in its rebirth, Wovoka awoke from his coma and regaled his amazed tribe with descriptions of the heavenly pure land he had been allowed to visit. From that moment on, his influence among all Indian tribes increased, spreading all the way across the Great Plains to South Dakota. Hundreds of Indians traveled thousands of miles to dance the Ghost Dance, which Wovoka said would protect them from the apocalypse of civilization. Perhaps it was this spirit that touched Emerson Smith and Billy Hawkins in that moment.

Jasper knew it was foolish to make plans to return to the Pine Grove Valley gold claim to supplement his Social Security and Veteran's Administration benefits, but he felt compelled to do so anyway. He had no additional income during his long stay in Honduras and feared depleting his meager savings.

Despite the pain in his stomach and the persistent lack of energy, he pushed himself out of bed to call Tommy. He asked Tommy to join him in the hard work. Tommy wanted to help his partner, but his duties at graduate school prevented a specific commitment. Tommy's hesitation disappointed Jasper. Tired and dejected, Jasper told him to forget the request. He would go by himself.

Tommy immediately realized guiltily how insensitive he had been. He was, after all, a full partner in the claim, and any gold that was recovered would have to be split evenly between Jasper, Tommy, and Grace, even if it had been recovered by the hard work of a single partner. Tommy called back Jasper soon after hanging up and told him he would pick him up in the morning. Then he promised to return on the following weekend to pan the black sand they were able to rinse from the riffle mats. Jasper grunted his satisfaction but still resented the secondhand treatment he perceived he had received from his young partner. Tommy was sorry he had not responded spontaneously to Jasper's original request.

When Tommy arrived at his house that Saturday morning, Jasper hobbled to the door. He silently motioned Tommy inside as he made his way back to the couch where he had been all night. One hand clutched his stomach, and the other reached out for the back of a chair to balance himself. It was clear to Tommy that Jasper would be unable to leave the house. Tommy asked if he should drive him to the doctor.

Jasper let himself down to lie on the couch. Even though it was a warm October morning, he pulled a blanket up to his chin. Tommy laid his hand on the old man's forehead. It felt warm, but Tommy couldn't tell whether that was the result of the humid atmosphere of the overheated room or a slight fever. He repeated the question, and Jasper shook his head in the negative.

Tommy had looked forward to spending the weekend at the gold mining claim below Mount Grant. He had rationalized abandoning a weekend plan of study for the exams he soon had to take by recalling the soothing but quietly exciting effect of the Great Basin desert. Though there was nothing distinctive in the landscape surrounding the gold claim in Pine Grove Valley, Tommy found the environment stimulated his senses. The Honduras jungle was equally wild, but its humid and densely forested landscape had never inspired him in the same way. In fact, as he reflected on this, he realized he distinctly developed a distaste for it. When he contemplated his return to Honduras, it was the thrill of a prospector's discovery that motivated him, not the new environs. In the mountains and desert of the Great Basin landscape, however, even without the search for gold, he found a strange and wonderful contentment. Life seemed complete, gold or no gold. Shoveling gravel into the sluice box provided the pleasure of exercise in what was for him a beautiful setting. At such times, he was happy to stay aware of the body, its strength, its flexibility, its power as he became mindful of the trees and great skies of the wide landscape with a mountain looming behind him. Sometimes as he and Jasper drove up the rough dirt road, which was nothing more than a dry creek bed, they disturbed a band of wild horses, whose stallion leader darted out from the clutch of trees and pranced away followed by his few mares. By the time he had completed the two-hour drive to Yerington from Reno to meet Jasper, he had forgotten his grad school worries and savored the expedition ahead of him.

Jasper refused to go to the doctor, but he could not accompany Tommy to the claim. He urged Tommy to spend the weekend there by himself, get as much of the gravel through the sluice box as possible, and return with the loaded riffle mats Sunday night. By then, Jasper indicated, he might be able to spend a few hours next week to rinse the mats and pan the black sand for gold. When Tommy returned the following weekend, he could receive his and Grace's share of gold.

Though he was concerned for his sick friend and partner, Tommy was faintly thrilled to spend the weekend alone at the claim site. He savored the opportunity to work alone, sleep by a campfire, and spend long moments contemplating his place in the universe. Lying in a sleeping bag under the Milky Way offered such potentials. October in wilderness Nevada was splendor.

Tommy pretended reluctance to leave Jasper alone when he suffered so greatly because he felt obligated to do so, but Jasper impatiently waved him out of the house. The old man promised his difficulties would soon resolve themselves as they had done before, and by the time Tommy returned, he would be well enough to pan the black sand.

"I need the dough," the old man said. "So bring back the mats full of gold."

Tommy feigned a military salute and joyously rushed toward his car for the thirty-mile drive down a lonely dirt road to the claim. By the time he arrived, it was noon. Without bothering to set up camp, he refueled the water pump, uncovered the sluice boxes, and retrieved his pickax, shovel, and plastic buckets from his car. He hauled the riffle mats from the car and set them in the bottom of the sluice boxes.

He set to work immediately, filling the buckets from the most promising places on the claim and dumping them near the sluice box. It was grueling work, and he was soon exhausted. He used a period of rest to slowly to spread out his sleeping bag and collect firewood for a campfire in the circle of stones they had used in previous visits. A little rested, he continued digging and hauling ore to the sluice box. Taking breaks occasionally to eat or to assemble the wood for a fire later in the evening, he worked like this until darkness set in. He knew a full moon would be rising over the shoulder of Mount Grant late that evening, and it would provide enough light to work for a few hours of the night. He lay down in his sleeping bag to rest and gaze at the dark night sky. The pleasant exhaustion of hard work released all tension, even in his thoughts, and he quickly fell asleep despite his determination to rise again. He wanted to stockpile enough gravel to spend the entire next day running it through the sluice box. Working by himself, he calculated he was able to move more ore than if Jasper had come to work with him.

He awoke with a start at midnight. The moon was just beginning its slow peek over Mount Grant's shoulder. His campsite hidden in a scrub of pinion pines stayed in the dark shadows. The campfire had dwindled to a few coals glowing dully in the ashes. He blinked his eyes to accustom them to the darkness, but even so, he was unable to make out any distinguishing form. For a moment, he thought he spotted the shiny eyes of a coyote or bobcat glaring from beneath a sagebrush. Uncharacteristically, this caused a shiver of fear. He scratched in the dirt by his sleeping place and found a stone to throw at the eyes. Before he could sling the rock from his prone position, the eyes disappeared. Still, he was glad he let the creature know he was not to be fooled with. He stood up and laid some dried sagebrush on the glowing coals. He knelt down to blow on the coals until the sagebrush ignited. Then he piled more of the collected wood on the fire to let it blaze, lighting up a circle around his campsite.

He was reluctant to resume his exertions, but he slowly gathered his shovel and buckets to go back to work even though the moon was still largely behind the mountain. By the time he could work in the moonlight, he had exhausted himself again and surrendered. He stopped his work, leaving the shovel and bucket where he dropped them, and climbed back into his sleeping bag.

He woke before the sun rose above Mount Grant. In the shadows and faint light, the air was chill. The fire had faded again to a mound of white ashes. He rubbed his hands over the warm ashes then crumbled some dry sagebrush branches over them to reignite the fire. As the fire began to blaze, he placed more wood on the fire then left to fill the coffeepot from the cold water of the creek.

As he waited for the water to boil, he pulled out his cell phone to check his e-mail and text messages, but there were none. He was out of range, as he knew he would be, but habit obliged him to make sure. Part of him was disappointed to not have received messages though there was none that he expected, and another part remembered the reason he enjoyed camping at the claim was because he was out of range. This contradiction amused him. When he analyzed this reaction, he determined he was resentful that modern life sentenced a person to this constant diligence. When such thoughts arose, he was grateful for the reprieve the Great Basin provided for him. A peaceful separation from the world was one of the hidden benefits of his commitment to the gold mining claim. He often wondered how others survived their busy lives without such an opportunity.

By late in the afternoon, he had run all of the accumulated ore through the sluice boxes. When he lifted the riffle mats from the bottom of the sluice, they felt much heavier than when he had laid them in the box the morning before. The extra weight indicated a thick layer of black sand captured in the mats. This was sure to please Jasper, and that made him smile. He was very happy he had decided to fulfill Jasper's request.

He drove directly to Jasper's home and arrived just as the sun began to set over the mountains in the west. The house was dark. He knocked softly on the front door, and when there was no answer, he pushed it open. Jasper lay on the couch where he had left him nearly two full days ago. As before, a blanket had been pulled up to the chin of the inert form. Tommy leaned over to look closely and was relieved to see the chest under the blanket rising and falling with the breath. For a moment, he had feared the old man had passed away.

He gently shook the shoulder, and Jasper awoke with a start. He sat up quickly and rubbed his eyes.

"Sorry, son," he muttered. "Just couldn't get myself out of bed. Maybe I'll ride to Reno with you and go see the docs at the VA."

Tommy offered the couch in his apartment. Jasper just nodded. He took Tommy's outstretched hand and allowed the younger and stronger man to pull him to his feet. Tommy was a little shocked to sense how light and frail he seemed. He must have lost weight since returning from Honduras.

Tommy pushed back the back of the passenger front seat and placed a pillow at the head before easing Jasper into the car. Jasper soon fell asleep, and Tommy drove in silence for the entire two-hour drive to his apartment in Reno.

The long stairway up the side of the hill where his small cottage-like apartment was perched was difficult for Jasper. He threw an arm over the young man's shoulder, and slowly, they ascended the stairs. Jasper gratefully lay down on the couch. Tommy had carried the pillow from the car under one arm and thrust that beneath the old man's head. He gathered up a blanket that had been thrown across the foot of his bed and spread it over Jasper.

It was a long night. Jasper got up frequently, sometimes requiring Tommy's help, for trips to the bathroom. He refused nourishment of any sort. Tommy was so concerned he spent the entire night in the armchair next to the couch. He turned on the television to distract himself and occasionally nodded off to sleep.

In the morning, Tommy had to surrender a full schedule of classes and planned study sessions at the university to chauffeur Jasper to the Veteran's Hospital across town. He helped the old man with the long shuffle from the parking lot to the waiting room. Though he wanted to leave for the university and his classes, he was so concerned about the old man's unstable gait he stayed with him until a nurse came out to accompany Jasper to an office for his meeting with a doctor. By now, he was curious to see what the diagnosis might be.

After another hour, he inquired of the nurse who had come to escort Jasper to his doctor and asked when the examination might be over. She asked for Jasper's name and tapped on her computer for a moment. She informed Tommy Jasper had been admitted to the hospital and that visiting hours began in the afternoon after four o'clock.

Tommy rushed to the university to catch what classes and lab times he could, and to cram in some study time for the exams he would soon have to complete. He was occupied until after five in the afternoon, and by the time he returned to the hospital, it was after six. He found Jasper in a two-bed room of the hospital. Jasper's bed was closest to the window, which had a grand view of the Sierras in the west. A curtain was stretched between the beds. As Tommy walked past the first bed, its occupant rose up as if happy to see him; but when Tommy stepped behind the curtain, he slumped back into his pillow. An unexpected surge of sympathy rose up in Tommy's heart for the old veteran, and he wondered why he hadn't at the minimum acknowledged him. He felt he should part the curtain and say something to the other patient, perhaps to ask if he needed something, but by then, Jasper also reacted with as much joy as his weakened body would allow at the sight of his young visitor. Tommy's smile was uncertain because he still felt guilty he hadn't been more considerate of Jasper's roommate.

Jasper needed no greetings, nor did he expect any. "Pneumonia," he announced, "and ulcers. A double whammy."

He fell back into the bed as if his brief remark and movement had expended all his energy.

"Pneumonia!" Tommy exclaimed.

Jasper nodded his head. "Don't know how. Don't know when. But that's what the doctor says I got. But the pain is ulcers."

"How long will you have to stay in the hospital?"

"Not long. I'm here to take my antibiotics for three days, then I can go home. But I can't take Tylenol because it aggravates the ulcers. They're giving me a prescription for that and a diet. You'll have to drive me home in a couple of days. You'll come back for me?"

Tommy was struck at how helpless Jasper seemed. Jasper always appeared to be a rough and ready fellow, rarely seeking help. Now he was dependent upon others. Tommy presumed this development bothered Jasper and was the cause of a different sort of illness, the mental pain of losing one's independence. He nodded to assure Jasper he would not be deserted.

Jasper was discharged late on Friday. Tommy met him in the lobby of the hospital. As Jasper came toward him down the sterile hallway, he seemed to Tommy much thinner, smaller, and unsteady on his feet. He frequently stretched out an arm to touch the wall for balance. Tommy went forward to help, but Jasper refused it. As weak and infirm as he seemed, Jasper clung to a fierce independence, the same spirit that inspired his

Libertarian views and lonely life on his ranchette and at the gold mining claim far out in the desert.

They drove directly to Yerington. It was obvious to Tommy that Jasper was too weak to pan the black sand still awaiting them in the stacked riffle mats he had left behind when he and Jasper drove to Reno the previous weekend. After settling him in the house, Tommy told Jasper he would sleep in the camper trailer Jasper left parked on his property, and in the morning, he would begin the arduous process of rinsing the mats and panning for gold. He urged Jasper to rest and refrain from the impulse to go back to work.

"Maybe it'll perk me up finding a little gold," Jasper objected.

"I'll pan it and show you the gold. That'll perk you up, won't it?"

"Yeah, but it ain't the same as finding it yourself."

Jasper's response made Tommy remember the project in Honduras where they had yet to find any precious ore. After seven long months, they had found nothing, and yet, that seemed to have little effect on their ambitions or those of the competitors for the property. There had been none of the eureka thrill of discovery, just the backbreaking work of tunneling through hard rock and the abstractions of corporate maneuvering. Even though they had tossed around figures in the millions, none of this speculation offered the concrete sense of finding what they sought. Always, the result was elusive and vague. He would find a greater sense of satisfaction finding a few flakes of gold from their small claim than all of his months of struggle and speculation in Honduras.

"It is about time we saw something real, don't you think?" he said to Jasper.

"I don't think I'll be going back to Honduras," Jasper said, picking up on Tommy's inference. "Can't stray too far from the doctors. And besides, I don't have the energy for it."

Tommy moved a chair closer to Jasper's bedside and sat on it. He leaned forward with his arms on his knees. "We know there is gold in our Pine Grove Valley claim. We just don't know how much. It's real. It's there. We've seen it. But we haven't had the same experience in Honduras. There's been nothing. Yet it has required all of our attention."

"And our money," Jasper added.

"Exactly. Were we crazy?"

"A bird in the hand is worth two in the bush, is that your meaning?"

"Is it?" Tommy asked.

"I don't know. It's more like two million birds in the bush. Now that would be something."

"Right now though, it is no birds in the hand and no birds in the bush."

Jasper laughed weakly and nodded his head in agreement as the laugh turned into an ugly cough. He held a tissue to his face and turned away from Tommy.

Benvolio held a small bouquet of flowers he had purchased just outside the airport terminal from a street vendor. It was a last-minute impulse when the vendor pushed the posies toward him. As he waited with the flowers for Pilar at the gate, he resisted the impulse to throw them into a trash bin. Pilar was not an easy woman to please, and he doubted she would appreciate his gesture.

Pilar's life was so strenuous and demanding and her character so strong and resolute, most who met her minimized her good feminine qualities even though she was a beautiful woman. She wore little makeup and no jewelry, though she was partial to long dangly earrings; her dark hair either flowed loosely around her face or was pulled up in an efficient topknot. Sometimes she wore a baseball cap that hid her eyes in the shadow of its bill. Her attire was predictable; the only variety was the color of the tank top and the condition of the flip-flops she had chosen for the day. Her jeans were often torn or smudged with dust. Another woman similarly attired would appear plain and ordinary, but Pilar's intense energy emblazoned her attire with purpose. It was apparent to all who met her, she had a mission, and her manner suggested she would persevere until her mission was accomplished.

But unexpectedly, Benvolio had touched her, which surprised her as well as Benvolio. She accepted the flowers with a sincere display of gratitude and wonder. He smiled broadly and was happy he had followed his impulse. She pressed the flowers to her chest as Benvolio removed her heavy traveling bag from her shoulder.

Feeling happily expansive, Benvolio suggested an early dinner in a nearby hotel restaurant before returning to the apartment in Santa Lucia. Pilar assented with a simple nod of the head as she slid into the battered and dusty Toyota pickup. Benvolio jammed her bag behind the seat; he couldn't leave it in the bed of the pickup because it would disappear as soon as he slowed the pickup in traffic. As he slid behind the steering wheel and inserted the key into the ignition, he looked over his shoulder at the woman beside him and smiled. She smiled back, though tentatively. He raised his eyebrows as if to ask permission and then, without warning, leaned toward her and lifted his right arm over her shoulder. Like a wilted but still beautiful flower, she allowed herself to sink into his embrace. He held her close as she laid her head against his shoulder and closed her eyes. After a few moments, she lifted her head to look him in the face.

"I don't know," she whispered in Spanish, slightly elated to rely on her native tongue once again after her two weeks in Nevada. "It's only been seven months."

"It doesn't have to be any more than this," Benvolio murmured.

Pilar let out what could be described as a slight laugh but was more like a sigh and nodded her head to show she understood, at least for now. Benvolio gently removed his arm and bent to turn the key in the ignition. She put her hand on top of his, as if to stop him, then let go.

"Dinner sounds good," she announced as she sat back straight in her seat.

After dinner, they drove to the apartment in Santa Lucia. Benvolio pulled her bag from behind the seat and led Pilar through the door. He opened the patio doors to let in fresh air and announced that the sheets on the bed were recently changed by the housekeeper at his request. On the bed were clean towels and a robe.

Pilar looked uncertain until he said, plainly, he would continue on to the mine and stay in the accommodations in the office shack. He would drive back in the morning to take her to the mine. He stood in the open doorway of the apartment as he prepared to leave. Pilar came forward and leaned her head against his chest.

"You can give me a hug," she said in Spanish.

He awkwardly put both arms around her, and as he increased the pressure, she moved closer to him. Then she pushed away.

"Thank you," she said somberly as she pushed closed the door.

Benvolio spent a moment staring at the hard wood of the shut door then turned on his heel to the truck.

For a moment as she listened to the truck engine echoing on the cobblestone street outside, she clutched at her cell phone thinking she might call him to return. But what she herself regarded as her good sense took charge, and she threw the phone onto the couch. She was tired from the trip and ached for a shower to cleanse her body and mind. She hadn't returned to Honduras to be with Benvolio; there was a higher purpose to be achieved, and that was the priority. At least in this moment, she was very thankful she would be alone when she finally allowed herself to slip under the clean sheets and just rest. For a while, the world would be just fine as it is.

Though he had a key, when he returned the next morning, Benvolio knocked on the wooden door. Pilar was already dressed. She jerked open the door with some authority and pointed toward the kitchenette against the opposite wall.

"Coffee," she told him abruptly, turning on her heel to the table where she had left her cup.

Accepting that today was for business only, Benvolio helped himself to coffee and sat at the table. "I got some news," he said quietly, peering into the coffee cup at the black liquid. "I don't know whether it's bad news or good news or no news."

Pilar wrinkled her brow and peered at him.

"Marc Cousineau showed up yesterday at the mine. He told Jorge he's coming back today to see me. When Jorge said you would be back from Nevada by then, he said he still would be coming."

The world was not fine anymore. Pilar's shoulders slumped a little then straightened up.

"I guess he's on a reconnaissance mission," Benvolio continued.

"What can he learn that he doesn't know already?"

"Miguel was with him, Jorge said."

Pilar let out a rough laugh. "He's like a coyote slinking around for a few scraps."

Benvolio nodded his head in agreement.

"You worried about seeing your old boss?" Pilar asked.

Benvolio shook his head in the negative. "No, that's all in the past. I'm with you." He paused to let his words sink in. "This is more than a job, I think you know."

"Technically, you don't have a job. You're just hanging around."

Pilar's comment made Benvolio chuckle. "Maybe I'm looking for a few scraps too. Ever thought of that?"

Pilar wanted to say she wasn't a scrap but wasn't sure that was his meaning, so she held back. "Why then?" she asked instead.

Her question was an invitation. His ostensible purpose was to help develop the mine as a means of compensating for his former employer's misdeeds, but what he really wanted to say was he couldn't leave her alone in this predicament. Giving up the effort—even the desire—to express these difficult thoughts, he merely shrugged his shoulders.

"You know why."

His response was vague enough that Pilar could read into it what she wanted to.

A Toyota Land Cruiser was parked by the office shack when Benvolio and Pilar arrived at the mine. Inside the office shack sat Marc Cousineau and two men, both of whom wore pistols tucked neatly into tiny holsters strapped high on the hip. Always hospitable, the cook had supplied all the men with coffee, which they sipped at contentedly as they watched Benvolio and Pilar ascend the steps into the office.

Cousineau's two bodyguards stood up and moved back against the wall as the couple entered, but Cousineau stayed seated. He didn't look up, but stared into the coffee cup as if deciding whether or not to have another. After a few moments, he turned in his chair, his back to Benvolio and Pilar, who waited in the doorway, and held up the cup for more coffee. The cook came forward with the coffeepot, and Cousineau thanked her in Spanish. He tested the coffee once then set the cup back on the table, ostensibly for it to cool. Only then did he turn to face the couple. He stayed seated.

Instead of initiating the conversation as she was wont to do, Pilar went to the kitchen and asked the cook for coffee. As the cook retrieved a cup and filled it with the black liquid, the two chatted amicably in Spanish about the cook's children. Cousineau let out a snort to show her and Benvolio the snub hadn't affected him. Benvolio followed Pilar's example.

As Cousineau put down his coffee cup, he tapped it lightly on the wooden tabletop as if bringing a meeting to order with a gavel. Pilar turned to face him but stayed in the kitchen behind Cousineau. To see her, he had to turn in his seat. Benvolio stood behind her.

"I've had enough coffee," Cousineau finally said. "How about you?" He looked at his watch. "You always come to work this late?"

"Where's Miguel?" Pilar asked, effortlessly turning to English.

"I sent him to see what the Chinese may be up to."

"They're not going to give him the time of the day," Pilar answered.

"We'll see. How about a tour? Your man, Jorge, told me he couldn't do it without your permission. Are you hiding the silver ore?"

Pilar turned to look at Benvolio. He and his former employer had yet to exchange any words.

"There's nothing to see—yet," Pilar said as she turned toward Cousineau.

"I see a lot of tailings out there. You made a dam out of them. Quite clever. Kostas told me he was going to do that. I told him it will just be a source of future problems."

"Helping others is a problem?" Benvolio spoke up at last. He shook his head as if with pity or with shame.

"It complicates things," Cousineau said to him.

"What do you want?" Pilar asked. "You know what a mine shaft looks like."

"You forget I have a copy of Kostas's model. I'm curious just how far along you are with the mine, and how close you think you are to the ore body."

"Thirteen hundred and thirty-five feet as of yesterday," Benvolio announced.

"So maybe another three hundred feet to go before you strike it rich. That is if the model is right."

"Sooner or later, we'll have silver," Pilar said.

"Then what? You raising the price? You don't have the resources or skill to mine it yourself. You'll have to sell, and that means you'll have to go through me. I can hold up a sale indefinitely, and I will unless we can make a deal."

"Trying to keep the price down by buying it now before we strike the ore body?" Benvolio asked.

"Silver or no silver makes no difference to me. Even if you find the ore where Kostas predicted it would be, you'll have no idea of the scale of the find without spending hundreds of thousands of dollars to drill in order to chart the deposit. You don't have that kind of money, not anymore, and no one is going to give it to you without some control over the mine. And in that case, you'll have to go through me. Mining is more than just extracting the ore. You'll have to haul it to a mill and refinery. How are you going to buy the equipment, the trucks, the labor to do that? Mining is big business. Actually, you'll need millions just to get started. And years of planning. Finding silver is just the beginning of your problems."

"So you're saying you control the mine?" Pilar asked.

"Well, isn't that the case? What can you do about it?" Cousineau turned in the chair, his back to Pilar.

As Pilar and Benvolio exchanged glances, he shrugged his shoulders. Pilar walked around the table and sat opposite Cousineau.

"No matter what, you're not getting anything," she said.

Cousineau shook his head sideways, back and forth, as if considering her remark. "As long as I'm in the picture, you're not either. Even with the Chinese."

"Why are you here?"

"Can't you see? I'm closing the deal."

"What deal?" Pilar asked quickly.

"Two million. You get back what you paid for the loan and nearly double your investment. A pretty good deal for an empty hole in the ground."

"If it is empty, why do you want to pay two million for it?"

"You've created a pathway to the treasure. But to go from here, it will take millions and years to develop. You have neither the resources nor the time. You can't do it by yourself, and you can't sell it to somebody else unless it's me, and I'm setting the price right now, which, by all accounts and purposes, is fair. Time to go home to your daughter with your new boyfriend, don't you think, before you find more trouble than you can handle."

"Are you making threats?" Benvolio asked as he moved to stand behind Pilar.

"And you," Cousineau said as he looked up at tall Benvolio, "you got troubles too."

"What troubles?"

"As an ex-employee, you've absconded with proprietary secrets."

"Like murder? Is that your secret?" Pilar hissed.

Unfazed, Cousineau slowly let a grin spread across his round face. He pointed to his two bodyguards still standing against the back wall of the room.

"Everyone needs protection in Honduras, even me. No telling what can happen in this godforsaken country. Just being here is hazardous to your health. You know that as well as I do."

"Would you be doing this if Kostas was still here?" Pilar asked. "Could you?"

"We had discussions. We were working something out."

"What?"

"A fair price."

"Not two million, I'm sure," Pilar responded.

"Well, he brought value to the table, I have to admit."

Benvolio placed the palm of his hands on the table-top and leaned over it to address Cousineau. "Are you negotiating? Is that why you're here?"

"This is due diligence. I'm inspecting what I am buying."

"Is that why you were in Schurz?" Pilar asked.

Cousineau held his forefinger up in the air as if to test the direction of the wind.

"I was testing the waters, so to speak. Your company is a mess. All I saw was a bunch of amateurs way over their head. All you are doing is wasting time. And money. Your own, I might add. Your hole just keeps getting deeper. You are past the point of adding value to the claim."

"Finding silver is not adding value?" Benvolio asked.

"We know it's there without finding it. That's the point. Otherwise, we wouldn't be talking about it like this. You're naïve. Geology is just an intelligent guess, but we've found a way to make money with our guesses. You don't know how to do that. You think mining is actually digging in the dirt and extracting a few shiny nuggets from it like the prospectors in the Wild West did a hundred and fifty years ago. Now it's speculation and manipulation. Sooner or later, someone will do the dirty work of actually digging and hauling the ore out of the mountain, but by then, everyone along the way will have already made their millions. Like I say, you are novices. Without a clue. Let an expert take over. Take my two million, and go home happy you hadn't wasted your time, and made a few bucks in the meantime. Everyone is happy. Honestly, I can't see why you have a problem with my proposal. It's not high enough? Okay. Maybe you should bargain a little. What if I doubled the offer? Four million. Four times your investment at least. What a deal!" Cousineau turned to look at his two bodyguards. "What do you guys think? Would you take a four hundred percent increase?"

Both nodded only to acknowledge that they had been addressed by their boss. Cousineau turned back toward Pilar and Benvolio. He spread his arms out wide. "And no problems! For all of you and your poor Indians in Nevada, the life of Riley. Why wouldn't you want to get out of this place and move to easy street?"

"Now you're offering four million?" Pilar asked. "Just like that? We didn't press you for anything."

"Not officially. Just talking, but you get the drift. I'm serious." Cousineau stood up quickly and motioned to his bodyguards. They moved outside to the Land Cruiser.

"I'm staying at the Marriott in Tegucigalpa. And you have my cell phone number. I'll be in the country for a couple of weeks to check out my other operations here. If I don't hear from you before I leave, I'll come back to give you one last chance to work out a plan. In the end, you have no option but through me. You may as well make it as profitable for yourself as you can and as trouble-free as you can, don't you think?"

Pilar watched the dust slowly settle as Cousineau's Land Cruiser drove down the gully and turn on the dirt road in front of the Lenca village. Only when the sound of the vehicle was gone did she lift her cell phone to see the time, knowing that Grace would be arriving at the clinic in Schurz about now. She dialed the number, and Grace, breathing heavily, answered.

"We just got here to the clinic," Grace told Pilar. "Antu is already on her way to the school with the other kids. You want me to call her back to the phone so you can talk with her?"

"No. This is business. Cousineau is here in Honduras."

Grace asked her to call back in a few minutes so she could settle herself in the office. She confessed the beautiful Nevada fall had arrived, and the air outside was already chilly.

"Cousineau must have come here directly from Nevada," Pilar told Grace as soon as she answered the second call. "And Miguel Tavares showed up too."

"You saw Miguel?"

"No. He was here yesterday with Cousineau. Cousineau was waiting for us when Benvolio and I arrived this morning."

"What did he want?"

"He's making threats."

"What kind of threats?"

"He says we won't be able to move forward even when we find the silver ore. He's threatened Benvolio too, I think. Legal threats, not violence. Now he says he'll give us four million dollars to get us out of the way."

"What do you want to do?" Grace asked.

"What would Kostas do?" Pilar replied.

"Is four million enough? We would net about three point four million after paying back the Chinese. That's almost five times our original investments. Everyone might be happy with that."

"Miguel would be happy too."

"What does Benvolio think?"

"He thinks what I think."

"And that is?"

After a pause to collect her thoughts, Pilar responded, "We press on, trouble or no trouble. We can't let Cousineau blackmail us like that. We're in it for the long haul, don't you think? And Cousineau disregards any of the environmental and social conditions we have planned. I couldn't live with that. And we can make more."

"Or lose more."

"I'd rather lose than give in to Cousineau."

"It's enough money to take care of Antu for the rest of her life." Grace waited for Pilar to respond, but getting none, she continued. "I'll call Emerson Smith. He'll know what to do."

"He represents the Chinese, not us," Pilar finally spoke up.

"True, but I believe he's on our side too. A good man. I trust him."

After Grace finished her brief report on the phone to Emerson Smith, he remained silent for a long moment. Grace recalled his kindly and fatherly face and presumed he was contemplating their options. She waited quietly. When he spoke up at last, his voice was light and cheery, which lifted Grace's spirits and removed the sense of foreboding any conversation about Cousineau always engendered.

"There's nothing to worry about," Emerson said. "We can fly to Honduras and confront him directly. My Chinese clients have a plan. They know what they want to do. Do you wish to be there too?"

"Am I required to be there?"

"No. But I think Billy Hawkins should. We need a representative of the Muhaluna Mining Company. He's generally in charge of financial arrangements and will have to approve whatever we arrive at."

"I'll call him."

"No need. I'll do that. Henry's assistant will make travel arrangements. Who else is there besides Pilar?"

"Benvolio, who used to work for Cousineau, but he has no official capacity. But he can be useful. He knows Cousineau."

"We'll interview him to see what he might be able to contribute."

"And Dave said he wanted to be there. And I imagine if Tommy's father is going, he'll want to tag along too," Grace added.

"So we'll have the whole crew there? Good! Maybe you should consider coming too. We'll book everyone at the same hotel as Cousineau. We can arrange meeting rooms at the hotel. We're getting close to resolving something. Don't you worry about Cousineau. Our strategy will make him sorry he tangled with you."

"And Pilar."

"Revenge is not a strategy. But we can get even."

"How?"

"Kostas understood the Chinese and Cousineau. I must say I admire him, as do my Chinese clients."

"So this is a plan Kostas put in place?" Grace asked, amazed again at her husband's clever stratagems.

"The clever part of the plan is, everyone else thinks it is their plan."

"Now I'm too curious to stay away. I guess I should come too."

"You should, for everyone's sake. We'll meet in Los Angeles for the flight to Tegucigalpa."

For Kostas, geology was promise. There was never a doubt in his mind that the earth contained treasures that would make him and his families rich. Gold, silver, diamonds—the entire periodic table of elements—had been stored in the planet somewhere, awaiting discovery by a shovel or drill, by a Geiger detector or magnetometer, even by accident. When he surveyed the desert, the mountains, the plains, the hills and valleys, the jungle rivers, he saw not landscapes but a planet seething and churning, endlessly empowered by vast volcanic and tectonic forces, and the slow and inevitable adjustment of wind and water, cold and heat, the pull of gravity. Rivers, creeks, streams, and flash floods carved canyons out of mountains, dispersing its wealth along gullies and riverbeds. Erosion filled steep canyons and made them flat and serene valleys over vast underground lakes and pools of organic fluids where pebbles of gold or crystal were disbursed by the forces of nature. Never distracted by the vegetation that covered most of the planet, he saw raw earth under its green carpets, earth containing nuggets turned into pebbles, crystals into sand, ore into dirt.

What had Kostas wrought? For all her life with him, she never inquired, and he never offered an explanation of his many mining activities. His heritage of Greek science and logic taught where to look; the patience of his Paiute ancestors turned looking into seeing; and his Irish luck gave him confidence.

Gradually, as he gained experience reading the landscapes and uncovering their secrets, he came to understand the same about humans. Underneath the soft landscape of skin and hair boiled forces as volatile and inevitable as lava and earthquakes. Within the timbre of their voices, he could hear the violent weather of greed and ambition erode trust. In the same way he judged a mountain, he judged a man. Where was the jewel? How deeply was it buried in the detritus of greed and self-interest? How could he turn this discovery into benefit for himself and others? In the end, he realized the real geology to be studied was human. That's where fortunes were to be made, and not in the blasting of rock or the excavation of earth.

At last, a showdown was set, Grace solemnly thought as she hung up the phone. She leaned over the desk and laid her head down on her folded arms. She was reluctant to begin another busy day interviewing and examining her patients, who already crowded the waiting room outside her office.

For all her life with Kostas, she understood in a moment of clarity—she let him carry the burden of uncertainty that troubles every life. He plunged into uncertainty while she sheltered herself in the career of serving others, certain that she was doing good and this noble service guaranteed her refuge from doubt. Kostas never complained. In fact, now she understood his service was to protect others from uncertainty. Wealth from his silver adventures brought a predictable future to many, to her, to Pilar and Antu, to the Lencas, and to his Paiute tribe. And he had died fulfilling this mission.

Her assistant cracked open the door to let her know Jasper was on the phone. He sounded weak and exhausted. After a brief description of Emerson's plan, she told Jasper she had not included him in the entourage that was to travel to Honduras with Emerson Smith.

"Do you need me to?" Jasper asked, his voice raspy and faint.

"Plenty of us will be there, but I don't want you not to have the option to be included."

Jasper stayed silent on the phone. "I'll go," he said at last.

"You sure? Are you well enough?"

"I want to see firsthand this Emerson fellow in action. A man of manners versus a ruffian."

"It's just a business deal. Not a gunfight."

"That's what you think."

Chapter Eight

Emerson Smith had cleverly reserved three separate meeting rooms at the Marriott Hotel in Tegucigalpa. Two were on opposite sides of the building on the mezzanine floor of the hotel, and the third was downstairs on the main floor. To walk from one room to another afforded the time to reflect on the results from one meeting before confronting the group in the next room. The Chinese executives and Grace's group waited in the rooms on the mezzanine floor. Emerson had invited Cousineau and his staff to gather in the room on the main floor.

Emerson was at the head of the long conference table, his assistant, Henry, on the side of the table facing the door, when Cousineau entered followed by two young men carrying sheaves of papers. Emerson stood up politely and shook hands with each person, who then took seats at the table opposite Henry. Cousineau took the chair farthest from Emerson, with a wide space between him and his two assistants.

"My client has made an offer, as you may surmise," Emerson started as he took his chair at the head of the table. "My client is the Yin Plata Mining Company, your competitor for the Muhaluna Mine project. I do not and cannot represent Grace Wilson and her crew. She'll be their spokesperson when it is required. Your interest, of course, is to match the offer of my Chinese client, or to reject it. If you reject it, we'll need a formal declaration in writing, which my staff has prepared here." Emerson nodded to Henry, and he pushed a sheet of paper toward one of Cousineau's assistants, a young man with dark hair and intense eyes. "If you wish to implement your claim to match or exceed this offer, then I've prepared another document certifying this, which you will have to sign and be witnessed. It includes a deadline for full payment, and if that deadline is not met, then we revert to my client's offer, who will assume control of the mining property once they have completed the transaction. Also, if you wish to match their offer, they have the right to add to their bid, in which case this entire procedure is repeated until we come to a final sum. One addendum to these conditions. The Muhaluna Mining Company will not pay Mr. Miguel Tavares a finder's fee as he may be expecting because of his original arrangement with Mr. Kostas Jack Wilson over four years ago. If he poses any challenge to our clients on this issue, they will delay this acquisition until you or my Chinese clients settle with him directly in such a way that Muhaluna is completely cleared of any responsibility."

Cousineau looked impatient and bored. "What's the offer?" he blurted.

"It's complex, but it totals twenty-five million dollars. However, that offer is in stages depending upon production. An immediate down payment of five million and then four payments of five million every six months. If during the two-year period the mine cannot be developed to its expected potential, the Chinese are free to suspend operations and return the property to the Muhaluna shareholders. Of course, Muhaluna keeps the payments they have received in the meantime with no obligation to refund them."

"So your offer is really five million."

"No, it's twenty-five million. That is the sum you have to match."

"In stages too?"

"No, at once. Muhaluna does not believe your company will be a reliable debtor, silver or no silver."

"You're expecting me to pony up twenty-five million immediately even though your client does not have to?"

"Yes."

"Technically, I don't think that is matching the offer. It is two different offers, so doesn't meet the requirements of my agreement with Kostas."

"My clients are ironclad. They'll put the entire amount into escrow. Therefore, you can say they have made their offer firm."

"I can put money in escrow too."

"As I said, Ms. Wilson will not extend that trust to you. If you don't accept these terms, I will advise my client to go ahead. It will be up to Ms. Grace Wilson to accept that offer. We, and they, are fully prepared to debate this arrangement if you wish to contest it in the future. In the meantime, they'll be developing the mine and profiting by it. It is our expectation that within two years, they'll recover this investment."

"If I agree to this arrangement, your clients can still come back with a higher offer. Is that right?"

"Of course. They're upstairs awaiting my report."

"You plan on going back and forth on this until you drive me out?"

"As you can see, we value this property highly. I think it would be to your advantage, if you wish to avoid that situation, to make an offer now that certifies your definite interest."

Cousineau leaned back in his chair and stared at the ceiling. "What I'm reading is twenty-five million all at once is a much better offer than twenty-five million over two years. That's a better offer in my book."

"It is."

"What I also see is your clients are tentative, so they've spaced out the payments to give them a way to back out if things go sour."

"It's just good business from their perspective. I wouldn't say they are tentative. In fact, it is the opposite. They're determined to get this property."

"And they'll still be determined to get it even if I win this round, is that it?"

"If you are intent on developing this mine, then they'll move on to their other sites on the mountain. As you know they have claims on the eastern slope where they have been drilling for a couple of years."

"Yeah, I know. Also, I know they came up empty. That's why they want this property."

Emerson pushed his chair away from the table and stood up. He paced back and forth for a few moments before walking down the length of the table to stand before Cousineau, who remained seated.

"Let's be frank. No one has any interest in selling the claim to you. Neither my clients nor Grace Wilson. They wish to be rid of you, if you want to know the truth. This meeting is just a means to make sure you're gone, or we're gone. We're just fulfilling the letter of the agreement you made with Kostas. Make your offer and we go from there." Emerson looked at his watch. "I'll come back in an hour. In the meantime, I'll report to my client what has transpired and to hear how they wish to address the outcome of this meeting."

With that, Emerson strode to the door and left without looking back.

He did not walk to the conference room where his Chinese clients were waiting but to the room where Grace and her crew sat around a table. Present were Pilar and Benvolio, Jasper, Dave, Tommy, and Billy. As soon as Emerson entered, Billy stood up.

"Well?"

"We have to wait."

"How much did you tell him?" Billy pressed.

"Twenty-five as we discussed."

Grace raised her hand slightly, and Emerson turned toward her. "And your clients? What do they say?"

"We're moving on their plan. I just gave it a voice."

"If Cousineau goes for the twenty-five million, then what?" Billy asked.

"As we discussed earlier, the Yin Plata Mining Company will make a counter offer of thirty million dollars."

"Six million down, and six million every six months," Tommy enumerated, eager to be part of the negotiations because his father was present.

Emerson nodded.

"Do you think Cousineau will go for that?" Billy asked.

"No, of course not. But he'll promise to cause legal action if his offer isn't considered equal or better because it will be cash in front."

"Why would he pay twenty-five million for something he only offered four million for?" Pilar asked.

"He thinks the Chinese know something he doesn't know—that there is a silver lode if they're willing to go to thirty million dollars, maybe even more. He knows they're not novices in this mining business, and much is at stake for them. Either he can find a way to develop the mine himself with his company or sell it to someone else, even to my Chinese clients, after he proves there is silver ore. He's counting on doing what you haven't been able to: to find and prove there is a silver lode. From his perspective, he already has a prospect in his pocket, the Yin Plata Mining Company. I think he's raised his sights. To a hundred million. I think he believes he is taking advantage of your naiveté."

"But he said his company is too busy with other projects," Pilar continued.

"He isn't planning on developing this mine," Benvolio offered. "He has said that all along. He is just trying to manipulate a mining property. He figures if Kostas was right, the mine will produce a billion dollars, even more, especially when you look at the history of this mountain. That's worth up to a hundred million right now to an operation like the Chinese, especially if the price of silver continues to climb."

"In other words," Grace said, "he thinks he can't lose as long as he gets the mine."

"Yes. We've got him right where we want him," Emerson replied.

"How do we deal with Miguel?" Pilar asked.

"He'll be Cousineau's problem, not ours," Emerson told her.

"Even from Cousineau, I don't want him to get anything," Pilar continued.

"What he'll get from Cousineau won't make him happy," Emerson assured her. "And it's not worth you fretting about, believe me."

After meeting with his Chinese clients, Emerson Smith, accompanied by Henry, who had been waiting in the room with the Chinese delegation, returned to the room downstairs. Cousineau and his two assistants were all talking heatedly on their cell phones when Emerson entered. They quickly hung up on their calls and signaled to Emerson to wait outside for a moment while they concluded their meeting. Soon, one of the assistants came out and ushered in Emerson and Henry.

"Thirty million," Emerson announced without preamble or fanfare. "As I said, they're serious. And they're not gaming you. They are fully prepared to advance six million and deposit the remaining in an escrow account."

"My offer stands," Cousineau asserted. "Twenty-five million all up front. Let's get Grace in here and see what she has to say. She can pick one offer or the other."

"And if she picks my client's offer?"

"We'll go from there. I stand on my offer. Twenty-five million up front will make up the difference in interest over two years, plus it is all in their hands right now. If Grace is wise, she'll take this offer."

Emerson reached for the house phone and rang up the meeting room where Grace waited with her crew. He faced away from the men at the table and explained the offer. Grace said she would be right down.

She arrived with Pilar and Billy Hawkins. The five men in the room stood as they entered. Emerson moved around to Henry's side of the table and pulled out a chair for Grace. Pilar leaned against the back of a chair without taking a seat. Billy sat down directly across the table from Cousineau.

Emerson explained Cousineau's offer of twenty-five million dollars paid within a deadline, but Pilar responded.

"Who pays Miguel Tavares?" she asked.

Cousineau sneered at Pilar as he responded. "He'll do what we say."

"And that is?" Pilar continued.

"I've called him. We'll give him twenty-five thousand if he signs off on the deal with you."

Grace raised her hand slightly for attention. "We've paid you back your loan," she started. "Six hundred thousand and something. I would like that added to the amount so we can pay back what we borrowed without touching the principal amount."

"Did the Chinese offer that?" Cousineau asked.

"They added five million, which we considered was sufficient," Billy Hawkins interjected. "We don't mind earning six million every six months for two years. I understand there are tax advantages for doing so. It is a very attractive offer."

"But you'll still be involved," Cousineau said as he stood up.

"We trust them," Grace responded. "But you're right. It would be attractive to be finished with Honduras, at least in this regard." She turned to look at Emerson seated at the head of the table, who seemed to give her a slight nod of approval. Turning back to Cousineau, she added, "Much could go wrong in two years. The price of silver may fall. Worldwide recession. A disappointing silver deposit. I've learned a lot about the mining business these last few months, more than I want to. After four years of my husband's hard work, all we have is a mine shaft. No silver yet, as you know. We, the Chinese company, and you are all moving on this property on the basis of my husband's measurements and projections. You are clear on that, aren't you? This is all speculation, and frankly, I would like things to be a little more certain."

Pilar, still leaning against the back of the chair across from Cousineau, spoke up. "Did you review our other conditions? The ones Yin Plata has agreed to?"

Cousineau waved his hand in front of his face as if impatient with Pilar. "We always comply with local environmental regulations. It's not a problem."

As they had planned earlier, Billy Hawkins stood up and feigned excitement and impatience, though it was not hard to do as he was amazed his son had brought him into a situation where they were discussing tens of millions of dollars. He turned to address Grace directly.

"As your financial advisor, I agree. Twenty-five million in hand now is worth more than thirty million over a two-year period. You're right, Grace. A lot can happen in two years. You want this to be your last trip to Honduras. I say we accept the offer from Global Resources."

Grace faced Cousineau. "Billy can give you the exact amount of the loan we have to pay back. I'd like that amount added to your offer before I make a decision with my team upstairs."

"If I do, it will seal the deal?" Cousineau responded quickly, leaning over the table toward Grace. He held out a hand as if to shake on a done deal.

Grace ignored his hand.

Pilar stood up. "And Miguel? He still gets his twenty-five thousand? You can guarantee he won't come to us for more?"

Cousineau nodded in the affirmative. "He'll be happy. It's more than he deserves since he had little to do with all of this."

Grace pushed back her chair and prepared to leave with her two partners. "Am I to assume you have approved adding the amount needed to repay the loan? Billy will give you the exact amount."

Cousineau cast a glance at his two assistants. One of them shrugged his shoulders to show it was a minor adjustment to the total. Cousineau nodded the affirmative toward Grace.

"Yes, you can assume that."

"And the deadline?" Emerson asked. "You agree to that." He looked at his watch. "Ten days from now, the money has to be in their bank, or my clients sign with Grace and her crew."

Cousineau nodded agreement.

Grace, Pilar, and Billy hurried out of the room toward the stairs leading to the mezzanine floor. Pilar seemed dissatisfied, Billy was elated, and Grace was thoughtful.

"Two things," Pilar started. "What if they find out there is no silver? And Miguel, I still don't like him getting anything."

"We never claimed there was any silver," Grace replied. "He knows we've been searching for it on the basis of the model Kostas created. He is as aware of that as we are."

Billy bounded ahead, taking long strides of two steps at a time. He stopped and turned to face Grace and Pilar coming up behind him.

"Don't forget. They're presuming the price goes up if we did find silver. In this case, for us, no silver is good."

Pilar stopped in her tracks to look up at Billy. "I don't understand. How can no silver be more valuable than actual silver?"

Billy held out his arms on both sides as if in exultation. "We're not miners. We don't dig for a living. We wheel and deal."

"But if we actually had silver, couldn't we wheel and deal more effectively?" Pilar asked.

"We could, of course, but it would be much more complicated. Clinging to the actual would be a burden. Maybe in the long-run, we would get more, but for that period of time, everything would be uncertain. How much silver would there be? What will be its price in two years, three years? Could we sustain an effort with our meager resources while we negotiate? Maybe, just maybe, we would become desperate. Besides, for all that you've put into it, don't you think twenty-five million is an adequate reward? We can't get greedy now. Otherwise, we'll be in the same boat as Cousineau. Don't you see how pleased he looks, thinking he is making out like a bandit?"

"I'm afraid," Grace said softly as she paused on the stairs with one hand on the rail, "we're the bandits."

Pilar corrected her. "Kostas is the bandit. Robin Hood."

"This is what he wanted all along, I suppose," Grace added.

When Grace entered the conference room, her smile announced the result of the meeting. Billy could not contain himself. He rushed toward his son and hugged him in plain sight of the rest of the crew. Dave wiped his forehead with the back of his arm, hardly believing this was happening. Jasper slumped down in his chair as if exhaling exhaustion, but he smiled faintly. Benvolio moved close to Pilar and gave her a reassuring smile, though Pilar appeared to be pouting.

"What's wrong?" Benvolio asked her.

"Miguel still gets something out of this," she replied so that everyone could hear her complaint.

Benvolio tapped her arm tenderly. "Twenty-five million dollars has a way of inspiring forgetfulness. So what?"

"He'll feel like he won something," she replied.

"I don't think so," Grace said thoughtfully. "I think he'll feel like he lost something."

Though it was rare for Miguel Tavares to be introspective, he became angry with himself as he reflected on the missteps that had reduced his monthly income by more than two thirds and precluded the chance of any finder's fee from the Chinese, who he believed held the most legitimate interest in Kostas's mine. Because Kostas had been such a good man, even in the eyes of Miguel, he now wondered why he had not surrendered completely to his leadership. Such devotion, he realized, would have provided more benefit than just a generous payday.

When Marc Cousineau first arrived in Honduras, before his meetings with Emerson Smith and Grace, he called Miguel to his hotel and offered him a revision of their contract. Miguel now understood had he been more perceptive, he should have limited his contracts to the Chinese and Kostas, and avoided the poisonous Cousineau. The additional income from the Canadians paled in comparison to what he understood the Chinese to be planning. His finder's fee arrangement with them could have been as high as a hundred thousand dollars. With Cousineau, all he could expect was a meager retainer.

But the die was cast. He was ousted from the operation Kostas had inspired, and also from the Chinese. He should have been able to ascertain the intentions of the Chinese when they began quizzing him about the ambush that killed Kostas, his friend and virtual partner for nearly four years. The savvy and perceptive Chinese reacted impatiently to Miguel's exaggerated expressions of ignorance and innocence. They just could not accept nor believe he had absolutely no suspicions about the ambush and who might have had inspired it.

Though rarely expressed as formal accusations, it was clear everyone close to the situation believed Cousineau, in an indirect and devious way, had created the causes for some desperados to presume they would profit by the murder. In Honduras, murder for hire was often instigated with a mere nod of the head or some casual and seemingly irrelevant remark. Everyone in the Central American mining industry knew Marc Cousineau was a ruthless competitor who was successful in operations around the world, many in lawless and wild places where the rule of law was weak and legitimate government was absent.

Now that he was the recognized representative of Cousineau, Miguel was in no-man's-land, caught in the open between the hostile Chinese and the dedicated entourage of the man who should have been his mentor. Like so many others, he regretted that he had allowed selfish impulses to influence his choices. And he wondered if his decision to secretly work for Cousineau had in some way contributed to the murder of his friend Kostas.

Suddenly, he was afraid. Not only did he have to worry about Cousineau but also Kostas's friends, among them the most threatening, Pilar, but also her Lenca compatriots. The lore in Honduras was that the ancient Lenca were fierce and merciless warriors, and she was a true daughter of that lineage. The Honduran legacy of murder and retaliation dated back to the days of the conquistadores. Though this history did not provide a rationale for such actions, it certainly inspired dangerous fits of outrage. As he contemplated his own fate, he understood he was at once the product and the victim of this outlaw culture.

When Cousineau called from the hotel conference room to let him know he would receive twenty-five thousand dollars if he cancelled his claim for a finder's fee from the Muhaluna Mining Company, he was relieved he didn't have to resort to an uncertain legal case in the slow-motion courts of Honduras. He even doubted he had the willpower to actually make a claim. Like Grace and her crew, he just wanted to end the intrigue and aura of violence that accompanied Cousineau.

Even so, Cousineau's last words on the phone startled him.

"Just don't cross paths with Pilar," Cousineau warned. He hung up before Miguel could question him further.

Settling with Cousineau for twenty-five million dollars, even with an additional sum to repay the loan from the Chinese, brought no happiness or elation to Grace or Pilar, though Pilar expressed some slight satisfaction that Cousineau had been outsmarted, and Miguel earned only a pittance. Grace hung her head low, not sure if what they had accomplished possessed some inner value, such as peace of mind or the inspiration of good deeds.

Jasper cautioned Dave and Tommy not to count their chickens before they hatch. "The money ain't in the bank yet, and that robber baron is a crafty one."

Tommy realized now that an agreement had been reached and a sum settled upon, he would fret until the money was in the bank. He couldn't bear the thought of not having it, though the very idea of twenty-five million dollars for their seven months of effort was inconceivable only hours ago. Already he suffered the great fear of losing something that he had yet to possess.

Mysteriously, Dave was silent after letting everyone know this experience was better than blackjack, but had been a gamble nonetheless, only the stakes were higher—much higher.

Billy Hawkins was a different story. He could not contain his excitement. He quickly pulled out his cell phone to use the calculator to figure the return on his twenty-thousand-dollar investment. He couldn't believe his eyes as he recalculated the sum, over a half million dollars! He looked at his son, Tommy, across the table from him. All those years, he had overpowered his son's initiatives in favor of his own conviction. His son's paltry investment of five thousand dollars had turned into more than a hundred thousand dollars in a matter of months, a feat accomplished not with business savvy and careful deliberation but from the simple-minded and pure loyalty of friends. Such loyalty, and faith, he realized, he should bestow upon his son and not continually second-guess his decisions. His son's purity created purity, and Billy understood in an uncomfortable moment of self-realization that from the impurity of self-interest, only impurity can result.

Pilar had no patience for the excited contemplation of their apparent victory. She signaled to Benvolio, and the two of them left the hotel to drive to the mine, though Emerson had reserved a hotel room for each of them. Pilar felt obliged, even eager, to inform the Lenca families their employment would end soon, but instead, they would receive generous bonuses, equal to two years' pay as she and Grace had already decided, in addition to the bequest to benefit the entire community.

As he drove the battered pickup, Benvolio could not resist reaching over to pat Pilar on the arm. She did not react but remained still and pensive.

"You look angry," he said at last, taking his eyes from the road to lean over to try to peer directly into her face.

Pilar jerked her arm from his touch to show that indeed she was angry.

"Grace told me anger is bad for me. She said to make it wrath, and wrath was okay. But I don't know the difference. Kostas is gone. Miguel got something out of it. And Cousineau thinks he outmaneuvered us."

"Don't you think you outmaneuvered him? Shouldn't that bring you some satisfaction?" Benvolio inquired as he turned back to the road and removed his arm from Pilar's side of the seat.

"What if he finds silver? We're not sure it is not there or is there. In fact, everyone says it is there, they just don't know exactly where to look and more looking takes money, lots of money. But with a billion-dollar prize, people are motivated to look."

"We don't have the money to keep looking," Benvolio reminded Pilar.

"We had a hundred yards to go. Did we quit too soon?"

"It's not the money, is it?" Benvolio asked gently. "You want control."

"I guess I have to be satisfied that we control twenty-five million dollars."

"That's a lot of control."

"After the money is in the bank, what do we do?" Pilar asked.

"With money in the bank, you and Grace have options you didn't have before."

"I don't want to be a bad person, but I can't think of Miguel without bad ideas. And Cousineau."

"You don't have any proof Miguel was in any way involved."

"But he used the situation to his advantage."

Benvolio shrugged his shoulders. "What else do you expect? Especially here in Honduras. There aren't many other options for anyone here."

"You say I should just forgive and forget?"

"What else is there to do?"

Pilar pulled her cell phone from the hip pocket of her jeans. "I can call him."

"And?"

"And tell him what I think."

"That's harmless enough, I guess."

"But so what? Is that what you are thinking?"

"I guess if it makes you feel better. What if he doesn't listen to you? Or begins to defend himself? Or worse, just sneers."

Pilar did not respond. She held the phone in her hand and stared at it as if deciding what to do or say.

Benvolio spoke up again. "You ought to be happy. Your families will be taken care of. You've done something good."

Pilar let the phone fall in her lap and turned to address Benvolio. "Kostas did something good. I think this was his plan all along. Somehow, he managed us all."

"So what did Kostas expect would happen to Miguel?"

"He'd let him go on his way. He did serve a purpose after all."

"You should remember Kostas then."

"W-W-K-D, what would Kostas do?" Pilar chuckled, though slightly.

"Why did your Chinese clients play along?" Grace asked Emerson as they rode in the limousine Emerson had engaged. "They certainly weren't going to give us twenty-five million dollars based on Kostas's projections?"

Henry, Emerson's assistant, sat in the front seat opposite the chauffeur as he talked with great energy on his cell phone. Another hired car with Billy, Tommy, Dave, and Jasper followed them as they made their way to the site of the mine.

Emerson leaned forward to tap on the window separating them from the front seat. Henry hurried to finish some remarks into his phone then hung up and pull backed the window.

"Tell Grace why our Chinese clients played along," he ordered Henry.

Henry sat up straight to speak through the opening. "For two reasons. One, to best an aggressive competitor, whom they hoped to weaken here in Central America. Two, for a million dollars. That's the fee your husband offered if we achieved the goal of twenty-five million."

"You mean they had this agreement with Kostas from the very beginning?" Grace asked. "Why didn't you tell me?"

As Emerson answered, he motioned for Henry to sit back down and close the window. "We thought your performance would be more credible if you actually believed the Yin Plata Mining Company wanted to make an offer for your mine. We didn't want to compromise your principles."

"This is on paper, what my husband agreed to?" Grace pressed.

"Yes, it is why my clients came to me in the first place after your husband was ambushed."

"But a million dollars hardly seems like it is worth their trouble, to say nothing of the risks involved, in the face of tens of millions of dollars? And you, why are you so helpful to us?"

"Actually, your husband promised them two million dollars if we reached the goal of twenty-five million. The other million dollars goes to my company."

"So we net twenty-three million, not twenty-five million?"

"Don't forget the six hundred thousand dollars you so cleverly added. A brilliant stroke, I might add. I should have thought of that myself. At twenty-three million, you and your friends increased your return by thirty times the original investment. And, finally, you are done with Honduras. And your husband's plan has been executed as he wanted it."

"That still doesn't answer my question. Why would the Chinese participate in this charade for a paltry million dollars?"

"Simple. A bird in the hand." Emerson patted Grace's hand on the seat between them.

"Don't your Chinese clients believe there is silver?"

"Your husband was an honest man. Even though he created the model that by all rights was the most accurate estimate of a silver ore deposit, he didn't for a second buy his own projections. He knew in the last analysis it was still a guess. But he needed material to build the dam. The best way to get that material was to dig it out of the mountain right next to the streambed. In addition, the water seeping from the mine would be pure and filtered by the Earth itself. You could say his real purpose was benefiting the Lenca tribe who had rallied around him, Pilar's community. In fact, his daughter's community. He figured he could kill two birds with one stone. Build a dam and convince a greedy man to pay him twenty-five million dollars for doing it. The Chinese, no stranger to complicated and devious strategies, loved the harmony of it. If they could make a few dollars on the side and deliver a blow to their chief competitor in Honduras, they were all for it. But I have to say, it was their shock at your husband's murder that motivated them. Like you, and like Pilar, they wanted to exact some form of justice. It was doubtful the Honduran legal system would ever be able to link Cousineau to the ambush. This was their best alternative, even if it later turns out Cousineau had nothing to do with the crime. We'll never know for sure, but we all know what kind of man Cousineau is and what he is capable of. If he is weakened a little, then that is a good result. We also think after his board of directors discover they wasted twenty-five million dollars, and the millions more they'll have to spend to find out they have bought an empty hole in the ground, Cousineau might be worried about keeping his job. Honduras is a complicated place. This is the Chinese way of making it a little less complicated. They are committed to finding silver here. Your husband's plan was one way. They have their way."

"So the model is an illusion Kostas conjured up?"

"It has merit, but it is just a starting point."

"Is there silver in the mountain?" Grace asked once again.

"Of course. There has to be. Five hundred years of successful mining activity proves it. But it may be buried a little more deeply than anyone thinks."

"Did we lie to get this deal?"

"You didn't lie. If you will remember, you yourself told Cousineau your husband's projections were merely that, estimates, an educated guess, and it was uncertain what actually would be revealed. You were truthful."

"But I believed there was silver."

"And there is. You just don't know where."

Grace shook her head as if confused. After a few moments, she turned to face Emerson seated next to her in the limousine. "Cousineau should have known better. After all, he's an experienced mining executive. It was he who started this whole scheme when he hired Kostas to do the original research and projections."

"And your husband did a good job. He painted the picture as he saw it. And Cousineau turned it down. If you will remember correctly, he turned down Kostas's original projections. If he had accepted them then, he would have saved himself twenty-five million dollars."

"Even though he rejected Kostas's projections, he kept his finger in the pie by requiring the right of first refusal."

"Miners always do that. They count on luck as much as they do science. If Kostas got lucky, they would have taken it over in a minute."

"But Kostas wasn't lucky. We never did find the silver ore."

"So he sold them on the science. Pretty damn clever of Kostas, I have to admit. He used his Greek logic, not his Irish luck."

Grace quietly smiled to herself as she responded to Emerson's closing remark. "And his great-great-grandfather's magic."

The limousines had to slow down after they turned off the paved highway onto the rough dirt track crudely carved out of the streambed. As they approached the Lenca village ahead, Henry drew Grace and Emerson's attention to the road ahead. On each side of the road, the villagers had lined up. Men, women, and children waved their hands. As the two limousines slowly passed by them, the villagers tapped the cars softly and fell in behind. Women held up their small children so they could see the occupants inside the cars. Grace rolled down the window on her side of the car and reached out her hand to touch lightly the outstretched hands of children and women. The men stood stalwart and alert, though all were smiling. Some offered a military-style salute as Grace's car crept by.

In the second car, both Tommy and Dave rolled down their windows. Billy sat in the front seat next to the chauffeur. He had pushed back the window that separated him from the passengers in the back so that he could watch his son happily greet the villagers. He was smiling broadly. His son's easygoing loyalty had benefited many, he realized. It was a rare illumination to learn that business could be guided by compassionate and generous impulses, and not just by the disciplined self-interest that had ruled his life for so many years. As he watched his son shaking the hands of the children who ran alongside the cars, he resolved to modify his business practices. He had never made so much money in such a short period of time than he had by following his son's initiatives. His own style of business was based on the presumption the work would be difficult, the people he had to deal with would be dishonest or disinterested, and an energetic devotion to his own interests would be required to protect his efforts. But now he saw that perhaps business was difficult simply because he thought it was that way. If he relaxed, if his mind broadened to include the needs and interests of others, success brought more than pecuniary award; it could include the satisfaction of knowing he had benefited others. In fact, he now realized, as he sat back down in the seat, his thorough focus on his own needs and desires might have brought trouble to others.

As he watched the happy villagers turning to walk with the limousines to the village, he felt ashamed that he might have caused harm rather than benefit.

This was the first time Grace had visited the place where her husband had died. She was a little apprehensive, despite the eager welcome of the villagers. In front of the village, before the road turned up the gully that led to the mine office shack, Pilar and Benvolio stood. Both were beaming. When Grace's car stopped, Benvolio stepped forward to open the door. He held out his hand and helped Grace step out into the bright sun.

As Pilar came forward, Grace was surprised by her broad smile. She could not remember a time that Pilar had smiled or seemed to appear anything other than grimly determined or angry. They hugged each other briefly. Pilar handed her a framed photo. It was a shot Jorge had taken with Kostas's cell phone at the request of his boss. Kostas stood with one foot on the streambed, the other against the flank of the mountain, with a pickax held high over his head as he prepared the first blow against the mountain. Below the photograph, in a small rectangular space in the frame, was the word *Aqui!* carefully printed in bold letters.

"Jorge made this for you," Pilar explained. "It commemorates a special day for him, for all of us. It is the day we started the mine. Over eight months ago."

She turned to invite Jorge to meet Grace. He came forward holding his baseball cap with both hands at his chest.

"My cousin, and our foreman. He has something to say to you."

Jorge gathered himself and, in Spanish, elaborately welcomed Grace to their home. Pilar did not need to translate as Grace understood the intent of his remarks. She held out both of her hands and clasped them over one of Jorge's hands. Jorge bowed down his head as if he had been blessed by a saint.

A long table had been set up under an awning. Two chairs were at its head. Plates of melon, corn, tortillas, mangoes, tomatoes, squash, and boiled eggs cascaded down the length of the table. In the tent behind the awning, women stood in front of hot ranges flipping tortillas and frying meat, fish, and scrambled eggs in big pans. Pilar led Grace to one of the chairs at the head of the table. Jorge pulled out the chair for Grace to take her seat.

Pilar and Benvolio led the remainder of Grace's group to seats on each side of the table near where Grace sat. Emerson took the chair closest to Grace, but the others of her group chose seats farther down the table so that they could sit among the villagers. As Billy Hawkins tried to pull out a chair next to his son, he was ushered by one of the Lenca miners to another seat near a group of miners. The table could only seat Grace's group and the sixteen miners. The women and children busied themselves with serving food. Pilar sat next to Grace at the head of the table.

After everyone was seated and food had been served, but before anyone could begin eating, Emerson tapped a glass with his fork and stood up. In excellent Spanish, he thanked the Lenca villagers for their hospitality and goodwill. When he was finished, Benvolio stood up and delivered an impassioned speech in Spanish about the strong will of Lenca women, the strong backs of Lenca miners, the kindness of Grace, and the fortitude of their protector, Pilar. He held up his glass of water toward Grace and Pilar. Everyone clapped when he sat back down.

For a while, there was silence. No one began to eat. All the men at the table, including Grace's group, leaned over to stare at the two women at the head of the table. Even the women in the kitchen and the children servers stopped their activity to see what was to happen next. Grace presumed she was expected to say something, but instead, she turned to Pilar and lifted her elbow to indicate she should stand and talk. Pilar looked down into her lap then reached over to pick up the photo of Kostas that Grace had laid down on the table in front of her. Pilar held up the photo so everyone could see it as she rose from her chair.

"Aqui!" she shouted, and everyone clapped.

Then there was silence. Some of the men turned to look at the place across the clearing at the edge of the woods near the office shack where Kostas was found by Pilar that fateful Valentine's Day. Dave and Tommy followed their gaze and understood its meaning. Each day, someone from the village commemorated the spot by refreshing the flowers in the small vase that had been wedged into the sand near the fallen tree that Kostas had leaped behind when he was attacked. A small white cross was planted in the sand behind the vase of flowers. Some of the men crossed themselves before turning back to the table and the meal before them.

Pilar made no mention of the memorialized site even though she knew it was the cause of the silent pause in the festivities. She breathed in deeply and wiped one of her eyes with the back of her hand.

"Dave," she said at last, "stand up." She waited as Dave awkwardly rose to his feet. "Tell us about the dam. I'll translate."

Dave pointed to the dam, visible up the creek bed from the site of the Lenca village.

"I just checked it out, the dam, I mean," he started. He looked around at everyone surrounding the table then peered into the kitchen to acknowledge the women and children there. Pilar translated briefly his few words before he continued.

"It's great! The dam! Did you see it? Did you see how much water there is behind it? Pure water too! I tasted it, right from the pond." He paused for Pilar to translate. One of the Lenca miners held up his glass of water to show his glass was full of it. "I'm so honored to be part of it. It's so beautiful."

After Pilar's translation, everyone remained silent, respectful. Billy Hawkins pushed back his chair and stood up to see the dam more clearly. It loomed fresh and large at the edge of the clearing.

"You built that?" he asked.

Dave pointed to some of the Lenca crew seated at the table. "They did. And Kostas engineered it. We even got engineering drawings, complete with an irrigation system. You know, there used to be dam there, not as good as this one, but it was washed away in 1998 by Hurricane Mitch. Hasn't been a dam there since. Now there is a dam." After a pause, a mischievous smile creased his face. "A dam good one at that!" he added.

Pilar had difficulty explaining the joke in Spanish, but everyone laughed even so. After a moment, she turned toward Tommy.

"Tommy, tell us about the mine."

It was clear Tommy was hoping not to be noticed by Pilar. He looked over at his father on the opposite side of the table. Slowly, he stood up then smiled in the same sly way Dave had a moment ago.

"The best mine by a damn site," he started.

Again, Pilar had difficulty translating the humor. His father, Billy, laughed heartily and slapped the back of the Lenca miner next to him.

"Mi hijo!" he told the miner in terrible Spanish.

The Lenca nodded his head and pointed to a young boy playing with a soccer ball in the clearing. "Mi hijo!"

Both dads smiled broadly as they admired and loved their sons.

Tommy continued. "The mine, it's not just a hole in the side of the mountain. It's engineered within inches of its projected track. At a precise 2 percent grade to allow seepage to drain easily from the mine, right into the pond behind the dam. It's a beautiful piece of work. Don't leave without taking a stroll in it. A quarter mile through solid rock. And right on target."

After Pilar finished her translation, Jasper spoke up. "On target to what? Ain't no silver yet!"

"Thank God!" Emerson Smith uttered in response.

"What do you mean by that?" Jasper asked, sounding exasperated.

Emerson pushed his chair away from the table but did not stand up. As he spoke in English, he paused for Pilar to translate for the others.

"Do you think we would be sitting here at this fine table with all these good friends if you had discovered silver?"

"Maybe it would have been a bigger celebration," Jasper challenged.

"What more do you want than what you have already gained?" Emerson asked Jasper directly.

Pilar translated his words again. The Lenca miners looked confused. They had just been blessed with more money than they had been able to earn during their entire lives; and their community would be receiving an endowment that would improve the lives of everyone. Why couldn't these gringos be content? Even Pilar looked confused.

Because Jasper didn't answer, Emerson continued. "Dave has a dam, Tommy made a fortune for himself and his father, Grace and Pilar can care for their child and their families. These men here can go back to what they love, tilling the earth to produce something of value. These women are happy their children and their men are safe in this violent country. Do you think we would have these things if you uncovered the silver lode for giant corporations, corrupt governments, and aggressive men who would kill for those fortunes? This village would be cleared away like so much debris, gone. Those farms would become parking lots for giant trucks. The pond behind the dam would become polluted with poison. Tommy is right. You were right on target. This," he said as he held out his arms to include all of the people around the table, the children running back and forth from the kitchen, the boys playing soccer, and the women in the kitchen who had turned around to watch and listen, "this is the target."

Grace stood up. Pilar began to sit down, but Grace held her in place at the elbow.

"You can translate for me," she whispered to her husband's mistress and the mother of his child whom she now considered her own daughter.

"Dave," Grace began, "you can take me to the dam and explain the irrigation system. I would appreciate that. And Tommy, please, let's tour the mine together, with your father. You can explain the engineering feat you fellows pulled off. No more talk about silver. Emerson is right. Our problems would be just beginning if we had, as they say, struck it rich. Let Mr. Cousineau worry about those kinds of problems. Don't forget there is another village, in Nevada, where people like you will also benefit from your hard work. I see now this was my husband's plan all along. He struck it rich once, ten years ago, with another silver mine. We got paid handsomely for it too. Some of that money enabled this enterprise. But he learned something from that first strike. He learned the lust for success measured only in money would never satisfy. So he transformed the mining business for himself and for all of us. His experience and wisdom became the means to satisfy and protect others. He was ingenious and patient. I am happy to be out of the mining business. Jorge and his crew, I daresay, are happy they don't have to ever again walk into a dark hole and work doggedly for days on end, though they never complained, and accomplished their tasks with vigor and good nature. There are men, and women, in this world who think what can be held in the hand is real. That's a vain dream. What is real cannot be grasped. It is the very spirit of life, the joy we wake up with every morning just to be alive, to breathe, to hug our child, to sip our coffee, to sit with our partners in life and make plans for dinner, for school, for the future. This was the rich ore Kostas mined. And we are the beneficiaries of his wisdom."

Grace had to pause from time to time for Pilar to translate. Both women became solemn as Grace's meanings took hold. After Pilar translated her last words, both women took their seats. After a long silence, everyone began to eat and talk.

Just as the celebrants began moving their empty plates into the kitchen to be cleaned, Miguel's Land Rover appeared on the road. As usual, he was driving too fast. One of the Lenca miners motioned to him to slow down. Miguel hit the brakes and slowly approached the group assembled around the long dining table. Tommy had already walked to the mine with his father, and Dave was busy with Emerson and Henry atop the dam. Pilar and Grace still sat at the head of the table, conversing pleasantly with two of the Lenca women. As Miguel came to a stop and emerged from his car, Pilar stood up suddenly to walk toward him, but Grace pulled her back by the arm and motioned for her to retake her seat.

Miguel doffed his straw hat and nodded politely to the two women. Benvolio was in the kitchen helping the women scrape clean the plates from their lunch. When he saw Miguel's Land Rover, he threw down the utensils and reached for a rag to wipe clean his hands. He strode quickly to stand near Pilar, who remained seated as Grace insisted.

One of the Lenca cooks emerged from the shade of the awning and gave Miguel a very friendly greeting. She asked him in Spanish if he would like something to eat, and Miguel muttered something she couldn't understand, but she took it to be acceptance of her offer. She turned around and came back with a plate full of food and placed it on the table near Pilar. Miguel, not knowing what else to do, pulled out the chair and sat in front of the plate of food. He thanked the Lenca cook. Her husband, one of the miners, greeted Miguel with a cheerful salute, and Miguel waved back.

"Well, eat!" Pilar said in English.

Miguel picked up a fork. "I didn't expect this," he said.

"What did you expect?" Pilar pressed.

"Cousineau told me not to cross paths with you. I expected some kind of trouble."

Grace stood up and poured Miguel a glass of water from the pitcher on the table. "Dave says it's pure, filtered by Mother Earth herself."

Miguel lifted the glass and sipped some of the water. "It's cool too," he told Grace.

Because Grace had risen to her feet, Pilar followed her example. Benvolio stood by, as if on guard, his eyes focused on the beautiful but angry Lenca princess.

"You came looking for trouble?" Pilar asked, her hands planted on her hips. "That's either brave or foolish."

"I'm sorry," Miguel said quietly as he laid down the fork without having touched the food. "I'm sorry," he repeated quietly.

"Sorry you didn't get more out of this?" Pilar growled.

"Sorry Kostas is gone. Sorry I didn't know what to do." Miguel paused to take in the activity in the village. "This looks like a very happy place . . . now."

Pilar waited, silent. Grace sat back down and propped her chin in her hands, elbows planted on the tabletop.

"It was an honor to work for Kostas. I realize that now. There is no honor in money. I am sorry I didn't understand," Miguel continued.

Pilar started to reply, but Grace held up an arm and stopped her.

"Kostas used you, you know," Grace started. "You couldn't have known his plan. And you've gotten paid for it. So all is well. There is nothing more to say or do. We'll soon be gone, back home in Nevada."

"Not yet have I been paid for it," Miguel replied. "And I am beginning to suspect I'll never see what Cousineau promised."

"We're not making up the difference!" Pilar announced abruptly.

"I don't expect you to. I already signed papers with Cousineau. I have no claim on you any longer. He is supposed to pay me in ten days."

"And if he doesn't?" Pilar asked.

"I guess I'll just go hungry. I should never have trusted him."

"So why did you drive all the way out here?" Pilar persisted.

"I just wanted to be close to something good, at least for a little while. I wanted to 'cross your path' so I could let you know I was wrong. That's all."

"We're done here in Honduras. We won't need your services, if you're looking for another job," Pilar responded.

"I don't want anything from you, nor do I think you need my help. You seem very capable all by yourselves."

Pilar could not let go of her suspicions. "You're not asking us to force Cousineau to pay you, are you? I think you know I would be very happy if you got nothing out of this other than what you have already earned."

Miguel chuckled. "I think that has been very clear from the very first. But no thank you, I don't need your help. I'll solve my own problems."

Grace leaned over the table to speak to Miguel. "Then why are you here?"

"I see now it is helpful to associate with good people." Miguel paused to wave an arm at the activity around him, women in the kitchen cleaning plates and packing food, boys who made the clearing in front of the mine office a soccer pitch, the Lenca miners enjoying cigarettes under the shade of a tree, the limo drivers leaning against their cars as they nibbled at the food the women had brought to them. "I just want to be happy like you are happy. That's all. No agenda. No plan. It's like starting over. I want to start over, and I thought by driving out here to see Pilar, to let her know I understand the way she feels, and to see how Kostas worked his plan, that's all. I know tomorrow it will be difficult for me to remember this moment. I will be wrestling with Cousineau, with others. I will be worried about money and how am I going to get it. I'll be worried about my enemies. But for a moment, even this brief time—" Miguel stopped to look at his watch. "These few minutes, I wanted to know what happiness was like. So thank you."

As he stood up to leave, he reached for his straw hat that he had set on the table.

Pilar moved toward him, and watchful Benvolio stepped toward her. He didn't think she was capable of physical violence, but he was prepared to stop her if she made such a move. Instead, she pointed to the plate of food the cook had set down before him.

"You haven't finished your lunch," she said.

Miguel sat back down and placed his hat on the table again.

"It looks pretty good," he said as he lifted his fork. "And I am hungry."

Grace had only one more obligation before she left Honduras. From where she still sat alone at the head of the long dining table, while the others in her party were busy touring the dam or mine with Dave and Tommy, she could see the spot, not even fifty yards away, where her husband had died—the place where his mistress found him behind the fallen tree he had used as shelter from the hail of bullets that killed him. From her vantage point, she could make out the bright splash of color of the flowers the Lenca placed there each day, and in the shadows, the faint outline of the whitewashed cross. Earlier, Pilar had offered to escort her to that spot, but Grace refused. She asked to be alone, to be given a few moments of quiet contemplation on what she and her husband had wrought.

In a few days, twenty-three million dollars would be in a bank account she controlled. The sixteen miners and the one cook would each receive ten thousand dollars, equal to two years of pay in Honduras. She would authorize a fund of two million dollars for the Lenca community, which would be managed by her husband's mistress. The Paiute community in Nevada would be bestowed with a similar amount, the fund administered by old, wise Sarah. Her Paiute friends and neighbors who had invested in this venture could receive up to twenty-five times their investment, for most of them, an astounding sum. The few who had invested only one thousand dollars because that was all they could afford would receive twenty-five thousand dollars. Even old and often drunk Eddie Tom, who tried to sell his one-thousand-dollar stake to Marc Cousineau for ten thousand dollars, would receive two and a half times that much. Tommy and Jasper's investment of five thousand dollars apiece would return a hundred and twenty-five thousand dollars. Lucky Dave, despite his girlfriend Jackie's warnings, had earned more than six hundred thousand dollars, and he was still in graduate school! Tommy's father, whose change of heart freed him to contribute, transformed his investment into a half-million-dollar bonanza. The investment of Grace and Kostas had become a four-million-dollar nest egg, more than enough to establish a trust fund for Antu and to finance Pilar's commitment to her Lenca community.

And they found no silver!

Grace shook her head with disbelief as if she had survived a sudden accident and only now realized what had happened. She shivered with the faint but pleasant terror of wonder. How had she persisted through these eight months without Kostas by her side?

She looked around as if to spot him someplace in the rough landscape of the mountain and jungle forest.

All this time he had been gone, just a memory, a photograph, an ache in the heart, a nighttime dream, but still a presence lingering at the edges of perception. She looked at the empty chair next to where she sat at the table and tried to imagine him sitting there, boasting about their accomplishment, laughing at the utter absurdity of literally making something out of nothing, of remembering what is not visible is as important as seen and touched things. He rarely brought up his great-great-grandfather Wovoka, Grace supposed mostly because Wovoka's dreams in the end did not protect his tribesmen, but his dream, Kostas's dream, now fulfilled that failed legacy. Kostas had protected his tribe, his family, and his adopted community in Central America. As she imagined him sitting next to her, she included in this vision little Antu standing between them, their daughter—yes, her daughter, the real prize Kostas had bestowed. The world would be, was, a better place because this girl of many cultures had appeared as a savior princess, to Grace's mind, a Native American Joan of Arc. Of this, she had no doubt.

In the midst of this vision Grace tried to maintain appeared Pilar, walking toward her from the dam. *What a beautiful woman,* Grace thought despite herself. No wonder her husband chose her as his alternate partner! Even though there was still some pain at what an ordinary woman would call a betrayal, Grace loved her husband's mistress. She admired her strength, her devotion to a higher cause, and her angry Lenca addiction to revenge.

Yet in the end, when Miguel came hat in hand to confess he had lost his way, Pilar didn't reject him. She pushed a plate of food in front of a hungry man, as she would for anyone who needed the moral sustenance of compassion. Pilar, as it turned out, in her own way was a wise woman.

Pilar sat down in the chair next to Grace and smiled. She leaned over to look into Grace's face, and Grace smiled, nodding her head from side to side.

"I am happy for Antu," Grace said quietly.

Pilar looked up at the people milling around the compound, the women busy cleaning up after the meal, the boys kicking a soccer ball around in the clearing, Dave and Jasper throwing pebbles into the pond behind the dam, the Lenca mining crew waiting outside of the mouth of the mine for the tour group with Tommy to appear, the cook sweeping the wooden porch of the office shack, the limousine drivers who joined the young boys at the homemade soccer pitch. She spread out her arms to take it all in.

"And I am happy for them," Pilar replied.

"Even Miguel?" Grace asked.

"Poor Miguel," Pilar said as she turned to face Grace. "Poor Miguel. He just didn't know any better, did he? I guess you were right. My anger would have harmed but not healed. I am still angry, but it doesn't have to be violent or nasty. I guess it could even be a sort of kind anger. Is that what you call wrath?"

Grace shrugged her shoulders. "I don't know. What about Cousineau? Are you 'unkindly' angry at him?"

"Of course. I would shoot him if I could get away with it."

"Well, I'm glad you can't get away with it," Grace replied.

Pilar stood up from her chair and held out a hand to help Grace rise from hers. "You want me to go with you now?"

Grace breathed in deeply before answering. "By myself, if you don't mind. Sometimes I get angry with you."

Pilar lowered her head. "I would too if I were you."

Grace started for the spot across the clearing where her husband had fallen. Pilar stayed behind by the dining table and watched her lover's wife slowly walk across the clearing but soon realized it was inappropriate to spy on these private moments. She turned her back to Grace and strode into the cooking tent to help the Lenca women clean the dishes and put away the food.

Grace stared at the sand behind the fallen tree trunk hoping to find some mark to reveal Kostas's presence, but the sand was ordinary, a few pebbles, a stray fallen leaf, an ant crossing the miniature landscape. The crude wooden cross, whitewashed, leaned to one side a little. Grace had to suppress the impulse to straighten it. The flowers in the ceramic vase were fresh, apparently put there only this morning. Grace turned around to see who was watching her. She could not see Pilar under the shadow of the awning. Dave and Jasper were now walking along the top of the dam, oblivious to her presence. Jorge and some of his crew still waited at the entrance of the mine for Tommy and his father. The cook sweeping the porch of the office shack had finished her chore and was happily surveying the results of her work as she wiped her hands in a washcloth. The boys and limo drivers had escaped the bright sun of the clearing to recline in the shade of a nearby tree, chattering loudly about their game. Faintly, she could also hear the busy chatter of the women in the cooking tent. She looked up at the sky. No clouds. Just blue and golden sunlight. She put out a hand to steady herself and sat down on the log.

Despite the flowers and cross, there was nothing special about this spot, a place she dreaded to visit because of what transpired here. If no one had thought to mark this place with a cross or to leave a vase of flowers, there would be nothing to distinguish this place from any other place. There was nothing, only a precious absence.

About the Author

A ce Remas grew up in the Basin and Range country of Nevada, where prospecting was a serious career option. Later in life, striking it rich became a metaphor for a different kind of prospecting, seeking the gold in one's own heart. He was a dedicated Buddhist student for twenty years and taught meditation classes in Northern California and Nevada. He is the author of three previous books, a novel entitled *Precious Time* and two memoirs. Just out of graduate school at the University of Nevada in Reno, he found his purpose as an author when he wrote for the famous Virginia City weekly newspaper, the *Territorial Enterprise*, where Mark Twain began his literary career. He subsequently became the publisher of a weekly newspaper in Marin County, California, where he now lives with his wife, Marsha. He is the father of two fine boys.

CPSIA information can be obtained
at www.ICGtesting.com
Printed in the USA
LVOW08s0422061216
515996LV00001BA/12/P